Evermore

An Era of Dawn Novel

Alexandra Lee

To:
Grandma

It was wonderful to see you. Thank you for your support! I'd love to come visit sometime!

Love, Chelsea

Copyright © 2016 by Alexandra Lee
All rights reserved. This book or any portion thereof may not be reproduced or used in any manner whatsoever without the express written permission of the publisher except for the use of brief quotations in a book review.
First Edition
This is a work of fiction. Names, characters, places, and incidents either are the products of the author's imagination or are used fictitiously. Any resemblance to actual persons, living or dead, businesses, companies, events, or locales is entirely coincidental.
ISBN 978-1-946212-14-6
Title Wave Publishing, LLC
www.titlewavepublishing.com

Dedicated to my brother, Andrew, for reading my book as I finished it. You are the most intelligent person I've ever met and one day will change the world.

And to my friend, Josh, who to this day is the only person to have read my first book. We will never speak of that story again.

"Insanity is the opinion of others and what they cannot see."

— *Alexandra Lee*

Acknowledgments

I've had an incredible team of people at my side to help get my book from the computer to your hands. Thank you, everyone!

First, I want to recognize my publisher, Beverly, because she said yes. She took a chance on me: a twenty-two-year-old with no awards or a college degree. She is one of my best friends now, almost like a sister, and I can't thank her enough.

Beverly then introduced me to my marvelous editor, Laura, who was brought onto the team last minute after some issues with my original editor (who despite our falling out I wish nothing but the best for in the future). We both are beginning our careers, and I can't wait for her to get her hands-on *Kismet*. She is determined, honest, patient, and a terrific friend. Thank you, Laura. You gave me confidence in both, myself and my ability to tell stories. I know now that this series will be *great*. Let me be the first to say that you aren't paid enough for the quality work that you do!

Laura then encouraged me to improve the cover of Evermore, which led me to Gwendolyn1.deviantart.com. She was very kind, easy to work with and finished the cover of Evermore in only a few days. I look forward to the future covers she creates for my books. I would also like to thank our generous stock providers: Almadediciembrestock.deviantart.com,Diza-74.deviantart.com, frozenstocks.deviantart.com,Ikrodreamsstock.deviantart.com, Lisajen-stock.deviantart.com, and Tinalouiseuk.deviantart.com.

Furthermore, I want to make a shout-out to all my friends who have supported me, especially Ethan and Kelly. You've always had faith in me and pushed me forward. Thank you!

Lastly, I want to thank my father, Michael, for encouraging me to finish my book. You saved my ass, Dad. So, thank you. Do not think for a moment, I don't appreciate everything you've done.

Dear Reader

At the time of writing this, I've been creating books for ten years now despite being only twenty-two. I don't remember a time where I didn't think about writing, and in fact, my father once told me that I've talked about writing since the age of nine. It amused him because I never expressed much interest in reading.

I still don't. I can't explain why I write because I am too young to understand many things, including about myself. What I do know is that I want to be an example. You don't need to be an avid book reader to write a book. I certainly am not. I used to think that without awards, and a college degree that I'd never get published. I want to show people that a piece of paper doesn't define me *or* what I'm capable of.

I'm not special by any standard. I'm an average woman with an average sense of humor, and probably an average IQ (though between you and me, I'm secretly a genius). My parents didn't own a publishing company. Neither of my parents were writers. In fact, neither of my parents have read my writing, but in my mother's defense, she passed away two years ago.

I want you to know how much I appreciate you. You took the time to listen to my words, to hear my story. And I hope I made you cry, laugh, and throw my book against the wall (I certainly did). I hope this was one of the best stories you've read in a long time. And even if it wasn't, I want to thank you for listening to my words and to tell you that I love you for doing so. If my next book comes out, and you've moved on, that my love is unconditional. All I will ever ask of you is to give me a chance. Thank you.

—Alexandra Lee

An Introduction to Insanity I

1. Reality is anything perceived by sight, sound, smell, taste, and touch as real.

2. Illusion is anything that deceives by producing a false impression of reality.

3. Sense impressions are dependent upon changes in the brain.

##

I am no wiser than the man before me, but from what I have seen on this world, I feel that illusions are no more than opinions. Opinions of a reality that we do not yet understand. For if both reality and illusions are dependent upon sense impressions — and they are — then how do we differentiate them from one another?
I don't think we can because I don't think we're meant to. At times, it's the things that others don't see or understand that make us stand out among the crowd and all the noise. Sometimes, they make us more creative or wiser of the world around us. However, I believe, wholeheartedly, that there's a place for madness in this world. For if we were all sane, then surely madness would become the inevitable.
By definition, illusions are deceivers, but does that make them any less real? We perceive them no different from what we consider to be our reality. We hear them.... We see them.... We smell them....
Does the fact that they are deceptive make them any less real? No.

He watched her as she laughed, wiping the tears from her eyes, though she spoke to no one.

She seemed broken, and though it was against his better judgment, he remained. He knew his duties, and though every move pained him, he worried a great deal about this woman.

He touched her arm gently, the unique perfume on her skin only making it harder.

She stared into the wall, her smile that he had become so accustomed to now withering away.

"I hear their voices. See their faces. Why can you not?" she inquired.

Every word she spoke only brought more agony, torturing him as much as his own words.

"They say the cause lies in your head. That you've gone mad," he said, pressing his hands to her arms.

"Enough!" she said, pushing his arms away, turning around and staring at his eyes, though she felt as if she were staring into an abyss. He was no longer the man she once knew.

He reached for her, disheartened when she stepped away.

She shook her head.

"Call it what you will! You describe my reality as if it is no more than lies! You are so desperate to label what you cannot see, that you brush it off as madness, when it could very well be that they are mad, and I am very much sane."

The man sheds tears reaching for the wall standing alone in the room before him.

Chapter 1

With a trembling hand, she reached for her handkerchief, dabbing at the sweat upon her face. Her breaths came quick, her chest tight, bright eyes watching her father behind his desk. His frail hands shook, struggling to light the pipe.

"Father, perhaps it is time you set the pipe down."

"Nonsense. I've almost got it."

She sighed, clutching her handkerchief to her chest.

She had been in her father's office many times before, though in the past, it had been in the company of her sister, who now waited outside its doors. Its walls reached high, covered in dark wood with candles circling the room, their flames casting a familiar glow almost as if it were sunset. It was the most color she had seen on his face in a long time.

The pipe caught fire, the tobacco becoming a bright orange. Her father took a deep breath, shaking the flame from the smoke coursing from his nostrils, hanging in the surrounding air. A cough seized him for a moment, the silver-haired man clutching his chest as well as the desk. He leaned back into his chair once it had passed, clearing his throat and resting on the hand who held his pipe.

"Marie, your mother and I, after an exhaustive search, have at last found a suitable husband for you."

Husband. The word formed knots in her stomach.

She stood in silence, waiting to hear his next words.

"Your mother will come see you in the morning to prepare you to meet him."

He spoke as if she were an elegant dish soon to be served to the most gluttonous of people.

"Marie, I can't stress enough how important it is that this goes as planned. It's because of this, that I must forbid you from breathing a word to your sister."

He lifted the pipe to his lips again. Breathing deeply, smoke filled the air once more.

"I understand, Father."

"I hope for your sake that you do," her father sighed, waving her off. "If only your personalities had been identical too."

She nodded, holding her tongue as she left the office, closing the door gently. She turned from the door, meeting the familiar eyes of her sister, a weight being lifted from her shoulders. She looked concerned, taking her hand, giving it a firm squeeze. Marie's chest and stomach relaxed allowing her to breathe easy again.

"You did nothing wrong," she assured her.

"I know," Marie said, squeezing her sister's hand in return.

Her sister started down the hall toward their chambers. Head held high. The guards looked at her bitterly, some whispering harsh words to one another. She, however, pretended not to notice them, glancing at Marie every so often instead. It bothered her how people constantly gave her sister the cold shoulder, treating her as if she were a plague about to consume them all.

She came to a stop before their chambers, letting go of her hand.

"Your choice, Sister."

"My room," Marie said, reaching for her door.

She entered her chambers, sitting before the pearl colored vanity, her sister closing the door behind them. They had always shared chambers despite their parent's best efforts to separate them.

She was her other half, the side she couldn't show the world. Her sister spoke when words failed her and acted when her hands were too weak to do so.

"I need the parchment, inkwell, and quill from my desk," Marie said, pulling the pins from her hair, platinum locks falling over her shoulders. She lifted her brush from the vanity, carefully pushing it through her hair.

"What for?"

"There is something you must know."

"Then speak."

Marie set the brush down, turning to look at her.

"I promised father I would not speak. However, I made no such promise for writing," she said, reaching for her sister's hand giving it a light squeeze. "Please, Thea."

She sighed, taking her hand away.

"Since you said please."

Thea crossed the room to the desk, retrieving the parchment and quill with one hand, using her other one to carry the inkwell to her sister.

"Thank you," she said, lifting the quill and opening the inkwell. She dipped the quill before scribbling along the parchment.

"You're telling me either way. Why not speak and save the ink?"

"It's not that I am telling you, but how I approach telling you that matters." She closed the inkwell, returning it and the quill to her desk before sliding the parchment over. "If people haven't learned yet that we do not keep secrets from one another, then they will never learn."

Thea sat before the vanity beside her sister, pulling the parchment close, as Marie began to pull the pins from her hair.

##

My husband has been chosen. We meet come morning. They've made plans.

##

"And you'll just marry this man because they tell you to?" Thea said bitterly, her dark hair falling over her shoulders.

Marie lifted the brush, pushing it through her sister's hair just as carefully as her own.

"It's not as if I have a choice on the matter, Thea."

"You realize this will separate you from everything."

"I do," Marie said, placing the brush on the vanity, staring at the two of them in the mirror. "Maybe he's a good man."

Thea's expression matched her solemn tone as she looked into the equally blue eyes of her sister.

"For you or for them?"

##

Marie rubbed the sleep from her eyes, sitting up, shielding them from the sun.

"Thea, why didn't you wake me?"

Emptiness filled her as only silence accompanied her words. Her chest felt hollow as she realized she was alone.

"Thea?" she said once more, nervously. She climbed out of the bed, sitting before the vanity, lifting the brush to her hair.

"Your sister is having her breakfast alone that way you'll be able to focus," her mother spoke, taking the brush from her hand, pushing it quickly through her hair. "No offense, darling, but your sister has never been the best influence."

Marie winced, watching her mother in the mirror as she tugged at her hair, forcing it into an elaborate braid.

"Mother, I didn't hear you come in."

"Of course not, you were still in bed. It seems you rely too much on Thea."

She spoke her daughter's name bitterly as she moved toward the closet.

Marie bit her tongue at her mother's words. She clutched her vanity, her knuckles paling. Her parents had always looked down upon her sister, ever since she had chosen to become rebellious.

Marie's mind returned to the days of their youth, recalling the many times Thea had spoken out against them. Though she was her identical twin, they had tried to marry her off first. They called her exotic with ice for eyes and dark hair against pale skin. However, she had always detested the idea of marriage, and had the strength to say no. They'd spent many years presenting her with suitors, trying their hardest to persuade the many dukes that they should marry her. Nevertheless, Thea did not waiver, going as far as to slap one of the first suitors. Their parents finally drew the line when she bit a suitor. For the time being, they would focus on Marie, and revisit the idea of marrying Thea off in later years, with hope they would not be too late.

Marie admired her sister, though her approach was brash. She, too, was growing weary of their parent's persistent remarks about her sister.

Her mother emerged from the closet, holding a dress the color of a lemon with a corset front and decorative lace cuffs. It sent shivers down her arms as she watched as her mother laid it onto the bed. She walked to her side, dragging her over to the bed by her wrist. She snapped her fingers impatiently.

"Get undressed, Marie. Honestly, what would you do without me?"

"Could I have some privacy, Mother? I am capable of dressing myself," Marie insisted, glancing in horror at the dress. She would have much rather worn orange or green.

"Absolutely not. Now undress."

Marie took deep breaths, swallowing every word that came to mind as she removed her nightgown, her mother squeezing her into the corset. Marie gasped, her hand on her chest as her mother pulled on the strings far too much. It was as if her mother were trying to suffocate her. Perhaps she wouldn't have to get married after all.

"You look sickly thin, Marie. You need to eat more especially if you are to get a husband."

"How ironic, Mother, seeing as my organs are now hugging one another."

Her mother gave one more tug on the strings, smiling as her daughter gasped for breath.

"I hope you understand that your father, and I searched for a very long time to find someone. If this goes south, then there's no telling what we will do" she said, reaching for the dress, forcing her daughter into it.

Marie swatted at her mother's hands, stepping away.

"I assure you, if this goes south, it will not be because of me."

"Then I should have nothing to worry about, right?" she said, turning her around to lace up the back of the dress.

Marie chewed on her bottom lip, wishing her sister were in the room with her. Thea would have never allowed her to wear yellow.

Her mother grabbed a pair of frilly tights, reaching for her legs. Marie removed the tights from her hands, slipping them on. She had managed to place one shoe on as her mother pushed her toward the door; Marie forced to hop upon one leg.

Her mother stared at her critically, her lips forming a thin line on her face.

"Chin up."

Marie lifted her head.

"Back straight."

Marie straightened her posture, holding her hands together against her waist.

"You look decent... wait." Her mother pushed up on Marie's breasts, forcing them closer together. "Perhaps we should try stuffing."

"Under no circumstances are we stuffing my breasts!" Marie said stepping away, covering her chest, her cheeks flushing as she glanced at herself in the mirror.

Her mother sighed disappointedly, looking at the clock.

"We don't have the time to do so. Your father is waiting in the foyer," her mother said, pushing her out the door, keeping close on her heels.

Marie tuned out her mother's voice, focusing on the windows as they passed them on their way to the dining hall. She felt as if she wore the curtains that draped around the windows.

Outside, the sky was clear and bluer than most days as it hung over the meadow that stretched endlessly beyond their estate. She would have rather been outside under the sun, tending to her garden, watching as the summer breeze caused the grass to perform a little dance. She loved the smell of roses, the many layers of the peonies, and the unique shape of jasmine.

"Are you listening to me?"

"Every word, Mother."

Marie's chest tightened as her attention was stolen from the windows, the two of them entering the foyer. Her eyes fell upon her father as he checked his pocket watch. He wore fine burgundy silks, his weary eyes on the doors.

"You're late."

"I know, Dear, but Marie overslept," her mother said, kissing his cheek taking her place beside him.

He put his pipe in his mouth, smiling briefly at his daughter, before returning his eyes to the doors, watching as the servants pulled them open.

Marie watched as their guest entered through the tall doors, a bottle of wine in his hands. He removed his hat, revealing hair like that of salt and pepper. Resting beneath his hair was eyes like that of a crows. He handed his hat to one of the servants, scratching at his beard. He was a large man with skin that reminded her of parchment, more so as he approached them. He extended his shaking hand to Marie, smiling politely as he kissed her hand.

Her father cleared his throat.

"This is the Duke of Heathford."

Marie smiled in return, wishing she had worn gloves, tempted to take her hand back, but remaining still.

Her mother spoke before she could have the chance.

"And this is our daughter, Lady Marie Elizabeth Leighton."

Marie curtsied before they began to make their way to the dining hall. Her parents sat at their seats at the table, placing their napkins in their laps. The servants brought their food on pristine golden plates, setting them before each person and removing the lids. Her parents only used them whenever they entertained guests, which seemed to be more often than not.

Marie thanked the servants before watching her father speak to their guest, waiting patiently for him to take his fork into his hand. She looked down at the eggs and sausage, her mouthwatering, seeing the potatoes next to them, the aroma causing her stomach to rumble. She blushed, hoping no one could hear it.

Her father, after some time, took his fork and knife into his hands, taking a bite of food. Marie smiled in relief doing the same, taking a bite of potatoes, chewing thoroughly before swallowing. Their guest looked at Marie as he continued speaking with her father.

"Marie is very beautiful, but I thought you had another daughter."

Marie sipped at her orange juice, meeting her mother's eyes. Her eyes spoke all: hold your tongue. That's how she spent her last few years, constantly holding her tongue and swallowing her words. Her mother would one day learn that she had a thing or two to say.

"Yes, Thea. She won't be joining us today I'm afraid. She is very into her studies."

That was the same excuse they told all their guests when they inquired about her whereabouts. Thea often wasn't allowed to attend their parent's parties; however, she would come anyway, conveniently done with her studies and never a moment too soon.

Though her parents used it as an excuse, it was no lie. Her sister was into her studies. She could always be seen with a book in her hands. She frequently kept Marie company in the garden, educating her on the things she learned. Thanks to her sister, she learned about languages, how to write, and her favorite being history. There was no book Thea would not read. Their parents were only concerned with their etiquette and making sure they could perform the duties of a duchess. Not if they were intelligent enough to hold a conversation, much less on the world outside their estate. She doubted they knew their daughters could write.

"She must be very intelligent."

"She does well for herself."

She could see her father straining himself to compliment his daughter. Marie could have named ten things in the same amount of time.

"It's a shame she can't join us."

"Perhaps some other time."

They continued to eat, silence falling over the table. Marie eventually placed her fork and knife together on her plate facing up, finishing her juice. The Duke, after some time, did the same, her mother and father following last.

"Would you be interested in seeing where the wedding will be taking place?"

"Of course, Duchess—"

Her mother laughed, covering her mouth with her napkin.

"You don't have to—"

Marie exhaled sharply, having seen her mother behave this way in the past with other suitors, though most were younger. She found herself constantly tuning out their chatter, even as they made their way onto the balcony.

Her mother smiled, her voice almost giddy.

"The wedding will take place in a fortnight. The servants will begin setting up three days prior to it in the garden. It has an absolutely breathtaking view, don't you think?"

"You have a beautiful garden, Ma'am."

"Thank you, but the credit goes to Marie. It's nearly impossible to get her to leave it. It's been like this ever since she was a child. Her skin was as pale as her sister's when she was a child."

Marie stepped to the edge of the balcony, holding onto the railing, smiling as a cool breeze rustled her dress. She stared into the garden, remembering the many hours she had spent within it. She was captivated by the variety of flowers, carefully clipping them, watering them, and even talking to them on occasion when she thought no one was looking.

"I see, but why not have the wedding there?" the Duke said, pointing at the blossoming meadow.

"The meadow is nothing special," her mother said.

"Except for our family name," Marie said, insulted by her mother's words. "If I had a say in the matter, I would agree with my mother. The garden has a beautiful variety of flowers that we could use at the wedding. It would also make for a lovely backdrop."

"Then we shall have the wedding in the garden."

Marie could see the relief on her mother's face.

The sun shined down on them, Marie lifting her hand to protect her eyes from its light. She was tempted to look up into it, though she knew better. Instead, she looked down, her eyes widening in surprise.

Her sister sat below at a table in the garden, a book in her hand as the sun bathed her in its light. Her hair shined like the feathers of ravens draped against a lavender colored dress, similar to her own. She met her sister's eyes, lifting a cup of tea to her lips, hiding the devious smile on her face. The guards stood in a line behind her, eyes on her like hawks. To ignorant eyes, they might have looked like they were protecting her when, in reality, their job was to ensure that she didn't disrupt their meeting. It made Marie smile wider to see her sister sit with such confidence and elegance.

"And tell me whom this woman might be?"

Thea's eyes narrowed, meeting the eyes of Marie's soon-to-be-husband. She grimaced, placing her teacup onto its saucer.

"They can't be serious," she said to herself, keeping her voice a whisper.

"That woman is my sister, Thea," Marie said, placing a hand over the frail hand of the Duke. She felt comforted by her sister's presence.

"She seems... bothered."

"She most likely is. My sister has been protecting me since we were children. I look forward to the two of you becoming acquainted at the wedding."

His hand was tense for a moment.

"As do I."

Marie met the eyes of her sister again, winking at her, the two girls grinning at one another.

##

"You did well to convince the Duke to have the wedding in the garden, Marie. A wedding in that meadow would have been so dull," her mother said, slicing butter from the tray, placing it on her plate, before pulling a piece off her roll and buttering it.

"My pleasure," Marie said, resting her wrists on the table on opposite sides of her plate. "However, you shouldn't insult the meadow. Thea and I have spent many days and nights in that meadow. Some of my best memories come from it."

"It's just grass, Marie," her mother said, sneering. "Get over it."

Marie bit her tongue, certain it was bleeding.

"While on the topic of your wedding, your father asked that I informed you that your sister won't be attending the wedding."

Marie placed her fork and knife on the plate, having lost her appetite.

"And where is father?"

Her mother reached for her hand, but Marie held it away.

"He's breaking the news to your sister as we speak."

Marie wiped her mouth conveniently at the same time.

"I insisted that he allows us to have our lunch at the garden, just the two of us."

Marie placed her napkin down, meeting the eyes of her mother.

"I will say this only the one time, Mother, so please pay attention for once," she said in a polite tone, as if she were greeting her. "If you insist I go through with this wedding, then you will not only allow Thea to attend, but you will insist that she is there. Beside me."

"What makes you think that you can talk to me like that?"

"The same thing that makes you think that you can separate my sister from me."

"You may have forgotten, but I certainly have not, when it comes to your sister's extensive history—"

"Which makes it even more shocking that you and Father thought it wise to keep her away from me." Marie took a sip of her tea, lowering the cup enough for her mother to see her speak. "After all, Thea does have an extensive history."

"This isn't for you to decide."

"I agree with you completely," Marie said, smiling.

"Your sister may very well put an end to this wedding."

Marie finished her tea, placing her cup back onto its saucer.

"I couldn't agree with you more. Tell me, Mother, did it once cross your mind that preventing her attendance would only result in the failure of this wedding? Telling her no only makes her more determined, especially with matters regarding me. Didn't you hear me on the balcony say that she protects me? She will find a way into this wedding. I assure you, and if you doubt our bond any more than you already have, then you are far more the fool than I expected."

Her mother's nostrils flared, the two women sitting in silence for a moment.

"Your father will not approve of this, but..." her mother closed her eyes briefly, "...if you insist your sister attends, then very well. That said, I expect you to keep her in line."

Marie's expression remained unyielding.

"That's the best part, Mother. I won't have to."

It made sense to her why her sister was as defiant as she was, now that she had finally shown the same defiance toward her parents.

Her mother's lip curled as she turned to one of their servants.

"Find Thea. Tell her that she is allowed to attend the wedding if she behaves," her mother said, before taking her leave to find her husband.

The servant waited until she was out of earshot before turning to Marie.

"Is there a message you wish to tell your sister, Lady Marie?"

Marie stood, removing her heels and lifting the skirt of her dress as she made her way into the garden.

"Tell my sister what transpired here, and that we will have tea in the garden this evening."

She lifted a white rose into her hand, smelling it before plucking the thorns from its stem with her other hand.

"Word-for-word?" the servant asked.

"Ignore my mother's words. Tell my sister the truth as you saw it."

"Yes, Lady Marie," the servant said before disappearing.

Marie watched as the servants collected the dishes from their dinner, returning with polished dishes for tea.

"Lady Marie, will you be having coffee or tea this evening?"

"Coffee."

"And what would you like to have with your coffee? We can prepare cucumber sandwiches, or perhaps some scones?"

Marie tapped her chin with her finger, her elbow resting in her free hand as she thought about it.

"Sandwiches... no. Scones, please."

"With cream and jam?"

"I wouldn't have them any other way," she said.

She spent the next few hours in the garden, tending to the flowers as she waited patiently for her sister to arrive for tea. She lost track of time, becoming concerned, not yet seeing any signs of her sister.

"A little birdie came to me and told me a story where my quiet and innocent sister stood up to our heartless mother. She was even able to convince her to allow me, *the devil*, to attend her wedding. Which is very ironic, since just a moment prior, our father had told me that 'under no circumstances was I allowed to be seen at the wedding.' I had already begun plotting," Thea said, taking a seat at the table, another book in her hand. "Surely, it wasn't you being defiant?"

Marie walked over to her sister, tucking the white rose behind her ear.

"It sounds like your sister learned from the best."

Thea smiled, closing her book and placing it on the table.

"I suppose she did, and I must say you were great."

"I'm tired of being quiet and innocent Marie. It felt good to take a stand."

"It always does, which is why I'm surprised you held your tongue about that dress, much less when you saw your soon-to-be-husband. He's got to be as old as Father, if not older."

Marie sat at the table with her sister, reaching for the lid covering the scones, her sister's hand resting over hers.

"There is a time and place, Thea."

"We must talk about this. I'm concerned," Thea said, lifting her hand, watching as her sister removed the lid.

"And we will, but first we eat," she said, pouring the coffee.

Thea accepted her sister's answer with a smile.

"Of course, you would choose scones," she said, as her sister handed her coffee on its saucer.

"I chose coffee, didn't I?" Marie said, pouring herself coffee and dropping cubes of sugar into it. "Who drinks coffee during tea time anyways? It's called tea for a reason."

"That's something else that we must address. You don't drink tea with scones," Thea said, pouring cream into her coffee, watching as the colors swirled before blending together.

"And you don't drink coffee with everything."

"That's because no one has yet to give me the option," Thea said, holding her finger up. "And the same goes for my cucumber sandwiches."

"Not everyone is as addicted to those bloody things," Marie giggled. "You must accept that my scones have their place in this world."

Thea smirked, holding her coffee close, smelling the aroma.

"Addiction implies that I have a problem, and I certainly do not have a problem."

"Eating them for every meal every day is certainly a problem, Thea."

"They have yet to give me the option," Thea said with a wink. "Now about that 'husband.'"

"I understand your feelings, and I agree he isn't the most pleasant to look at, but he seems to be a decent man, Thea."

Marie took a scone, breaking it in half before spreading jam on it and taking a bite. She didn't understand her sister's fascination with tea sandwiches. To her, nothing was better than a sweet treat in the evening.

"You deserve better than decent, Marie," Thea said, blowing the steam from her cup, before sipping at her coffee. "I'm sure when we were small, we thought the same of our parents. Now look at us, you just told mother no."

Marie sighed, placing her elbow on the table, resting her chin in her hand.

"I suppose you are right," she said, before finishing her scone.

Thea grabbed a scone, breaking it in half, spreading a light layer of cream on it as she spoke.

"Listen, Marie, I still think you should go through with this, but I'd stay away from him if I were you."

She took a breath before taking a large bite out of the scone.

Marie reached for another.

"Thea, what aren't you telling me?"

"Nothing, I've just got a bad feel—"

Marie dropped her scone on her plate, shushing her sister.

"Don't say that. Bad things always happen when you say it. Take it back."

"Fine, I take it back," Thea said, amused by her sister. "But Marie, I'm serious."

"I'll keep my distance if you'll stop saying that."

Thea grinned, leaning forward, holding what remained of her scone up.

"Only if you promise to have cucumber sandwiches and coffee tomorrow night," Thea said, knowing her sister's response. "And I won't tell mother you put your elbow on the table."

"Tea," Marie laughed, putting her other elbow on the table.

"Deal."

Chapter 2

Marie's heart raced, her hands holding the bouquet of flowers firmly. They were the only thing she could take solace in, her sister behind her with five other bridesmaids carrying her train as she walked. The bouquet consisted of roses in white, peach, and orange, which paled in comparison to the rest of their estate that had been decorated in the same, colors adorning the doorways, halls, and windows.

Her eyes fell to the carpet of white petals beneath her feet as she clutched the bouquet tighter. Her mother though disappointed at the lack of yellow roses did well for planning the wedding in less than a fortnight. The dress she wore must have been stolen from her dreams: white satin, trimmed with peach rose blossoms. Her headdress was equally beautiful with a wreath of peach roses and a veil of white lace. Her bridesmaids too wore dresses of white and lace a wreath of roses and ribbon decorating their heads. However, unlike her bridesmaids she wore her mother's blue diamond earrings and a new blue diamond necklace her sister had given her.

They approached the doorway that led into the garden. Its twin doors pulled open by the servants. Marie lifted her head, hands shaking seeing the many faces of her guests, their sears circling the altar. She took a deep breath, trying to cease her trembling hands, focusing on the aisle. Flowers decorated the bases of the candles that lined the remaining carpet that seemed to go on forever. The altar waited for her at the end, a priest behind it, her soon to be husband standing at its side. He wore a frock coat of wine. His waistcoat was white, and his trousers were of lavender doeskin.

She continued down the path to meet him, beneath multiple arches adorned in matching roses. She smiled as much as she could muster, seeing the faces of her parents among the crowd. It bothered her to see her mother dressed in black satin though many deemed it appropriate. It made her think of a woman in mourning, but she knew her mother would, in fact celebrate the marriage of her daughter though perhaps not for the kindest reasons.

The Duke stepped forward taking Marie's hand guiding her to the altar where the priest met their eyes. The bridesmaids took their places beside Marie, Thea standing beside her sister like Marie had insisted. This too, eased Marie and through her sister's strength, she maintained the urge to run away.

The priest inhaled, his eyes meeting those of the guests. "Dearly beloved, we are gathered together here in the sight of our makers, and in the face of their worshipers, to join this man and this woman in holy matrimony."

Thea took her sister's bouquet from her, holding it as firmly as she had. Marie smiled, trying to find the strength to steady her hand as her soon to be husband held it in his.

She wanted nothing to do with neither this man nor the life that awaited her beyond the safety of her family's estate. She would have been perfectly content spending the rest of her life within its walls, her sister at her side, protecting her from men like this. Her sister's words gnawed at her memory. She believed Thea wholeheartedly and didn't doubt her when she warned her to stay away from him.

"I require and command of you both, as you will answer at the dreadful day of judgment when the secrets of all hearts shall be disclosed, that if either of you knows any reason why you may not be lawfully joined together in matrimony, now is the time to confess it."

Marie smiled at her husband trying to convince him that she was happy to be doing this. She knew, however, he was wiser than to believe such lies. What lady of so few years would be pleased to marry a man of so many as him?

Certainly not her.

"Will you have this woman to be your wedded Wife, to live together after our makers ordinance in the holy state of matrimony? Will you love her, comfort her, honor her, and keep her in sickness and in health? And forsaking all other, keep you only unto her so long as you both shall live?"

"I will." Spoke the Duke.

"Will you have this man to be your wedded Husband, to live together after our makers ordinance in the holy state of matrimony? Will you love him, comfort him, honor him, and keep him in sickness and in health; and forsaking all other, keep you only unto him so long as you both shall live?"

"I will." Spoke Marie.

She felt sickened by the words hoping it was illness about to take her life. Her sister too felt the same, swallowing nervously as the ceremony's end finally neared.

Marie felt as if for a moment, she were miles away. Her mouth spoke the necessary words, but her mind was elsewhere. Her hand had ceased trembling. Her heart no longer raced in her chest, but she did not feel peace.

The Duke placed the ring on the finger of her left hand, speaking the words told to him by the priest. Marie did the same as the Priest told her the same words. She could see out the corner of her eye how their guests did not appear moved.

The priest finished a prayer before speaking to them. "I now pronounce you husband and wife."

There it was again. Husband. Only now it was real.

The Duke took Marie's hand the two looking ahead, their eyes not meeting those of their guests as they made their way to the estate's dining hall. Thea trailed close to her sister followed by their parents, the other guests behind soon after.

Marie had completely disappeared from the world, her fingers tapping away endlessly on the table as the piano played softly in the background. Her sister sat beside her, watching her for a moment before placing her hand over her sister's.

"It's an itch I can't scratch." Marie said, looking at their hands.

"I know but do stop your tapping for the time being. You're driving me mad."

Marie was relieved when one of the entertainers lifted a violin, beginning to play with the pianist. She was captivated watching them perform together, continuing to ignore the world around them, the many eyes that rested on them.

That was until her husband sat beside her stealing away the attention of their guests. She exhaled quietly, taking her sister's hand as the toasts began, her sister eventually having to recite one herself.

She loathed being the center of attention, her knees weak as she stood beside her husband. She did all that she could to resist the urge to cover her ears, to leave the room. Her sister's hand was the only thing keeping her in place. She was content being quiet among parties though now she was confident enough to speak her mind. If she could tell her mother how she felt, then she knew she would be able to hold her own with the rest of the world. Her sister being near made it easier. Thea was her strength.

She looked up when her husband took her hand, leading her to the dance floor. She forced a smile as the violin came to a stop leaving only the pianist. She clutched his hand tightly, staring into his face.

"You look ravishing, Marie."

"Thank you, Dear." She said. "You look handsome yourself."

"I apologize for the small gathering we have here today. I assure you that when we return home you will not have to deal with this."

"I am content either way."

Thea watched her sister as she danced gracefully though uncomfortably along the floor, counting the seconds until it ended. Though her sister did not show it, she knew that she was eager to sit down again. She watched as her parents joined the floor as well as other guests. A man approached her, but Thea held her hand up before the man could get his first word out. She had heard of many odd arrangements in the past, some of which had been her own but their parents had married her sister off to a man triple her age.

Thea's fist balled as she waited, relaxing once Marie placed her hand over it. "Did you see the cakes?" She whispered. "I could go for some cake."

Thea looked over to the table that held the wedding cakes: a simple white cake to the left, a more elaborate, multi-tiered cake in the center, and another simple cake to the right, this time black.

Marie stared out the window, pleased to see the sun at its highest point, the day still clear. She did not enjoy traveling in the rain.

Thea nudged her sister. "It's time for dinner."

##

"They tell me it is customary for a bride to bring with her a traveling companion. I was hoping you would come, Thea." Marie said softly, closing her last suitcase watching as the servant took it away.

Thea closed her own suitcase, a servant taking it away leaving the girls alone. "Naturally. I mean who else would join you? Mother?"

"I think not." Marie said with a smile even as tears rolled down her cheeks. "I'm glad you will be joining me because I don't think I am quite ready to leave."

Thea made her way over to her sister, placing a hat on her head. "But you are, Marie. You may not want to but of the two of us; you were always more prepared for this. I'm more of the kicking and screaming type."

Marie chuckled knowing her sister spoke the truth. "I wish I was more like you, Thea." She wiped away at her tears, more following in their place. "What if I can't stay away? What if something happens, Thea?"

"Then you come home." She said, wiping the tears from her sister's eyes.

Marie smiled, taking her sister's hands. "I will."

Thea hugged her sister, tightly pressing her hand against her head as a servant spoke. "Duchess Marie, your husband is waiting at the carriage."

To Marie's surprise their father entered, pushing the servant out of his way. "But before you ladies go, I wanted to have a few words with my daughter before she left. That is if you don't mind, Thea."

"Oh I do mind but for Marie's sake, I suppose I can allow you this one time." She said sardonically, letting go of her sister. "I'll be outside." Thea walked past her father, watching as the door closed behind her. She stood against the wall, staring at the door with a sigh. It was the office all over again.

"I thought it best for you to know some of the rules of marriage ahead of time. It's simple things that will allow you to have a prosperous marriage like your mother and I. Why don't you have a seat, Marie?"

Marie sat at her vanity looking up into the eyes of her father.

"Never oppose your husband's wishes. You are to support him unlike how your mother allowed Thea to attend the wedding." He said, placing his pipe in his mouth, lighting it.

"Let me stop you right there, Father." Marie said standing, watching as smoke filled her chambers, displeased that her father would smoke his pipe in her room. "I insisted because Thea would have come regardless."

"Your opinion, like your mother's, doesn't matter." He coughed for a moment, clutching his chest.

Marie smoothed out her peach-colored dress, straightening her hat. "Do try not to cough up a lung in my absence, Father. And if you do, don't do it in here." She said making her way towards her chambers.

"You don't know it yet Marie, but you're making a mistake." Her father said, sitting on the vanity's bench, smoke following him. "You won't have Thea to protect you unless you are able to persuade your sister to stay. And honestly, you would be doing me a favor. She's a thorn in the flesh."

"It's quite ironic you should say that since Thea was always a rose among thorns." She said closing the door gently behind her.

Chapter 3

"I expected more of you." Marie's husband told her, sitting across from her as the carriage as it pulled up to the doors of his estate. "I noticed you faltering during our ceremony."

Marie looked at him, forcing a smile. "I shouldn't have and for that I'm sorry."

The carriage came to a stop her husband opening his door. "I will send for you soon." He said before disappearing behind the doors of the estate.

Thea stared at her sister, breathing through her nose. "Did you just apologize to him?"

Marie laughed, getting out of the carriage. "I did. You should try it once or twice."

"I have apologized. *To my sister.*" Thea said, following her. You might have met her, kind of looks like you but with her dignity still attached."

"Oh I have!" She said, resting a hand on her hip. "I heard she got married to a man the age of her father."

Thea rolled her eyes, defeated, speaking once she turned to look at the estate. "So this is where you will be a prisoner." She covered her mouth. "I'm sorry, I meant living."

"You're funny." Marie laughed, looping her arm through her sister's, their eyes wandering over the light stone of the estate. There were tall windows on every side, with an equally large entrance. At its center sat a fountain, its waters casting small rainbows in the air.

"At least the grass is green." Thea said as her sister led her to the back of the estate.

"I do not want to lay with that man, Thea. What should I do?"

"I hate to say this, Marie, I really do, but you don't have much of a choice. Once the honeymoon phase passes you need to keep your distance. You're good at hobbies. I'm sure you will think of something."

Marie's lip quivered. "Then I swear to you that today is the only day I allow him to lay with me."

"I'll hold you to it." Thea said, the girls coming to a stop in the back of the estate, standing on its brick stairs. "For the time being, how do you intend to deal with it? The staying away part not the—"

"Thea." Marie said.

"You're in a stiff position, Sister." Thea said with a chuckle.

"Thea. Please, stop." Marie said, her sister's idea of humor enough to drive her mad from time to time though she could never stay angry at her.

Thea sighed. "You're no fun sometimes. Maybe you can use that to your advantage!"

Marie looked at the lush grass as it stretched forever before finally touching the forest. "What do you see here?"

"I see you about to put a garden."

"Just like back home only this time I have the luxury of starting over. I want topiaries and everything. Perhaps over there I can put some horse stables. Do you see where that path is?" She said pointing to an opening in the trees. "I'll take lessons of course, horseback riding, dancing, piano—"

"Marie you are the best pianist I know."

"That isn't saying much." Marie said. "But he doesn't know that regardless." She said calmly before a voice came from behind her.

"Duchess—" A servant spoke from the entrance. "—His Grace waits for you. I will show you to your quarters."

"Have any jokes now, Sister?" Marie said kissing her cheek.

Thea kissed her cheek in return, whispering. "Close your eyes."

"You can bet on it." She laughed, leaving with the servant.

Marie waited until she was no longer in her sister's view before holding her one hand tightly in the other. Her eyes trailed along the blue and gold walls of the estate, accented with purple in some places. Her heart felt heavy in her chest as they stepped up the stairs, their steps echoing.

The servant came to a stop, leaving her before the door to their quarters. She stayed there for a moment, studying the patterns in the wood until she heard his voice on the opposite side of the door.

"Is that my wife outside?" The word wife twisted her stomach into knots.

Marie swallowed, opening the door. "I apologize, Dear. I was looking at our beautiful home."

He sat with his back propped against the pillows, the rest of his body bare beneath the covers of their bed. "There will be time for that tomorrow. I need you now."

She stepped closer to the bed, forcing another smile. "I didn't mean to make you wait."

His eyes wandered over her body as he spoke. "It's well worth it."

She removed her clothing except for her underclothing, climbing onto the bed. "You're too kind."

"Then I shall remedy that." He removed the last of her clothes, pressing her down onto the bed. His lips met hers then her skin, his hands wandering over her adolescent body. She closed her eyes, her cheeks reddening as he touched her body, pressed into it.

Her body betrayed her.

Marie lay on her side in the bed, holding the covers up to her neck, her knees pulled to her chest. She could not rest, unable to get past his insufferable snoring.

She breathed deeply, getting out of the bed, pulling fresh clothes on quickly before leaving the chambers quietly. She stared at the wall across from her, her heart relieved to be away from him for the time being. She continued down the hall, the colors of the estate more vibrant under the morning light. She soon found a window, holding her hand up to shield her eyes from its bright light. She smiled tenderly at its warmth before looking for the stairs, descending onto the main floor. She stared at the front doors eagerly, wishing she could leave with her sister. She turned, searching for the dining hall.

She took a seat at its long table, a servant approaching her, eyes wide as they rubbed their hands together. "Your Grace! I must apologize. We weren't expecting you so early. Please allow me to-"

Marie held her hand up, giving them a reassuring look. "It's perfectly fine. I would like a cup of coffee and some cubes of sugar if it isn't too much trouble."

"Of course!" They spoke, standing straight, looking at the entrance. "And for you, Lady?"

Marie clasped her hands together in her lap, smiling as Thea entered the room. Thea avoided the eyes of the servant even as she sat down across from her sister.

"Coffee. Cream. No sugar."

Marie laughed at her sister. This was the first time she had to wake herself up. She could only imagine how her day would go if there wasn't coffee.

"Thank you." Marie said watching the servant leave before meeting her sister's eyes.

Marie watched as her sister tapped her fingers on the table, her head resting on her other hand as she stared out the window. She found it amusing while most people found her to be insulting.

The servant returned, setting coffee before both sisters, Thea dismissing them immediately. "If nothing else, your husband knows how to decorate his estate properly, except for the gold. If I were you, I would do away with that at once." She said, meeting her sister's eyes from behind her cup of coffee.

"I'm afraid the gold is the only part I like, Sister." She chuckled, dropping her sugar into her coffee, stirring it. "You were right. So after you return home, I will begin my work here. I am rather talented at keeping myself occupied."

Thea chuckled. "Did you just compliment yourself? That's unlike you. In fact, that's something I would do." She took another sip of her coffee before placing the cup down.

"Would or have done?"

"Take your pick." Thea said with her brow raised. "Teasing aside, I am glad to hear you say that because if I have your approval, then I will be leaving tomorrow morning."

Marie nodded. "Of course, you have my approval." She said, finishing her coffee. "But I wish I could keep you here longer."

"If I stay here any longer than I may never leave, Marie. You're going to be an exceptional duchess."

"Thank you." She said, her eyes tearing up.

"I think lessons are your best course of action." Thea set her empty coffee cup aside. "I'm going to recommend that you learn something to defend yourself with. Archery sounds like you."

Marie laughed, shaking her head. "For as much as we have in common, Thea, fighting is not one of them. I use my words."

"And he's going to use his hands on you."

##

Thea hugged her sister tightly. Behind them, the servants loaded her few suitcases into the carriage. More than anything, she wanted to bring her sister home with her but knew she could no longer be selfish.

"Thank you for the gifts, Marie. They're perfect." The servants closed the carriage, returning to the estate. "If anything happens, come home."

"Have faith, sister." She said holding her hands. "Though if something does happen, I will be at your door."

Thea let go of her sister, approaching the carriage. "You are going to do great things, Marie. Just you wait."

"That was always my intention." She said with a smile. "Stop worrying so much, I'll be sure to come home and tell you about everything."

Thea nodded, opening the door of the carriage, taking one last look at her sister. "I love you." She stepped into the carriage, closing the door.

"I love you too." Marie said, watching with teary eyes as the carriage rolled away. It wasn't until the carriage was no longer in her view that she felt alone for the first time. This did not deter her. Marie returned to the estate, joining her husband in the dining hall at the table for breakfast. She met his eyes, smiling, sitting across from him.

She stopped a servant. "Could I have a fresh coffee? This one has cooled." She said though steam still rose from the new cup.

"Of course, Your Grace." The servant said, leaving with the cup, replacing it with a new cup as well as sugar cubes.

"I hope you slept well, Dear."

"I did." He said, holding his napkin over his mouth. "Thank you for convincing your sister to leave so early. I don't doubt that your parents spoke truth regarding her behavior."

Marie sipped at her coffee before cutting into a piece of sausage. "It's no trouble really. I have quite the schedule ahead of me."

He looked at her curiously. "Are you willing to share?"

"I noticed yesterday that there wasn't a garden. I enjoy gardening. I thought that I would have one planted. It would also add some color to the estate's exterior. I also wanted to get into music, perhaps even dancing. It's embarrassing being a Duchess with no talents."

"Especially being married to the said duchess." This caused Marie to hold her silverware a little more firmly. "Then after breakfast I will look into hiring a tutor. I know of one who will be able to teach you multiple things. Are you interested in horseback riding by chance?" He said, sipping at his coffee.

"Yes, Dear. Could we see about having stables put in?"

"Certainly."

"When will I meet this tutor?"

"Tonight. I, like your parents, am fond of hosting parties. He often performs at them."

"Sounds delightful." Marie said, continuing to eat her breakfast.

##

Marie met the eyes of the crowd as her husband led her through them over to the piano. A man sat on its bench, flipping through the pages that rested on it. She was convinced his hair was spun from gold. Upon their approach, he stood shaking the Duke's hand, bowing to Marie. They met eyes, his sharing the same color as the meadow of her homeland.

"It's a pleasure to meet you, Duchess. You are younger than I had expected."

"As are you." She said, her heart beating faster. "The pleasure is all mine."

"I look forward to speaking with you in the future but for now I must return to the piano. Excuse me." He said, taking a seat, beginning to play music. She watched as he moved with grace, playing effortlessly. Her fingers itched to play again, the feel of the keys as they fell under the weight of her fingers.

Her heart ached when her husband pulled her away so that they could dance. She would have rather spent the night under the moonlight, playing until her fingers bled, watching as the guests danced instead. It wouldn't have hurt either for the tutor to sit at her side.

Instead, they stood at the center, dancing to his music. She met eyes with her husband from time to time, even allowing him to steal a kiss from her once.

She was grateful when the song ended, their dance coming to a stop. Her husband held her hand tightly, leading her to the guests, though he did all the talking. Unfortunately for her, she was the shiny new toy to them. Soon after she was stolen away be a group of women. They surrounded her, speaking too fast for her to keep up.

She took a deep breath, smiling and nodding, occasionally laughing with their conversation.

"Do you wear makeup?" One lady asked. "I just started a few months ago. It's made with arsenic to make you look younger."

Marie genuinely laughed at that. "If I look any younger than my husband will need to hire a tutor to teach me to walk."

The woman scowled at that, another woman immediately replacing her. "Well I make this mixture with arsenic, chalk, and vinegar. You eat it, and it does the same thing. It doesn't taste very good, so I have it with a little wine in the evenings."

"I prefer to spend my time in the sun gardening."

"Oh, you have to try it! The sun is terrible for your skin. You'll look as bad as Charlotte over there." The woman said, hiding behind her hand.

"Perhaps some other time, if you'll excuse me." She looked over to see the piano vacant, taking the opportunity to sit before it, brushing her fingers against its keys. She balled her hand up, forcing herself to step away from it. She could see the tutor, in the distance, speaking to her husband. It had been months since she had last played; even then it was at night with her sister. She watched her dance with grace around their family's ballroom with only her shadow. On occasion, she joined her, the two humming a tune as they spun in circles in the light of the moon. She missed those days.

She pressed her fingers to one end of the piano, playing a tune quickly on its keys before a voice startled her.

"Have you played before?"

She looked up to see the tutor sipping on a glass of wine before he set it down on the piano, taking his place on the bench.

"I apologize. I will leave you to your music." She said with a deep breath, making her way to her husband. The music started again, her husband leading her to the floor. She did her best to resist humming the tune. She could name many of them by heart.

Marie was grateful when the party ended, the guests returning to their homes. "Did you enjoy yourself?" Her husband spoke.

"I did, thank you." She said, watching as the tutor approached them.

"I hope to see you in the morning, Duchess." He said.

"I will make sure she is there." Her husband said, giving her shoulders a squeeze.

Marie placed her hand over his. "I wouldn't dare to miss a lesson. Thank you for performing tonight."

"The pleasure is mine but it will one day be you who performs." The tutor said before looking at her husband.

"You did a good job tonight. I hope my wife learns to play just as well."

"She will. I have faith in her." He said meeting her eyes. "Until tomorrow, Your Grace." He said shaking his hand before taking his leave.

Marie looked at her husband curiously noticing how he made his way up the staircase. "He lives here?"

"Yes, it's part of our contract. I find it more convenient this way. You won't even notice he's here."

##

Marie's eyes opened long before her husband's. She climbed out of the bed, dressing herself before leaving the chambers. She wandered around the estate before she was approached by one of the servants. A woman with silver hair and a kind face. She took Marie's hand as she spoke.

"Duchess, can I help you find something?"

"I'm looking for the parlor. I would like to write a letter to my sister."

"There's a desk in your quarters if you prefer."

"I would prefer the parlor and with a cup of coffee if it isn't too much."

The woman led her to the parlor. "With sugar?"

"Please and thank you." She said, taking a seat on the plush sofa before the small table. She smiled, waiting until she had left before sinking into the purple velvet.

The servant returned with an inkwell and parchment in one hand, her coffee in the other. "If you wish, Your Grace, there is a door here that leads to the balcony. It provides a nice view. You can almost see the lake beyond the trees."

"Thank you for everything." Marie said. "I will come find you once I have written the letter."

"Nonsense, leave it beneath the pillow, and I will collect it when I come to clean."

"Are you sure?"

"Of course." She said. "Your breakfast has been prepared ahead of time since you are early to rise."

"Then I will make my way to the dining room after I am finished here." Marie said opening the inkwell. She grabbed the quill, quickly scribbling along the parchment. She could not wait until she saw her sister again to tell her of the tutor. Perhaps her time here would not be so grim after all.

She made her way to the dining hall, sitting at the table where a coffee sat on a saucer, ready for her.

"Could I trouble you for a fresh coffee?" She said with a smile, the servant nodding. "Thank you."

"That's the last time I do something nice for you." The tutor smirked from across the table. "I suppose I shouldn't take it easy with your lessons either."

Marie looked at him. "I don't trust a drink I didn't ask for."

"You are wiser than your age suggests, Duchess."

"I have my sister to thank for that." She said as a servant arrived with her coffee and sugar, setting them down before taking their leave. "Though her reputation would say otherwise, my sister is very intelligent." She dropped cubes of sugar into her coffee, stirring them.

"Your husband compares her to a wildebeest."

"Forgive me for saying this but my husband is ignorant. He has not known my sister longer than a day and only knows of rumors."

"And are these rumors true?"

"Only some but if you were to compare my sister to an animal, you would be wise to choose wolves. They are beautiful, intelligent, and dangerous."

"And is your sister dangerous?"

"Well I did say some of the rumors were true. There was an incident where she bit a suitor."

The tutor laughed, watching as she sipped quietly at her coffee. "Oh, you're serious."

"Quite." She said. "And that's why I have always looked up to my sister."

The tutor stared at her, watching as her husband joined them for breakfast. Marie lifted her fork and knife, beginning with her eggs as she met his eyes.

"And when will you begin lessons? I wish for my wife to perform as soon as possible."

"It will take a couple of months before she is ready for a performance, Your Grace. It is not a skill taught overnight." He said, meeting Marie's eyes. "We will begin whenever Her Grace is ready."

She swallowed, wiping at her mouth before, looking at him. "Then once I have finished my breakfast, we should begin."

"As you wish, Your Grace."

Marie sat in the ballroom, making a small tune with the keys as she watched her tutor set up. "I suppose we should begin with songs that we often play at the parties." He said, sitting beside her. "But before you can play you need to understand how to read the music."

Marie listened, watching as he showed her how to identify what each note meant and how they translated into the keys. It amused her, having learned everything he spoke of when she was very young.

She nodded occasionally, her hands on her lap, watching as he played the first line. When her time came, she made a fool of herself playing off tune and even missing keys. She was relieved when her tutor sighed, more so when he began to rub his temples.

"I apologize. I have not done this before." It wasn't a lie. She had never pretended to be bad at the piano. She was for a long time and then she became good, very good at it according to her first tutor.

"It's all right." He said, repeating himself before instructing her to try it again. She did as he asked, hitting the keys more accurately but still keeping out of tune.

"Is that better?"

"A little bit, yes. Do it again."

She continued to play the same line over and over, tempted to play it correctly. After an hour of the same line she finally leaned forward in frustration, soft curls falling into her face. It was far more difficult to pretend to be a novice at something she had been doing for many years than to learn something new.

"Can we please try the next line? I'll do better."

He laughed. "We'll practice three lines today. Does that satisfy you?"

"It does." She said looking at him, moving her hair from her face.

He cleared his throat, moving to the next line. "Now place your hands here and start with this key." He said pressing down on a key, its deep sound reverberating through the ballroom.

Hours continued to pass, her tutor rubbing his temples again. "Again."

She resisted a chuckle, allowing herself to do better this time, her chest tightening when she saw her tutor's brow raise.

"Much better. Do it again."

The hours continue to pass, the sun reaching its highest place against the sky. Marie did a little worse at the end but mostly out of frustration. She was tired of playing the same three lines over and over. She just wanted to play a song again.

"That's enough for today." He finally said, taking over the keys. "Do you want to hear the song you are practicing?"

"I would enjoy that."

He smiled, both relieved to hear the song as it was meant to be played.

##

The months passed, Marie counting the number of songs she had completed in her head as her husband led her into yet another party. She was quickly becoming tired of the parties, of being her husband's favorite accessory.

However, tonight was different. He led her over to the piano, encouraging her to sit before it. She looked at him nervously. Though she wished to play, she did not feel comfortable being in the spotlight. She only performed for her sister in the past and now her tutor.

"You've completed enough songs to perform tonight." Her husband insisted, giving her shoulders a squeeze.

Marie could not speak, the tutor joining beside her. "Not quite, she's still short about three."

"Just have her repeat the ones she's good at. If she gets too off key, take over."

"As you wish, Your Grace."

Marie's breath was caught in her chest as her eyes skimmed the pages. She paused, tapping on the page as she saw words.

"I don't sing." She said. "I don't sing."

"Just play." Her tutor said, putting her hands on the keyboards.

Her eyes met the crowd as she began to play. Only this time she wasn't pretending to be a novice. Her nerves consumed her and her ability to play.

"Stop looking at the crowd. Just play." Her tutor whispered, looking at the crowd.

Marie took a deep breath, her eyes on the keyboard as she continued to play. With the music replacing her nerves, her skill begun to shine though she did her best to seem like a novice. She was convinced her tutor wasn't fooled anymore. He did not look at her, opening his mouth as they reached the words.

She opened her mouth in awe, watching as he sang the words on the page. She continued to play, softly now, her cheeks flushing as he sang. She looked over the crowd again, unable to see her husband any longer.

The song ended, Marie pulling her hands from the keys. However, the tutor placed her hands back on the keys. "Next song. I'm going to grab a drink. Do you want anything?"

"Some water would be nice."

He nodded, standing from the piano. Marie watched him as he walked away, seeing her husband enter from the corner of her eye, a woman following behind him only minutes later. She scowled, not even noticing as the song became something darker.

The tutor sat beside her, nudging her. "Softly, play softly." He said, placing their drinks on the piano.

"My mistake." She said, taking her eyes off her husband, a tear falling down her cheek.

She woke some time later, the moon's light flooding their chambers. She was careful as she climbed out of their bed, leaving the chambers in nothing but her nightgown as she made her way to the ballroom. She needed to play in the moonlight like she had so many times in the past. Her bare feet stuck to the smooth floors of the ballroom as she hurried to the piano, sitting down on the bench. She checked to make sure no one had followed her before sitting at the piano, running her fingers down the keys. She paused, their sound echoing as she turned her head to see if anyone had noticed.

When no one came, she began to play the first song that came to mind, a lullaby her sister used to sing.

She stopped every so often, to write on the nearby parchment, a letter to her sister. Her father had always kept parchment at their piano as well, hoping Marie would be as talented a songwriter as she was a pianist, but she was always content to play the music that other people created.

She soon turned to the song that her tutor had sung, beginning to play. Once she reached the words, she came to a stop. It was easier this time, no one watching her. She began to sing, her fingers continuing once more. She started softly, her voice growing louder as she progressed through the song.

From afar her tutor watched, staying out of her sight. He watched her fingers dance along the keys of the piano more graceful than her feet.

"I have become quite fond of your voice." He said, approaching the piano, placing a hand on the side. "However, I wouldn't suggest a singing career."

She gasped, leaning away from the piano, folding her hands into her lap. "How long have you been watching?"

"Long enough." He said, taking a seat beside her, placing his hands on the keys as well. "Why insist on piano lessons when you're more talented than the tutor?"

She covered her mouth, laughing. "And don't you forget it."

He took her hand. "Marie, why did you insist your husband hire a tutor?"

She bit her lip, taking her hand back. "My sister has warned me to keep my distance from my husband since the day she laid eyes on him and again before she returned home. So for these past months I have done just that."

"What if she's wrong?"

"She's not wrong." Marie said confidently, sitting straight. "I think my husband has finally realized that I want nothing to do with him."

"What makes you say that?"

"His behavior tonight was...strange."

"I was hoping you hadn't noticed, but I suppose that explains the change in tempo earlier."

She looked away, holding her arms close to her body, the strap of her nightgown falling. "I apologize for that."

The tutor leaned in close, kissing her exposed flesh before returning the strap to her shoulder. "There's no need to apologize. I would, however, like to know why you are wearing only a nightgown."

She scooted away from him blushing. "I assumed no one would hear me."

"I didn't mean to offend you, Your Grace."

She shook her head, holding up her hand with her wedding ring, its gold band shining in the moonlight. "I know but I can't be with you."

"Your husband doesn't seem to share the same way of thinking."

She smiled, looking him over, wishing she could have married him instead. "I am not my husband. I will respect my marriage to him, though I may not agree with it."

"Then I will do the same even though it pains me, Your Grace."

"Thank you."

He covered the keys, leaning against the piano. "So what will you do? You cannot hide behind the piano much longer."

"They finished planting my garden and are nearly finished with the stables. I will be taking horseback riding lessons from you. That is according to my husband."

"Then I will look forward to our next lesson." He pulled the music sheets off the piano, revealing the keys again. "Play a song for me and not as my student."

Marie nodded, closing her eyes as her fingers met the piano keys again. Thea's lullaby played softly in the air around them.

With the piano lessons coming to an end, her husband satisfied with her performance, though she was sure, he did not see past the first song. That was assuming he stayed for the entire song. She did not mind, now able to play her heart out every night at her husband's parties. She would watch him disappear and return after sometime, her suspicions confirmed. Her tutor was kind enough to stay close and provide her with good conversation and the occasional break. She enjoyed the attention from their guests regarding her performance and enjoyed chatting with them about music.

But like all good things it came to an end.

Marie pretended she wasn't bothered by it, often sneaking out of their quarters to play, her tutor no longer joining her. He would lay in his quarters awake, listening to the sound of her music. At least they could be in love with something.

The tutor sat on the balcony, a book in one hand, coffee in the other as he occasionally would sneak a peek at Marie below as she wandered through her garden. It was enormous, and he was rather confident she was lost within its walls of flowers and different sculpted hedges. She would often visit the one shaped like a man, draped in a robe. In his hands, he held a book and quill. There was a certain air about it that she admired and would often clip flowers that were nearing their end and give them a new home around the man's feet.

Marie had once missed the sea of color and many different aromas of flowers. She leaned into a rose, holding it between her fingers, carefully to avoid its thorns, as she smelled the sweet center. They had always been her sister's favorite, and they were quickly growing on her too. She took a second look at it before snipping it, removing its thorns and placing it into her hair.

She heard gunshots nearby in a rapid succession, birds flying up from the trees of the forest, cawing loudly as they flew overhead.

She looked up at the balcony to see the tutor with his eyes on a book. Beside him her husband handed off his gun to a servant, replacing it with tea as he watched her. She had never seen him visit while she was in her garden.

"You spend a lot of time with my wife." He said, lifting his tea to his lips.

"You should try it sometime." He said, looking at him. "I'm her tutor, Your Grace, and I'm afraid that requires that I actually be in her presence."

Her husband looked at the stables he had put in upon her request. "My wife wishes to learn horseback riding. Seeing as you work for me, I want you to teach her to ride a horse. Perhaps even a bit of sporting but do see that my wife doesn't get injured."

"I wouldn't dream of it." The tutor said, stealing one more look at Marie before closing his book and taking his leave.

##

Marie pet the face of the horse as she fed it what the servants had brought her from the kitchen. The horse was beautiful, white with dark eyes. The servants prepared the saddle as she continued to feed the horse.

"I see you've already chosen one." The tutor said, approaching her.

"I will ride them all. They deserve as much attention as possible." She kissed the horse's face before looking at him. "They have feelings too."

The tutor laughed, helping her onto the saddle, mounting his horse afterwards. Marie held onto the saddle, blushing at her pale knuckles. She held her head up, trying to seem like she knew what she was doing. "Speaking of their feelings... what if my horse gets startled?"

"That's very unlikely but is a risk you have to take." Her tutor said, petting his horse as they rode into the field.

Marie loved the view of her garden from here, turning to look at her tutor as they made their way through the forest. "Like how you spend time with me outside of lessons despite my husband's aversion towards you? I find it rather amusing since he had spoken so highly of you."

The tutor looked at her, blushing. "Your husband spoke highly of me? Well, it must be for my musical talents, though I doubt he has need for me now that he has someone such as you."

Marie laughed, petting her horse like the tutor had. "I think there will always be a place for you within our home."

"Though I'm afraid it's not the place I would like to be."

The two horses stood next to one another, Marie staring into the distance. There were hills for as far as the eyes could see. She sighed, the lush green reminding her of the meadow at home.

"And what place is that?"

"Your Grace, I think you already know." He said, leaning over to steal a kiss from her.

She moved out of his reach, looking away. "I cannot. I'm married." She looked at him with tears in her eyes. "Do not think for a moment that I don't want to. If I had the opportunity I would give myself to you."

His heart ached as he stared into her eyes. "I apologize, Your Grace."

"Don't. My name is Marie."

He was silent for a moment. "I envy your husband, Marie."

"What could you possibly envy about that man?"

"He had the chance to marry you and did."

"I would have preferred to marry a man such as yourself."

"No one of class would allow their child to marry a man like me."

"Maybe they don't have a choice." She turned her horse round, following beside him as they made their way back to the estate. Her mind raced with the thought of having the chance to be with him. She wanted to feel his touch, his lips against her skin. The very thought brought color to her cheeks. She could imagine it, finding herself holding onto the reins a little more tightly.

Marie looked at him, changing the subject, hoping her mind would cease with the images. "Do you know a reliable courier by chance? I fear that my sister has not been receiving my letters for I have received none from her as well."

He smiled, meeting her eyes. "I do, there's a friend of mine that could deliver it for you. This city is not as large as the Duke would have you believe."

Her heart felt heavy as they approached the stables. "I'd really appreciate it."

Nearby she could hear a gun fire, the horses rearing up. The tutor fell off his horse and onto the ground, his body no longer moving. Marie's horse fell backwards, crushing her leg, her head hitting the ground hard enough to cause her to take a sharp breath. She could see the balcony, her husband disappearing into the estate. A gun draped over his shoulder.

She came to in her bed, fear seizing her as the smell of smoke filled her nostrils. Her eyes watered until she looked up to see her husband standing by their desk. In his hand, he held a letter. The candlelight reflected off of it, allowing her a glimpse of the words. She recognized it as a letter she had written to her sister weeks ago. He placed the letter over the flame from a candle, throwing it into a bowl where it burned with her other letters.

"You've been burning my letters!" She said, seething.

Her husband sighed, beginning to read another letter. Marie forced to watch as her letters burned. "I've been meaning to speak with you, dear. You see I've learned a lot about you by reading your letters. I must say that I am proud of you for keeping your hands off the tutor. I didn't expect a woman such as yourself, so young, to be able to resist temptation."

"If only I could say the same for my husband."

"Marie, don't you know that I only have eyes for my wife?"

She narrowed her eyes at him. "Perhaps I should speak with the promiscuous women who seem to come and go as they please at your parties."

"I don't know what you're referring to-"

"Where's the tutor?" She said, sitting up, seeing the cast on her leg. "My leg-"

"The horse broke your leg when it fell. The doctor says you're lucky you didn't die from head trauma."

"And the tutor?" Tears gathered in her eyes but not from sadness. A familiar burning returned to her chest.

"He was not as lucky. He suffered a blow upon the head. The doctor says it was-"

"The doctor is wrong. I saw the gun." She said, meeting his eyes. "He died from your bullet."

He smiled. "A blow to the head all the same." He placed the letter over the candle and into the bowl of ash. "I can see how much you love your sister. It's a shame that letters can get lost somewhere in between hands."

"Then I will take them to her myself!" She said, swinging her good leg off the bed.

"Careful now." Her husband said, grabbing her leg and forcing her back into the bed. "I wouldn't want you to get hurt trying to walk. The doctor says you need to stay in bed for a few months. That leg won't heal if you try walking." She watched as he made his way to their window, closing the curtains.

He approached the door, locking it. "Which means you can't leave."

Fear seized her, the anger that once consumed her chest vanishing. She crossed her good leg over the cast, holding her nightgown down. She watched as her husband slowly removed his shirt and trousers, approaching her. He separated her legs, standing in between them as he fought to push her hands away.

"Get away from me!"

He grabbed her by her jaw, holding her tightly, running his thumb over her lips. "You don't know how long I've waited Marie. Did you think you could honestly get away with giving yourself to me only once? I am your husband." He said, squeezing one of her breasts. "You've forced me to wait the last eighteen months. I will wait no longer."

Marie screamed at the top of her lungs as her husband moved her good leg around his waist, forcing himself into her. "I know you want to perform your wifely duties Marie. You have done a decent enough job thus far."

Marie cried as he forced himself deeper inside her, the pain no longer just in her leg. She listened as he groaned, removing himself before turning her onto her stomach before plunging himself inside her a little higher.

She screamed again, louder, the pain shooting up her spine as the force ripped at her flesh.

But no one came.

Chapter 4

Marie laid on the bed, holding the comforter to her body, the sheets beneath her smelling of dry blood. She was unable to sleep, forced to listen to her husband as he snored beside her, dead to the world.

Marie swung her leg off the bed, collapsing once her broken leg met the floor. She slammed her fist onto the wooden floor, crying from the pain as she struggled to get to the desk. She reached her hands to the desk, feeling around until she touched the remaining letters, pulling them to her chest as the chamber's door opened.

She gasped, taking her hand back, her heart racing in her chest as she watched the door slowly open. She watched as the familiar face of the servant entered, helping Marie onto her good foot before leading her to the bed.

"Your Grace." The woman said. "I heard you fall—"

Marie smiled into the familiar face of the woman. "Take me to the room my sister once stayed in." She said, grabbing the remaining letters on the desk as they passed, holding them close as they made their way to the other chambers.

Marie's stomach was nauseous. She had never been forced to rely on someone so much before. Her sister had always helped her when she fell but allowed her to stand on her own feet. Now she could no longer stand without assistance. She was all but useless.

The woman helped her into the bed, noticing the blood on her underclothes. "Your Grace, you're bleeding. Let me run you a bath."

Marie stared at the blood stain, holding her good leg closer to the injured leg. The woman probably suspected the blood was due to natural causes. She worried what she might think when she learned otherwise. Would she see her duchess as weak for being unable to defend herself? She wouldn't be entirely wrong for thinking so.

Marie listened as the woman ran the bath, watching as she left briefly, returning with a fresh change of clothing.

Marie lifted her letters, throwing aside those she had written, already knowing what their contents held. It was near the end of the stack before she found a letter from her sister, her parent's handwriting scribbled across the front, addressing it to her husband. She loathed her parents for stepping between them. What did they have to gain by separating them?

She threw aside the remaining letters after she had confirmed that no more were from her sister. She clutched the letter, tears falling from her eyes as she read the contents, her sister's pain evident from her words. She memorized the date scribbled on the bottom, grateful that she had another year, before ripping the letter into the smallest pieces.

The servant stepped into her room, looking at the shredded pieces of the letter before helping Marie from the bed to the bathroom.

"My husband had my letters." She said, removing her bloody gown.

The woman nodded. "Your husband has been confiscating them from the couriers, threatening to kill any servant who breathed a word to you. I apologize, Your Grace."

Marie stared into the water, watching as the servant placed a pillow beneath her injured leg. She stared into the water, watching as it reddened from her blood. She could not blame the servant. However she loathed her husband now as much as her own parents.

Marie was still as she watched the woman bathe her, the woman resting a gentle hand on her foot. The woman gave her a kind smile before continuing to bathe her. Marie took a deep breath, leaning into the warm water. The woman was careful as she washed Marie, her eyes falling on her wounds. She kept silent continuing to bathe her. Once finished she dried her and helped her into the bed, returning the pillow beneath her cast.

"If you would like, Your Grace, I can bring your meals to you in here."

Marie held the covers close. "I'm afraid I'm in no shape to go down the stairs." She said with a laugh. "Thank you. I know I am causing you more trouble than I'm worth."

"It is no trouble at all, Your Grace."

"Could I ask another favor? Could you light a fire? I wish to burn these letters." "Which of the letters?"

"All of them."

The woman nodded, setting fire to the wood on the hearth. "Would you like me to draw the curtains?"

"That would be perfect."

The woman closed the curtains. "I will be gone only for a moment." She said, taking her leave. Marie worried about her safety. She didn't know these servants any better than she knew her husband and now her leg was broken.

The woman returned some time later with a tray. On a plate was something simple, with a glass of juice beside it. She placed the tray down, grabbing the letters as well as the shredded pieces of her sister's letter. The woman threw them into the fire, returning to Marie's bedside where she handed her the juice.

Marie sniffed the juice before sipping from it. Once she was sure it was only juice, she continued to drink it. She listened as the parchment crackled on the hearth, consumed by fire. She wished she could be like the fire.

"I can't thank you enough for your help." Marie said, placing the juice down, reaching for the fork and knife.

"It's no trouble at all, Your Grace." The woman said as she made her way to the bathroom, lifting her bloodied gown from the floor. "May I ask you something personal?"

Marie chewed a piece of bacon, avoiding the gown as she swallowed her food. "My husband doesn't know of a gentle touch."

The woman frowned, starting for the door.

"Burn the gown too." Marie said, taking a bite of the eggs.

"Yes, Your Grace." The servant looked at the dress before throwing it into the fire.

Marie paused for a moment, looking up to watch as the fabric burned. Satisfied, she continued to eat her meal.

Marie did not leave the chambers, unable to find comfort in the same walls her sister had once slept within. Perhaps it was her fault, she was in this situation. Thea should have stayed. She had always protected her before, there wasn't any reason for her to stop now. Their parents didn't even want her; it would be beneficial to them both.

Marie closed her eyes, biting her lip. She couldn't force her sister to stay. She deserved to live her own life. She should have been stronger, like Thea. This wouldn't have happened to Thea. She would have escaped, even with a broken leg. Her sister had always been better than her.

The weeks passed her by slowly, her dreams plagued by her memories of her husband as he had forced himself onto her. Occasionally she would wake up sick, her servant having to help her to the bathroom where she would vomit into the chamber pot. There had been a few times where they hadn't made it in time. The servant did all that she could to console her, but nothing seemed to help.

She was grateful when the doctor came to her chambers to remove the cast, checking her leg. He allowed her to walk again with assistance, giving her only a few more weeks of recovery time.

"That's terrific news, doctor. I know it has only been two months, but it feels as if I've spent much longer in this bed."

The man smiled. "You should definitely try walking around but try to keep it to a minimum. Just because the cast is off doesn't mean you can hop onto the back of another horse."

"I will keep my distance from the horses."

"That's good to hear." He said, standing up. "Has your nausea improved?"

"I'm afraid not. I've also been feeling more tired than I normally do."

"How long has this been going on?"

"Almost two months." Marie said, resting her hands on her stomach.

"That would explain the swelling." He said, taking a closer look at her. "Your Grace, I believe you're pregnant."

Marie's eyes widened in shock. "Are you sure, Doctor?"

"I am fairly confident. I'll visit again a month henceforth to check up on you and make sure that leg is still healing well."

Marie picked at her dinner that evening, glancing at the water as the servant tidied around her quarters. "Could I have coffee with my scones tonight?"

"Your Grace, I don't think that would be wise." Marie took a bite looking at her curiously. "Your nausea has yet to improve and if the doctor is correct — I do believe he is—"

"Do you have children of your own?"

"I do. I also have children with children. Nausea is common."

Marie looked down, pressing her hands to her stomach. "Are you sure?"

The servant removed the tray once she was sure that Marie was finished with her meal. "I am, Your Grace." The servant said, placing more pillows down. "Get some rest, I will see you in the morning."

Marie returned to her garden the next day, her servant at her side. She saw no sign of her husband though it did not bother her. She was more concerned with the state of her garden. If she was to have a child, it too would love her garden as much as she did. And if not, she would make sure her garden was somewhere safe that they could escape to like she had.

"Tell me, if I have a child do you think it will be a boy or a girl?"

"When, Your Grace." The woman corrected her, smiling.

"When I have a child."

"I think you will have a boy."

Marie paused, looking at the woman. "I think I'd like to have a girl. The two of us would spend every moment in this garden."

"Would it be any different if it was a boy?"

"Completely different. Boys don't want to sit here and stare at flowers all day. Boys explore and fight."

"I think if you were to have a boy, Your Grace, he might surprise you."

Marie smiled, placing one hand on her stomach as she turned her attention to the flowers. "I think you're right. Whether my child is a boy or a girl, I will love them."

The woman smiled, watching as Marie continued to clip at the flowers.

Marie's symptoms persisted, her servant remaining at her side. She was upset that she refused to bring her coffee but as her stomach continued to swell she understood her reasoning. The doctor spoke true.

The doctor returned, checking her leg, pleased to see that she had made a full recovery. "And the nausea has persisted?" Marie nodded. "Your stomach is continuing to swell, Your Grace. Should I tell your husband the news?"

"No, I will tell him myself. I think he will be overwhelmed with emotion." The doctor nodded in response, taking his leave.

"I'm having new dresses made for you, Your Grace as you get bigger. For the time being we will have to squeeze both of you into the old dresses."

Marie shook her head. "I am in no hurry. I will wait until the dresses have been made."

"As you wish, Your Grace."

Another month passed, her servant returning with new dresses in a variety of colors and sizes. She helped Marie into one of them, smiling at her in the mirror. "You're halfway there, Your Grace."

Marie covered her face, blushing. "I can't believe it has been four months!" She said, her hands resting on her stomach. "I would like to have breakfast in the dining hall today, but first I want to retrieve a few books from my quarters. I hope they are still there."

"I can check the library if you don't find them."

"Sounds good. I will see you soon." Marie said, taking her leave, returning to the room she had once shared with her husband. Her pace was slow, her hands shaaking as she reached for the door knob. She swallowed nervously, opening the door cautiously. She came to a stop, the door groaning at the hinges as if fell open.

Marie watched as her husband lay on top of one of the servants. The fire from the hearth filled her chest as she crossed her way to the desk, lifting the few books from its surface. It was sickening to watch her husband. She couldn't help but feel disappointed that her husband was unable to keep his hands off every woman who crossed his path.

"Your Grace!" The woman said, pushing against her husband, though he continued to force himself upon her.

Marie met eyes with them both, as she made her way to the desk. "Get out." The servant pushed her husband off, reaching for her clothes. "*Get. Out.*" The servant grabbed her remaining clothes, running out in nothing but her tights. Marie then met her husband's eyes, waiting for him to speak.

"I thought you were in your garden."

"No, I've been staying in another room, broken leg." She said turning to look at him. "You need to watch yourself lest you have another child."

"Another – *you're pregnant?*"

"Four months." She said. "I suggest you be more careful when rolling around in the sheets with the servants. I will not be returning to this room. My servant will bring my things to my new room."

She did not look into her husband's face. His silence was all she needed.

Marie was excited to watch as her stomach swelled more with the passing months. By the eighth month, she was literally being squeezed into her dresses for the few times she left her quarters. She felt more tired than she had before.

"Your Grace, is there anything I can do for you?"

"I need to check on the garden. It's been a week. There's no telling what state it's in."

Her servant shook her head. "And there's no telling when you might have your baby. You're not having your child in the garden."

"My child can wait until my garden is fixed. You can accompany me if you wish."

Her servant sighed, helping her into a dress. "I'll give you a few hours in your garden, but then you need to go back to bed."

"And I will." Marie said, rubbing her stomach as they walked. It was instinctive for her, to always have her hands on her child.

"Are you excited to meet your child?"

Marie smiled as they walked into the garden. "More than you can imagine—I mean— "She said, blushing.

She laughed, sitting in the chair as Marie happily snipped at her flowers. "I know what you mean, Your Grace."

Marie hummed softly, one hand constantly rubbing her stomach as she snipped away. She paused for a moment when she felt a warm liquid run down her leg. She continued to snip, so close to having her garden cleaned up enough that she would be able to sleep at night.

"Your Grace?"

"I'm almost done." She said, hurrying as she snipped. Pain shook her as she accidentally cut a flower. She fell upon her knees beside it, one hand on her stomach, the other holding the peony carefully in her hand.

"Your Grace!" She said, running to her side. "You should have listened to me! The garden can wait!"

Marie forced herself to her feet. "Apparently, my child agrees with you."

Marie screamed in agony, the sun setting behind them.

"One more push Marie." The doctor said confidently as he stood ready to receive her baby.

Marie cried, squeezing her servant's hand. "I can't."

Her servant squeezed her hand back, her daughter standing beside them.

"One more." The doctor said again.

Marie screamed at the top of her lungs as she pushed her baby out, its screams filling the room. Marie cried as she let go of her servant's hand, reaching for her baby instead.

"Give me a moment." The doctor laughed, happy to see her enthusiasm even though she was so young to have a child. "It's a boy!"

Marie cried harder, reaching for her son. The doctor cleaned him up, wrapping him in a blanket before handing him to Marie. She continued to cry, holding him close to her chest, gasping when he latched onto her breast. Marie looked down, watching as her son suckled though her body gave him nothing. Her lip quivered, realizing that she would not be able to feed her child on her own.

Her servant placed a hand on her shoulder. "Your Grace, your child must eat." She said in a soothing voice. "Let my daughter feed him, and then you may hold onto him for as long as you like."

Marie cried as she handed him over, watching as the servant's daughter fed her son. Even if she could not breastfeed her child, she was just happy to see him.

##

Marie carried her son with her everywhere she went. She was elated to be back in her regular size dresses again. Her servant and wet nurse were always close, in case he cried. She spoke to him often spending many of their days in the garden.

"What will you name him, Your Grace?" Her wet nurse said as she fed him, watching as Marie tended to her flowers.

"His name will be Ciel."

The ladies chuckled. "That's a *girl's* name."

"Perhaps. Nevertheless, it means from Heaven." She said coming to a stop, approaching her wet nurse who handed Marie her son. "And he must be from Heaven because I have never loved a boy so much in my life."

"Not even your husband?" He spoke as he entered the garden, his eyes on his son.

Marie looked up at her husband, holding her son protectively. "Especially not my husband."

He approached her, Marie stepping away as he grew closer. "*Do not come near my son.*"

"He is my child, Marie."

"No!" She said, holding him close. "He is *my* child. You couldn't be bothered to be there as I bore him. So you will not touch him, and he will never see you." Marie handed her son to her wet nurse and servant, leaning in close enough that her husband could not hear them. "My husband and I will be leaving here tomorrow and won't be back for a couple of days. I need you both to take care of my son while I am away."

"Of course, Your Grace. He will be safe."

"I know he will be." Marie smiled, kissing her son's forehead. "I love you more than anyone, Ceil. I will see you soon."

The ladies stood, taking Ciel away with them.

"Where are they taking him?" Her husband said.

"They are going to watch over my son while we are away. I'm sure you knew we would be leaving soon."

"To visit your parents?"

Marie smiled, smoothening her dress. "To visit my sister."

He scoffed. "Why on earth do you need to visit your sister?"

"My sister is getting married."

Chapter 5

Thea stood on the balcony. Her arms crossed over her chest as she gazed at the garden. The wind was cool, no more than a soft breeze against her skin. Her expression was solemn, her stance rigid even as petals from the garden floated past her. It wasn't enough for her.

She spent many days and nights on the balcony unable to tear her eyes away from the garden, hoping that one of these days she'd see her sister tending to the flowers again. At the least, she wanted a letter, some sign that her sister was safe.

But none came.

Things changed after Thea had returned home. Once she realized she would never receive a letter from Marie, the troublemaker within her perished and like her sister, she became a peacemaker. She had only agreed to marry her suitor - who was far more tolerable than her sister's: a man barely twice her age with a mess of red hair and olives for eyes - in hopes her sister would return home. It was ironic really. The last two years had felt like an eternity but her sister's wedding felt like yesterday now that her own was only days away.

"You look beautiful, Thea." Her fiancé spoke from behind her.

"Which brings me to question if you are a natural red head."

He laughed pushing his fingers through his hair. "Of course, I am."

Thea held onto the balcony railing, looking over her shoulder with a smirk upon her face. "How unfortunate you didn't turn out as handsome as the other red heads I've met."

"Is that really necessary?"

"No and neither is your presence."

He leaned back for a moment, smiling, hands over his heart. "You wound me with your words, Thea."

She turned around, leaning against the railing of the balcony, her arms resting on top of it. "Then could you imagine if someone locked us in a room together?"

"I won't have to in three days."

"That depends on if you can still see."

"It's no wonder your eyes are blue - you're cold, the very persona of winter."

"Brrr."

He stepped closer to her, though he kept a fair distance between them; she had not bit him as of yet. "Have you always been like this?"

"Ever since I realized that my middle finger could speak my mind."

He stepped closer to her, standing almost too near. "Even with your parents?"

She pressed her finger to his chest, turning her head slightly to the side, the smirk ever present. "I have problems with authority, especially my parents."

He shook his head, crossing his arms over his chest. "Yeah, I've heard about it."

Thea laughed, pressing her hands to his chest, leaning against him, her eyes wide in excitement. "How delightful! People really love to gossip! So, tell me, what stories have you heard? My favorite one has to be that I feast on the hearts of sleeping children."

She pursed her lips in thought. "But then again, there is also the rumor about my previous suitors. Some say I killed them and hung their testicles like trophies in my chambers. But then they also say I kick puppies."

He shifted uncomfortably, a look of concern on his face as he stared into her eyes. "You wouldn't though?"

She pouted. "*I'd never kick puppies.*"

Thea turned her head to gaze into the garden again, placing her hands on the rail, her face returning to the somber state many had become accustomed to. She tried to hide her fear from others and had been successful, for the most part. However she wouldn't be able to hide forever.

"Have you heard anything regarding my sister?"

"You still think about her?" He said almost surprised.

She turned with a quickness, pressing her finger to his chest, her eyes armed with daggers. "I haven't received a letter from my sister for two years and you're going to stand here and ask me if I still think of my sister?" She shook her head, starting towards the entrance to the balcony, stopping before the doors, giving him a fierce look. "Let me make something very clear. I would ravage this world and the next for my sister."

"I apologize." He said, approaching her.

Thea held her hand up, clenching her teeth. "Don't."

"Thea, c'mon. You didn't reject me before-"

"Day's not over." She said, turning on her heel, looking at him from over her shoulder again. "I could make you my next trophy."

"I don't find that to be very amusing." He said curtly.

"It wasn't meant to be." She said icily, leaving through the doors, ignoring her fiancé as she made her way to the parlor for tea.

Thea sat comfortably in a chair looking out the window before her, the sun setting filling the parlor with its warm glow. Since her return, this became her favorite place to have her tea. She foolishly hoped every day that she would see a carriage pull around, her sister stepping out of it. Though her imagination varied day to day as to what her sister would look like. Some days she was sullen and others she shined bright as if she had never left.

She sighed, watching as a carriage pulled around. This was normal, her parents now having parties as often as they could to change her public appearance now that she was behaving. Four servants hurried past the parlor and out the door to the carriage. Three lined up against the steps, soon joined by her mother and father. The remaining servant opened the door to the carriage, extending a hand.

Thea's eyes widened as she dropped her tea cup, listening to it shatter against the wooden floor. A servant hurried to her side, picking up the pieces from the cup, wiping at the liquid on the floor. Her heart ached in her chest as she watched the woman step out of the carriage.

Marie had come home.

There was something different about her, though she couldn't name what. She looked the same as she always had. Her skin tanned slightly from her time in the garden. Her mother embraced her, the Duke stepping out afterwards, forcing a smile. Thea could see past it, however. Marie repulsed him. Her very presence seemed to offend him. Her stomach became nauseous as she watched the Duke.

Thea lifted the plate of cucumber sandwiches, throwing it into the wall with a scream, the plate shattering on impact.

"Clean it up." She said before storming from the parlor.

Something seemed wrong.

Thea returned to her chambers, sitting before the vanity, staring at herself. She hadn't worn her hair up since her sister had left. She could no longer remember how to put it up. That had been their routine: Marie woke her, fixed their hair, then the two dressed and left together. During the day, she would act as her keeper, doing everything in her power to protect her. She took the blame for her sister's mistakes refusing to allow them to treat her so cruelly.

It wasn't until two years ago when her sister had agreed that she return home that she stopped. Marie had told her to have faith and Thea had been foolish enough to listen to her. She should have stayed, hidden from the Duke and watched over her sister. However she hadn't, and that was her biggest mistake.

##

Marie forced a smile as her mother embraced her. "I'm glad you could make it. I'm sure your sister will be too."

"Where is Thea?"

"I haven't seen her since dinner. She normally has her tea alone so I doubt she even knows you're here. Speaking of tea, we're having your favorite. You will join us, right?"

Marie shook her head. "I'm afraid not but thank you. Thea and I have always had tea together, so I'm going to find my sister. I will see you in the morning for breakfast. Mother. Father." She stepped past them, pacing herself as she made her way up to the stairs, grateful to get away from her parents and her husband.

She stopped before the parlor, watching as the servant scrubbed the walls, another picking up a plate and cucumber sandwiches. She clasped her hands together, taking a deep breath, her heart heavy in her chest. She had no doubt as to where her sister was.

She couldn't move fast enough, relieved when she reached her door. The silence on the other side troubled her, but she was determined to see her sister again. She opened the door, surprised when the room was empty. She closed the door, opening her sister's room, still decorated in a mournful style. She met the familiar form of her sister as she sat before the vanity.

"You need to redecorate, Thea. It's no wonder you spent so much time in my chambers."

Thea stared at the mirror, biting her lip, tears threatening to flow down her cheeks. "I can't remember how to put my hair up. Marie."

Marie closed her door and opened the curtains. The room flooded with light, bringing color to the now purple walls. She stood behind her sister, fastening it into place before sitting beside her.

"You look better with your hair down, sister."

"I wrote you every day." Thea said. "Why didn't you wr back?"

"Because I did, my husband made sure they never reached your hands. I suspect mother, and father did the same." Marie took her sister's hands, folding them firmly. "Except one, that's how I knew to come here."

"At least one of my letters reached you." Thea took her sister's hand, holding it tightly. "You seem different but I—"

"Thea." Marie said, her chest aching. "I have a lot to tell you though not all of it is as bad as it might seem."

"Like what?"

Marie took a deep breath. "I have a son now. He's four months old and his name is Ciel."

"You had a baby?" Thea said, her breath pulled from her chest. "What does he look like?"

"He has my eyes and your hair." Marie laughed. "Okay, he looks completely like you."

Thea smiled, hugging her sister. "I'm so happy for you. What does your husband think?"

Marie pulled away from her sister, beginning to pace about the room. "I told him he was not allowed to see Ciel."

"You did what?"

Marie stopped pacing looking at her sister. "He raped me Thea. However, it's not Ciel's fault and so he will be staying with my wet nurse and her mother. They've watched over me for the last year."

"How did he—"

"Because I conveniently broke my leg, and he raped me." She took a deep breath, sitting with her sister again. "I had feelings for my tutor, but I was a fool and respected my marriage. In response my husband shot him in the head which caused the horses to rear. My horse lost its balance and fell over, breaking my leg."

Thea stared at her with tears in her eyes. "I should have stayed."

"I stand by my decision to let you come home. However, what I don't understand is why you agreed to get married."

married you would come home. It seems I

came home. Your efforts are not in vain." She said, taking her sister's hands again. "You are my strength because I watched you for years endure and prosper."

Thea couldn't hold back her tears any longer, hugging her sister. "I'm sorry-"

Marie hugged her back. "Don't be. It's not your fault. Stop blaming yourself." Thea pressed her hand to Marie's stomach, Marie placing her hand on top of hers. "I hate him for what he did to me, but Ciel will never be to blame for his actions. I want my son to be just like you, or at least, I did."

"What's that supposed to mean?"

"You say it's because you wanted me to come home, and I understand that. However, is it possible that somewhere along the way, you gave up? It would explain why in three days you'll be married just like me. I want my sister back."

"I had surrendered like you did."

"I don't want you to be like me. Fight back, Thea. You're good at it." Marie pulled the pins from her hair before pushing a brush through it. "Because if you don't, my husband will do everything in his power to get to Ciel, and I will not let him touch my son." She placed the brush on the vanity, pulling the pins from her hair.

Thea sat in silence for a moment, watching as her sister let down their hair.

"You look better with your hair down."

Thea smiled this time, looking at herself in the mirror as her sister pushed the brush through her hair.

"Join me for tea, Thea. I miss my garden." Marie said, placing the brush down.

"I would love to." Thea said, approaching the door.

Marie followed her, placing her hand on the door. "I'm going to sleep in here with you tonight. Promise me that I'll have my sister back in the morning."

"I promise." Thea said, following behind her, closing the door.

Thea could not sleep, watching the hours roll by, her sister sleeping soundly against her. She watched her sister sleep, her hands on her stomach. She felt guilty that her sister had to endure in her place. She kissed her sister's head once before moving away from her, positioning a pillow in her place before slipping out the door.

A guard stopped her immediately. "Thea? You should be asleep."

"Marie wished to have a snack from the kitchen. You won't tell anyone, will you?"

"Of course not but hurry back." The guards had stopped watching her as closely since she had begun to act favorably around her parents. She watched the guards in front of the Duke's chambers door, having learned their shift changes as a mischievous child. She slipped inside his chambers as the guards made their way to their next shift. She wouldn't allow herself to be seen by the guards. There would be no telling what they would suspect.

She watched as her sister's husband laid on his stomach, sleeping soundly, his snoring muffled by the bed. The man had grown in size since she had seen him at the wedding. The thought of him lying with her sister was disgusting. She stepped to the bed, grabbing the pillow meant for her sister, hugging it to her body, her lips twisting into a smile even if only for a moment.

"You will never touch my sister again."

Thea was careful as she climbed onto the bed, straddling his shoulders placing the pillow on the back of his head, using her weight as she forced down. The Duke eventually woke up, struggling against her though it was difficult with both their weights pressing on him. He grabbed at her nightgown, choking against the bed. Thea did not remove the pillow when his arms fell to his sides. She remained there, continuing to press on the pillow. She had to be sure this man would never see her sister again.

After many long minutes passed, silence hung in the air, Thea quietly stepping on the floor. She fluffed the pillow meant for her sister before placing it beneath his arm. She stood against the door, pressing her ear to the wood, listening as the guards conversed before taking their leave once the shift change came again. It was now that she took the opportunity to leave his quarters.

She made her way towards the kitchen, stealing a sweet roll before returning to her quarters.

"Do you think you will be able to sleep now, Lady?" The guard said as Thea approached.

She pretended to yawn. "Of that I have no doubt." She said, opening the door, slipping inside, speaking through the crack in the door. "Good night."

"And to you, Lady."

Thea placed the sweet roll on the table beside her sister. She then took her pillow away from her, lying in the bed, falling asleep with ease.

##

"I'm afraid we have serious news." Spoke their father, his hands unsteady as he tried to light his pipe, a loud sigh coming from him once it caught fire. "Marie, your husband breathed his last during the night. We have a doctor on the way but your mother, and I suspect his health may have finally caught up with him." He brought the pipe to his lips, taking his wife's hand in his as smoke coursed from his nostrils.

"You're welcome to stay home as long as you need." Her mother said.

"Thank you both." Marie said, clasping her hands together, meeting the eyes of her sister.

The day carried on, people extending their condolences to Marie that evening as her parents hosted another party. It was hard for her to hear the sadness in their voices. She worried for Ciel now that her husband had died. Would she be forced to remarry? Marie hadn't prepared herself for the idea that he would never have the chance to meet his father. Though she had despised him she would have never wished him dead. The reality of her situation scared her.

In her mind, one question stuck out among the noise. How did her husband die?

Marie sat at her vanity, pulling the pins from her hair as she watched her sister in the mirror preparing the bed. "You've been quiet today, Thea. Is something the matter?"

Thea glanced at her sister, making her way to the closet. "I just feel more like myself today. I do worry for you now that your husband has passed."

Marie watched her hair fall, placing her hands on her stomach. "Have you? Then may I ask you something?"

"Of course."

"Last night, I told you my husband wouldn't stop if you didn't fight back... did you fight back?"

Thea lifted a pillow, fluffing it. "Fighting implies there was a struggle."

"I didn't want him harmed." Marie said, standing.

Thea looked at her sister, narrowing her eyes as she sat the pillow down. "I suppose I did."

Tears flowed down Marie's face as she made her way to the door. "He may have been unkind to me, but I have a child! A child who now is without a father because of your selfish actions!" She bit her lip. She had planned to keep Ciel away from her husband, but she wasn't prepared to rule over a territory without him.

Thea sat before the vanity, staring at herself. "You are a fool, Marie if you think he wouldn't have harmed your son too. Trust me when I say that one day you will be thanking me." She smiled, brushing her hair. "This way you can remarry."

"The man I wanted to marry is dead." Marie left the room, wiping at her tears as she hurried down the hall. She ignored the guards as they called to her. She shuddered with the thought of her sister killing anyone let alone her husband. She may have not liked him, but he was still her husband. She knocked at the door of her father's office, grateful when he opened the door.

"Father, I must speak with you."

He looked at her, seeing the tears in her eyes. "Marie, it's late. I was just about to retire to my chambers."

"It's urgent." She pressed a hand to her stomach, her chest tight.

"Fine but speak with haste, Marie." He said, returning to his desk, handing her a half-empty glass with water in it. "Calm yourself, dear."

"Thank you." She said taking a seat in front of him, drinking the water. She watched as her father grabbed his pipe, avoiding her eyes as he lit the pipe with ease. He shook the match, setting it on the desk.

"Father, I feel that you must know that..."

"Yes?" He said, meeting her eyes. His expression troubled her, almost as if he was searching for something.

"My husband forced himself on me—"

He raised his hand, stopping her. "I don't know what to say."

Marie was taken aback by his tone. It was not remorseful rather disappointed.

Marie finished her water, setting the glass on his desk before standing up. "I apologize for bothering you. I will see you come morning." She kissed her father on the cheek before moving towards the door, peeking back to see his face. She just needed to know if her suspicions were warranted.

His face appeared as if it were made of stone.

Marie held her tongue, leaving the office. She had hoped to be proven wrong, but now she was sure. The first sign had been that her sister never received her letters and now her father showing no emotion at her news. She owed Thea an apology.

She returned to her sister's room, saddened that her sister had already fallen asleep. "I'll just apologize in the morning." She climbed into the bed, snuggling against her sister.

##

Thea woke early the following morning, her guilt like acid in her stomach, eating away at her. They had never argued before, always able to find a solution even if it meant suffering the consequences together.

"Marie." She said, gently shaking her. "I'm so sorry." Marie had always been a light sleeper, waking at the smallest of sounds, especially Thea's voice.

Her sister didn't move.

"Marie?" She said, shaking her again.

Thea's nostrils flared, her eyes widening. "Marie?! Wake up! Wake up!" Panic seized her, joining in her guilt.

She screamed her sister's name, tears streaming from her eyes. Her body did not move. She pulled the body of her sister near, solitude closing in on her.

The guards forced the door open, storming in. Two guards tried to pull Marie away from her, Thea biting the hand of one of the guards first before another punched her in the face. The remaining guards seized Thea, dragging her down the hall towards the office. The guard she had bitten carried her sister's body away, swearing beneath his breath.

News must have travelled fast within the walls of the estate. Thea's parents stood inside the office, waiting for her. Her mother held a match, lighting the pipe for her father. He took a deep breath, exhaling, the smoke hanging in the air around him. Her mother blew the match out, placing it on the desk before standing behind him, her hand on his shoulder. In the room stood her fiancé as well who watched the door, a bruise on his cheek.

Thea struggled against the guards as they dragged her down the hall. "Unhand me!" She screamed, the guards dragging her into the office, throwing her into the floor before the desk. She stood, smoothening her nightgown as she met the eyes of her father.

Her mother narrowed her eyes. "As if you weren't a failure enough, you kill your pregnant sister and her husband."

"I loved Marie more than either of you swollen swine. I would *never* kill my sister."

Her mother approached her, striking her with the back of her hand. "You will not speak to me in such a manner! Much less plead for innocence when the evidence is against you."

"Pleading for innocence? Mother you must have me confused for someone who is actually guilty. What evidence do you possibly have?" Thea said ignoring the burning feeling on her cheek.

A guard stepped forward. "The night of the Duke's death, she had left her quarters to retrieve food for her sister only returning with a sweet roll. It was never eaten. However, and remains on their bedside table."

Her mother never took her eyes off Thea. "And the next day he was dead."

Thea laughed in her mother's face. "That's because I smothered him with his pillow though technically I used the bed. The pillow was so that I didn't have to touch him. After all, he was far more of a swine than you." She smirked, prodding her finger to her mother's chest. "You're just a bitch."

Her mother seethed. "You ungrateful child! I wish it had been your body the guards carried away!"

Thea turned to look at the rest of the room, gesturing to them. "Listen as it squeals! Perhaps you are a swine after all."

Her father stood, slamming his pipe onto the desk. "Enough! You will not continue to speak to your mother in such a manner!"

She continued to stare at her mother though her words were directed at her father. "Then I suggest you tell your wife to get out of my face."

Her mother opened her mouth to speak, but her father spoke first. "Come here, my dear." He said, her mother returning to her place behind him. "Last night, Marie came to see me, saying you had threatened her, and she was frightened. I see now that I should have never allowed her to return to her chambers."

"*You lie through your teeth, Old Man.*" Thea said looking daggers into her father's eyes.

Her fiancé stepped forward, now. "We had a conversation recently on the balcony. She had told me she felt envious of her sister for the life she had, but I had never thought she would kill her."

"You red-headed bastard! If I kill anyone again it will be everyone in this room. I will set fire to the halls of this estate and watch you burn."

The guards restrained her again though Thea did not fight, her eyes on her father.

"Throw her into the dungeon. You have killed your flesh and blood, now you may live to see yours rot."

##

Thea could no longer recall how much time she had spent on the floor of her cell, though it had been long enough that the light of day had died out. She remained still, watching a spider as it crawled along its web on the ceiling, the guards returning to light the candles that lined the halls. She felt numb, betrayal and misery clouding her mind, hunger consuming her.

She'd never experienced hunger before. Her adolescent years were spent on a constant schedule. She watched as the guard approached her cell, setting something foul on the floor of her cell. Her stomach heaved, the smell enough to deter her from eating.

"Dinner, Prisoner." The guard said, his footsteps now fading into the silence.

She forced herself to move to the front of her cell despite the stiffness. The food looked raw and decayed, though she saw no other choice. She began to shovel the food into her mouth, hunger winning despite the turning of her stomach. Her skin crawled, her chest heaved, eyes watering as she consumed the food. Once the plate had been cleaned, she returned to her previous place, forcing herself to rest.

Hours later, she was stirred from her sleep. Feeling nauseous, she hurried to the small bucket in her cell, covering her mouth with her hand. She closed her eyes, vomiting. The sickening feeling remained though her stomach was now empty. She crawled to the corner of her cell where the light did not reach, desperate to fall asleep again.

The same food was brought again the next day.

"This food is rotten! I demand something else! Bread will even suffice!" She yelled to the guard, kicking the plate over.

"Perhaps you should have eaten the sweet roll you had stolen." The guard said, walking away.

She wrapped her hands around the bars, staring at the foul mash as she grit her teeth. "Then I shall starve! I will die by my own terms!" Silence accompanied her words, sorrow filling her chest as she returned to her corner.

She continued to stare at the plate from her corner when a small rat appeared. It peeked from a hole in the cell, looking around before approaching the plate. He sniffed at it, making a small noise before beginning to eat.

"It'll kill you too." Thea whispered, pitying the animal.

The rat never returned, the plate remaining to be consumed by flies.

##

"Prisoner." The guards called to Thea as she sat against the wall of her cell. They lifted the third plate she'd left for the flies, swatting at them. Another guard went to light the candles that lined the walls.

She looked up at the guards. "I need water." The guard looked at her amused, clearing his throat before spitting onto the floor of her cell. "I am at the mercy of my oppressors." She said with a chuckle, staring into the night sky through the small window in her cell.

She pressed her back against the wall as she sat on the stone floor of her cell, her arms crossed over her chest. She tried to imagine the different ways her conversation could have gone with Marie. She began to think about the many difficulties she had caused over the years, the many regrets she felt. Over and over she imagined how things could have happened, things she could have said. Her regret consumed her until she realized that there was nothing she could do about it any longer. Marie had moved on perhaps it would be best if she did too.

"I'm sorry, sister." She said, tears streaming from her eyes as she stared at the walls of her cell. "I will be with you soon."

She was stirred from her sleep some time later from the loud sound of iron clashing together as the prison door opened. Thea sat up, meeting the eyes of the guards as they entered her cell. They lifted her from the stone floor, dragging her out of the cell. She struggled against them as they dragged her down the hall. There was an almost hopeful feel about it from the many candles that flickered in the darkness, giving the hall a warm glow. However, it was a false hope for what waited at the end was only despair.

The guards entered a room shrouded in darkness, a stone vat sitting at its center. It was no more than waist high, round, and filled with arctic water. The room felt strangely cold, as if people had died here but never truly left. It was enough to make her skin crawl.

They secured her wrists onto the edge of the vat, one guard grabbing her by her hair, submerging her head in the freezing waters. She was surrounded by blackness, seeing nothing more than the bubbles in front of her created by breathing through her nose. She struggled against the restraints, screaming though it was muffled by the water. Her lungs, quickly emptied of air, water filling them in its place.

Under different circumstances she might have found the cold water to be refreshing.

The guard pulled her head out of the water not a moment too soon. She coughed the water out of her lungs, taking in deep breaths.

"Why did you kill Marie Leighton?"
"Her death is not on my shoulders."

The guards looked at one another, the senior officer sighing. "Again, it will take time before she confesses."

The guard's grip on her hair tightened, submerging her head once more. Thea struggled against her restraints, kicking at the guards, screaming into the water again.

The guard pulled her head out. "How's the water taste?"

Thea spit the water in her mouth into the guard's face, coughing through her laughter. "Why don't you tell me?"

The guard smacked her with his hand, the sound echoing through the chamber. He pulled her head back violently before submerging her again.

The impact from his hand stole the air from her lungs. What remained wasn't enough to keep the water from filling her lungs even without her screams. The guard waited longer before pulling her out this time.

Thea choked violently. Her hair was soaked, her head now pounding. Her chest felt like fire, sore from the lack of oxygen. She watched as the restraints were unlatched, the guards dragging her back to her cell. They slid the iron door open, throwing her into the cell, locking it behind them.

"We will return for you."

"I look forward to it." She said nearly out of breath.

She remained still, lying on the floor, pulling her knees to her chest. Her body trembled both from the cold and the pain. She couldn't decide which she dreaded more, the return of the guards or the plate of rotten mash.

She woke the next morning, watching as the guards came, blowing out the candles that lined the halls before taking their leave. She spent the day fidgeting with her nightgown, until the sun faded away, the cover of night replacing it. Thea stopped handling her dress, choosing instead to hold her knees to her chest. The guards returned once more, lighting the candles that lined the halls, but never stopping before her cell.

Thea stood, running to the front of her cell, wrapping her hands around the bars. "Where's my food?!"

The guards ignored her, continuing back to the surface of the estate.

"Answer me, damn you!" She sat against the wall of her cell again with her knees to her chest, waiting for them to return with the plate in hand.

Only the plate never returned.

A second day came with no visit from the guards, not even a look, then a third, the same as before. Though she no longer desired to eat, it troubled her that they made no attempts to feed her.

She remained in the corner of her cell, watching the guards as they went about their business, only moving when absolutely necessary. The door would open again. It had to, even if it was only to collect her body.

The days became a blur, the guards returning. The most heinous of smiles was stretched across their faces as they dragged her from the cell. She stared at the floor as they dragged her back to the room with the vat, restraining her again. The guard held onto her hair, wrapping the dark locks around his hand, holding onto her skull.

"This could be over now if you acknowledged your sins."

Thea smirked. "I stole an apple from a table as a child. And I ate it too."

"You think this is some kind of joke because you were once the daughter of a Duke? You're no better than the dirt on my boots!" The guard said submerging her head again.

She continued to smirk, watching as the bubbles formed before her, decreasing in number with the passing seconds. They held her head in far longer than they had before, pulling her back to watch her choke.

"Admit that you are responsible for the death of your sister!" Spoke the senior guard.

"I would sooner drown."

"So be it." The guard grumbled, submerging her again.

The guards watched the bubbles, smiling to one another. "She's getting better at holding her breath."

The guard holding her pulled her out of the water, smiling maliciously as she choked on the water, gasping for her breath. Once she could breathe again she began to laugh. They wanted her to lie, to confess to a crime she did not commit and for what? To ease the burden on the souls of her parents for killing their daughter? She would never give them the satisfaction they sought, so she continued to laugh.

The guards were taken aback by her laughter. They released the restraints, dragging her still laughing back to her cell, throwing her into the stone floor.

"What's so funny?"

She refused to speak, lying on the floor of the cell continuing to laugh.

The guards stopped returning after that, not even to light the candles on the walls. She did not mind the darkness, instead choosing to welcome it with open arms. Somehow she could find peace in the combination of darkness and silence.

She slept more soundly than she had in days past despite her constant stomach pains. She would be able to die without them interfering any longer. However, after several days had passed, the guards returned once more, with two more men than normal.

"We are offering you one last chance to atone for your sins."

She laid in the center of the floor, basking in the moonlight like a cat. "I do not seek atonement. I only want to see my sister again."

The guards unlocked her cell door, stepping inside, locking it behind them, throwing the keys to the one man who remained outside the cell. Her cheeks flushed, her heart racing at the sound of their metal belts snapping loose, their trousers falling to the floor. The three of them pressed their hands to their genitals, rubbing them as they stared at Thea ravenously.

She pulled her knees to her chest, holding them tightly enough that her skin paled in places. A guard laughed as he grabbed her legs pulling them straight. He got on his knees, grabbing her soiled underclothing, pulling them off before throwing them to the side. The other men got onto their knees, one grabbing her breasts, pinning her to the floor while the other held her by her jaw, running his dirty fingers across her lips.

Thea screamed at the top of her lungs until the guard holding her jaw covered her mouth with his hands. The guard holding her legs spread them around his waist so that she could no longer close them. He ran his hands up her exposed flesh, squeezing her rear. He forced himself into her, groaning, pushing deeper, thrusting against her.

"I never knew the Duke's daughter was so tight. I had always assumed she, and her sister were close for a reason."

She screamed against the man's hand, tears falling from her eyes, stopping at his hand. The man moved his hand, rubbing her tears on his genitals before forcing her mouth open.

"You scared?" He said, no longer able to wait for the other man to stop. He placed two fingers into her throat for a minute before putting his dick in their place. He held her mouth open by her hair, pulling it tightly, his other hand on her jaw.

Thea tried to scream as she choked. "Scream for me baby." He said, thrusting against her face.

The last guard got tired of watching, ripping off her nightgown before turning her onto her side, the other guards adjusting their positions. The last gentleman pressed himself to her rear, forcing himself inside.

Pain seized her body, her screams muffled, as she cried again, all three men thrusting against her body, squeezing it. The guard on the outside grinned, his trousers around his ankles as he touched himself, watching the others as they thrashed against her.

Two of the guards finished inside her before standing, pulling their trousers up, fastening their belts. The final man forced her onto her back, taking one of her legs, forcing it to the other side of his body as he groaned, thrusting harder into her body, finishing inside her.

"Are you sure that is wise?"

"She won't live long enough to bear a child."

The guards chuckled, leaving the dungeon.

Thea pulled her knees close, holding the tattered remains of her nightgown to her chest. The smell of copper strong around her, blood staining her skin, soaking into the floor beneath her. She refused to move, her body writhing in pain. She found no comfort in the moonlight any longer.

For the first time since her imprisonment, Thea sobbed.

She laid there for hours, sobbing, her body trembling. The pain grew worse as the time passed her by. How could her parents allow their guards to rape their only daughter no matter what she did?

Thea couldn't fall asleep that night, afraid that they might return. As the hours passed she could hear the sound of wings fluttering in the distance, a large bird now sitting at her window, the light from the moon revealing its lustrous black feathers. The bird cawed, beady eyes the color of charcoal focused on her.

She could swear the bird was smiling at her.

Thea held her nightgown tighter, pulling her knees to her chest, burying her face into the dirty flesh. She ignored the bird continuing to sob into the fabric of the gown, her tears collecting the dirt on her flesh as they fell leaving only her pale flesh behind.

The bird began to cackle.

Her body now trembled for another reason. She slowly made her way to the wall, leaning against it for support as she climbed to her feet.

"Enough! Away with you bird!"

The bird silenced turning its head curiously as it watched her. She scowled, her legs giving out beneath her, bones sore from trying to stand. Though the bird appeared like any other, except for the voice that emitted from it, she could see something different about this one in its eyes. She could sense something very dark and powerful about the bird.

The bird's beak parted slightly. "I find it rather ironic, Thea that I am the bird, and you are the one locked within a cage."

"Oh sweet raven, I have suffered enough at the hands of man." She said, still holding onto her nightgown.

"I once admired you for your strength but have watched as you succumbed to weakness."

"I want nothing more than to be released from this weakness." Thea took a deep breath, trying to cease her tears. "Oh sweet raven, I'd give anything to leave this place."

The raven closed its beak, smiling once more. "Understand Thea that the price of your release may prove to be worse than death."

"Take what you will, raven. I can take no more."

The bird flew into her cell, landing on her leg, meeting her eyes. "Then this once I give you power equal to an unkindness of ravens. Ravage this land, take your revenge, and make your escape but know that you will not get far."

"So be it but I will not die within the walls of this prison." Thea said, reaching out to touch the bird. The bird latched itself onto her finger, drawing blood. She screamed, shaking her hand, clutching it to her chest once the bird let go.

The bird cackled once more, her blood staining its beak. flying to the window. It looked into her eyes one last time.

"You will be the undoing of this world, Thea, but only if you desire." The bird cawed loudly, flying into the cover of night.

Thea looked down at her finger, the wound closing quickly. She took a deep breath, closing her eyes, her trembling coming to a stop. She no longer felt burdened by hunger nor pain. Her energy returning to her tenfold.

She stood, dropping the nightgown where she once sat, returning to the place the guards had left her, in the center of the blood-stained floor. She closed her eyes, lying as if she were dead. Days passed but her hunger never returned, her body never becoming stiff. She did not waiver until she could finally make out the familiar sounds of the guard's footsteps. She listened as they approached her cell, resisting the urge to smirk as she listened to their conversation.

"Starved herself to death." The guard said, opening her cell. "A pity too, I had hoped for one last touch."

"She can't fight you this way." The other guard said, placing a hand on her forehead. "Body's still warm. Just pretend she's alive."

Thea's eyes opened wide. "Who's pretending?" She said, kicking the man in the chest. She stood up, grabbing the man by his throat with both hands, choking him. "I can see the appeal now." She laughed as the man gasped before she crushed his windpipes.

"The bitch is still alive!" The other guard said, hurrying to the cell's door.

She approached the man, grabbing the back of his skull, turning, crushing his skull on the wall. She watched coldly as his body fell to the floor, leaving a blood smear on the wall of her cell. She approached the other man as he sat in the floor, watching as he clutched his neck, unable to breathe.

She ran a finger along his lips, smiling. "Now you know how I felt when your dick was in my throat. Only difference is you will die here, and I will walk out that door."

She was quiet as she made her way up to the stairs, killing all guards that approached her, painting the walls in their blood:

##
If you want to kill me, try harder.
##

She dragged her bloodied fingers along the wall as she leisurely walked down the hall, making her way to the entrance.

"Lady Thea!" spoke a servant as she dropped her tray, plates smashing to the floor. "Where are your clothes?"

She placed her bloody finger to the servant's lips. "Ask the guards who ripped them off me." She said, continuing to walk past her.

Guards watched over the entrance, their eyes widening when they saw Thea. "She's still alive?" One spoke, looking nervously at the other guard.

Thea smirked, recognizing their faces. They had been with the other two guards the night they had forced themselves upon her.

She approached the one on the right, kicking him in the knees, listening as the bone snapped. The man fell onto the floor, holding his leg. The other guard ran at her, Thea turning her head, grabbing him by his uniform.

"You should watch." She said, smashing his skull with her foot. She let go of his uniform, using her hands on both sides of his head to crush his skull. His body fell onto the floor, Thea dipping her fingers in their blood writing for the last time on the estate doors:

##

I will set fire to the halls of this estate and watch you burn.

##

She threw the doors open, the doors creating a refreshing breeze. She enjoyed the view of the courtyard as she made her way down the stairs of the estate. The dew-covered grass was refreshing against her feet. She took a deep breath, eventually reaching the meadow beyond the estate.

Thea could hear a howling in the distance. She looked in the direction of the noise, gasping as dogs larger than a man came at her. Their bodies were emaciated, flesh rotted away in different areas exposing muscle. Their ribs could be seen though mostly covered by flesh. Chains dangled from their necks, their eyes hollow. They latched onto her, grabbing her limbs.

Thea stared in horror as the sky turned to red, the meadow dying beneath her, the ground painted in black. The ground trembled as it split, a river forming, its waters painted red.

She could hear the cawing of ravens in the distance.

Chapter 6

    She woke, in taking breath, staring into the space around her. There was no other way to describe it other than space for all she could see was white. It did not feel hollow rather as if someone were shining a light in her eyes. She lifted her hands to shield her eyes but could not see them.

    She started to walk though she wasn't sure she was going anywhere. Her pace was slow in the beginning, fear holding her back. As she continued to walk the fear dissipated, leaving the most peculiar of feelings. It was as if she were in the center of everything no matter how far she walked. And though she was lost, she had never felt more at peace than she did now.

    The white began to fade, her hands now clearly visible before her, platinum locks resting against her chest. She came to a stop, her cheeks reddening as she crossed her arms over her chest, her pale skin fully exposed.

    She stood still, frightened of the world before her. Everything was painted in various blues as if the world had been brushed with ink made of sapphires. Little white lights peeked out through the clouds, dancing on the waters beneath her. The sky was the darkest of sapphires fading into their natural color. Words failed her, tears rolling down her cheeks.

The world became something unfamiliar. It was like she had become part of an elaborate painting. The world around her seemed to be painted in watercolor. She could almost make out the brush strokes as they had created the clouds. Some parts of the clouds were more vibrant than others. The clouds met the edge of the water in the distance never coming closer. It was almost as if the world had become flat just like a painting. There was no depth, and a small part of her was reluctant to move forward.

"Thea?" She called out. "I'm sorry for storming away." She stared into the water as tears rolled down her cheeks. In her reflection, she could see the truth. It felt like a heavy burden on her shoulders, bringing her to her knees.

She had died. She couldn't deny it. The evidence was all around her. She closed her eyes, unable to look at the beautiful world around her as she balled her hands into fists. She felt foolish calling for her sister knowing she would never see her again. The pain made her chest ache but only for a moment. It was as if the world was forcing her into a state of peace. She wiped the tears from her eyes forcing herself to face the world before her.

She extended her leg testing her toes on the surface. She didn't want to remain in the same place but the idea of walking on water caused just as much fear as remaining. When her toes did not pierce the surface, she allowed her entire foot to press down, the water rippling for a few feet before fading into the vast body of water. She allowed her next foot onto the surface the water rippling again. Confident she wouldn't fall into the darkness she pressed on walking forward watching as the water continued to ripple into the distance around her.

"What is this place?" she said, stones forming in the water beneath her feet.

The water became clouds painted in gold, divided by a stone path that extended as far as the eye could see. The path itself was light in color like the sun had bleached it. She stopped, looking around but there was neither a sun nor moon. She was careful with each step, her eyes never wavering from the clouds in the distance.

"Where am I?"

She would have been content to walk forever but in the distance, she could make out large gates of gold and ivory.

She came to a stop seeing a creature guarding the gates. Its head had four faces: an eagle, a lion, an ox, and one of a man. Its body was the same as that of a lion but with the feet of an ox. The creature held a sword consumed by flames ever turning. On its back spread four conjoined wings covered in eyes. The creature though terrifying in appearance also seemed majestic surrounded by the soft glows from the clouds and the golden gates.

"You are trapped in Limbo, Child. Worry not, for behind these gates is the kingdom of Heaven. It is home to our brethren." The creature spoke through the man's face, beckoning her forward. "Enter but no longer as the human you thought you once were. Enter as a Stronghold addressed only as the virtue Humility."

"What are you?" Her voice was faint but gentle. The creature intimidated her but she approached with caution, her breath caught in her chest.

The creature's faces watched her as she approached, speaking through the face of the lion now. "I, Humility, am a cherub. Now enter, for there is much work to be done."

Heaven.

Humility passed through the gates as large white wings emerged from her back. Her body felt weightless, no longer bound to the surface. The cobblestone path continued into Heaven, extending in all directions. Many of its paths led up to grandiose temples of pale marble with statues made of the same stone decorating their entrances. Along the paths were many fountains decorated with images of putti across their bases. The water within the fountains was full of color from the way the sky reflected off it.

There were no artists on earth that would be able to recreate the sky of Heaven for it was beyond human ability. Like the clouds before she had passed through the gates, these too seemed as if they had been painted on but by the angels. There was no way to tell where they began or if there was a beginning for where there was no stone path, there were clouds. Heaven was a place of color: pinks, oranges, yellows, pale blues, and soft purples. The only white was that of thousands of angels as they danced across the sky, flying from temple to temple.

She held her hand above her eyes, the colors so bright they were radiant.

She took a breath, suddenly bumping into someone. "I apologize..." The angel's appearance was breathtaking and fitting. She had always imagined angels to be otherworldly in beauty. This angel met her imagination with perfect curves and a muscular physique. Its eyes were constantly darting from angel to angel as it issued commands and directions. From its tone, she could tell it had been doing this for quite some time. It spoke quickly, almost in a blur, directing the angels who approached it with the scepter in its hand. Atop the scepter was an orb that shined brilliantly. Its other hand held a clipboard that it occasionally would suspend in the air to write on its pages. The angels approached it in a flurry quick to receive their orders and depart.

"Name?" The angel said, looking at her impatiently.

She looked up at it, surprised that it had noticed her among the madness. "*Me?* M-Marie Leighton." She said, stammering.

The angel looked at the clipboard, running its hand over the pages, mumbling. "I have no record of that name." He cleared his throat, flipping the page. "Do not tell me you've *forgotten* your name."

"Humility?" She said quietly.

"Are you asking me if that is your name?" The angel said looking through the pages of the clipboard, tsking.

"*My name is Humility.*"

It ran its hand over the pages again, flipping them occasionally before smiling from ear to ear as it checked off on the clipboard. "Ah, yes, the new stronghold." The angel beckoned her forward, the clipboard disappearing. "Come this way."

She followed closely, awestruck by the appearance of the other angels. Some looked like horrors while others seemed as if they had come from the paintings she had seen around her family estate as a child. She had once believed that every angel was beautiful like the one beside her. However, she now understood this to be wrong. It was nearly impossible for her to believe that she was one of them. It felt more like a bad dream.

She looked at the angel again curiously. One of its faces looked at her in return.

"What is it?"

"I was wondering why you carry a scepter?"

The angel sighed as if she should have already known. "I am a dominion. We all carry a scepter, and it is our duty to make sure that *you* are doing *your* job." It cleared its throat. "As a stronghold you're assigned a virtue, in your case humility. You will be expected to bring blessings from Heaven to Earth, to create miracles, and to influence humanity by bringing them courage. You can even cause acts of heroism."

Humility smiled. Perhaps she would have the chance to help the people she had been forced to leave behind.

"However, you must wait until the Elders command you to so don't get any ideas. Until you are called upon by the Elders I will leave you to help Azrael for he has requested assistance. It would be in your best interest to see to his needs since he is unable to leave his temple. Hurry inside, Humility." The angel said, stopping before a temple larger than any other, ushering her inside.

"Thank you," she said.

Pillars lined the entrance into the temple. Ivy wrapped loosely around them. She ran her fingers across the marble, staring in wonder. The walls reached high, light pouring in through the large windows of the clerestory. The hall seemed to glisten in the light. She held her hands close to her chest, turning as she walked looking at everything. The ceiling though far away unmistakably bared a never-ending mural.

The mural was vivid though it was so far away. Images of angels warring with others of their kind were painted. Some angels kept their distance such as the principalities but many wielded their weapons, dressed in complete sets of armor as they charged into battle. Leading them were four heavily armored men riding immense steeds. Behind them stood a large angel wielding a book with seven seals.

Then they turned to look at her. The angels emerged from the ceiling, flying at her. Their weapons poised to strike, their eyes piercing through her.

Humility fell upon her knees, covering her head, desperate to defend herself from her attackers. Her screams pierced the silence of the temple but the angels did not show mercy, as they grew closer.

Chapter 7

She came to screaming her sister's name in the darkness wrapping her arms around her body as she lay against the dark wood of the boat. Her hair was like shadows as it struggled to cover her body, most of it trapped between her and the boat itself. Before her was a torch providing her the light she needed to see as the boat slowly drifted down the river towards the gates of Hell. The river seemed to reach into eternity flecked with light as the boats guided souls.

Thea took solace in the fact that she wasn't the only sinner. Though she had read the stories of Hell as a child, they had described it with few words. Souls cast into a furnace of fire where they shall wait and listen to the rasping of teeth until the end of time. Even the angels were not spared, cursed to spend their remaining days in the shadows of hell bound to chains of darkness.

Though she had screamed for her sister she knew she would never answer. Thea had always known her sister would make it to Heaven to fly among the angels. Marie deserved only the best, and she hoped that she would find it for her final days would be for nothing if her sister didn't receive the fate she deserved.

She had taken the raven's words with a grain of salt.

Thea sat upright in the boat surprised by the fact that she felt the very same as when she had made the deal with the raven. In the boat, beside her laid a white dress, which she quickly donned. It brought a small smile to her lips. She didn't particularly enjoy walking around fully exposed.

The world before her was like nothing she had ever seen before. She had read hundreds of books, perhaps thousands but none of the words prepared her for what she saw now.

Hell was beautiful in its own chilling way.

The shore looked like the charred grass of the meadow, black as the night sky with a thin grey mist hanging above it. The air around her was still, the smell of burning wood pungent though far more pleasant than the smell of her cell. The torch crackled, piercing through the silence keeping her affixed to her new reality.

The water that the boats gently floated through was a deep shade of blue like that of the evening sky. It rippled away from the boats as they grew near the gates. The gates though still far away seemed larger than anything else she had seen before. There was nothing for her to compare them to for they seemed to have no beginning and no end. They stood within the waters, closed and waiting.

Beside them a beast stood diligently on all fours, large enough to view the length and breadth of the river. His eyes were watchful, a bright gold embedded into his head. His fur was darker than the grass on the shore. At his side were two pups, striking and large like their father. He stepped forward, nudging the gates open with his head, the river's glasslike surface torn apart by waves. The boats drifted through crashing upon the shores of Hell, the gates closing behind them with a decrying sound.

Thea held tightly onto the edges of the boat, the sound ringing through her body. She felt hollow, her fear being the only thing reminding her that she was still alive in some way. She watched with wide eyes as a man approached her. He towered higher than any man she had met before by several feet at least, his limbs covered in images of war. He carried a great sword equally large, piercing the earth before her with it. He picked her wilting body up with one arm, placing her on his shoulders before lifting the sword from the earth.

She had never felt such terror, her heart racing in her chest and beads of sweat trickling along her skin. She stared before them as he made his way along the charred ground towards a mountain reaching higher than any she had seen before. Although she had only seen mountains in the books she read over the course of her life and had been left to imagine their immense size.

The cavern entrance was shaped like the face of a man, withered and time worn, though he smiled almost as if he were laughing. His eyes remained closed. His mouth was the entrance, veiled in darkness, the screams of souls within the cavern resonating out of the mouth like a cruel laughter.

The entrance into the cavern swallowed the man. Stone spikes reached high to his left. To his right were braziers twice his size built into the walls, their flames untamed. Thea watched in the distance as a lesser demon with bellows in his hand took a deep breath, exhaling strong winds, fueling the fires. His face was dismayed. She could see that he had lost hope now living his days out as a slave to the bellows.

She gritted her teeth refusing to allow herself to give in so easily. She pressed her hands to the demon's shoulders, pushing her body off and falling to the ground beneath him. She forced herself to her feet though her body aching from the impact. She ran in every direction, in search of a way out. However, each direction was the same, demons carrying souls further into the mountain. Their stone walls blocked her escape at every turn. Her chest ached as her eyes searched. For the first time in her life she could neither think of nor see an escape.

This was Hell.

The man's voice thundered as he placed his sword in the earth again moving leisurely as he retrieved Thea, grabbing her by her wrist. He pressed his mouth to her ears, his voice causing her to tremble.

"I'm sorry." The man said, returning to his sword, dragging her with him. He lifted his sword, resting the blade against his shoulder as he continued down the path.

Thea closed her eyes, unable to shed tears for she had asked for this despite not knowing that this was where fate would take her. "So sweet raven, this is what you meant."

The cavern opened into a large room that split into hundreds of halls, some demons coming to a stop, others pressing forward. The demon unfortunately was one of those who came to a stop. He placed her into a chair, his sword standing before her. She swallowed nervously looking at her reflection in the steel.

The demon pinned her to the chair with one hand, the other reaching into his pocket pulling out a small blade. He held Thea by her hair, allowing her shoulder to recover. He brought the blade up to her hair, cutting the long raven locks before throwing them onto the ground beneath her. He then pressed the blade to her scalp continuing to remove her hair.

Thea watched as her hair fell upon the ground beneath her, biting on her lip as her tears flowed down her cheeks. She closed her eyes, trying to resist the pain that consumed her. Though the blade did not cut her, the love she had felt for her hair was now torn from her. She had never imagined that there would be a day where someone took from her something that had always been a part of her. However, this wasn't the first time.

The demon forced her to stand, his hands grabbing the fabric of her dress, ripping it from her body piece by piece. She screamed, desperate to hold onto her dignity. Her memories of the guards ripping her nightgown from her body flood her mind. She fought against him screaming at the top of her lungs. The demon brought the back of his hand across her face, the sound resonating through the room. He ripped the last of her dress before throwing her onto the ground. She reached for the chair her heart sullen as she watched the demon kick it from her grasps.

She struggled as she climbed to her feet, tears streaming from her eyes as the demon grabbed her, dragging her down one of the halls. She continued to scream, fighting against him though his strength was unrivaled.

He threw her into a room, bringing his hand across her face again. She clambered to her feet, the hands of another demon now holding her in place. She looked up into the face of a raven, its head sitting on the body of a man. Wings extended from his back, their feathers the same color as those on his head.

The demon with the sword growled, pulling her from the bird demon, taking her into a smaller room that was connected though sealed off separately. He placed her within it, sealing the door close behind him. The room was painted shadows. Sound could not pierce its walls. Even the screams of the other souls could not pierce its walls.

She closed her eyes unable to sleep, to pretend this was a dream. That she would wake up and her sister would be beside her. She would finally have the chance to apologize to her.

##

The sword demon returned to the main room, staring into the other demon's eyes. "You aren't welcome here, Gluttony."

Gluttony sat in a chair, crossing one leg over the other, his arm resting against the back. "I will be here for only a moment, Wrath. That is assuming you are willing to cooperate." He said with a smirk.

"What is it you have come for, Scavenger?" Wrath spoke, pointing the sword at Gluttony.

"That girl's soul belongs to me. You may not see me as a demon, but I assure you I have earned my place here." He said, standing from the chair, pushing the sword away with his hand.

"I will not deny that you earned a place in Hell, but I can't surrender the girl's soul. It has been so long since I've eaten."

"Then perhaps you should try harder."

Wrath sneered. "You speak as if it's so easy. Not all of us are burdened with physical changes."

"You're a poor son of a bitch. How dare they bestow upon you empathy." He said, approaching Wrath, pressing the tip of his finger to his chest. "I'm taking her soul one way or another. It would be easier on us both if you handed it over."

"You dare to mock me and then threaten me? An angel who pretends he's a demon because he killed a few people."

"I've killed far more people than you can count." Gluttony said, stepping away.

Wrath watched as Gluttony disappeared from the room, spitting where he once stood. "Eat a corpse scavenger."

Gluttony rolled his eyes, leaning against a nearby wall. He could sense a powerful force grow near. He kept silent, hiding himself in the illusion.

A demon entered the room, twice the size of Wrath, his entire body made of the faces and bodies of the countless souls it had consumed over the centuries. Though they were a part of his body, hands reached out wrapped in his flesh, their mouths open to scream though no sound came. The worst of them was a child whose face protruded from the chest of the demon. Its face still held the same innocence as it once did when it lived.

"First I deal with the cursed bird, and now you have come." Wrath said disgustedly. "This is why I never get a meal around here."

The demon looked at him. "Gluttony was here? What for?"

"The girl."

"How unusual. I've not heard of him taking an interest in souls before."

"It was bound to happen one of these days. Perhaps he's giving them to Sloth since she can no longer leave her bed."

"That's why she has dolls, Fool."

"You can't tell me you haven't noticed how close they've become."

"I've not paid attention seeing as there are more pressing matters at hand than their affection towards one another." He said looking down at Wrath. "I wish to see this girl. Bring her to me."

##

Thea laid in the dark room curled up like a child hiding from monsters. She knew this was no different than being in her cell again. However, unlike her cell it was warm, quiet, and shrouded in darkness. She couldn't see her hand even when she placed it in front of her.

The only thoughts that came to mind were those of the raven's warning.

Perhaps she was wrong. She had been a hundred times before. At least here, she still had options though bleak they may be. If she were to die, then she wouldn't be able to avenge her sister's death. And maybe the opportunity would never come for her to but this way she could try. For if she could never see her again then she could at least try to get even with those that had stabbed them in the back.

She forced herself to her feet, walking around the small room. She came to a stop, turning her head when the door opened before her. She shielded her eyes from the bright light, Wrath reaching for her. He forced a cowl over her face, tightening it around her neck making it hard for her to breathe. She grabbed at it for a moment before he grabbed her arms holding them behind her back.

They moved quickly, Wrath holding her arms with a harsh grip. The light grew brighter, shining through her cowl as they entered the large room. Fear seized her body, her heart racing as she sensed something else in the room. Though she could not see it, she could feel its power.

Thea jumped, throwing herself forward as she landed, trying to break free from his grasp. She did not care how it knew her. Only that she could escape from them.

Wrath planted his feet where he stood, holding her despite her struggles. He looked up at Greed.

"Place her in the chair. I think it's time we had a little talk." Wrath placed her in the chair before removing the cowl. "Give the girl some space, Wrath."

Wrath mumbled insults to himself but did as he was asked, standing on the wall opposite Gluttony.

"What have you done to end up here, girl?" Greed spoke, standing before her.

"I made a deal with a demon. It didn't exactly work out in my favor."

Greed laughed though Thea tried to remain calm in the face of danger. She couldn't hide her trembling hands from the demon or the unsteadiness of her breathing. They knew she was terrified but there was something amusing about her false bravery.

"Well then perhaps you're willing to give it another go."

"Make *another* deal with a demon? I don't think so. It didn't exactly fair for me well the first time."

"There is no deal with a demon whom you can make where you come out on top."

"Then why would I even consider making a deal with you?"

"Because your only other option is death."

She took a deep breath, exhaling through her nose. "I'm listening."

"You're too young to be down here because of greed. Was it a man?"

"I killed my sister's husband."

"A little thing like you?" Greed said with a laugh. "So it was envy."

"He raped my sister. So, I made sure he would never lay a hand on her again."

"You think of yourself as her protector."

"I am her protector." Thea said standing up.

"From what I can see you aren't doing a very good job."

"That's because we're both dead." Thea took a step forward towards the demon. "What is it you are offering me, Demon?"

"You are filled with pride, and I think you would benefit from joining us. Unless you would rather be *killed.*"

She crossed her arms over her chest. Though she didn't want to sacrifice her humanity her only other option was to sacrifice her life. That was a sacrifice she could never make. If she were to become a demon, then she would be able to achieve revenge at least.

"I accept your offer, Demon, but on one condition. I have yet to finish my business on Earth. There are people that must die for what they have done."

Greed laughed, approaching her. "While I like your spirit, Girl, you are in no position to make an ultimatum."

"I will find a way to kill them. With or without your help."

"You should be grateful I'm allowing you to live regardless."

Greed leaned forward, plunging his hand into her chest. "From this day forward, Thea is dead. You will be referred to as Lavanah."

Thea coughed up blood, looking up into the eyes of Greed as his bloodied hand pulled a bright blue light from her chest. He swallowed the light, his flesh stretching into an exact copy of her. She could see in her own face the fear that she felt now.

She fell on her knees, holding the gaping wound with her hands. Her blood was warm as it slipped through her fingers. She collapsed to the floor, closing her eyes.

"Wrath I want you to find Gluttony. Tell him the girl is his. I'm curious what he will do with a doll of his own."

"What if he rejects her because she no longer has a soul?"

"Throw her onto the streets with the other lesser demons. If she isn't to become a doll, then she is of no use to us. I have what I want." Greed said before taking his leave.

Gluttony stepped forward, continuing to keep himself hidden. He adjusted the illusion so that Wrath began to walk in place. He watched for a moment as he opened a door that wasn't there.

He knelt beside Thea lifting her body into his arms. "The last thing I need is a doll." He said digging into his own chest where he produced an orange light. The light split into two, one returning to his chest, the other being absorbed by Thea.

Her eyes opened wide, her chest healing as she began to scream. Gluttony covered her mouth, looking at Wrath who was talking to a nearby wall. Thea stopped screaming after a moment looking at Gluttony. Words failed her, but she knew something was wrong. Her head felt as if it were trying to explode.

"Gluttony, you're a bastard." She mumbled behind his hand.

"I didn't do this to you, Thea." he said. "But I wish I had."

She pushed his hand up, quickly standing up. Little black dots danced in her vision for a moment before she found herself lying on the floor again.

##

Lavanah was roused by a constant pricking on her back followed by the wiping of a cloth against her flesh. She lay on her stomach. Her limbs stretched out and restrained to the bed she laid on top of. The pricking continued, a strange cold air seeming to have wrapped itself around her body. She shivered as the needle pricked her skin again.

Attached to the needle was Wrath who focused on her pale flesh. "She's awake now." He said moving the needle away. "I am nearly finished but I can't have her moving if you want this done."

Gluttony sighed, motioning to a nearby doll. "Check her."

The doll approached her, standing in front of her face where it looked at her closely. The doll's face revealed little emotion as it looked at her. Lavanah kept her eyes closed long enough that the doll looked at Gluttony, nodding.

"She's fine. Carry on." Gluttony said motioning to Lavanah impatiently.

Wrath smirked, moving his arms away from her. "Wait."

Lavanah snarled whipping her head back, long platinum curls landing on her wet back as she thrust her head into that of the doll. The doll pressed their hand to the top of their head briefly before pulling it away. They looked down to see blood, their face frowning slightly as they held their hand out to Gluttony.

"It appears I am mistaken."

"No shit." Gluttony said, pushing the doll out of the way, stepping in front of Lavanah. He wiped the blood from her forehead, pinning her head to the bed by her neck, his eyes meeting Wrath's.

"Finish already."

Lavanah continued to snarl as she bucked against her restraints like a wild animal. Her head was sore though it pained her more on the sides than on her forehead.

"I have a bleeding doll because of you." Wrath said, snorting like an angered bull, glaring at Gluttony. "I told you she must be still!"

Gluttony sighed equally frustrated, wrapping his hands around her throat, watching as Lavanah choked, her body becoming still. "How about now?"

Wrath moved her hair from her back, continuing the pricks. "See, Gluttony, was that really too much to ask? I'm doing you a favor."

"Oh? And here I thought this was your idea of charity."

"Never heard of such a thing."

Gluttony shook his head. "Of course you haven't." He looked at Lavanah with a mischievous grin, squeezing tighter on her throat. He couldn't help feeling a sort of thrill with her being restrained against the bed, tears rolling down her cheeks. He resented Wrath for being on top of her bare body though it was only so that he could focus on his work. Still, something about Lavanah was appetizing to him.

"What have I done to you?" She choked out, looking to the side seeing that her arm was covered in something black. "I don't even *know* you."

"For those who gorge and those that squander will come to be clothed in rags, plagued by an ever-present hunger." He grabbed her by the two small, pale-colored ram like horns protruding from her head. They were delicate, her head still tender from where they had grown shaped in tight curls. She screamed as he pulled her head down, pressing her face into the bed with enough force to suffocate someone.

"I am Gluttony."

Chapter 8

Humility's scream echoed through the temple, shaking the windows. Azrael dropped his quill, the sound piercing the silence he had become so accustomed to. He had listened to the screams of man for centuries but never had they been outside his own head.

He lowered his head as he stepped through the archway. Before him sat a woman holding her head as she screamed. He looked down the hallway to find what had brought her such terror but saw only the marble walls of his temple. He knelt beside her, tried to comfort her but nothing stopped her screams. He forced her to her feet, leading her into his office. She kept her arms over her head in fear they might follow.

"Humility." he said, softly.

She silenced her screams lowering her arms from her head. Turning her attention to the arms that embraced her, she could see eyes staring back at her, tongues licking her flesh. She pulled away from him, pressing herself against the farthest wall, covering her mouth as she stared at the angel before her.

He was considerably larger than the average man wearing long white robes. The hood was lowered, revealing four faces, their eyes watching her curiously. His body was covered in thousands of eyes and tongues. The wings upon his back were in as great of a number, white like the other angels. One of the faces smiled, intrigued.

"In all my years, you are the first angel I have seen to express fear." Azrael said, returning to his table, a thick-leather bound book sitting in its center. The book was no smaller than a window. He lifted his quill beginning to write on its pages.

She lowered her hands, keeping her back pressed against the wall. "Are you trying to tell me that angels don't feel fear?"

He paused for a moment, the face on the back of his head meeting her eyes. "I am beginning to believe that there is something in our programming that makes us immune to things like fear and joy." He turned the page creating a small rush of air as the page merged with the others. "You, however, do."

She stepped forward, her nostrils flaring. "I was attacked. Of course I felt afraid."

"I saw nothing out there."

"It was real."

The face in front focused on the book while the side met her eyes, watching as she moved. "I'm sure it was to you."

She stepped closer, her heart racing in her chest. "And who exactly are you?"

"I am alpha and omega, the first and the last, the beginning and the end." He laughed, striking against the pages. "But the elders have named me Azrael."

She took a deep breath attempting to calm herself. "I am Humility."

The angel's faces laughed together. "I know who you are."

She crossed her arms over her chest. "Is that so?"

"Changing your name doesn't change who you are, who you were." He flipped the pages of his book back, holding them with one hand, his tongues licking at the corner. He tapped on a name that had been crossed out.

"You were born as Marie Elizabeth Leighton, daughter to a prestigious family, and twin sister to Thea Ares Leighton. You had a son named Ciel—"

She clutched her chest, eyes widening as her son's name echoed through her head. She had barely had the chance to spend time with her son and now had been ripped from his life.

"How do you know that?"

"I'm not just another pretty face." He said, smirking.

A look of concern befell her as she stood beside him, keeping her distance from his tongues. She could see in the pages before her that her name, and her sister's names were both scratched out. She watched as he flipped the pages forward. Every page seemed to be the same as the one before it, name after name going down each page in multiple columns.

"Why have you written down the names of people?"

Azrael began to write as he spoke. "It's my duty to watch humanity. As you are born, I record your names. Then I watch your lives and upon your death, you are scratched out. Even the angels forget about you."

"So you can see my son?" She said, trying to hide her pain as she longed to see him – to hold him – again.

"I can." Azrael said, seeing through her. "He's doing well and lives with your wet nurse and her mother. He cries for you often."

"How do you know it's me he cries for?"

"Because I don't simply watch, I'm in the heads of every soul. I can feel his confusion and his fear." A tear slipped from Humility's eye as he began to laugh. "I'm only joking. Could you imagine if I had to hear all of humanity's thoughts? I would go mad."

"I think you already are." she said holding her hand up, shaking her head as she remembered the sound of his cries, imagining how he must feel now that his mother was no longer there. "And my sister? You crossed her name out."

"I don't remember you being this inquisitive when you were alive."

She watched as the eyes and tongues changed with the names. "Being alive just wasn't as interesting."

He laughed, finding her to be far more amusing than other angels. "Not from what I've seen, and I see everything."

"If what you say is true, then Azrael, what has happened to my sister? How did I die?"

The sound of the quill against the parchment seemed to echo in the silence.

"Humility, I have a project I'm working on. If you agree to assist me in my work, then I may answer some of your questions."

"Why ask me?" She said, skeptical about his proposition.

"You're the only angel with something to gain. The others had no lives before Heaven for this is both their beginning and their end. For you, it is neither."

"I'll take your word for it." She took a deep breath. "What is it you ask of me?"

"I need you to return to Earth and retrieve samples of blood from a handful of different animals. I've made a small list along with the amounts. After you have collected the samples, I need you to hide them at the location I have written on the bottom. Make sure no one can find them. Since I am unable to leave this temple, I am forced to rely on you." He sighed, hating the thought of trusting someone else with his work. "Do this and I will give you some of your answers. If you continue to assist me in my work than I may continue to answer your questions." He said producing four small vials and a list from a pocket in his robes.

"What do you need blood for?"

"She continues to ask questions." He said, lifting the quill again, her constant questions beginning to sound like nails on a chalkboard. "If I answer all of your questions then I stand to gain nothing."

Humility's brow rose, startled by his tone as she took the list and empty vials from his hands. "Then I will return soon."

She returned to the gates of Heaven, surprised to see the dominion with its clipboard still at the gates. Did it not steal a moment for itself from time to time? Angels continued to approach it from all directions listening as he gave instructions one by one.

Humility approached it, smiling, beginning to find it amusing. In a way, it reminded her of her sister.

"I have a question."

It looked away from the clipboard for a moment, meeting her eyes with a sigh. "They always do." The clipboard's page flipped over, allowing him to scribble quickly along the fresh page. "Speak with haste, Stronghold. My time though immense is also limited."

"If I needed to get to Earth, how would I do so?"

"The same way you got here: through the gates." It said, returning its eyes to the clipboard as it pointed to the gates with its scepter.

"Don't know what I'd do without you."

The angel ripped the page from the clipboard, handing it to an angel as it gave directions, waving the angel away. "I would have more time to do my work." It said, waving her off as well. "Now away with you. There is still much to be done."

"That's what they keep telling me." Humility said, taking her leave. "Always a pleasure."

Humility left through the gates, glancing at the cherub, as it stood vigilant. The world became a bright white like the first time she had come here. She placed her hands up to shield her eyes, surprised that she could see them from the moment she stepped through the gates.

The white became green, the dew-covered grass tickling her bare feet. She stood before a forest, trees going as far as the eyes could see. Shadows covered the ground under the trees, rays of light piercing through their leaves, speckling the shadows with little green spots every so often. She held the list tightly, looking at the first animal: sharp-beaked ground finches.

She started into the forest, absorbing the world around her with every step. The rays of the sun pierced through the trees spreading in all directions bathing the forest in a warm glow. The ground beneath her bare feet was damp with morning dew. The only sound around her was that of the birds as they sang to one another.

She came to a stop when a voice called to her. It was rough though deep and fierce as if it belonged to a warrior in the heat of battle.

"Foolish girl, you're going the wrong way."

She gasped, looking behind her, but she stood alone.

"Where are you?" She said quietly, staring into the forest as it stretched behind her.

"You will not find the bird among the trees."

"*It's a bird—*"

"Not all birds live in trees." He said in a demeaning tone. "Far from here there is a group of islands. Go there and you will find your bird."

"How can I trust you?"

"Perhaps you can't. Until you've decided on whether you will or won't, it may be in your best interest to listen to me." The man's voice said.

She smiled at the irony as her wings lifted her into the sky above the trees. "All right, Stranger, I will give you a chance. It's not as if I have much of a choice."

The man's voice laughed. "No, *you don't.*"

##

Azrael placed the quill inside its inkwell, stepping away from the desk as he lifted his hood. His many wings extended from his back lifting him into the air effortlessly despite his size. He flew through his temple into another room that looked similar to his office. This room, however, was disorganized. Pages of research were scattered among the table and floor. The bookcases were broken in many places, some with their shelves barely holding on. Books were piled on the table as well as scattered about the floor, some stained from blood.

He lifted the pages from the desk, quickly reading over them. After a minute, he clenched his teeth, slamming them onto the desk, pushing all the papers and books off the desk. They floated into the air gently falling to the floor.

He watched as they fell, slamming his fists on the table. "I must take action sooner. Time is running short."

He watched through the eyes of humanity as children were born, his skin itching now that humanity's numbers drastically outnumbered the eyes and tongues on his body. He watched, as another eye appeared staring into his own. His body grew larger to accommodate the eyes and tongues that appeared on his body.

He leaned back, the hood falling as he covered two of his mouths, screaming. His body continued to grow, tongues and eyes appearing on his flesh. In his head, he could hear the screams of a thousand infants. Many were experiencing their first breaths but for some, it was also their last.

Humility entered Azrael's temple, holding the warm vials of blood against her chest. Her face was tear streaked, her eyes aching. Her bare feet made muffled sounds against the marble as she walked along the cold floor. This time she kept her eyes fixed on the entrance to the office, studying the veins in the marble.

She was still getting used to having wings, trusting her feet over them. She stopped in the archway, watching Azrael as he worked, the only sound coming from the quill and parchment. He had become larger since she had last seen him; the flesh around many of his eyes and tongues was swollen from their growth, the flesh around them red.

"Does it hurt when they grow?" She asked, approaching his desk where she placed the vials. She flew closer to him, carefully pressing her hand against the swollen flesh around one of his tongues.

"No." He said meeting her eyes. "I'm pleased to see that you were successful."

She forced a smile, though she kept her hand against his flesh. "Would you mind if I asked a question?"

One of his faces returned her smile though it was sincerer than her own. "I think I owe you that much."

"I want to know of the events leading to my death. Last I remember I had seen my father after becoming upset with my sister." Her voice was weak and filled with regret.

Azrael turned away from her, writing the names of many people as he spoke. "Do you know how many eyes and tongues I have on my body?"

She looked over what exposed flesh she could see though much of it was hidden by his robes. "I don't know."

"Humor me."

Humility took a moment, trying to count them but quickly lost track. "I'm afraid not."

"More than the wings on my back and I have four thousand." He said, his wings extending briefly before folding again. "I need you to understand that I can only see events, and that I cannot always tell you why those events happen or what happened afterwards. I can't see everything."

"He's afraid of how you may react." She looked around, realizing that it was the same voice from the forest. "You're still just a child, Humility. Perhaps you aren't ready for the truth."

Humility landed on his desk, looking up into his face. "Azrael, I need to know my past. It's the only way I can decide what I do with my future."

Azrael placed the quill inside its inkwell before turning to face her. "Your past matters not, Humility. Like the others of our kind, we are but servants to the elders." He said, meeting her eyes. "So what is it you hope to gain?"

"I am a servant to no one. Including the angels." She said with a fierce expression. It surprised her how much she sounded like her sister.

"You think you can get away with ignoring their orders?"

She laughed. "I don't care, Azrael. I didn't ask to come here and will not feel sorrow if I am forced to leave. I would rather spend eternity among the humans then be here."

This brought a smile to Azrael's lips. "Can I tell you a secret?"

She nodded.

"I too would rather be among the humans." He lifted his quill from the inkwell as he continued to speak. "The night you visited your father in his office he killed you by poisoning the glass you drank from. Your death was then used to frame and imprison your sister."

Her eyes widened, taken aback by his answer. "Why poison me?"

"I don't know."

"I don't mean to question you but how is it that possible?"

"It troubled me for a time. I worried that I was losing my power. That somehow I had angered the elders and was being punished." His face turned serious as it stared into her eyes. "I know now that I was wrong."

Humility took a step back. "What are you saying, Azrael?"

"I'm saying that whatever wanted you dead isn't human."

"Can you see other angels?"

"Could you imagine how large I would be if I could? These eyes and tongues aren't for show, Humility." He said taking her wrists in his hands. "I would no longer fit inside a temple."

Humility pulled away. "Then why did my father kill me if he didn't want me dead?"

"I'm not saying that he didn't. You're not the first to be killed this way, and you certainly won't be the last."

"Azrael, we can't let this continue to happen. Humanity doesn't deserve this."

"Humility, it's beyond our control." He said.

"How so?"

"Your parents were fully aware of what they were doing, I assure you."

"Azrael, what aren't you telling me? Why did they hold my sister responsible for my death?"

"I'm led to believe that your death was a sacrifice so that your parents can remain in the good graces of the Grigori that watches over their land. From what I've observed I believe they feared they might lose their wealth. By pinning your death on your sister no one would suspect them of murdering their own child."

Her nostrils flared as she stared into his eyes. "They sacrificed me to an angel?"

"Not just *an* angel but a fallen angel."

"Why are fallen angels watching over humanity if they encourage the slaughter of innocents?"

Azrael laughed though not from humor. "You speak as if the elders care about the fate of humanity. Angels are selfish and violent creatures."

She closed her eyes for a moment, breathing through her nose. "Then you certainly don't belong here, Azrael." She made her way towards the archway before opening her eyes again,

"Humility." He said dropping the quill. "Where are you going?"

"I'm going to do something about this. I don't know how and I don't know if I'm going to succeed."

"You won't alone." Azrael said. "I will do what I can to be of assistance.

"Aren't I supposed to be your assistant?" She said with a chuckle.

"How do you feel about making one last errand for me?"

"I'm sure I can make the time."

"I need you to go to the Garden of Eden and retrieve the fruit from the Tree of Knowledge."

"The forbidden fruit?"

"There are twelve, bring them to me and I will be able to aid you in your fight against the Grigori."

"How will I know which tree is which?"

"It's across from the Tree of Life on the opposite side of the river. It's the one farthest away from the Elder's temple."

"Then I suppose I will need to find a bowl." She said turning away.

"Humility?" He said quietly.

She looked at him from over her shoulder.

"You don't belong here either."

Humility left Azrael's office. A smile spread across her lips. Her joy, however, was quickly spoiled.

"He may be surprised." The man's voice returned.

"I think you have me confused with my sister." She laughed. "I simply wish to have a conversation with the Grigori. Nothing more." She said with a faux innocence.

"Your words can be like daggers, Humility."

"Then let them strike where it hurts my enemies the most."

The man's voice gave a sinister laugh as he continued to whisper in her ear. "I will be the hand that guides them if you ask."

"I am beginning to think you are a side of me I have never known before."

"Am I unwelcome?"

Humility came to a stop, looking in the distance, watching as the angels flew above her. "No. On the contrary, I don't think there's been a time where I needed you more."

"I am pleased to hear that, Humility, for I am never leaving your head."

She sighed though she smiled through her words. "I suppose I could've had a worse fate." Her wings spread, lifting her into the air.

Chapter 9

Lavanah woke with a gasp, staring at the grey walls of her room. Though it was small, it did have a few furnishings: a mirror over the bed, another in the corner, and a desk near the window. She sat up, swinging her feet off the bed and onto the floor. She stumbled for a moment, pressing her hand to her head, wincing, as it remained sore from Gluttony grabbing her horns. She approached the mirror poking at the tender places curiously.

Platinum curls draped down her back, hiding most of her horns. Her flesh was pale, for the most part. Her arms now decorated in ink. It graced her body painting it in different shades of black.

Her right arm looked like witchcraft, arrays drawn onto it in thin elaborate circles from her wrist to her shoulder. She couldn't understand the meanings behind the symbols within them or why there were so many, some small, others as large as her palm.

Her left arm was like a painting made in watercolor. It began at her wrist, wrapping around her entire arm like the arrays on her right arm. Only instead of symbols she saw water reflecting the scene above it. Above the water was a forest that stretched for miles, tiny black birds flying through the evening sky. The moon graced her shoulder, its light reflecting into the waters below.

Her back was ominous, depicting a fierce battle between a wolf and a raven. The wolf howled at the moon, the raven on the other side, flying towards the wolf. It's claws ready to strike. The feathers of the raven drifted through the air, fading into the arrays on her right arm.

She turned her back in the mirror, trying to look at the entire image, fascinated by its beauty until she heard the door opening from behind.

She watched as the door slowly opened, a woman looking no different than any living woman, entered. In her hands, she held clothes, approaching Lavanah, extending them to her. Lavanah glanced at her body, realizing she was still bare. She accepted the clothes, the woman helping her into them. They seemed odd at first though beautiful. A corset made of dark leather and lace that covered her left shoulder but left her arrays completely exposed. Her trousers too were made of dark leather, tall boots covering them.

"Is this really necessary?"

"It was a request made by Lust." The woman spoke, her voice drained of emotion. "He has requested your company."

Lavanah tugged up on her corset though it did not budge. "Then I suppose it would be rude of me to keep him waiting."

The woman nodded, guiding Lavanah from her chambers to those of Lust. She followed close behind her. The walls around them were decorated in red, purple, and gold. She watched the lamplighters travel down the halls, replacing the candles as they burned out. Another demon followed in his wake, cleaning the excess wax. Eventually, the two demons disappeared into the end of the hall bathed by the shadows.

The woman came to a stop, pointing to the door. Lavanah looked at her, bemused by her behavior. She reached for the doorknob, turning once more to look at her. However, the woman had already disappeared half-way down the hall.

She pulled the door open, stepping inside, immediately greeted by a pillow to her face. She caught it, looking at it for a moment, running her hand over the colorful silk and lace before looking up to see Lust draped in an armchair, crown in hand.

"You're late."

Lavanah's brow rose. "You're a *man*."

"Sometimes." He said, standing, a smile stretched across his face as he bowed, his eyes not once leaving her. "I am many things, Dolly." He said standing straight, placing the crown on his head. "Though I much prefer the appearance of a man."

"You've peaked my curiosity, Lust. Why choose to be a man?" She said, approaching him. "I'd like you either way."

He held her by her chin as he spoke. "Despite what the humans say, being a man is far more pleasurable. Women are too often mistreated."

She chuckled, pushing his hand away. "Sounds dreadful."

"Dolly, you laughed!" He said in excitement, cupping her face, a wildness in his eyes as he spoke. "Come quickly, I wish to enjoy you before your new soul takes over."

"My what?" She said as he took her hand, leading her further into his chambers. She was surprised by the softness of his hand despite his firm grip. There was something daunting about him, though he hid it well. It was not in his words for his intentions were clear. It was as if the air around him bodes evil.

He opened the doors to his private chambers, securing them behind them. "Tell me, Dolly, have you ever defiled a human skull before?"

She shook her head, terrified with the thought.

"The eye socket is a tight fit, but it's absolutely delightful once you get past the eye. It's another reason why I prefer the appearance of a man."

She stepped away, struggling to breathe. "Is that what I'm here for?"

"Of course just not in your skull." He said pressing a finger to her eye. "You have beautiful eyes. I can only imagine Gluttony's reaction if he learned I had popped one out of your socket. He has a thing for eyes."

She felt as if she were made of stone, sinking into the countless pillows as they covered the floor in a sea of bright-colored silks. The walls around her threatened to close in, decorated with curtains of red and purple hanging around the walls. It was as if she were a child living through a nightmare disguised as a dream.

"Wrath took care of your flesh despite losing another soul, though I suppose he will eventually claim more. Allow me to see his art." His grin faded, a thin line stretching over his lips as he approached her. He unlaced her corset with ease, throwing it to the floor. His hands were ravenous as they ran over her smooth flesh. He chuckled, allowing himself to smirk as he ran his hand over the arrays on her arm.

"It must be rather convenient for Gluttony to have bound his magic to your arm instead of him having to teach you himself." He moved her hair away from her chest, staring at her breasts. "I have always found his arrays beautiful. They remind me of something else."

She blushed, covering her chest with her arms. "Thank you, I suppose."

He grabbed her arms, holding them with one hand, covering her mouth with his free hand. "You are quite the talkative doll. It is in your best interest that you stop." He released her only to unbutton her trousers, pulling them down. He ran his hands along her delicate body, getting on his knees as he removed her boots and her trousers with them. He hugged her body, pressing his face to it.

"You're so new, so innocent. I almost feel bad." He said as he pulled her into the floor, removing his own clothes. "*Almost.*"

His mind was poisoned by his insatiable desires, driven further into madness by her cheeks. They were red as the inside of her flesh. His body ached with the need to make her as obscene as the other demon,s though he knew she would inevitably become like the other dolls. For the moment she was exotic, still full of life as all new dolls were.

She reached to cover her body, looking away as Lust spoke. "If I were Gluttony, I would never let you go. You're not the kind of doll that one should share." He lifted her leg, placing it around his waist as he gave into desire.

She made a small noise, closing her eyes, as he rolled her onto her stomach burying her face in the pillows, as he pressed deeper into her. He lifted her waist with one hand, continuing to press down on her head with the other.

"Oh Dolly, though I may not be able to touch your skull, defiling you will be exciting all the same. Perhaps Gluttony will realize the mistake he has made in allowing you freedom because I would chain you to my wall for eternity."

There was something vile about the glint that appeared in his eyes. He released her, quickly making his way across the pillows where he threw open the curtains. Lavanah's eyes widened in horror as she saw a woman chained to the wall. She made a muffled sound like that of a yawn though her mouth was gagged.

"Hello, darling." Lust said, caressing her face. "It's time to play." He removed the gag, releasing her from the chains. Her body fell to the floor before him, following him on her knees.

He moved to the next set of drapes, staring at a man as he too was bound and gagged to the wall. He pressed his hand to the man's genitals, pulling on them enough to get his attention.

"*Shh*, I didn't mean to hurt you." Lust said releasing the man. "Help me release the rest of our family. I want to introduce you to someone *new*." He said moving to the next set of curtains, the man climbing to his feet before going in the opposite direction to aid him in releasing the dolls. Once finished Lust and the dolls joined Lavanah among the pillows. Their bare bodies met on the floor, Lavanah stuck in the middle with Lust.

He wrapped his body around Lavanah, forcing her to go first, squeezing her breasts as he held her in place. Another doll approached, licking her soft flesh.

Lavanah closed her eyes, squirming against Lust uncomfortably. She had never been touched in such a way when she was alive. As time became little more than a figment of her imagination, she could see that Lust was a beast in the form of a man. The cries of the dolls only fed his desire. Her struggles eventually turned to cries of pain but even that became nothing more than silence. Her body gave up on struggling beginning to enjoy it, though she never gave it away.

Lust lay upon his back, pushing a doll off him, forcing Lavanah to take her place. He watched as she moved against him, though she was unaware of what he expected of her. After a moment of watching her struggle he placed his hands on her hips guiding her movements. Her mind was clear, and her face began to mirror that of the other dolls.

"And here I had hoped you would keep that look of innocence a little longer." He leaned forward kissing her breast. "Still, this desire will not quench itself." He said leaning back, watching as two dolls began sucking on her breasts.

The days passed like a blur, Lust lying upon the floor with his dolls piled on top of him. Somewhere along the way he had taken the form of a woman. He kept Lavanah closest despite the many dolls he had to choose from. He often grew tired of the same dolls, sometimes killing one to replace it with another. No matter how many dolls he had, or how long he spent with them it wasn't enough. His desire could never be quenched.

He held Lavanah by her hair, kissing her pale flesh, licking it from time to time. He almost wished he were Gluttony though it would be a waste to eat a woman with such beauty.

He finally pushed off several of the dolls, standing. "Back to your chains." The dolls crawled to the wall, Lust fastening them into place before closing the curtains. He watched as Lavanah reached for her clothing, taking them from her.

"Follow me." He said changing back to the form of a man.

She did as he asked, watching as he ran a bath. He took her hand, helping her into the warm water. He began with her hair, thoroughly lathering it before moving over her body. He watched, as the bubbles covered her body but never fully, taking care of even the smallest of details like flesh from underneath her fingernails.

Her skin took on a floral scent, making Lust bite his tongue. He rinsed the soap from her body, his tongue bleeding as he watched the water roll down her skin. He took her hand once he could no longer handle bathing her, helping her out of the tub. The water drained behind him as he covered her with a towel. He was quick to dry her before helping her into her clothes. He then brushed her teeth before combing her hair. The soft curls returning as it dried.

"Thank you." She said though her voice was void of emotion.

"You were in no condition to leave." He said shrugging, surprised to hear her use manners. Gluttony had never made a doll before. It was unlike them to retain fragments of humanity though it was not unwelcome. It only served to remind him how much of a fool Gluttony was to allow her to be used by all demons.

Lavanah pushed her lips into a smile.

Lust moved her hands, holding them tightly at her sides. "Don't do that again."

She nodded slowly as he let go of her hands.

"It's time for you to go." He said beginning to run a new bath, avoiding her eyes.

"Okay." She said, reaching to touch his face.

He lifted his hand to block her hand. "*Just go.*"

Lavanah watched him for a moment as he returned to his chambers to retrieve a doll. He placed her in the clean water beginning to bathe her too.

Lavanah took her leave, the doll that brought her clothes, waiting for her outside.

"Your eyes have dulled."

Lavanah looked down for a moment. "What do I do now?"

"You wait."

Lavanah closed the door of her chambers, climbing onto the bed. She could not sleep and instead rolled onto her back, reaching towards the ceiling. She continued to stare at her arrays on her arm, understanding a few of the symbols, though she did not understand how they worked. Her arm eventually fell as she sat up, staring at her desk. She watched as the wind caused the journal to flip open, its blank pages flicking past before stopping.

She moved to the desk as the wind died down, flipping them to the first blank page. She lifted the quill, opening the inkwell where she dabbed it in the ink. She wrote only three words: I'm a doll. She placed the quill down, closing the inkwell and the journal; the wind stirring again sending chills over her skin. She looked over, surprised to see her window open. She approached it, leaning her head out curiously.

Hell was a world that had perished, its land consumed by ice. Though she could not yet see the skies of Hell – buildings of great heights blocking her view. She watched as the pale snow fell to the ground beneath her. The snow shined bright amongst the shadows that painted brick buildings in deep shades or red and grey. Lampposts stood along the streets, little white candles revealed the way for the demons though its light could not pierce far into the shadows.

In the distance, she could see a girl twirling about as she walked down the street though her face did not possess emotion. There was a childlike curiosity about her, the way she stopped occasionally to look at the world. That was until she approached a group of demons that lay on the side of the street. The cold had stained their skin a pale blue. Their hair was equally pale. They cried out, reaching for the doll as she ran away. The darkness had stolen their vision and left them to wander blind in search of souls even if it meant hunting the dolls. For a fake soul tasted better than no souls.

Another icy wind came, Lavanah pulling her head back inside, closing the window as she continued to stare at the frosted glass. She pressed her face to it, surprised by how cold the glass remained.

A hand grabbed her shoulder, causing her to turn around.

"You've been placed on cleaning duty in Sloth's chambers." Spoke another doll, one she had not yet seen.

##

Lust was silent as he approached Greed, watching for a moment as he counted coins on a table. The coins were lined in straight rows, each with the same number of coins. He lifted one of the coins up, looking at it for a moment before Greed took it from him, placing it back in line. He could see Lavanah's form on Greed's body looking sullen. He smiled, crossing his arms over his chest.

"I've met Gluttony's doll."

Greed stopped, though his eyes remained on the coins.

"She doesn't look like her soul."

"That's because she has no soul. These souls are mine." Greed scoffed, placing a coin, listening as it landed with a hollow sound. He held his finger on the coin, looking up at Lust.

Lust sat in one of the chairs around the table, rocking back in it. "Of course, how could I forget." Lust removed his crown from his head, twirling it in his hand. "So, Greed, what is it I can do for you? Bear in mind I can be quite charitable with my time."

"A charitable sinner? I think not." He adjusted himself in his custom-made chair, which was beginning to feel tight on his sides. "We share a lot in common with our brothers and sisters."

"I've noticed but what exactly are you referring to?"

"I have taken to Pride's idea of displaying my souls though not as quite in the open as she does."

"You may have to if you're going to continue to fit in that chair. The demon who makes your precious chairs is dead, remember?"

"I am painfully aware of that." Greed said. "I want you to watch Lavanah. There is something strange about her."

Lust reached into his pocket, producing a nail file which he pointed at Greed. "Spying on a doll? What's the occasion?" He said returning to his nails.

"I suspect Gluttony has an agenda for this doll, though he has not made his intentions clear. He can't be trusted; he never has been."

"Do you trust Envy?"

"No more than I would trust Gluttony. Angels can't be trusted." Greed pushed his coins into a large box, sealing it closed before his doll returned it to its place. "I find his sudden interest in dolls to be disquieting. I want to know what power he has placed within her."

"Greed, he has one power."

He shook his head. "The dark arts are made of many smaller powers, some with infinite power such as telekinesis. His power and now hers are only limited by their own strength."

"Gluttony has never displayed telekinetic powers."

"That is what concerns me. We aren't fully aware of what he is capable of. We've seen him crumble buildings and deteriorate limbs but what else is he hiding?"

"So the man is a little destructive. Dolls rarely use their powers. What is there to fear?"

"With destruction comes creation. If my theory is right, we may have a lot to fear."

Lust allowed the chair to fall to all four legs as he rested his arms on the table. "She's a doll, Greed."

"She's the doll of an angel, Lust."

"Envy has a multitude of dolls. I don't see you complaining."

"Envy doesn't have a motive."

Lust stood, making his way towards the doors. "You're paranoid for no reason, Greed. Sariel was just as confident as we are that Gluttony will never escape."

"Lust! I am warning you—" Greed said, standing from his chair. "What happened to being charitable?"

Lust laughed. "Demons don't give a damn about charity."

"Where are you going?"

"To get sucked."

##

Lavanah opened the door, stepping inside, closing the door gently behind her. The room smelled of filth, the floor covered in clutter and trash, dishes with food still piled about the built-in kitchen. It was the largest of chambers she had seen yet. As she walked through the filth she came across the occasional candlestick, broken glass on the floor, their light still flickering against the floor casting ominous shadows on the walls. She continued forward until she reached a door leading into the chambers.

The brick walls remained in their natural color though instead of a bright red, they were grey. Blank paintings hung crooked on their walls. The entire room felt as if life had been drained from the world around her. There was a dresser off to the side with thick layers of dust on its surface and the occasional blank picture frame. In the center of the room was a bed large enough for six people and made of black wood with grey and white bedding. In its center laid a woman, young in the flesh but thin and frail. Many pillows surrounded her, the same kind she had seen in Lusts chambers only grey and white. The woman laid still. Silver hair draped around her. In her hands was a thick book which she closed as soon as she noticed her presence.

"You must be Lavanah."

She nodded.

"Help me sit up if you would."

Lavanah approached the woman, careful as she lifted her, using the pillows to support her body. "How may I be of service?"

"I apologize for the poor state of my living conditions. If you would start in my chambers, I would be grateful."

She nodded, beginning by fixing the frames on the walls so that they sat straight before dusting them, sneezing occasionally. She then picked up the clothing from the floor taking it into the bathroom where she washed them. She hung them around the room wherever they fitted. Finally, she grabbed a small bucket from the kitchen, filling it with soapy water, before returning to her chambers. She dipped the rag in the bucket, getting on her knees where she scrubbed the floors.

Sloth watched her with a kind smile, returning to her book as she cleaned.

Finishing the chambers, she made her way into the main room where she began by sweeping the broken glass from the floor, placing it into the trash. She stood the candlesticks, surprised that their flames never died. She carried on with the next candlestick, then another until all had been cleaned and stood again on their feet lighting the path to Sloth's chambers. She lifted the plates from the floor into her arms taking them into the kitchen. She filled the sink with water, gathering the remaining plates from the sofa and table before cutting off the water. She scrubbed at them for what could have been hours before putting them away in the cabinets. To her dismay, their unpleasant smell didn't leave her mind.

Holding the last plate in hand, its smell had been fouler than the others. She froze in place, her hands suddenly weak as she dropped the plate to the floor where it shattered into many pieces.

The smell was like that of meat, images of wolves entering her mind. The wolves became dogs as they fought over a human arm, one holding it between its teeth. The dogs snarled at one another as they circled one another before a tall man shooed them off. He was dressed in tattered clothes, a long bloodstained apron tied around his waist. In his hand, he held a cleaver, the body of a platinum haired woman lying on the table before him, missing one arm.

The man had a wicked smile upon his face, the cleaver coming down on the woman's remaining arm as it tore through flesh. He brought it down again, this time harder, striking the bone. On his third strike, the arm was finally separated from her body.

One of the dogs returned, the other tearing at the flesh of the woman's arm behind them. It sat with the man, waiting patiently for a moment before whining as the man lifted the arm off the table.

"Away with you mutt!" The man said, waving the dog off with the cleaver.

The dog whined again, looking at the man with sad eyes.

He sighed, dropping the woman's arm onto the floor. "I suppose I can feed Lady Thea a foot. She won't know the difference."

The dog barked happily, biting into the arm before carrying it off. He lay on the floor, biting onto one of the fingers, the bones snapping as the dog ripped it off her hand, his tail wagging.

Lavanah lay on the floor, pressed against the sink cabinets, gasping for air. Her arms wrapped around her body as she shook.

Was that her on the table? The woman certainly looked like her.

"Have you finished, Lavanah?"

"Nearly done. I request only a minute more."

Sloth held her book firmly, a concerned look on her face though her words hid it well. "You owe me another plate."

"I will replace it once I have finished my work here."

"Thank you. See me once you have finished cleaning."

Lavanah nodded, finishing the dishes before straightening the tablecloth on the small nearby table. She then began to dust, disposing of the trash from the floor as she made her way around the room. Finally, she grabbed the bucket of soapy water, getting onto her knees again, scrubbing the floors clean before dumping the water out where she placed the bucket in a cabinet below the sink.

She straightened her clothes before looking around at the clean room. The smell has even improved though not by much. She returned to Sloth, realizing the smell came from her now.

Sloth lay in her bed, a book in hand, holding her finger up as she read a page. She licked her finger, turning the page, continuing to read. Every so often she would smile or laugh as she continued to turn the pages. After some time, Sloth marked the page, closing the book before tucking it beneath a pillow where it sat among many other books.

"I apologize. I hate stopping in the middle of a chapter." She then held her arms out to Lavanah. "Could I trouble you for a bath?"

Lavanah approached the woman, lifting her from the bed, surprised by how light she felt. She carried her to the bathroom where she sat on the edge of the tub.

Lavanah removed her nightgown, placing it to the side. She eyed her curiously, lowering her into the bath carefully.

They sat in silence, Sloth relaxing into the water as she watched Lavanah begin to bathe her.

"You're wondering why I do not bathe myself."

Lavanah paused but shook her head.

"It's all right to ask. All demons dolls or lesser always have the same question."

"Are you unwell, Sloth?"

She chuckled at that. "Demons do not face illness. However, the archdemons are cursed as a price for their power." She said hiding behind a smile. "When I became an archdemon, it felt as if my body had become lead, and I could no longer move. It was scary at first, to have lost freedom so quickly, but I have made my peace."

"You possess a great kindness."

Sloth laughed, splashing Lavanah with her other foot. "Perhaps you are right. I don't wish to treat the dolls with disrespect since they are responsible for tending to my needs."

Lavanah smiled even if only a little, working her way up to Sloth's legs.

"You are a very different kind of doll. I had been wondering when Gluttony would finally make one of his own."

Lavanah looked up at her as she moved to her silver hair.

After the bath, Lavanah lifted Sloth onto the edge of the tub again where she dried her body off. Sloth watched her, surprised by how light her every touch was. She treated her carefully as if she were, in fact, the doll. Lavanah then unpinned a nightgown from where the clothes had been drying, putting it on Sloth, brushing her hair afterwards.

She then carried Sloth to the chambers, placing her into the bed. She arranged the pillows with Sloth's guidance, watching as she stretched as much as she could manage before grabbing her book, hugging the bedding, a book in hand.

"I don't understand why Gluttony shares you. You're much more conversational than the others of your kind."

"I couldn't tell you. I have only met him once."

Sloth looked up from her book for a moment. "Once?" She pondered it for a moment before returning to her book. "I must say, Lavanah, it has been a pleasure, but you must go now if I am ever to finish this story."

Lavanah nodded politely, taking her leave from Sloth's chambers.

##

Gluttony entered Sloth's chambers, running his finger along a table before rubbing them together, pleased. "Hey, Sloth, it's me." He paused, seeing the broken plate among the trash.

Sloth set her book aside in the middle of the chapter, looking up as Gluttony made his way into her chambers. She smiled widely, watching as he made his way to the bed, pressing her knuckles to his face since he could not kiss them.

"Come closer, Gluttony. Give this old woman a hug." She said holding her arms open.

Gluttony wrapped his arms around her, keeping his beak away from her face. She pressed his head to her lap where she preened the back of his hand for him knowing it was a difficult area for him to maintain.

"I met Lavanah." She said, throwing the feathers to the floor, pulling one of the good ones for a bookmark. "She's a very kind doll." She placed the feather into her book, closing it before continuing to work on his head.

Gluttony stood up, looking at the feather with a solemn expression as it rested between the pages of her book. "Is she?"

Sloth nodded. "But she won't always be that way, will she?"

Gluttony turned his attention to her, sitting at the edge of her bed, taking Sloth's hands in his. "Whatever do you mean?"

She leaned her head to the side, holding his hands firmly as she tried to sit up, Gluttony helping her. "You go all these centuries never once showing an interest in the dolls except on the few occasions you need help preening your feathers. Even then, you normally come to see me for such help. Now, you suddenly have your own doll. It can't be for personal use if she has only met you once. Tell me, what is it you hope to accomplish?"

He pressed his hand to her cheek, the words caught in his throat.

"Whose soul does she have? I know you saw the broken plate." Sloth said, waiting for a moment, sighing when Gluttony remained silent. "It's all right, Gluttony, you don't have to tell me."

It pained him to keep secrets from Sloth.

She brought his hands to her lips. "I have nothing against angels."

"If only there were more demons like you, Sloth."

She smiled, giving his hands a light squeeze, her pain evident in her face. "I would *never* wish this burden upon anyone."

"I can think of one person." Gluttony said meeting her eyes.

Chapter 10

"You're wasting your time."

Humility sighed as she flipped through the pages of Azrael's books. The voice of the man had returned. She knew him well now. He was aggressive and though he at times angered her, he was often right. He never tried to lead her astray, always pushing her forward. It was almost as if her sister was with her again.

"Maybe the Grigori is in the Garden of Eden?" A woman's voice said. Humility neither liked her nor disliked her. She was kinder though not always honest. She acted the way Thea had as a child, often playing games and trying to lead her astray. However, the gentleman often put her in her place, which amused Humility. The woman's voice had only begun to speak up recently but she was just as welcomed as the man.

"Nonsense." Humility said, closing another book and returning it to the bookshelf. "Grigori are only allowed in heaven when they report to the elders. No detours like the garden."

"Maybe they went anyway."

"They would be killed on the spot." The man's voice said. "Struck down by the cherub who guard its entrance."

"Exactly." Humility said lifting another book, flipping through the pages. "Am I missing something? I swear every book is the same as the one before it." She was beginning to get frustrated. Each book was the same holding only names. The further back she searched through the books, the more frequently the names were scratched out.

"Humility, I warned you that you're wasting your time." The man's voice said with a sigh.

"You're also the one who insisted Azrael is hiding something from me."

"I didn't mean in these dusty books. I meant somewhere else in the temple perhaps."

Humility sighed, putting the book away. "*Now* you tell me. Next time, start with that."

The man laughed for a moment. "Eastern hall."

"How can you be sure?" Humility said flying out of the office. The temple never seemed to feel smaller no matter how much time she spent within its marble walls.

"Western."

"*Stop with your nonsense, Woman.*" The man said as Humility sighed taking the eastern hall.

Humility came to a stop, looking up into the many eyes of Azrael. She swallowed uncomfortably.

"I told you to go into the west but no one listens to little ol' me." The woman's voice giggled.

"Hello... Azrael."

"Are you snooping in my temple?" He said knowing the answer.

"*Busted.*" The woman's voice sang loudly.

"No!" Humility said until she saw his face twist in disbelief. "*Yes* but it's not what it looks like!"

"It looks like snooping."

"That's because I am snooping but not for the reasons you might think."

"You're trying to track down a Grigori in hopes of finding Thea before you visit the Tree of Knowledge."

Humility swore under her breath. "How do you know me so well?"

"Because I've watched you your entire life."

"You make a very strong argument."

"Humility, do you not trust me?"

She took a deep breath. "Sometimes. It's not... you... as much as it is that I lack patience when it comes to my sister. I've never been forced to live without her before. *Not like this.* I can't live like this, which is ironic since I'm *dead.*"

He crossed his arms over his chest, some of the eyes looking around spastically as tongues licked at them. "Go to the Tree of Knowledge, Humility."

"That's all you're going to say?"

"What do you want me to say, Marie? Chase after your sister? Because I want to tell you that, I do, but I *need* your help."

"What exactly am I helping you with?" She said, caught off guard by hearing her name again. She had almost forgotten it.

"I want to leave my temple."

She sighed imagining how it must feel to be confined to one place for millennia. "I should go. I still need to find a bowl."

Humility left the temple, visiting the Dominion by the gates. It took one look at her before sighing in frustration.

"It's you again. *Hello.*"

Humility smiled widely. "I need to find a bowl. Preferably a larger one."

"Take the northeastern path, third temple on your right, and speak to the principality inside."

"How will I know which is a principality?"

"Look for an angel holding a scepter *and* wearing a crown." It said as if she should have already known. She was starting to notice a pattern with the angel.

"He's a bit callous." The man's voice said as Humility flew away, taking the northeastern path like the angel had instructed. She didn't expect the temples to be so far apart, but perhaps it was necessary with the number of angels and their various sizes.

"Be kind." Humility said, landing on the steps of the temple, quickly making her way up the stairs.

"Humility, that's as kind as I am capable of."

"You're just like my sister." She said entering the temple, looking around for an angel wearing a crown. "Do you see it?"

"Eight o'clock and it's quite the looker."

Humility turned around, her eyes widening at the angel. It wore loose-fitting trousers made of an expensive white cloth. Its figure was closer to that of a human than Azrael, who hid beneath his robes. She had become accustomed to Azrael's appearance and was no longer bothered by his... imperfections.

"Perhaps I can carry the fruit in my arms-" She said watching the angel as it spoke to a standard angel.

"Don't be ridiculous, Humility. You're just asking for a bowl." The man's voice said. "Although I do not envy you."

The angel while its figure was recognizably human was also ghastly. Like other angels it had a pair of white wings but unlike the others it had a longer torso to accommodate an extra pair of arms. Its entire body was muscular even its neck, which was thicker than any other angel she had seen before it. Its neck supported three separate heads. Long hair flowed from these heads, wild and untamed. He looked more like a warrior than an angel.

"Don't make me speak to him."

"You have to do this for Thea." The woman's voice said.

Humility took a deep breath. "*Only* because of Thea."

She approached the angel, her hands shaking as she grew closer. One of its heads glanced at her, its eyes struggling to look down at her.

"Humility. How can I be of service?"

"I am looking for a bowl, preferably large."

"If you have a seat, I will return in a moment with your bowl."

Humility watched the angel fly away with grace. She found a seat on a bench among other angels.

"Now was that so difficult?" The woman said.

"Hush your mouth."

An angel sitting beside her turned its head, shushing her. "Try to show some restraint, Humility."

"Bugger off, Temperance."

The angel was taken aback but stood up and walked away.

The principality returned, in three of his hands were bowls, each made of a different kind of wood. Humility stood looking over each bowl before grabbing the one made of a dark wood.

"Thank you for your help."

The heads struggled to nod and instead just stretched up before speaking. "Your welcome."

Humility kept her pace light as she left the temple, waiting until she was outside to run down the stairs.

"Well done." The man's voice said.

"Shut up!" She said, leaping into the air, flying to the Garden of Eden.

Humility landed softly on the green path leading to the river of life, a cherub towering before her. They nodded politely to one another, the cherub stepping aside, allowing her to pass. She walked leisurely, the bowl tucked under her arm, clouds extending along both sides of the path.

In the distance, Humility could see a temple facing east, before it standing four angels who looked no different than elderly men, in their hands they held within wheels covered in eyes. Each angel's wheels were a different shade of beryl. A river flowed from the southernmost part of the temple. The river was like a sea of diamonds, feeding the Tree of Life on the left side of the river near the temple and the Tree of Knowledge on the right side of the river. The trees were enormous, larger than any temple, each bearing twelve fruits.

"This can't be the Tree of Life."

"According to Azrael, *it is.*" The man's voice said. "I don't think the angels have enough power to move them willy-nilly."

"I always imagined them to be something beautiful, maybe even inspiring." She said, tears welling in her eyes. She felt as if all the things she once imagined as a child were crumbling before her. The part that perplexed her most was that the forbidden tree, her entire purpose for being here, looked the most beautiful.

The Tree of Life was not only tall but also wide. She could have spent an eternity trying to walk around it in a complete circle and never reach where she stood now. The roots acted as bridges, connecting it to other grassy islands that hovered above the clouds. However, it wasn't the size of the tree that caused chills in her bones.

The tree itself looked like a sinister royal oak the color of dusky grey. Its roots and trunk appeared as if spines had grown over the wood, reaching all the way to its branches, which looked no different than those of an oak tree. The leaves were a pale shade of green, the fruit ivory instead of the bright red she had imagined as a child.

On the other hand, the Tree of Knowledge almost seemed lonely. It was the only thing on the right side of the river. It didn't connect to grassy islands like the Tree of Life but instead continued to stretch endlessly into the sky. She wondered how long it might take her to reach the top.

The roots of the tree hung off the edge of its island and were a pale blue in color. The trunk seemed as if it had split in two as it grew twisting as it reached the sky, its branches connecting in the center like a twisted ladder. The blue became a pale green and eventually yellow. At the top of the tree it held no fruit and in fact was mostly bare. The few leaves that clung to the tree for dear life would often fall gently towards the clouds. However, with every leaf that fell, a new one grew in its place.

"Where's the fruit?" She said, looking the tree over.

"Look at the flowers." The woman's voice said.

Humility flew into the tree, the flowers, each unlike the last looked no different than those her sister had shown her in books she read growing up. There were exactly twelve, each attached to the trunk as it spiraled towards the sky. Humility was careful as she plucked them, placing them in the bowl.

"When he said *fruit* the last thing I expected was pretty flowers." Humility said, carefully flying back to Azrael's temple.

"Heaven is full of surprises." The man's voice said.

"I have a strange feeling that says it hasn't revealed a fraction of its secrets." She said, glancing back at the trees and the cherub who guarded them. "It might never reveal them all."

"You aren't ready for all its secrets, Humility."

"I might never be but that doesn't mean I won't turn over every stone trying to unearth them."

The woman's voice laughed. "You said '*unearth*'."

##

The Tree of Life and the Tree of Knowledge continued to haunt her as she returned to Azrael's temple. She placed the bowl of flowers on his desk, worried when his face became one of concern. He did not speak however, instead walking to his bookshelf, lifting a marble mortar and pestle from it, setting it beside Humility. It was specially made for Azrael's size and stopped just below her knees.

"Are we going to talk about my sister?"

"You should sit down." He placed the flowers inside the mortar and pestle before moving it out of the way.

She crossed her legs, sitting down on his table. "Azrael-"

"You were lucky to have died in your sleep. When your sister woke the next morning, she shook you. She held you in her arms until the guards dragged her out of the room, carrying your body away."

"What did they do with my body?"

"They butchered it and fed it to your sister."

Her eyes widened in horror, her stomach doing flips.

"Your sister was pinned with your death and imprisoned. They would bring her a plate of... meat every day, but she became ill after eating it. So she stopped eating."

"Then what?"

"The guards tortured her for some time but then stopped visiting her. When they finally returned, your sister had starved herself to the point she could barely move. Three of the guards took advantage of your sister in her weakened state."

"*Three?*" She said, tears streaming down her eyes. Her husband had been cruel to her, but she had been able to take comfort in her sister. Her sister hadn't been as fortunate.

"They left her bleeding on the floor." Azrael took a deep breath, "I still remember your sister's cries, Humility."

Humility's lip quivered as she struggled to speak. "So where is my sister now?"

"I don't know."

"What do you mean 'I don't know'? That's your job." She couldn't bring herself to accept that she had finally hit a dead end.

"I can't see her soul any longer. *It's gone.*"

"I have to find out what has happened to her, Azrael. I don't care how but she's my sister. I owe her that much."

Azrael grabbed her by her shoulders. "You owe her nothing."

"If you've truly watched my entire life as I have, then you know that I owe her everything." She said standing up. "Azrael, it's time I visited the Grigori."

He took a deep breath. "Use caution, Humility. The elders are watching you."

"I don't give a damn." She said, hopping down from the desk. "They can kick me out of Heaven for all I care. I will find my sister and more importantly I'm going to stop the Grigori."

"I wouldn't tempt fate."

"Then perhaps you don't know me as well as you once did." She said making her way towards the archway.

"Humility, wait!" Azrael said, placing his hand on her shoulder. "The Grigori value power. There is only one way they will stand down."

She didn't look at him. Instead, she placed her hand over his though the feeling of the tongues and eyes still made her skin crawl. "Will you tell me?"

Azrael hesitated. "I may never see you again if I do."

She squeezed his hand comfortingly. "I can't remain apart from my sister, Azrael. I'm sorry, but she's my other half."

Azrael looked down at her, knowing that she spoke the truth. "If you are to save humanity from the Grigori, then you will have to become a God. A force they can no longer challenge."

"Thank you, Azrael." She said with a smile, looking at him over her shoulder as she let go of his hand. "I hope to see you again one day."

Humility hurried out of the temple, coming to a stop when her world shattered. It wasn't so much as shattering like when Thea had busted their mother's favorite vase as children out of spite but as if her world had been torn to pieces. She stopped, taking deep breaths, the tears slowly becoming seamless again. It was frightening in a way as if the world might peel away.

She found an angel, and quickly approached it. "I need you to visit Earth and seek the location of a Grigori. Preferably close to the Heathford Territory."

The angel nodded, flying away and disappearing through the gates of Heaven.

Humility found herself walking in circles around the fountain, though she could not explain why. It was the strangest feeling, like her mind had been switched off, her body acting on its own.

"Are you really willing to risk everything for your sister?" The man's voice said. "She would want you to remain here and be happy. *With Azrael.*"

"You're mistaking slavery and blind loyalty for freedom. These angels aren't happy. They've never known anything different. Thea could tell me right now to stay and I would still do all that I could to escape. This isn't the place for me. I belong on earth with other humans."

"Though you will never be human again?"

"I could be invisible walking the earth and I would still be happier than I am here." Humility's nostrils flared. "And I would finally be able to apologize to my sister." She said as she imagined what torment her sister had went through in her final days. She could feel tears in her eyes, the sound of the water flowing unable to soothe her. She ran her fingers along the images of the putti before sitting on its edge. She watched as the water poured in a colorful stream.

"What if she is dead?" The woman's voice said. "What will you do?"

"I will continue to fight until I no longer have a reason to." She bit her lip.

"Humility!" The angel called, appearing some time later, stopping before Humility. "I've located a Grigori by the name of Sariel presiding over the territory and surrounding areas."

"Thank you." Humility said, waving the angel off as she stood up, breathing deeply. "I suppose this is farewell to the angels. Ironic."

Chapter 11

"Are you finished yet? Never in my life have I met a woman who spends as much time before the mirror as you." Gluttony said, his stare nearly shooting daggers at Pride.

Lavanah looked at him for a moment as she plucked the feathers from his head, a sword catching her eye from the corner of the room as it lay against a table near Pride. It shined bright, with little blue floral ornate designs etched down its blade. It glistened under the light and though it was small, Lavanah had no doubt that it was more than a decoration.

"Hold your tongue, Birdy. You would return to your beautiful state if you could." Red hair flowed down from her back, piercing green eyes meeting the dull black eyes that belonged to Gluttony.

"I prefer having a human head over that of a raven's. To answer, yes, I would but not out of vanity." He said, resting his head on his hand. "You can't imagine the maintenance I go through with these feathers."

"Gluttony, are you calling me vain?" She said, almost as if she were offended, her hand on her chest.

"Pride, do not play a fool with me. You know as well as I do that the only important thing in your life is that of yourself."

She shrugged, smiling conceitedly, pushing the dolls out of her way, stepping forward as one finished pinning the last piece of lace to her dress. Her red hair was braided in an elaborate fashion, her beauty only able to be described as venomous. She motioned for the dolls to leave as she looked into the mirror. She ran her hand along her face before kissing the image of herself.

"Perhaps I am, Gluttony, but I think I look quite eye-catching."

"Is that supposed to be funny?" He said, watching as his feathers fell to the floor beside him.

"Is it not?"

"No. Your humor is weak, distasteful as a matter of fact."

Pride narrowed her eyes. "Very well then. You may leave with the dolls. I have Lavanah here to keep me company."

"I thought you'd never ask." Gluttony said, standing as he turned to face Lavanah. He grabbed her by her chin, lifting her head up.

"I will call for you soon."

"Yes, Sir."

Pride looked at him, still smiling. "I'm surprised you chose a woman like her. I would have thought you were into red heads."

Gluttony let go of her, looking in to Pride's eyes. "I have no need for personal dolls like the rest of you. Do with her as you will." Gluttony said before taking his leave.

Pride sighed, approaching Lavanah. "Lust and Sloth spoke highly of you but I see nothing remarkable about you. They say you're a different kind of doll but in my eyes, you're no better than other of your kind."

Lavanah stood still, expressionless.

Pride leaned forward, pressing her finger against her face. "You're toys for play and slaves for work." She turned away, approaching a lofty chair where she took a seat. Beside her was the table with the sword. A doll stood next to her, placing a plate of food on the table before walking away.

"Would you like something to eat, Lavanah?"

"I do not require food."

"Please, I'm offering. Don't be rude."

Lavanah nodded. "Thank you."

Pride lifted the plate, dumping the food onto the floor before handing the plate to the other doll. She looked at Lavanah as she pointed to it.

"Eat, Dog."

Lavanah looked at her for a moment before approaching the food on the floor, lifting the food with her hand, taking a bite from it. There was nothing wrong with the food other than the fact that it was on the floor.

Pride smacked her hand. "Dogs do not eat with hands."

Lavanah leaned forward, eating the food without the use of her hands. Pride reached down, grabbing her by her hair where she proceeded to rub her face in the food. Lavanah's chest ached but she ignored it, continuing to eat. Pride let go of her hair, smacking the back of her head.

"Messy dog."

Pride waited patiently until the food had disappeared before pointing at a large display case that sat near the entrance to her room, lights glowing from within it. "I want you to clean my display of souls." She said, entering the kitchen, throwing a towel to Lavanah. "It must be spotless."

Lavanah started with the base, meticulously running the towel along the wood though it appeared spotless. Pride grabbed tomatoes from a bowl in the kitchen throwing them at her, laughing when they hit her in the head or hung from her hair. She reached for the eggs next, throwing them at her, watching as they shattered on impact.

Lavanah sighed, rubbing the fog off the glass, grateful when Pride no longer threw food at her. She suspected that Pride worried about the glass having nearly cracked it in a few places. She stared into the glass, the souls within its walls glowing in a variety of colors. They lined the shelves of velvet for Pride to stare at like trophies.

"Aren't they beautiful? The blue ones are my favorite."

Lavanah nodded, continuing to clean, wiping the food splattered against the glass. Once she finished she turned to look at Pride waiting for further instruction.

"Polish my sword."

Lavanah approached the sword, turning the cloth inside out, running it along the blade carefully her eyes not once leaving the blade. She jumped, a cold and yellow liquid landing on her head, slowly running down her cheeks. It dripped from her chin and onto her body. Her hand slipped from the cloth, cutting it on the edge of the blade though she did not feel it. She watched her blood as it mixed with the substance.

She touched it with her fingers, sniffing it, the scent of vanilla strong.

"Your kind are rather fond of pudding, but I don't care for it myself. That said, I can't imagine wasting it." She looked at her sword seeing the pudding dribble onto the blade. "Continue polishing, Dog."

Lavanah continued, Pride watching her from afar, waiting until she had set the sword down, holding the towel against the cut on her hand.

Pride approached her, sighing. "Oh no, it looks like the dog got into the pantry again. I suppose I should give it a bath." Pride said before dragging Lavanah by her hair. She entered her bathroom, running a cold bath, another doll arriving soon after.

Pride removed Lavanah's clothing, throwing them at the doll's feet. "Wash these immediately. I would be very upset if a dog had to wear any of my clothes."

"I wouldn't dream of it." The doll said, taking the clothes before disappearing.

Lavanah tried to look at the doll as it left but was placed into the icy bath where Pride submerged her head under the water, holding her there as she washed her hair. Lavanah's eyes were wide beneath the water even as it filled her lungs, causing her a great amount of pain.

Pride let go of Lavanah, watching as she sat up. "Dogs aren't supposed to sit during a bath. You must stand like the dog you are."

Lavanah got on all fours, coughing out water, her chest aching.

"Bark."

Lavanah trembled, looking at Pride. "Woof."

Pride laughed in joy, picking eggshells off her as well as tomato seeds, her skin dotted with faint bruises. Pride grabbed the soap, rubbing it along her body, stopping after a moment to scratch behind her ear.

"Bark."

"Woof." Lavanah said, her pain in her chest growing.

Pride splashed water against her, rinsing the soap from her body before draining the bath. Lavanah stood up, Pride immediately shaking her finger at her.

"Lavanah, sit."

Lavanah did as she asked, sitting down.

Pride left for a moment, returning with a towel where she began to dry Lavanah off. Once finished she pointed at the floor, forcing Lavanah onto all fours again. The doll returned with her clothing, holding it out to Pride.

"Dogs do not wear clothing, set them on the table."

Pride dragged Lavanah by her hair into her chambers where she sat beside the bed, allowing Lavanah to sit with her. She grabbed the brush from her bedside table, running it through her tangled hair. She pulled roughly on it, dragging the wire bristles down the flesh of her back. Lavanah stared at the wall, her lip quivering, tears coming to her eyes.

Pride threw the brush aside once finished. She looked at Lavanah with a disappointed expression having quickly become bored. She returned to her living room, sitting in her plush chair. Lavanah did not react like her dolls who often became agitated though they continued to obey. She whistled for Lavanah as she crossed her legs.

Lavanah walked out to the main room but Pride shook her finger, pointing to the floor, watching as Lavanah stood on all fours again. She made her way to Pride's chair. Pride pointed to the space before her feet, stopping her with a tug of her hair. Lavanah gasped, Pride's feet suddenly resting on her back.

"Perfect."

Lavanah lost track of the hours that passed, her arms and legs burning from remaining in the same position. Each time she began to give into the pain Pride would dig her heels into her back. The pain in her chest now matching that of the rest of her body.

Pride sighed after several more hours had passed, removing her feet from Lavanah's back, knocking her onto her side. "You bore me, Dog. Get out."

Lavanah stood, fumbling as she redressed herself, leaving Pride's chambers.

##

"Sloth." Pride yelled, storming into her chambers. "You lied to me, Sloth. There is nothing special about that doll. She did not look at me any differently than when she first entered my chambers. My dolls don't hide their emotions."

Sloth laughed, closing her book as she looked at Pride. "Then she must possess great strength. I would have killed you if you treated me like you do the dolls."

Pride was almost hysterical, her eyes falling onto the black feather inside her book. "Kill me?" She said pressing her hands to her chest. "Sloth, you can't even move. You're completely useless."

Sloth continued to smile, amused by Pride's behavior. "Just you wait, Pride. You'll be the first to die one day and for that I envy you."

"How can you be so sure?"

"Because you're the first one I would go after."

Pride approached Sloth, slapping her across the cheek. "You know nothing of the world outside your chambers."

Sloth held her cheek, giving her a devious look. "I know far more than you give me credit for, Pride. Don't let your superiority blind you."

"I shall laugh with my brothers on the day you die."

Sloth set her book down, laughing so hard she began to cough. "I wish someone would come kill me. Then I wouldn't be forced to listen to our brothers complain. Not enough souls. Not enough dolls. Not enough blood. Not enough sex. Tell me Pride, when is it enough?"

"Surely you joke, Sloth. It's never enough."

"Then like a balloon you are nothing but air."

Pride scoffed, storming out of the room where she threw over the candlesticks as she left.

Sloth sighed heavily, reaching for her book. "And I just had my room cleaned." She said, tracing the array on the leather cover of her book, calling out to her dolls.

"Lavanah." A doll spoke to her as she sat behind her desk, writing in her journal, the pages quickly filling. The ink began calm, growing angry with each page she passed. "Wrath wishes to see you." Though the doll's expression was no different from the others, their tone spoke volumes: no good would come of this.

Lavanah finished the sentence, turning the page before putting the quill in its place, closing the inkwell.

The doll approached her, looking at her bruises which had reddened in the passing hours. "We will come for you as soon as it's over."

Lavanah nodded, standing. She followed the doll out of her chambers, the journal still open behind her as she closed the door. She ran her hand along the walls, the candle lights casting a warm glow over them as they made their way to a grand staircase that spilled into a large foyer.

The foyer was decorated differently with grey tiles and purple walls which faded into the walls at the top of the staircase. The fires of the candles were untamed as the doors were opened.

"I've never been outside before." Lavanah said, rubbing her arms as snow crunched under her feet.

Lavanah took a breath, exhaling a silver mist as the doors closed behind them. She looked into the purple sky, its color nearly black in places. The snow continued to fall, sticking to her skin. She brushed it off, following close behind the doll, breathing into her hands in an attempt to keep warm. The icy breeze played with her hair, sending chills over her skin.

Buildings stretched towards the sky, casting shadows on the streets below, every so often a room would light up, shadows flickering in the distance. Among them lived the lesser demons, watching with ravenous hunger as they passed. Though they could not see her, they could sense her soul. Some were covered in blood, occasionally missing a limb or two from their engagements with archdemons. She was petrified by the thought of ending up like them but as a doll there was only one of two places she could go.

##

Lavanah's breath caught in her chest as she stared into the distance. The world before her like the sky above was painted in black and purple flecked with white. Behind her the buildings had become snowy plains leading to a mountain that stretched higher than any building and extended beyond the reach of the snow. A cavern led into the mountain its entrance shaped like the face of a man, withered and time worn like the face on the opposing side. However, this face frowned and could only be described as lachrymose. His eyes remained closed, the snow acting as his tears. His mouth was the entrance, obscured in darkness, the wailing of souls within the cavern serving as his cries.

Lavanah brushed off another layer of snow, the dolls coming to a stop before his mouth.

"This is as far as I go. Wrath isn't hard to find."

"Lavanah nodded, entering the cavern. She wandered past the tortured souls, stopping Wrath as he carried his sword. His arm had been restored. However, close to his shoulder a scar circled where the wound once had been. She could see on his limbs that there was more than one of the scars.

"Come with me." Wrath spoke, leading Lavanah to his chambers high within the mountain. She followed obediently, surprised by his tone. Wrath was different from the other demons she had met thus far.

From Lust, she could sense his desire.

From Sloth, she could sense her burden.

From Pride, she could sense — no, see — her vanity.

In Wrath, she could sense an incessant feeling of regret.

His chambers were barren, chains hanging from the walls, a wooden table off to the side that he leaned his blade against. The table did not budge against the weight of the blade. Wrath dragged her over to the chains, fastening her in place before running his hands over the ink that graced her back almost fondly.

"I'm sorry." He said though it was not to her but the art he had created on her skin. He then began to strike her.

Lavanah's eyes widened, Wrath striking her with all his force. His sorrow consumed him, becoming the anger he used against her. Her armor tore as well as the flesh beneath it. The wolf's head was first to go. The raven's wings ripped from its body afterwards. She was fragile against him, blood staining the leather of her trousers as it trickled down her legs. She tried not to wince but felt herself quickly losing control.

If her eyes could have pierced stone, a statue would have stood before her. Her chest ached again, like it had with Pride though her pain only intensified the aching. She held onto the chains, clenching her teeth with each hit. Her wrists turned in the chains, the skin becoming raw, and blood flowing from her flesh trickling down her arms.

Her screams echoed through the cavern, her vision fading to black.

She no longer screamed for the horror before her only brought silence.

The ground beneath her feet had been stained in blood, the sky above her orange where the sun had started to set. Fire ravaged the city before her, smoke beginning to hide the orange sky. To her right stood an angel with large black wings extending from his back, dark hair dripping with blood though not his own as he submerged a child in water.

"No!" Lavanah said, stepping forward, reaching for them. She was too late, the child flailing, screaming, the water bubbling around his head. She watched as the number of bubbles dropped before ceasing altogether, the child's limbs falling still in the arms of the angel.

He pulled the unconscious child from the water. Wet red hair hung from her head, her freckled skin pale. He pushed in her eyes, removing them from her skull before dropping her body to the ground beside him. He rolled them in his hand for a moment, looking at their color, disappointed at how lifeless they had become. He brought the eyes to his lips eating them, savoring their taste.

He turned to face the other humans, watching as they crawled along the ground, their eyes hollow, and blood pouring down their cheeks. He tried to step out of their path, smacking them as they clung to his limbs, crying, screaming, and begging for answers.

One of the humans quieted, falling over. He grabbed them by their hair, dragging them into the pile of corpses, watching as those who were still alive stumbled over the dead bodies of their family.

He approached another human as they fell over, dragging it by its arms onto a large pile of corpses that he had created. The child's corpse was last to join the pile.

He held his hands out, chanting words Lavanah had never heard before, their bodies set ablaze. He watched for a moment as they burned, the pungent smell of death staining the air around him.

His wings extended, lifting him into the air where he flew into the orange sky, the humans screaming below him as they burned.

Lavanah woke inside a room, no longer in the mountain. She screamed, struggling against the dolls as they pinned her down. A doll stood above her, his hands casting a bright glow. Her back burned where the skin was stitching itself back together, her tattoos being restored in the process with faint scars. She cried, burying her head into a pillow realizing she was inside her chambers.

The dolls stayed until the last bit of flesh had stitched, her wounds healed; even the bruises inflicted by Pride. She could no longer hide from the pain finding it to be too much to bear. The demons were wrong, all except Pride.

One of the dolls reached out to her but Lavanah smacked their hand away. "Leave me alone."

The doll took its hand back. "Some days are harder than others. However, you've been summoned."

"Get out!" Lavanah said, getting into the doll's face. The pillows flew off her bed, her window slamming close where a small crack formed in the glass.

"Envy requests to see you." The doll said almost eerily calm before taking its leave.

"Lavanah, I was afraid you wouldn't come." Envy spoke, approaching her. She was the size of a young child with large black wings extending from her back. Her chest was flat, her arms and legs like twigs attached to a dress the color of leaves, white lace decorating its edges.

Lavanah crossed her arms over her chest. "What is it Envy?"

Envy was taken aback by her tone, smirking as she spoke. "The archdemons consider me to be the weakest of the sins. Can you believe it?" She said, stomping her feet as she walked away. "Even Gluttony looks down on me. How is that fair? We're both angels. Both come from the same place. I should be in his place. I would rather be despised than disrespected."

"Get to the point, Envy."

Envy took a deep breath, reaching for Lavanah's hands surprised when she pulled them from her reach. "Souls are the source of their power. Bring them to me. In Pride's chambers, she has a collection of souls. Bring one to me. She'll never notice it's gone."

Lavanah smiled. "I will do this."

##

Pride stood, staring into the mirror, speaking to herself as she frequently did, the dolls around her changing her clothes as well as unbraiding her hair. Lavanah watched from the corner of the display case.

Pride shouted, pulling a pin from her side. "Watch what you're doing." She said jamming the pin into the eye of the doll, blood staining her hands. "Now fetch a rag to clean this blood."

The doll held its eye as it approached her.

Lavanah covered her mouth, lying on the floor against the case. She closed her eyes, listening as the doll fumbled, accidentally pushing the rag off the display case. She jumped, the rag landing on her leg. The doll sighed, making its way around the display case.

"Stop." Pride said, disgusted as she wiped her hands onto the clothes of another doll. The doll stopped on the corner, standing above Lavanah, meeting Pride's eyes as she threw her sword, piercing both the doll and the wall. Blood ran in lines down the wall, pooling next to Lavanah.

Pride turned back to the mirror, shouting commands at the dolls. Lavanah was slow as she slid the glass door of the case open.

"Did you hear that?" Pride stopped, turning around.

Lavanah froze, trembling as she covered her mouth again. Beside her the doll's body flinched, still alive. It's foot occasionally hitting the display case.

"Someone kill it." A doll started its way towards it but stopped when Pride grabbed its hand. "After you finish this dress."

Lavanah squeezed her hand into the small opening she had made; grabbing the first soul she touched before closing the case and slipping out the door.

##

Envy took the soul from Lavanah's hands as soon as she returned, jumping with joy. "I didn't think you could do it."

Envy approached her doll as it sat on the sofa, holding the soul out to her. "A gift for you." She said, watching as her doll took the soul and consumed it. The eyes of the doll lit up even if only for a moment.

"Tell me Lavanah, have you ever strived to become better than someone but forever remain at the bottom?"

"The thought has crossed my mind lately."

"That is what it feels like to be me. Always being the weakest link." Envy said, sitting in her settee, hugging a feather pillow. "I want you to return to Earth and collect souls. It's best you leave for a bit."

Lavanah squinted her eyes as a doll handed her a rather large basket like one might use for picnics. "Is that so?"

"Pride will undoubtedly be here soon."

"You said she wouldn't notice."

Envy smiled, looking at her. "I lied."

Lavanah scoffed, leaving the estate, wandering the cold streets until her arrays glowed. Their light consumed her as she watched the world become that of a blue sky hanging above a meadow. She shielded her eyes from the bright light at first, cautious as she made her way along the meadow, a small town standing in the distance.

##

"You're lucky I don't hit children." Pride said, entering her quarters, sword in hand. She had since cleaned it of blood, its blade shining in the candlelight.

Envy looked at Pride as she sat beside her doll while it brushed her hair. "What do you want Pride?"

"I want my soul back." She spoke quickly before Envy could make a snide remark. "The one you stole from me."

"I have no need for your souls, Pride. I can't even consume them."

"Don't play innocent, Envy. I know better than to believe an angel of the fall." Pride seethed. "You sent that dog into my room. There was an interesting silhouette in the blood on my floor."

"So maybe I did take it. However, I no longer have it."

Pride clutched her sword tightly, calming herself. "And I assume you will tell me where it is..."

"I knew there was something different about you. Your head got bigger didn't it? You're no different than a puffed-up mutt."

"Envy. Let's be civil." Pride said twirling her sword. "If I were you, I would call for one of your dolls. There's quite the mess to clean up." She stopped twirling her sword, raising it into the air.

Envy's doll stood protectively in front of her with its arms stretched out.

"What are you going to do Pride? Destroy my room like you did to Sloth?"

Pride threw her sword, the blade piercing through the skull of the doll as it pinned her to the wall. She approached it, retrieving the sword where she wiped the blade on the body of the doll. She immediately returned to Envy, pressing the tip of the blade to her chin, drawing blood.

Stay out of my room, Envy. That includes your pets. If you don't you'll end up like your doll over there." Pride laughed as she left the room.

"Damn it. Now I have to start over." Envy said reaching for her pillow, flipping it to reveal an array. She pressed her hand to it, a green light glowing from it as she spoke in tongues.

##

Lavanah stumbled her way through the snow, the soft glow of her arrays fading. She had draped a cloth over the basket to try and hide the rainbow of glows that seeped through the woven basket. Her pace picked up as she entered the estate, making her way to Envy's chambers with haste.

To her surprise a new doll sat on the sofa, waving her closer. "Over here." The doll called out.

"You're not the same doll as before."

"Pride killed the other doll. It's not unheard of."

Lavanah removed the blanket from the basket, the room filling with a warm and colorful glow. "And now Envy has placed this burden upon you."

"Burden?" The doll laughed though there was no emotion to her voice. "You clearly have never eaten a soul." She took the basket from Lavanah, opening the lid. She held a soul out to Lavanah, eating it when she refused.

"What's it like?"

The doll consumed several others before speaking. "Corruption. I can feel the shadows growing closer but the more I consume them the less I care. Once you've eaten one soul, there is no stopping. Perhaps it is best you don't."

Lavanah watched as her basket quickly emptied, the doll returning it to her. "Then I suppose I should collect more." She looked down watching as a blue soul rolled around in it. "You missed one."

She held the soul out to the doll, but she shook her head, holding a hand up. "Keep it. You won't know the meaning behind my words without it. Consider it a gift from another of your kind."

"You show me great kindness." Lavanah said, placing the soul into the basket.

"I can't succumb to the curse yet like the archdemons." The doll said, its lips curving into a small smile. "Because there can only be seven at once. Once one is killed, another takes its place. Normally a doll but *sometimes* the lesser demons take power. They don't last long though. Too weak."

Lavanah returned the smile before leaving for her chambers. She placed the soul inside the drawer of her desk. Her arrays then glowed again, the sky becoming a bright orange as if it had been painted with fire.

Only then did she smell the smoke as it burned her nostrils.

Lavanah dropped the basket, coughing, her eyes burning as she struggled to look upon the world around her. She was in the same city that she had left, of that she had no doubt. However, she did not remember seeing flames before she had left.

"You're becoming rather adept at magic, little demon. However I am all too familiar with your tricks." Came a voice belonging to a man with hair the color of sand, neatly combed to one side. He approached her, his eyes were piercing and the color of silver. He dressed like a king though a sword rested on his side. Two white wings extended from his back as he drew his blade. His wings came down, propelling him towards Lavanah, his sword prepared to strike.

Lavanah crossed her arms together, holding them in front of her face as she tried to leap out of his way. She knew her flesh wasn't strong enough to stop his blade but perhaps they would ease the blow.

A hand grabbed her by the strings of her corset, pulling her out of the angel's path. "Lavanah, run." A familiar voice shouted from beside her.

The angel stopped, stumbling as he tried to regain his footing, the ground beneath him crumbled into a chasm.

"I can see through your illusions, Solas!"

Gluttony came down from the sky, his boots landing on the face of the angel, burying him in the snow.

Lavanah held her arm out, the arrays glowing where they returned her to her chambers.

Chapter 12

She stood before a palace cast in shadows, the sunset like a painting behind it. There was something sinister about this place as it looked down on the territory before it. She could feel the Grigori's power. It caused chills to her bones, made her tremble with each step forward. It was hostile and hungry.

However, she felt as if this was her last chance to find her sister. Her hope was beginning to dwindle, and if she did not find her, she feared that she would become the lost child her sister had once protected.

She watched as people passed by her in pairs dressed in elaborate gowns and suits. They wore masks as they filled the halls of the palace, laughing, oblivious to the darkness around them.

She had never been so grateful to be invisible as she was now. Her search had led her to the throne room where the darkness was most prevalent. She felt hollow, the Grigori's power seeming to echo in her bones.

The King and Queen rested on their thrones watching as their guests danced around the floor in blissful ignorance. She watched as their hands clasped together, their daughter no older than six sitting on her mother's lap. She conversed with the guards, two of them striking her as unusual.

The two guards turned to look at her. The King's eyes followed shortly.

"They're Grigori." The man's voice spoke.

"Which one?" Humility said, staring at them.

"All of them."

"That really narrows my options. *Thank you.*" She said.

"Humility using *sarcasm?* Thea would not believe this."

"I've used sarcasm before." She said with a blush as they made their way through the crowd. "Just not very often."

The man coughed, swearing quietly.

Time seemed to slow around them, shadows bleeding down the walls until they had swallowed the room. Humility could no longer see the guests as they danced. Only the two guards and the King. She landed on the floor before them, curtsying politely though she wore no clothes.

"So kind of you to visit Humility." The King said, standing. "Though I had hoped this day would never come."

Humility took a deep breath. "Then you are Sariel, I presume?"

"I am." He said calmly, taking his time as he made his way down the stairs. "And you look beautiful for a dead woman."

"So does my sister from what I've heard." She said watching him approach.

"She's absolutely a doll." He said pressing a hand to her breast, squeezing it lightly. "I almost regret not taking you as my wife when you were still alive. I would have had better control over you and your sister. I suppose it isn't too late. Perhaps one of my men would take you. What say you?" He said, turning his attention on the guards.

Humility slapped his hand away, looking up at the guard as he polished a knife. "Maybe back in the days at the estate but I have no interest in her now."

"Humans are more appealing though easily broken. Remember what Solas did to that village in a single night?"

She glanced at the two men, recognizing their faces. They had once been guards at her parent's estate.

"They were at my parents' estate. *Why?*"

"Because this is my territory." Sariel said. "And they watched your parents, watched *you.*"

"Your territory? It belongs to the people."

"Nothing belongs to the humans. They need stability. That's why the Grigori were created. Despite a little naughtiness, the elders saw the value in keeping us above ground. They named us the watchers."

"And how exactly is an angel going to provide stability to thousands of people?"

"I pull the strings for them. I underestimated your power, Humility. I expected your parents to be able to properly deal with two teenage girls but they're incompetent."

"We did nothing to you!"

"I knew as soon as you were born you would become trouble for me and thought it best to get rid of you. However as time passed you grew and I was forced to deal with more pressing matters."

"Me?"

"You are the problem." Sariel said, sitting on his throne again. "You never thought it strange that your hair was different from your sister's?"

"Mother told me I was blessed."

"Because that's what I told her. I was hoping she'd take more of an interest in you. You're the one with the Holy Spirit inside you and she goes after the vile one. Humans need a lot of hand holding and I only have two hands."

"You're a liar."

"Don't be so naïve. The platinum hair? The fact you're an angel? Newsflash; Humans don't become angels. They die. The end."

Humility ran up the stairs, the guards grabbing her by her arms. "And what of my sister? What have you done to her?"

"We framed her to look like she had killed you. It didn't take much with Sariel's control over the humans." The guard spoke, laughing maliciously. "I watched as the guards took advantage of your sister, her screams as they raped her."

"I hope my sister comes to kill you all."

Sariel stood, laughing as he held her chin in his fingers. "Your sister doesn't even know who she is. The demons pass her around like their bitch."

Humility laughed. "My sister is a slave to no one."

Sariel let go of her. "It matters to me no more. You're both bound to your masters. If you kill me, then you're no different than I am."

"I don't have to kill you Sariel." Humility said as the guards let her go. "Someone will come for you."

"Send my regards to Azrael." Sariel said, watching as she flew away. "*Watch her.*"

The darkness faded away leaving the King alone in the room to watch as his guests danced in circles before him. He lifted his hand, moving his fingers up and down as if strings were hanging from them.

##

"I met Sariel." Humility stood on Azrael's desk, using both her hands to crush the flowers into a fine powder in the mortar and pestle.

"What did you learn?"

"My sister doesn't remember who she is. Somehow her memory is missing." She struggled to keep her voice calm. The thought of her sister being out of reach was difficult to bear but the thought of her having no memory of their years together was unbearable.

"They must have removed her soul." He said, continuing to write, watching her from time to time. "I'm not surprised your sister chose to become a demon. She has always displayed a strong will."

"I don't see a way for me to see my sister again." She said, her words bringing tears to her eyes. They slowly rolled down her cheeks, dripping into the powder created from the flowers as she continued to crush them.

"Marie, I can think of one angel in hell who *might* look after your sister." Azrael said, finishing the page, placing the quill inside the inkwell. "There is no way to know for sure, but I have reason to suspect he's involved."

"An angel? Looking after my sister?"

"He's a fallen angel similar to Sariel." He said moving the mortar and pestle away from her, wiping at her tears with his hand. Though Humility appreciated the gesture, the tongues against her skin made her skin crawl. She wasn't sure she would ever become accustom to the feeling of the eyes and tongues on her skin. She no longer was afraid to look at him and for him that was enough.

"Though I must warn you that his crimes were more atrocious than those committed by Sariel."

"I'm not sure that's possible."

"What if I told you that Sariel is part of the reason why he's in Hell?"

"Is that what you're telling me?"

Azrael nodded.

"Then what reason does he have for helping my sister?"

"Because for one reason or another, he sees purpose in her." He said, taking her hands in his. "Like when I asked you to become my assistant. It's because I knew you were capable of great things, Marie."

There her name was, *again.* The cherub had told her she would be addressed as only Humility but Azrael was quickly returning to her *real* name. It brought a smile to her lips to know that someone cared about her past.

"What's his name so that one day I know who to thank?"

"When he was in Heaven his name was Solas. I couldn't tell you what the demons call him. However, he was a powerful angel and one of the angels responsible for a battle that took place a very long time ago.

"Where was this battle?"

"In Heaven. Many of the rebellious angels were killed but the ones who survived were divided into Grigori and prisoners."

"And he was a Grigori?"

"For a time until he became Sariel's prisoner."

She was quiet for a moment, taking her hands away from Azrael. "There is something I must do, Azrael."

"You're going to leave Heaven again,"

"I will return as soon as I am able." She said giving him a reassuring smile.

"You're going to visit your son."

She nodded. "I want him to know that his mother is watching over him. I want him to know I'm still here."

"Then give him something that once belonged to you."

"There is nothing of me left in that world."

"Your son is still there."

Humility looked at him, taking a deep breath. "Yes, he is."

Humility watched as her son cried, her wet nurse holding him, his tiny hands pushing against her. Tears streamed down the woman's face as she tried her best to quiet him, placing him in his crib after a moment. She sat next to her mother, placing her hand on her forehead.

"I don't know what to do. He won't eat. He won't sleep, and he certainly won't stop crying."

"Neither can you." Her mother said, wiping at her cheeks. "I'm sure he misses his mother. Wouldn't you?"

"I just can't believe her sister would kill her."

The woman shook her head. "And I've told you before, I'll tell you again, Thea is innocent. I may not have known her long but I saw the bond those sisters had. I'm telling you for the last time that something else happened. Something we don't know."

Humility took a deep breath, approaching her son. His crib was in the nursery, the only chambers their small cottage had. She didn't hesitate, revealing herself to him as she lifted him from his crib. His cries became choked up sobs before silencing all together as he stared into the face of his mother. A smile spread across his face as he began to laugh, reaching for her. She held him close to her bare body, the warmth from his skin stealing her breath. She folded her wings close as she sat in the rocking chair with him, cradling him with one arm so that he could suck on the thumb of her other hand. She ran her fingers along his cheek as he closed his eyes. She couldn't stop the tears as they streamed from her face, falling onto his pajamas.

"I love you, my son." She whispered. "Ciel, my baby boy."

"Do you hear that?" The mother of the wet nurse spoke. "Poor thing probably cried himself to sleep."

"*Thank goodness.*" The wet nurse said, relaxing into a chair.

"Why don't you check on him? I'm sure he would like his bear." The mother said, lifting the stuffed bear from the floor before dusting it off.

"Absolutely not. If you're so concerned, *you* go check on him." She said waving her mother off.

The old woman huffed, disappointed in her daughter. "I will be in the nursery with my grandchild."

"He's not my baby." The wet nurse said offended by her mother's words. "*He's not my responsibility.*"

"And most days I'm not even sure you're my child." The older woman said. "But you can bet your behind that Marie was like a daughter to me. So, her son may not be your responsibility, but we are going to raise him with all the love and support he deserves."

She held the bear close as she entered the nursery, shutting the door quietly behind her. "Ciel, sweetie, I brought Mr. Bear for you." She said in a playful tone as she turned around.

She gasped, dropping the bear, as her eyes fell onto the bare body of Marie as she held her son. "You're alive."

"*Shh.*" Marie said quietly. "Come, sit with me."

The older woman lifted the bear, grabbing a small stool as she sat with Marie. She placed her hand on Humility's leg to make sure that she was real, relieved when her skin felt warm to the touch.

However, she was in disbelief at the sight of the white wings that extended from her back. She couldn't deny that despite her sitting before her that she had indeed died.

"I want to thank you for taking care of Ciel for me." Humility said with tears in her eyes. "I had to come to see him, to hold him one more time."

"You may come see him whenever you wish." The woman said handing her the teddy bear.

Humility placed the bear close to Ciel, watching as he wrapped his arms around the bear, burying his head into the soft head. Humility held him closer, kissing his head.

"I wish that were true, but the truth is that I am no longer the same woman I once was. I'm not able to return and be his mother again. I am... an angel." She said though it broke her heart to admit that she had lost her humanity. "The others will not approve of my being here. I was warned shortly before I left that there would be consequences."

"Heaven isn't like that." The woman said.

Marie smiled. "It's no different than the governments of man. Only those with power and privilege rule." She rocked her son gently in her arms. "I want Ciel to know that I will always watch over him from afar. That he is never alone. I will always support him even though I may not physically be here. I love him and would do anything for him."

"I will make sure he knows every day how much you love him." The old woman said with tears in her eyes.

"And that I love you because you are raising him though it shouldn't be your responsibility."

"All I will ask of you, Marie, is to answer one question that has plagued me for so long."

"Anything."

"Who took your life?"

"My parents poisoned me and forced my sister to take the fall. She is no longer alive either."

"Is she with you?"

Humility shook her head.

The woman wrapped her arms around Humility, rubbing her back. "I'm sure you miss her very much."

"As much as I miss my son." She said looking down into his innocent face. "And I miss you more than you can imagine."

The woman shed tears as she watched Humility kiss her son's head again. "I need you to raise him to be a good man. One day soon, this world will undergo a change that it may not be prepared for. When that time comes, I need my son to live up to his noble blood. He has the heart of a King, not just a Duke. One day, the world will see that he'll do great things."

The woman nodded. "I will make sure he lives up to your words. He will be the greatest man."

"I have faith in you and in him." She said, running her hands through his blonde hair. "I don't want to let him go. I would stay here in this nursery with him forever if I could."

The woman gave Humility's knee a firm squeeze. "Ciel will always be here for you. Just promise him you'll visit."

"*I promise.*" She said kissing his head. "You will do *great* things, my son."

The older woman's lip trembled as Humility handed him back to her. "Thank you for taking care of my baby."

The woman reached out for Humility but she had already disappeared. The woman kissed Ciel's head as he began to cry again. She placed him in his crib with his bear, putting a small blanket over him.

"She'll come home one day, Ciel. She promised." The woman said before joining her in the living room. She waited for a moment before looking into the hazel eyes of her daughter.

"What?" She said curtly.

The old woman smiled. "I was visited by my daughter just now. I watched as she held Ciel with more love than I could ever hope to give that child." She said as he cried in the background. Only now she fought hard not to cry herself.

"I've been in this chair the whole time." She said.

The older woman laughed, speaking gently as she stared into her daughter's eyes. "*You* are *not* my daughter."

##

Humility entered Azrael's temple surprised to see the angels dressed in full suits of armor there. One held its spear towards Azrael, its helmet lying in the floor beside them. They met Humility's eyes briefly before directing their attention towards Azrael once more.

"Humility, it's them!" The man's voice said. "From your meeting with Sariel. Those were his guards. Look at its face."

Azrael looked at Humility. His expression more relaxed than she would have expected in the current situation. He pushed the spear away, meeting the eyes of the angels.

"I think it's time the two of you took your leave."

The other angel holding a shield, placed his hand on the other angel's shoulder. "I think it's time we leave. There will be more opportunities."

"No." Humility said. "*There won't be.*"

The two angels looked at her, almost intimidated by her words. The one angel retrieved his helmet before following behind his partner. Azrael and Humility stared at one another in silence until they were sure they had left the temple.

"What did they want with you, Azrael?"

"It's nothing to concern yourself with, Marie. Authorities have always been rough around the edges."

"On the contrary, Azrael. Those were the same angels guarding Sariel when we had our little chat. So yes, I think this is definitely something I should concern myself with."

"They were there?"

"Azrael, they watched my sister suffer." She said placing her hands on his desk.

Azrael stood in silence for a moment, watching as she began to pace through his temple. He scribbled down more names into his book before closing it. "Stop your pacing, it's disturbing the silence."

She came to a stop, looking into the face on the back of his head. "Your face is disturbing." She took a deep breath for a moment. "I apologize for that. It was inappropriate."

Azrael's faces laughed at her comment. "They could fall if the Elders were to catch wind of this."

"Then I will make sure a breeze goes through their temple."

"Humility you'll be creating a storm that may drag you with them."

"My sister would do the same."

"You aren't Thea." Azrael said, lifting his quill, placing it into the inkwell. "I wish you would seek justice in another fashion."

"I can think of none other."

"Power is a fickle thing and can be attained in a variety of ways. Angels attain power from the faith humanity places in us. The Grigori are disgraced angels but still have the ability to become Gods because they aren't human. What's to stop you from doing the same?"

"Then I have nothing to lose."

##

Humility tried to keep calm as she landed on the steps of the temple that housed the elders. She hurried up the stairs, surprised to see so many angels in one place. It was enough to make her head spin. Angels spilled into it just as quickly as they exited creating a small breeze that felt cool against her face and feathers.

It was the largest temple in Heaven able to be seen from everywhere. She approached the front desk, smiling at the angel. It looked no different than a human except for the wings that graced its back.

"Where can I direct you?"

"I would like to request an audience with the elders. I have something they should be aware of."

"I see, that is quite the request. What is this regarding?"

"I have reason to believe that a group of authorities are conspiring with the Grigori."

"I see. That is a very serious accusation. However, I will see to it that you have your audience. If you'll have a seat for a moment."

"Thank you."

Humility watched as the angel scribbled something onto a piece of parchment before handing it off to another angel.

She sat patiently among other angels watching as others came and went through the temple. She couldn't believe that there was so much work to be done for eternity.

She did not have to wait long, the angel soon calling to her. "Humility, the elders will see you now."

She stepped out from behind the desk, Humility following her through the temple to its main chambers. It took her breath away, a room made of marble, with an incredible view of the Tree of Life and the Tree of Knowledge. She could see the River of Life as it flowed between them. The walls reached higher than those of Azrael's temple, light pouring in through their stained-glass windows. The marble floors were bathed in color.

"Your name?" One of the elders spoke.

There were exactly twenty-four of them, mature men with wrinkles creasing their skin. They dressed in long white robes and held in their hands wheels within wheels covered in eyes, each a different shade of beryl. It was the only way she could tell them apart from one another. The eyes of the men themselves were clouded, the men seeing through the wheels. They sat comfortably in thrones that circled part of the room. At their feet Seraphim sang praise in soft voices.

"I am the Stronghold Humility."

"Welcome to our temple Humility." One elder spoke. "You have news of angels betraying our order to conspire with the Grigori?"

She nodded. "I do. I witnessed two authorities conspiring with the Grigori Sariel. They aided his plans to have a human woman named Thea Leighton framed for the murder of her sister, Marie Leighton, which resulted in two innocent deaths."

The elders held their hands up in unison, the seraphim silencing.

"*You.*" One spoke.

Humility froze, watching as another Throne raised his hand. "What are the names of these authorities?"

"I don't know their names, but one carries a shield and the other a spear."

There was grumbling among the Elders. "We can't act on this alone. There are many authorities that meet such a vague description."

"You're looking for Shamsiel and Jeqon." Came Azrael's voice from the back of the room as he approached. "They showed up at my temple threatening me if I didn't release Humility to them. So not only have they gone against your orders, but also they've threatened the lives of their fellow angels. Is this not enough to act on?"

The elders looked at Azrael in awe as he approached Humility. "Azrael?" The elders spoke, shocked by his presence. "What part do you play in this?"

"I sent Humility to Earth because I had been having trouble seeing a group of humans. I learned through her that this was because my visions were being interfered with by the authorities aforementioned with orders from Sariel."

The elders looked at one of the angels. "Seek out the authorities. We need to verify this information before proceeding."

The angels nodded, taking their leave.

Humility took a deep breath, looking at Azrael. "Thank you for coming."

"Don't thank me yet. This isn't over."

"What will they do to those authorities?"

"The other authorities are going to use magic on them. If it affects them negatively, and it *will,* then they will be stripped of their wings. Once that happens they will be destroyed. Conspiring with Grigori is an offense punishable by death."

"That's enough for me."

"I was unaware you had a dark side, Marie." The two shared a small smile as they continued to wait.

The angel returned after some time, speaking quietly with the Elders before taking their leave. The Elders spoke amongst one another for a moment before directing their attention to Humility and Azrael.

"The authorities were able to verify the information you have presented us. Shamsiel and Jeqon are no more. It is always a shame to be forced to put down our own, although we do what the situation calls for." The elders said though their tone did not seem grateful. "However, that is not the only thing that has been brought to our attention."

Humility's breath caught in her chest and for the first time she feared for her well-being.

"Humility, we expected so much of you. You are the first human that has been blessed with the Holy Spirit. We will not make this mistake again. When Azrael came to us regarding the success of your birth, we knew immediately that upon your death — though it was untimely — you were destined to join our ranks." Archangels began to fill the room, waiting for the Elders to speak. "However, you wasted no time proving to us that our gift was wasted. Humanity is not ready for powers they don't understand. They may never be. When you began to invest researching into your previous life which you should have abandoned, we knew then that you would have to be dealt with."

"This is injudicious! She was only acting under my orders!" Azrael said, stepping forward.

"You told her to visit her child?"

Humility flew high enough to place her hand on his shoulder, meeting his eyes. "I accepted the consequences of my actions long ago."

"We see all, Azrael, angels and humans. Did you think we wouldn't learn of your experiments and research?"

Humility looked at him. The word *experiment* filled her with concern.

"She did as she was ordered."

"Do not try to save her from her fate! Humility chose to act out of selfishness, seeking only the things that would benefit her."

The elders in the center stood. "We have been watching your actions for some time now, Azrael. We feel that this path you are on will only lead to destruction."

Azrael laughed, approaching them. "If you forsake me, then know that I will forsake you as well."

"The path you are on, Azrael can easily be summed up by the words of the divine: 'A charismatic leader will fool the whole world, rise to power, institute a worldwide dictatorial regime and finally bring about the apocalypse'."

"Then let this be our final words to one another, Elders. For I will no longer call you my brethren. I will call you my adversary." Azrael said bitterly, reaching for the Elders as the archangels restrained him. It took ten of them to hold him down.

"Azrael the Archangel of Death, you will spend your days amongst the humans as a Grigori in their form and never able to die." The Elders turned their attention to Humility, the archangels grabbing her arms. "The Stronghold Humility will too spend her days as a Grigori never to bear another child of your own. Because of your selfishness Azrael has come closer to creating children of his own."

The remaining archangels approached Azrael from behind grabbing his wings and ripping them from his back. They threw them into a pile on the floor, his blood staining the marble red. Humility watched as he screamed, hundreds of his wings piling on the floor around him.

She screamed, the archangels ripping the wings from her body before throwing them aside. They let go of her, her body falling onto the temple's floor. At the same time, she felt as if something was being carved into her stomach before being set on fire. She cried as she felt her blood pool around her body.

The world became eerily familiar, bathed in a white light.

Chapter 13

Lavanah was puzzled as she stared at the estate before her. It was made of a dark brick with large arching windows. Black gates wrapped around the land but not for protection. It would take more than steel to keep out demons. She couldn't understand why such a beautiful building existed in Hell. That was until Gluttony approached, pushing open the gates.

"It's time you and I spoke privately."

She hid her anger well as she spoke, following behind him. "I have visited Earth on multiple occasions. This was the first time I found myself standing before someone's sword."

"You would be dead if I hadn't stepped in. His sword was forged in Heaven." He said opening the doors, ushering her inside. "Why were you on Earth in the first place?"

"Envy sent me for souls to feed her doll."

Gluttony sighed, the doors closing behind him. "Of course she did." He followed her into the parlor, watching as she sat upon the sofa. "It's time you did the same."

"It's not necessary."

"Don't argue with me." He approached her, pressing his hand on her cheek, rubbing his thumb beneath her eyelid before forcing it into her socket. He pulled the eye out with his beak where he then swallowed it.

Lavanah screamed as she held her face in her hand, warm blood dripping through her fingers. Her heart raced in her chest though she could not see through her other eye. The world around her was consumed by darkness.

Her screams turned to silence as suddenly her vision became clear. It was as if her eye had grown back.

In the center of the room before her stood tall steel posts with dark chains hanging from them. The chains themselves appeared as if they had rusted though she knew otherwise. The longer her eyes remained on them the more nauseous she felt.

A man, dressed in armor was forced into the room, large white wings extending from his back. He held within his hands a sword and shield as he tried to fight against the demons who approached. He pierced one with his sword, using his shield to hold another off. However; he was outnumbered, the demons ripping his shield from his hand, others taking the sword. Though disarmed he continued to fight but the demons latched onto his limbs. They ripped the armor from his body leaving the angel bare. He was then forced into the chains where he screamed.

"These chains will not hold me!" He said, thrashing against them. The demons bound his wings despite his struggling.

"I will not succumb to demons!" His voice echoed through the chambers.

The demons drew their weapons, beating the angel though he took each hit without a sound. The demons continued to beat the angel until his blood began to pool beneath him.

The demons came to a stop as a man entered, his hair the color of sand, white wings extending from his back. Lavanah stood between the two angels, watching the memory play before her. She remembered the second angel from her encounter with him on the surface.

"Solas, I never thought I'd see your beautiful face here of all places." He said grabbing the hair of the other angel, pulling him forward. "That was until I smelled the burning flesh of your victims."

He laughed, looking into the eyes of the angel. "You hide your betrayal well, Sariel. Tell me, who is it you fight for now?"

"My allegiance remains with Heaven as it always has, Solas. Do you speak out of regret?"

"Only that I did not taste the eyes of an angel when I had the chance."

"You disgust me." Sariel spoke, using his finger to draw arrays in the air before the angel. "You will forever be bound to this place, Solas. You showed your true colors, acting gluttonous, wasting the lives of thousands of humans. Had Azrael not sent an angel to inspect this plague — he called it — you would have continued to sin. You are a harbinger of death and shall be cursed to see yourself as one."

The angel screamed as his skull transformed growing a beak and raven feathers. His eyes darkened. His white wings now stained black.

Lavanah gasped, covering her mouth though they could not see nor hear her.

"You are now the omen you created." Sariel said. "What the demons will do with you I hope to never know."

Though the angel was in pain he forced a laugh through his beak. "You call me a harbinger of death. Then let this be a warning to you Sariel: I will see to it that you meet your fate."

Sariel chuckled, spreading his wings and flying away leaving Solas bound to chains.

The demons looked at him, raising their weapons. Solas hissed, pecking into the eye socket of a demon, swallowing his eye. The demon screamed, the others beginning to strike Solas.

##

Lavanah gasped, suddenly in the parlor floor, staring up into the eyes of Gluttony. She held her hand over her socket as she watched him. He leaned forward, beckoning her closer with his finger.

She cowered, scooting away from him. "Please, don't take my other eye."

He pointed to the floor before his feet. "Though your eyes are sweet I don't want seconds."

She crawled over to him, sitting before him. She flinched when he grabbed her by her chin.

"I am getting out of Hell, Lavanah but to do so I need you. Tell me what you have seen thus far."

"There was a woman on the table who looked like me —" She said, tears mixing with blood as they rolled down her cheeks.

"But she wasn't you. She was your sister." He said, wiping off her tears. "And she was killed as a sacrifice to Sariel. The same man who did this to me."

Lavanah pressed her free hand to his face, running her fingers through his feathers.

"Sariel."

He nodded. "The same angel who attacked you."

She tried to stand, but he held her down by her shoulder. "Why do you need me?"

"Because you have as much motivation to get out of Hell as me." He said pressing his hands to her head. Images flashed before her eyes of the platinum haired woman as a young girl playing with her dark-haired sister. Then again, of the times they had been in trouble and others of when they had danced in the ballroom under the pale moonlight.

Once Gluttony let go of her she found herself holding onto his leg, her head spinning. "I had a sister."

"*Have* a sister but you won't see her unless you leave this place." He pushed her off his leg. "I watched you grow up, waited until you had exhausted all other options and then made our contract."

"How do I leave?"

"The same way I leave. You need to reclaim your soul." He cupped her face, kneeling before her. "I want you to listen very carefully. After you leave here Greed will demand your presence. Act as the doll I created until the moment you return to your chambers. Consume the souls I have placed within your desk."

"You want to turn me into the doll Envy was trying to create." She said, stepping away.

Gluttony held out a basket of souls to her. She stared at them and their bright colors, trembling as she reached for one.

"I will succeed where she has failed." He said, placing the basket on a nearby table. "Know that I own you Lavanah and that my word holds more weight than that of any other demon."

She took a deep breath, prodding her finger into his chest. "I'm only doing this for my sister—"

"Marie."

Lavanah was taken aback, her eyes widening in surprise. "What?"

"Marie is her name."

##

"Remove your shoes." Greed said as Lavanah entered his chambers. "I do not want snow on my floors." He said, slowly making his way towards a long table, its surface covered with food that stacked high. Greed pulled her chair out, waiting for her to have a seat before sitting at the opposite end of the table.

"How may I be of service, Greed?"

"This is all I ask of you. To sit with me and watch as I eat."

Lavanah folded her hands into her lap, watching as Greed gorged himself, feeding the many souls on his body. It disturbed her to watch as the many hands reached for food, feeding Greed. It was nauseating to watch as his flesh stretched and tried to place food in its many mouths but fell upon the floor instead. Once the end of the table had been cleared of food, Greed began to make his way around the table, continuing to consume the food.

Greed eyed her curiously but couldn't see any evidence of Gluttony's influence. Still he did not doubt that she would play her part soon. He had been expecting this for some time and had learned quickly that Gluttony did not act spontaneously. Everything was done for one reason or another even if it was nothing more than a waste of time in the end.

Lavanah resisted the urge to shudder as Greed stood beside her, consuming the food before her. One of the arms of his body reached out and touched her face, pulling on her nose. Greed smacked the hand off her, speaking to it.

"That's bad table manners. We do not eat our guests."

Lavanah breathed deeply, watching out the corner of her eyes as Greed made his way around the table though he did not clear the table of food. There remained a large pile of food in the center of the table, which he avoided.

The doors to the chambers opened, a doll entering, standing a fair distance from Greed. "I bring a message from Envy: She demands that you hand over the doll in your possession for play time is not yet over."

Greed stopped eating, approaching the doll. "Why does everyone accuse me of stealing?" He said placing his hands on the doll's shoulders.

"What is your message to Envy?"

Greed grabbed the doll by its arms ripping them from its body. He then opened the doll's mouth, placing the fingers inside before closing it.

"There's her message. Be sure you don't drop your arms." Greed wiped his hands on his gown as he met Lavanah's eyes. "I apologize for the interruption. Where were we?"

##

The doll returned to Envy, dropping its arms on the floor in order to speak clearly. "He declined to release the doll."

Envy picked its arms up, placing its hands on her face. "Oh my, I suppose I'll have to do this myself." She said, handing the arms to the doll sitting beside her. "Make sure it gets fixed. I will go deal with Greed."

The doll stood, nodding. "Of course." She said, holding the arms with one hand, opening the door with the other.

Envy kicked open the doors of Greed's chambers, storming in. "What makes you think you can just dismember one of my dolls?" She flew to his face, prodding him in the chest. "I had Lavanah first and you need to give her back!"

Greed laughed, flicking Envy in her forehead as if she were an insect. "You may take her with you if you wish, Envy. I have finished my meal and no longer require her company but know that you don't own her. *In fact, you own nothing.*"

Envy flew over to Lavanah, taking her hand as she landed on the floor. "Come with me, I want to have a tea party. The other dolls are waiting!"

"But I have no souls for you." Lavanah said as Envy dragged her down the hall.

Envy stopped, staring at her bitterly before forcing a smile. "Then you have to prepare the tea."

"I was attacked by Sariel and lost my basket in the fight."

Envy opened her mouth to scold her but decided against it seeing her empty socket, her skin crawling. She had only seen one angel cause that kind of wound before.

"Return to your chambers, Lavanah. I will send some dolls to fix your eye."

"Thank you."

Gluttony sat in Envy's chambers with his waist wrapped in a white cloth. It continued to bleed as he waited for her to return. Her dolls sat before him conversing monotonously as they shared a plate of souls and a pot of tea. It bewildered him how he and Envy shared a similar fate. Not only were their appearances changed but somewhere along the way, so were their minds.

"Gluttony?" Envy said entering her chambers, the smell of blood pungent in the air. "You're bleeding." She hurried over to his side, examining the wound.

Gluttony chuckled, leaning forward. "As a matter of fact, I am and so is my doll. Have you seen her?"

"Lavanah told me about the attack. How you lost my souls."

His amusement quickly turned to disgust as he grabbed her throat. "You worry over souls when she could have died, Envy." He clutched her tighter, standing up, holding her in the air. "I will not allow harm to come to her."

"Other than the eye you ate?" She choked out. "Just my childlike curiosity."

"I own her." He said, dropping her onto the floor, watching as she gasped for air. He placed his foot on her chest, pinning her to the floor.

Envy's eyes widened. It finally made sense to her as to why he needed a doll. She felt like a fool for not having seen it sooner.

"You're going to use her to leave this place."

"And then I'm going to kill Sariel."

Envy laughed hysterically despite the pain in her chest. "You've gone mad, Solas. Sariel will kill you."

Gluttony removed his foot. "Until I have the opportunity to find out, stay away from Lavanah."

##

The dolls pinned Lavanah to her bed as she struggled, the pain in her head was almost too much to bear. She could feel her eye as it regrew in her skull, surfacing as it expanded, her vision returning as if it had never left. She tried to scream but another doll covered her mouth, muffling the sound. It didn't last long, the little blue sphere moving in unison with her other eye.

Gluttony entered the room as the dolls tested her eye one more time before taking their leave. "My turn."

Lavanah covered her eyes. "Why should I?"

"Did you know ravens will often first peck out the eyes of their prey when they attack?"

She lowered her hands, approaching him cautiously before pressing her hand to his stomach. "I did not."

"Neither did I until this happened to me. I would sit around and watch the birds for days." He said watching as the wound stitched closed.

Lavanah approached her desk, staring at the colorful glow emitting from its drawers. "These weren't here before, Gluttony."

"Perhaps I've intercepted a couple of deliveries to Envy."

She opened the drawer, running her hand over the souls. "I don't want to eat people. I don't even know why you're doing this."

"If for no other reason than because we have a contract. I am bound to make sure you remain alive long enough that you get your revenge. You would be too if you had your soul."

"I want to see my sister again."

He smiled, crossing his arms over his chest. "Then commit the taboo. Reclaim your soul."

"You should go." She said, returning his smile as she opened the door. "I'm afraid I have work to do."

"Then you better get started." He said leaving her chambers.

Chapter 14

Marie stared into the blue sky above her, watching as the soft clouds rolled by. She had watched the sun rise into the sky many hours before and had wondered if somehow it was a dream. It wasn't until the dew-covered grass had dried, now still between her fingers that she realized that she was finally home. She took deep breaths, enjoying the fresh air, unable to tear her eyes from the sky above her.

Though she felt joy she also felt fear. She knew Azrael was beside her. She had reached out to touch him, feeling his nose and lips for only a moment before taking her hand back. She didn't have the courage to look at him, afraid that he would still be covered in eyes and tongues. How would she explain his appearance to the humans? Would he have to spend forever hiding from them?

He had remained unconscious much longer than her and for a moment she wondered if he would ever open his eyes again. She felt foolish knowing that the Elders words were not to be taken lightly. They would never let him die, and though it was selfish of her, she was grateful.

Earth was no different from Heaven in the sense that all the colors were luminous. However, the world seemed fragile almost, tearing apart as she stood. It took her breath away; fear causing her to tremble, her knees weak. She controlled her breathing, focusing on the pieces, her world sewing itself back together again. She had experienced this before in Heaven but hadn't thought it would follow her to Earth.

She felt as if she had become a stranger in a land she was once so familiar with; this frightened her.

Beside her Azrael stirred, opening his eyes as he pressed his hand to his head. He trembled as he felt the hair on top of his head.

"Azrael?" She said, turning to look at him, grateful to see only two eyes right where they belonged. "How do you feel?"

He rubbed his hands over his head and body, fear seizing him. "Marie." He spoke softly. "I am afraid to look at myself."

"You shouldn't be." She said, placing her hand on his cheek.

He struggled to climb to his feet, falling to his hands and knees. "I feel heavy, Marie." He said, clutching her leg tightly. "I can't get up."

She wrapped an arm around his waist, helping him to his knees unable to resist the smile that spread across her face. "You'll get used to it. I promise." He placed his arm around her, moving slowly with her help. The crisp breeze sent a chill over their skin.

"I can't stand the silence."

"What are you talking about?" Marie said, lowering him onto the ground. She pushed his hair out of his eyes, gasping when she saw the tears welling in his eyes.

"I can't see them anymore. I can't protect them anymore. If someone is in danger, there is nothing I can do." He said, tears rolling down his cheeks as he stared at his hands. "Is there nothing I can do for these people?"

Marie held his hands in hers. "You don't need to burden yourself with the problems of others any longer. We will help those that we can and know that we tried for those that we can't."

He looked up into her eyes, nodding as she helped him stand. They continued to walk, eventually reaching a small town with farms stretching for miles before them. Marie had never been so happy to see chickens and cows. People stared at them as they made their way down the dirt road, an older man finally approaching them, throwing a blanket over their shoulders. He led them into his house, his wife preparing a pot of tea.

"I don't mean to be rude." The man spoke. "But where are your clothes?"

Azrael looked up at the man. He had seen him many times before and his wife as well. He could remember watching as they had grown up in this small town as neighbors. They spent every moment together until the man finally proposed. She hadn't hesitated, crying as she had accepted. It wasn't long until she was with child, in the end the couple having three children. They had grown up however, leaving their small home to live lives of their own outside of the town.

Marie squeezed Azrael's hand as she spoke, bringing him out of his thoughts. "We were robbed and now are just looking for shelter."

"Even your clothes?"

Marie blushed. "It was in the middle of the night—"

"You're a liar. You don't deserve to be an angel." The woman's voice said.

Marie smiled wider though now in frustration knowing that the voices remained.

"She can't just tell them she's an angel. They'd never believe her, and it doesn't matter any longer." The man's voice said.

"That's because she's a liar." The woman contorted.

"Says the woman who cries wolf at every turn."

Marie sipped on her tea as the voices continued to banter within her head.

The man held his hand up. "Say no more. There are plenty of empty houses further in town. Some say we were attacked by demons but I don't believe in such nonsense."

Azrael's fist clenched, Marie lacing her fingers with his. His brows arched in frustration as he opened his mouth to speak. Marie kissed his cheek with the lightest touch, catching him off guard enough that he held his tongue.

The man's wife approached, pouring the hot water over her husband's tea bag. "You two are so young. It's just awful that you were robbed during the night."

This amused Azrael enough that he set aside his comments.

"We may have some spare clothes in a cupboard upstairs. The children have grown and left the nest. However they never take everything with them. It's like they expect to come home one day." She shared a laugh with her husband before heading upstairs to look for the clothes.

"Don't drink it. *It's poison.*" The woman's voice said.

She could hear the man's voice howling in the distance, mocking the woman.

"Could I trouble you for a few cubes of sugar?"

"Of course, would you like cream too?"

"The sugar will be just fine." She said, turning to Azrael. "Try the tea."

Azrael nodded, taking the hint, sipping at the tea with his free hand.

Marie dropped the cubes into her tea, stirring them before taking another sip. "You don't believe in demons?"

"No. I believe there was a plague. It's the only reason that makes sense."

"Plagues don't just disappear like this, Dear." His wife said, placing clothes on the table. "You're welcome to use the room down the hall. We'll be preparing dinner in a few hours if you'd like to stay the night."

"We couldn't." Marie said, surprised by their kindness. "You've done so much already."

Azrael squeezed her hand. "Thank you for the offer. We will certainly join you for dinner."

"That's fantastic." The man said. "I apologize. I never asked your names."

"My name is Azrael and my wife is Marie."

"Azrael? I've heard that name before. Like the angel of death?"

Marie's breath caught in her chest.

Azrael chuckled. "Something like that."

"Well, I suppose the two of you should get cleaned up."

"Thank you." Azrael said, handing Marie the clothes, struggling to stand. Marie held him up, the clothes under her arm as they made their way to the back room.

"They're killers. That's why the town is empty." The woman's voice insisted.

"Look how old they are." The man said. "They could never take down that many people."

"Not unless she poisoned their tea."

Marie helped Azrael onto the bed, setting the clothes beside him. In the corner she spotted a mirror, hurrying over to it. She looked at her reflection, grateful that she appeared no different than before she died.

"Back it up." She said, speaking to the voices. "How many people died?"

"If the town is as empty as they implied, then probably a hundred or more. I'm sure some people have fled in fear."

"Do you think Thea could be behind this?"

"Marie?" Azrael said softly, watching as she conversed with herself.

"I don't believe your sister could be responsible for this. She has killed many people, but I don't think she has the heart to take this many lives."

"She doesn't know who she is."

"*Bull shit.*" The man's voice said. "You never truly forget who you are."

"How can you be sure?"

"Why are you asking me? *She's your sister.*"

Azrael placed a hand on her shoulder, struggling to stand behind her. "*Marie?* Are you feeling all right?"

"I think he's right." She said, her eyes wide as she turned to look at Azrael. "I don't think my sister is responsible for the deaths of these people."

"I'm sure she had something to do with it." He said, beginning to dress himself. "Do you mind covering the mirror for me? I would like to wait until tomorrow to see myself."

She turned him around before taking the blanket from the edge of the bed and throwing it over the mirror. "I think that's a wise decision." She reached for the dress, blushing as she watched him get dressed. "At least you aren't ten feet tall."

"I'm rather grateful. Humans build shorter doors than angels." Azrael said though he could not find humor in his words.

She approached him, taking his hand. "I want us to keep our past quiet. They don't need to know."

"Does that include your son?"

She was taken aback by his words. "What are you saying?"

"You're going to be on Earth for the rest of time, Marie. Do you want to keep that a secret from your son too?" He pressed a hand to her face. "You don't have to answer me now. I just want you to think about it."

"Those clothes seem a bit loose on you." The man's wife said as Marie and Azrael entered the kitchen. "My sons are a bit larger in the waist."

"They take after their dear old dad, I'm afraid." The man chuckled. "There's a tailor in town that could fix that for you."

His wife looked over Azrael as she served dinner. "The two of you look so polished. Where are you coming from?"

"We lived near the Heathford Territory for some time before moving south." Marie said. "And now we're here."

"Well you're never far from home, Dear." She said.

The man took the large pot from his wife, setting it in the center of the table as she took her seat. "And what was it you did over there?"

"I was a writer." Azrael said. "I've written many books over my lifetime."

"Unfortunately, I can't read but my wife loves books."

"Anything I've read?" She said.

"Probably not. They aren't all that interesting."

"Take my word for it." Marie said with a smirk.

Azrael placed his hand on her cheek. "That's because you love stories of heroes. Not of the past."

"Then maybe it's time you wrote a new story." Marie said, placing her hand over his. "Where *you* are the hero."

Azrael took his hand back from her. "I'm afraid I only tell events as I've seen them, my love. I don't possess the imagination that you have been blessed with."

Marie smiled. "All we have is time."

The man and his wife held hands as she spoke. "I agree with your wife, Azrael. You have so much time left. Go see the world and write a new story. I would love to read it one day."

"Thank you for your encouragement." He said.

"Enough chatter." The man said, lifting his spoon. "It's time to eat."

The man and his wife lifted their spoons, dipping them into the bowls before them. Marie waited until they were chewing their food before beginning to eat.

Azrael stared curiously at the food within his bowl. "What is it?"

"It's a stew." She said. "We made it all the time when the kids were still home. We grow the ingredients ourselves." She spoke proudly of her husband's hard work.

Marie swallowed her food before speaking. "I loved stew as a child. Our parents never allowed seconds. My sister would often switch bowls with me so that I could have a little extra."

Azrael smiled, recalling the memory as he lifted a spoonful to his mouth. The flavor surprised him, tender but also a bit salty.

"It's very good, thank you." He said.

"Thank you." The woman said before turning her attention on Marie. "You speak fondly of your sister. Where is she now?"

"She's on an adventure further south. I'm going to see her soon." Marie said confidently. "From what I can recall, this is the longest I have spent away from my sister. For as long as I can remember we have remained inseparable."

"I think it is important that family remains together." She said. "Though our children live in the northeast, they write to us every week. There have been many times when we've received an extra letter from their children. Though it can be difficult to read, it is also very sweet."

"I look forward to reuniting with my sister." Marie said, wiping off her tears with her napkin.

##

After dinner, the two returned to the chambers where Marie ran a bath, ~~getting inside~~ it. She breathed deeply, lowering herself into the water, her knees poking out from the surface. It had been so long since she had bathed despite the fact in Heaven there was no need for baths. The angels relied on magic for all their needs.

Azrael watched as she bathed, smiling when she caught him peeking. He watched as she splashed water at him, her cheeks a deep red.

"Do not sit there and watch me bathe! Light a candle and grab a book. I will be more than a minute."

"You can't wash away the past." Spoke the woman.

"She can, however, wash away the smell." The man said. "No offense."

Marie pouted, blowing bubbles in the water. "Some offense taken."

Azrael did as she asked, lighting a candle on each side of the bed with a match. He then rolled down the blankets covering the bed. He sat on the edge of the bed, his legs weak, as he removed his clothing. He then lifted his legs into the bed, pulling the covers close enough to cover his privates.

"I think I am beginning to grow accustomed to walking."

Marie lifted her arms out of the tub, letting them hang over the side, her feet sticking out from the end of the tub. "Have you never walked before?"

"Never." He said looking over the various books he had picked from the shelf.

"Do you think we will be able to sleep tonight?" Marie said, looking out the window by the sink. "I *really* miss sleeping."

"I'm afraid angels don't sleep, Marie. We also don't have to eat or bathe."

She pulled her limbs back into the water, turning around to face him as she clutched the side of the tub. "I am *not* giving up my baths. I can give up food and rest but bathing? *Absolutely not.*"

Azrael opened a book with a chuckle. "That is why we possess magic. I may not have my wings but like all angels I possess some kind of power."

"Is that how Sariel controls people?"

"That is what I suspect." He said, flipping the page.

Marie stood from the tub, draining the water. "Why do they put us on the same level as Sariel?"

"Because we are being punished, Marie." He said, flipping another page. "We are recognized by our own kind but without our wings we will surely be rejected."

She stepped out of the tub, wringing her hair over the drain before wrapping a towel around herself. "I do not seek acceptance from angels. I never felt I belonged there in the first place." She said entering the chambers where she pulled a book from the shelf. "Wings only make life more difficult anyway."

"How so?"

"Such as wearing clothes. It's no wonder everyone in Heaven is naked."

"I certainly was not and neither are the elders."

She rolled her eyes, sitting on the bed beside him. "All of twenty-five angels out of *thousands.*"

"The authorities are always in a suit of armor. So that's more likely a few thousand out of *millions.*"

"Millions of angels?"

Azrael nodded, licking his thumb before turning the page.

Marie opened her book for a moment before closing it. "There was something else I wanted to talk about, Azrael. Something that has been plaguing my mind."

"And here I thought for a change I would have the opportunity to read a book instead of writing in one." He said with a laugh, marking the page before closing it. He set it on the table beside him before looking into her eyes.

Marie placed her book on the table beside her before meeting his eyes. "I wanted to talk about what the Elders said about you."

"If it will ease your mind."

"It certainly will."

He tucked loose pieces of her hair behind her ear. "For many years I watched humanity, saddened that they didn't have the chance to see more of the beautiful world they lived in. So I began to research into the animals of Earth and the things we had access to in Heaven. I realized by combining the blood you had collected with the fruit-"

"*Flowers.*" She corrected him with a laugh. "An apple is a fruit."

"And like many fruits come from a flower." Azrael said with a smirk. "I believe that by combining the blood with the powder created from the flowers, I can create a solution that will allow humanity to live longer, healthier, and thus fuller lives."

"Why do the Elders disagree with such an idea?"

"Because angels don't want to compete with humans, Marie. They see themselves as superior beings."

"That is unfair."

Azrael shook his head. "No, *we are* superior, which is why it is our duty to protect humanity."

"Does humanity need our protection? I thought angels didn't pick sides."

"Angels have always remained a neutral force, aiding when given the order and hindering their growth when humanity seemed to be growing beyond their control."

"Is changing them the best way to save them? Is there not another way?"

"If I cannot protect all humans with my own hands then I want to give them a way to protect themselves."

"I can stand behind that." Marie said, reaching for her book. "However, the blood and powder created from the flowers are still in Heaven."

Azrael smiled, grabbing his book, opening to where he had left off. "You let me worry about that."

The following morning Marie and Azrael put their books away on the shelves before straightening the covers on the bed. They clothed themselves before walking into the kitchen. However, the man and his wife were not there. She walked into the living room, but they were nowhere to be found.

"Perhaps they're asleep." Azrael said, reaching the door finding it unlocked. "Marie."

She stepped through the door where the man was plowing their farm, his wife under the shade milking their cows. They talked about their children fondly, remembering the days when they had been able to help them on the farm.

They came to a stop when they saw Azrael and Marie, "We didn't expect you to be up so early or I would have prepared breakfast." The man's wife said.

"That's quite all right." Marie said. "But I think we should head into town for a place of our own."

Azrael closed the door behind him as he stepped outside. Marie looked at him, fixing the buttons on his shirt before folding down the collar. He looked away, embarrassed that she was fixing his clothes.

"The two of you are always welcome to come visit." The man said. "Do take care of yourselves."

"Thank you for your hospitality." Marie said, leading Azrael away. She kept her pace light, Azrael following her stride with little trouble. He kept his arm around her shoulders as a precaution.

The wooden houses and the various stores captivated Marie. Some were still open for business while others had been closed down for some time. She had never had the chance to go into town much as a child and was grateful to have the opportunity to live within the town.

They wandered in and out of the vacant houses, occasionally stopping so that Azrael could rest. He was adjusting to gravity rather well but found it difficult to walk for long periods of time. They finally decided on a home closer to the center of town. Marie was pleased to be close to the shops while still being far enough that Azrael would have to practice walking more.

He rested on the sofa, watching as Marie looked around their new home. It was larger than some of the homes, possibly used as a shop at one time. As she tidied the home she could see things such as clothes and toys that had been left behind.

She lifted a child's teddy bear, thinking of Ciel. "Where do we go from here, Azrael?"

He joined her, running his hand over the bear's head. "Why don't you gather the toys together and give them to your son. I'm sure he would appreciate them. They don't do us any good here."

"Really?" She said with a sparkle in her eyes.

"Yes." He said making his way up the stairs to the largest room. "I have business to take care of while you're away."

Marie placed the bear on a table, following behind him. "You're going to continue your experiments."

"I've come too far to stop now." He said entering the bathroom, running a bath. The hot water filled the room with steam, clouding the mirror. Azrael listened as the water flowed, approaching the mirror.

She took his hand, rubbing her thumb over the back of it. "Do you want me to be here when you finally look at yourself?"

"I can handle it." He said kissing her forehead. "Why don't you take some things from the house and trade them in town? There is more here than we will ever need."

"I will call to you when I am leaving. Until then, why not take a bath?"

He let go of her hand, smirking as he reached for the top buttons of his shirt. "Then you should go, Marie. I don't want you watching me bathe."

"Don't make fun of me." She said with a pout. "It's weird if the person watching isn't in the bath."

"I've noticed that the humans enjoy bathing together."

"Just call them people Azrael. Why must you separate everyone?" She said, taking a basket from the chambers, beginning to fill it with various items from their home. "On Earth, we are all one and the same."

Azrael removed his clothes, getting into the warm water. "I've not heard that before."

Marie filled the basket, carrying what remained in her arms as she made her way to the front door. "I'm leaving, Azrael. I'll return later." She called out to him before closing the door behind her. She couldn't help but worry that she was making a mistake.

Azrael avoided looking at his body, making no real effort to bathe himself. After sometime he drained the bath, glancing at the mirror. The steam cleared from its surface, the room reflecting in the mirror.

He took a deep breath, approaching the mirror with his head down. As he exhaled he questioned if he was ready to see himself. He closed his eyes, knowing that if he did not look now that he may never look. He breathed through his nose, filling his lungs with air as he looked up into the mirror.

And he screamed.

"I don't deserve to look like this." He shouted at his reflection before shaking his head. "I have only one tongue and two eyes. Where did the rest of them go?"

He rubbed his hand along his face surprised by his prominent jawline and the lean features of his face. On top of his head was a mess of straight black hair.

"I hate the color black." He said before looking into his eyes. They were grey and reminded him of smoke only they were missing the fire behind them. "Why are my eyes grey?"

He grabbed at his hair, ripping it out in chunks. "I'd rather live without hair." With each handful he ripped away, more grew in its place. It piled on the floor below him, clinging to his wet feet.

Tears filled his eyes as his hair remained as if he had never touched it. "Why have you done this to me? Why won't you let me change?"

He turned his head, wishing he could see his other faces but he only saw ears instead. "These eyes must be broken! I do not deserve to look like those that betrayed you!" He reached for his eyes, clawing them out of their sockets before removing them, throwing them onto the pile of hair.

"Give me new eyes to see with."

His eyes grew back in his head still as grey as before he had removed them.

"I can accept immortality but let me control my own body!"

He stuck his tongue out, biting down on it until it came out. He then used his nails to cut open his arm, trying to place his tongue inside it, hoping it would stay. The tongue however fell to the floor, landing on the pile of hair. Blood filled his mouth, spilling out the corners of his lips. He grabbed his bloodied teeth, ripping them out one by one, throwing them into the pile of hair.

He continued to mutilate himself hoping that somehow his body would give up on repairing him. He would have rather existed as a mutilated creature than a perfect man. He felt as if he had lost a sense of control by being impervious to both harm and death.

"I'm home!" Marie called sometime later, closing the door behind her. She quickly put away their new belongings before making her way upstairs smiling from ear to ear. Behind her she held an ornate box that had been a gift from one of the merchants. She found herself falling in love with their small town.

"Azrael?" She said as she entered their chambers. "If you're still in the bath, let me know, and I will give you privacy." She entered their bathroom, dropping the box as her eyes fell upon Azrael.

He lay upon the floor beside the pile of hair, teeth, and tongues. He could not speak, his tongue still growing back. The bathroom smelled like copper, blood staining their sink and floor as it continued to drip from his body.

"What have you done to yourself?" She trembled as she stepped inside, sitting in the floor beside him. She pulled his body into her arms, forcing his hands to stay at his sides.

"Doesn't it hurt to injure yourself?"

His tongue grew back into place. "I hate your fleshy, human forms."

She let go of him, standing before him. "Then do you find me to be hideous?"

Azrael stood, cupping her face. "Marie you are the most beautiful of angels."

"No!" She said, pushing his hands away. "I am but a *woman*. The entire time I was in Heaven all I wanted was to be home again, and now I am."

"You can't erase the past, Marie. *We're angels.*"

"But we are also people." She said. "So if I am not ugly to you, then what is the difference between me and you?"

She stopped him before he could speak, pointing to the mirror. "I want you to *look* and tell me what the difference is." She stood before the mirror, pulling him beside her.

"I am a man."

"And?" She said staring at them in the mirror. "What else?"

Azrael touched the thin hair around his jaw. "I have hair on my face."

"Keep going." She said crossing her arms over her chest.

"I..." Azrael's forehead creased as he struggled to find more differences between them. "I don't know."

She turned to face him. "That's because there is nothing different between you and me other than the fact that you are a man and I am a woman. So, I will ask you again. If I am not ugly, then what is the difference between us?"

"There is none." He confessed.

Marie took a deep breath, wiping the blood from his face as she spoke. "Then what the fuck is wrong with you?" She said just above a whisper.

Tears streamed down his face, as he looked into her eyes, ashamed that he had hurt her. He never wanted her to see him broken, to see him looking defeated.

"I can't change my appearance. I can't die. I'm a constant in this world, Marie." He said putting his hands on his chest. "The elders have forced me to take the appearance as one of the fallen."

She found herself sounding more like her sister. "Why do you give a shit? They're in Hell, and you are *here*. With me."

"I hate the color black."

"Well that's too bad because my sister has black hair."

"My eyes no longer hold color."

"Then I suppose it's a good thing you look me in the eyes when you speak to me." She covered his mouth with her hands before he could speak again. "I'm tired of your excuses. So what if you're a constant. You need to appreciate what you have instead of reminiscing over what you've lost."

He removed her hands from his mouth. "It must be easy for you to say that having never lost anything."

She smacked him with as much force as she could muster. "I lost my sister and my life because your elders whom you're so fond of allowed Sariel to kill us both." She approached the doorway. "Don't speak to me as if I've lost nothing when I have lost everything I once cherished. The difference is I'm not so weak as to let it hold me back."

Azrael looked at her, his cheek red from her hand.

"I will speak to you once you find your balls." She said leaving the room before smiling. As children, she had always found her sister to be rude but she was beginning to like it. It made her feel more confident though she wouldn't allow herself to speak like her sister too often She had to remind herself that she was more polished then her sister.

"Thank you, Thea." She said above a whisper as she entered the kitchen. "Your bad example all those years has proved very useful."

Azrael looked at himself in the mirror. With a heavy sigh, he cleaned himself up before disposing of his mess. He cleaned the floor before looking at his body.

It was the same as other men in the fact that soft flesh hung from it below his waist. However, unlike most humans he did not possess scarring or any form of blemish. His shoulders were broad, his muscles defined and toned. He ran his hand over his collarbone, curious by how it could be seen on the surface of the skin.

He had not lied when he told Marie that he found her to be beautiful. The way she had spoken led him to believe that he needed to see that same beauty in himself. It would take time, but he believed that one day he might see himself as... appealing.

He cleaned himself up, combing his hair neatly before pulling on fresh clothing, joining Marie in the kitchen. She hid her smile from him well, looking at him in the same way she would if it were Sariel standing before her.

"Well?"

He smirked, unable to speak his words with the seriousness she expected of him. "I found my balls. I didn't have to look far."

Her eyes widened and she laughed out loud. She snorted in her laughter, blushing as she covered her mouth.

"Marie I meant it when I said that you were beautiful."

She approached him, nudging him with her fist. "*And so are you.* At least to me." She said, still blushing. "Isn't that enough for you?"

He cupped her face, her hands around his wrists. "If it pleases you..." He said, his words drifting off as something caught his attention out of the corner of his eye. "What's on the table?"

She let go of him, turning around to grab the small box she had dropped. "I got you a present because I was proud of you for having the strength to face yourself."

"Can I have it?"

She held it close to her chest, pouting as she spoke. "I'm not sure you deserve it."

He stepped closer to her, placing a hand around her waist. "*Please, Marie?* I promise I'll be good from this day forward."

She threw the box in the air with a laugh. "I don't believe that for a second but knock yourself out."

Azrael got the box, ripping the colorful paper from it. Inside the box was a small leather bound journal and a selection of different pens.

"I have heard of these. They are like quills but the ink is inside them." He looked up at her. "Marie, thank you."

She stood on the opposite side of the table. "I thought if you were going to continue your experiments you might need something to write your notes in."

He set the box on the table. "It's a very thoughtful gift. I love it." His heart felt heavy in his chest as he looked at her. He felt as if she had given him a part of himself again.

She smiled at him, focusing her attention on the basket in front of her. She wrapped pale blue ribbon around the handle, securing it to the basket. Inside the basket was a blanket with little puppies on it. She had placed a variety of bears along the back with smaller toys in the middle. In the front of the basket she had placed a variety of books in different sizes. She lifted another blanket with kittens on it, using it to cover the books and toys.

"That's a very nice gift basket." Azrael said. "Are you going to take it to Ciel?"

She looked at him, nodding. "I'm going to go spend some time with my son. I know you want to finish your experiments-"

"I'll come for you as soon as I've finished. I won't be long."

"You don't have to do that. I can meet you at home."

"I want to meet your son."

She held the basket tightly. "Okay." She didn't know what to think of his words. "I'll see you soon then?"

Azrael approached her, kissing her forehead. "You will. Travel safely, Marie."

She laughed, pushing him away. "I'll be fine."

Azrael took her hand. "Humor me." He worried that something might happen to her if she travelled alone.

"I'll go into town and see if someone will accompany me. Will that ease your mind?"

"Yes." He said leaning in to kiss her lips.

She grabbed the basket, turning around. "Good! Then I'm off!" She hurried out of the house, her cheeks burning from his show of affection.

Azrael tied his horse to a post outside the tailor. Inside the building was a woman he had watched for many years. She lived in a town in the northwest far from where Azrael had settled with Marie. She was unmistakably human with strawberry blonde hair and green eyes. Her husband spent much time away on business, which was inconvenient for him today.

Azrael entered the tailor looking over the faces as they worked until he spotted the woman behind the counter. She smiled delightfully as she polished the wooden surface.

"How can I be of service to you, Sir?"

Azrael leaned against the counter looking the woman in the eyes. "Where can I find your dear, *dear* husband'?"

"Excuse me?" She said stepping away from the counter.

Azrael was quick, grabbing her hair and slamming her face into the counter. The employees stood, scared that he may come for them. He then turned to them; speaking words known only to the oldest of angels for it controlled a very powerful magic.

The humans returned to their seats ignoring Azrael as they continued to work.

"Your husband." Azrael said leaning casually against the counter, still holding the woman by her hair. "The Son of God."

"I-I don't know where he is. He just comes and goes."

Azrael chuckled. "I'm sure he does."

Azrael pulled on the woman's hair until she began screaming. He did everything within his power to keep her screaming until a man rushed in through the doors of the tailor. He looked no different than the average man though he was exceptionally handsome. His eyes fell on Azrael, though he did not recognize him, his lips curling in anger.

"Let her go."

"I've no use for her." Azrael said letting go of the woman, putting his hands in the air. "It's *you* I've come for."

She held her head with one hand, her swollen stomach with the other as she hurried to the man's side. She spoke to him quickly, tears streaming down her face.

"Go home." The man said, meeting her lips briefly. "I will come see you after I've finished my business here."

The woman did not hesitate, leaving the tailors.

"Who are you?" The man said approaching Azrael, reaching for his throat. "What do you want?"

Azrael grabbed him by his wrist, pulling him forward before grabbing his hair with his free hand. He smacked the man's head onto the counter, using his leg to keep the man's apart.

"I'm hurt that you don't remember me." Azrael said looking into the man's eyes. "*My name is Azrael.*"

The man's eyes widened. "The archangel is now a Grigori? *Oh,* the irony."

Azrael gave a faux laugh. "Yes but the Elders could only take away my wings."

"So what is it you want from me?"

"You're going to go to Heaven and retrieve something for me."

"And why would I do that?"

"Because I'll kill your wife and child if you don't."

The man looked away for a moment. "What do you need?"

"Within my temple-"

"*Your temple?*" The man sneered. "Grigori can make no claims to any part of Heaven. You should know this, Azrael."

Azrael slammed the man's head onto the counter again, blood trickling down his face. He used his free hand to push his black hair back, smiling wickedly.

"I'm sorry. I find myself losing my temper now and again." He looked the man in his eyes as he spoke. "Within *my* temple is a powder inside a mortar and pestle made of marble. You will bring it to me." He said pulling the man's head off the counter. "And there are four vials of blood in a room to the east."

"What do you need blood and powder for?"

"I'm creating a medicine with them." He said letting the man go. "*Bring them to me.*"

##

Marie knocked on the wooden door nervously before taking a step back. She clutched the basket tightly, her palms sweaty as she studied the patterns in the door. She had imagined how this day would go a hundred different times and worried if her son still cared about her.

The door was opened by the wet nurse, Ciel crying behind her. "Can I help you?"

"I brought a basket of books and toys for Ciel."

The woman looked over Marie suspiciously. "Why?"

She swallowed her nerves, tightening her grip on the basket. "Because he's my son."

The woman laughed. "I highly doubt that."

In all her scenarios, Marie hadn't imagined herself being rejected. "Believe what you will but I bore that child."

Behind the wet nurse, her mother stood, staring at Marie in disbelief. "Invite her in."

The wet nurse turned her head. "Absolutely not." She said beginning to shut the door. "I don't know this woman nor do I believe her."

The mother approached her, holding Ciel in one arm, grabbing the door with the other. "You continue to show me that I've raised a fool. It is because of this that I do not deserve the right to raise this woman's child." She forced the door open, holding Ciel out to Marie. "Will you hold him for a moment while I speak to my daughter?"

Marie set the basket down, taking her son from the woman. "Of course I will." Ciel's cries stopped as his mother held him close. "How are you my baby boy? You've grown so quickly."

The woman dragged her daughter into the home, the basket of toys in her other hand. She gently placed the basket in Ciel's room before meeting the eyes of her daughter. She had learned more about her daughter in the last year than the entire time she had raised her.

"I've never felt more disappointed then every time you open your mouth. Here Marie stands before us and you are going to lie to her face?"

"She doesn't deserve him."

The woman slapped her daughter. "And what makes you think *you're* worthy?" She took a step towards the door. "I don't want to see your face until Marie has returned home and I *pray* she takes Ciel with her."

"Mother I'm sorry-" The woman said holding her cheek.

"It's not me you should be apologizing to." She said holding the door open. "That woman has literally died and come back to us. *She is an angel* sent to us from Heaven. She is watching over our home and her son. You need to show her some gratitude."

The woman nodded, returning to the entrance. "I must go into town for some time but it was nice to see you, Marie." She said before leaving.

Marie watched the woman leave in confusion before turning to her mother. "If it's too much trouble I can go."

"Don't be ridiculous." The woman said pushing her inside. "We have much to discuss."

Marie smiled at the woman, taking a seat on their sofa. "I only saw him what feels like yesterday and he's already so much bigger!"

The woman prepared tea, bringing two cups with her when she joined Marie on the sofa. "That's because it's been a little over a year since you died."

Marie looked at the woman as Ciel smiled, reaching for her face. "It's been that long?"

"Time must seem nonexistent when you're dead." The woman laughed.

Marie recalled the first time she had gone to limbo, how time felt as if it had disappeared altogether. She looked into her son's eyes, watching as he smiled at her. She began to bounce him on her lap, listening to him as he laughed.

"He can talk now."

Marie looked at Ciel. "You can talk? Say something to me, Ciel."

"Angel." Ciel mumbled.

The woman laughed. "Yes, Ciel, mommy is an *angel.*"

Marie laughed, gently hugging her son. "But mommy is here now."

The woman smiled, placing a hand on her lap. "It would warm my heart if you would take Ciel with you."

Marie looked at the woman, tears streaming down her face. She had never thought they would ask her to take Ciel. She had imagined them saying it to them but hadn't thought she would hear the words. Now that she did she wasn't sure what to say.

Azrael sat with the wife of the Son of God, sipping on a cup of tea she had prepared for him. She had poisoned it; of that he was sure but it did nothing but make his stomach a little nauseous.

"This tea is *absolutely* lovely." He said. "What kind is it?"

"Why are you not dead?" She said, her hands bound to the table by magic.

"I can't die."

He looked at the clock, finishing his tea. It had been a little over three hours since the angel left and he was quickly growing impatient. He stood, entering their kitchen.

"Where do you keep your knives?"

The woman panicked, struggling against the table. "What on earth do you need a knife for?"

"I remember." Azrael said amusingly as he pulled a knife from one of the kitchen drawers.

The woman watched as he stood in front of her. "I apologize for not answering your question sooner." He said, placing the large knife on the table. "I'm going to kill you."

The woman's eyes widened. "Don't hurt my baby."

"I'd never harm an unborn baby." Azrael said almost offended by her words. "Though judging by how swollen you are and from what I've already seen, he's got some time to save your child."

Azrael grabbed the woman by her hands, the knife in his other hand as he dragged her up the stairs. "*Please, stop!*" She said, screaming, tears flowing from her cheeks.

Azrael threw her onto the bed, using his hand to hold her down as he brought the knife down towards her head.

The Son of God stormed into the room and grabbed his wrist just before it could pierce the woman's flesh.

Azrael looked at him before handing him the knife. "Did you bring what I asked for?"

"*Yes.*" The man said with shaking hands as he extended the fine powder and blood, all safe within their vials. "Don't hurt my wife."

Azrael took them from him, placing them into his pocket. "I'd never hurt your wife. In fact, you should thank me. I'm about to save her entire race."

The man held his crying wife as he stared at Azrael. "What do you mean?"

"This medicine will cure her people." Azrael said as he left the room.

"Humanity isn't sick." The man whispered as he held his wife, her tears dripping onto his skin. "*I'm here. I'm here.*" He said, trying to comfort her.

"I can't." Marie said, Ciel now asleep in her lap. "I can't take him with me."

The woman looked at Marie. "Why not? He's your child."

Marie held him close. "The life I live is no place for a child."

"What do you mean?"

Marie kissed Ciel's head. "I'm going to go find my sister and bring her home. And at that point, I'll come for him. Until then, I can't take him. He doesn't need to see the awful things I'm about to cause."

"What are you talking about, Marie?"

She took a deep breath. "I love my son. I love him more than life itself, but that's why he must remain behind. He is *safe* here. *Loved* here even if it isn't by your daughter. I know that life will not be easy for any of you, but I assure you it is a much better place than where I am now."

The woman took Marie's free hand, holding it tightly. "You're still not answering my question."

Marie looked at her with tears in her eyes. "There is an angel out there. He is watching over the land I now live in. The same land we once lived in. And he wants my sister and I *dead*. If Ciel comes home with me, then he might kill my son."

The woman took a deep breath, looking at Ciel. "I understand."

"Do not think for a moment that I don't want to bring him home. I want nothing more. However, alone I'm not safe and neither would he. I can't risk my child's safety because I chose to be selfish. I need him to be with someone I trust. Someone I *love*."

The woman kissed, Marie's hand. "I will watch over him as if he were my own.

"I know that and I swear to you as soon as it's safe that I'll come for him."

"He deserves better than this." The woman said. "He deserves better than my daughter and better than me. Though his mother is an angel and his aunt a..."

"Thea is a demon now."

"He deserves to be with his family. I've no doubt that you, and your sister will give this boy the best life."

"Tell him to wait for me." She looked at Ciel. "Mommy is coming home for you. *I promise.*"

A knock at the door pulled her out of her sadness. "I think that's my husband."

The elderly woman stood, opening the door. "Ah, you must be the husband I've heard so much about."

"I am. Thank you for all that you've done for my wife." Azrael said, stepping inside. He knelt beside Marie, pushing Ciel's hair back.

Marie blushed, looking at Azrael. "This is my son."

"I've got a trunk for his clothes and belongings. Should I go grab his basket?" Azrael said smiling hopefully. "The family is waiting at home."

Marie's eyes widened. "You were successful?"

Azrael nodded. "I'm sure Ciel would like to meet his cousins."

Marie laughed. "One day soon but not today." She took his hand, holding it gently. "I'm not bringing him home yet."

Azrael frowned, looking at Ciel. "Though it pains me, if you want to wait, then I will wait too." He said kissing the boy's head.

Marie let go of his hand, touching his face. "I think it's time we went home. I want to take care of business so that he *can* come home."

Azrael held Marie's hand as she stood, kissing the boy's head one more time. Marie handed him back to the woman, kissing his head as well. The woman cried as she hugged Marie. Though she understood her reasons and deep down she was grateful that she put Ciel's safety first, it also pained her. She wanted him to be somewhere far away from her daughter.

"Thank you." Marie said from the doorway.

The woman shook her head. "*No.* You come home for him, Marie Elizabeth Leighton. You come home for your boy. You hear me?"

Marie gave the woman one last hug. "I'll come running home. In the meantime, make sure he wears out his new toys. I'll buy him new ones when he comes home."

The old woman wiped at her tears as she waved good-bye to Marie, watching as their carriage pulled off.

"Why did you leave him behind?" Azrael said once the cottage was out of view.

"Because the world isn't safe. Not with Sariel out there. Not with my sister unaware of who she is. Once the world is ready, I'll bring him home."

"Do you believe that this world will ever be safe?"

She smiled, looking up at him. "*That* is what you're working to do, is it not?"

He smiled, leaning over to kiss her forehead when the carriage hit a bump. Marie chuckled at his miss, reaching to touch his face. He leaned down, kissing her.

She closed her eyes, blushing as she wrapped her arms around his neck. Azrael pulled her onto his lap as the carriage went over a series of bumps.

"It's going to be a bumpy ride." He said lifting her dress.

She blushed, meeting his lips again as he lowered his trousers. "You can't wait for us to be home?"

"No." Azrael said hugging her body close. "I can't explain why but I need you *now.*"

She gasped, looking into his eyes. "That's right. This is your *first* time."

"It certainly won't be my last." He said meeting her lips again, the carriage hitting another bump.

##

The carriage came to a stop in front of their home, Marie and Azrael stepping from the carriage. He paid the man before leading her inside. He closed the door behind them, grabbing her arms before she could walk further into the house.

"I need to warn you Marie that they are going to seem different."

She looked at him. "We're helping these people to live longer and healthier lives. A life I never had the chance to experience."

Azrael let go of her. "Of course."

Marie made her way through their home until she reached one of the chambers. Inside it she saw two men and two women. They did not display emotion like the angels. One of the men looked at her before lunging forward.

Azrael stood beside her, stopping the man. The man kneeled before Azrael making a low growl.

Marie's eyes widened, horrified.

"These people are like animals, Azrael!" She said as he closed the door. "How many more are there?"

"Six, three men and three women."

Marie stepped back, looking at him. "I need to be alone." She said going upstairs to their chambers. She grabbed the clothes they had once borrowed from the man and his wife.

"Marie, it's probably just a side effect."

"*Probably.* However, we don't know. This might be permanent. Until I know for sure I'm going to return these clothes." She hugged the clothes close. "And then I'll come home and we can talk about it. However, if this is permanent... I can't stay with you. I can't support what you're doing to these people."

Azrael grabbed her arm, but she yanked it away. "I assure you that what I'm doing is best for these people, Marie."

"I hope for your sake as much as theirs that you are *right.*" She said leaving the room. "Otherwise, I will spend my time on Earth looking for my sister."

"And what about Ciel." He said, yelling from the top of the stairs. "What happens to your boy?"

"I don't know." She said looking back at him. "Just like I don't know where to start with my sister. But you can bet that I'm going to find out."

##

Marie returned to the man and his wife who had helped them some time ago. She was glad to see them, to return her dress — they had disposed of Azrael's clothes after his incident. As she was leaving they stopped her, concerned.

"Are you and your husband doing all right?"

Marie forced a smile. "Yes."

The man wasn't as convinced as he held his wife close. "Well, you be careful out there. The palace caught fire today. Some worry that its flames will travel this way."

Marie smiled. "Don't worry, I will put a stop to the flames."

"I don't think that's necessary. There's a storm coming. I'm sure the rain will take care of it." His wife said.

"Regardless, I want to make sure that the town is safe." She said, her attention stolen away by the sky in the distance as it had greyed.

"Then take one of our horses. It's a long distance by foot."

"Thank you." Marie said, making her way to the stables. She mounted one of the horses, petting it before taking off.

Marie had never seen the world beyond her home neither as a child nor since she and Azrael had settled in the town. The wind was pleasant through her hair though it did not comfort her. The horse neighed in fear of the foreboding grey sky and thunder, which sent shivers over her skin. The horse neighed again, finally coming to a stop near the palace.

Marie pet the horse again, shushing it as they slowly made their way towards the palace. Marie could feel it too. There was something wrong at the palace. As they approached, Marie's heart sank in her chest. However, it was not the fire she feared.

Chapter 15

Lavanah paced in her chambers, her eyes often meeting her desk. The glow from the souls turned her stomach. What quality of life could they have crammed inside her desk? The lives of hundreds of people were trapped within its wooden walls. Mothers, fathers, brothers, sisters, friends, enemies....

They weren't people any longer. That was what she had to tell herself as she approached the desk, pulling the drawers open, her room filling with color. Even if there was a chance they could live a full life in this state it wasn't worth sacrificing Marie.

Lavanah lifted one of the blue souls, closing her eyes as she bit into it. She shuddered, reaching for another, this time a pink one. Many of the souls tasted sweet or sour but some were spicy or even bitter. It was almost terrifying. The more she ate, the less she felt bad about it. It consumed her, Lavanah slamming the drawer closed once it had been emptied. She pulled open the next drawer, consuming the souls.

She took a deep breath once she had finished, kneeling on the floor. She stared at her empty desk, no longer feeling like the doll they had created.

She climbed to her feet stumbling over to the mirror where she stared at herself with a smile. Her eyes widened, remembering the glass display case in Pride's chambers. If she could get her hands on the best souls, then perhaps she'd have an even greater chance of defeating the other demons.

She hurried out of her room, pushing dolls out of her path as she made her way to Pride's chambers, throwing the door open. Pride stood before her display case, running her fingers along the velvet. She met Lavanah's eyes with a familiar bitterness.

"Dogs belong on the floor."

"Then perhaps you should get on your knees." Lavanah said, kicking over the display case.

Pride's eyes widened as she watched the glass shatter, souls rolling along the floor. "We were beginning to wonder when Gluttony might turn on us." She said reaching for one of her souls. "I've put down a doll before, and I am happy to do it again."

"I am a doll no longer." Lavanah said, stepping towards her.

Pride backed up, reaching for her sword, holding it in one hand as she turned, striking at her throat. Lavanah was surprised by how natural her spells felt to her, the arrays on her arm glowing. The glass formed a wall, protecting her from the blade but shattering on impact. Pride planted her foot, her sword tapping the floor before coming around at Lavanah again. Lavanah stepped forward, catching her wrist before striking her in the ribs with her fist. Pride sneered, holding her side briefly as she struck at Lavanah, slicing her leg.

Lavanah bit her lip, running at Pride who struck again. She brought her sword towards her head, Lavanah's hands separating at an angle. Her left arm stopped the blade, her right arm rising to carry Pride's arm with it, trapping it in her hand. Her left arm pushed Pride forward, trapping her against her body, before hooking her leg with her foot where she fell.

Lavanah's arrays glowed again, the glass becoming spears that struck at Pride who blocked them with her blade. Pride appeared behind her, kicking her through the nearby wall. Pride ran behind her, leaping through the hole in the wall, turning with her sword in hand, using the momentum to strike. Lavanah rolled out of the way climbing to her feet before striking Pride in her ribs with enough force to crush several of them.

Pride smiled, watching as Lavanah disarmed her, taking her sword from her hands. "It seems my skills have slipped and now my title."

Lavanah plunged the blade in the woman's chest. "The thing we fear most is fear itself. Tell me Pride, are you so hollow as to deny it even in the face of death?"

"I fear nothing, Dog."

Lavanah removed the blade from her chest, watching as she fell to the floor. She wiped the blade clean, taking it with her as she climbed through the hole in the wall. She lifted the souls from the floor, consuming them, savoring their taste.

The door opened, a doll looking at Pride's body before meeting her eyes. "Pride, Wrath requests your presence."

Lavanah smiled at the title change. "I will be there shortly." She approached the mirror where she healed her wounds before fixing her hair.

The doll nodded, closing the door.

She took a deep breath, looking at the sword before setting it down. With her next target in mind, she left the room. She did not want to bring an end to the sins but it was the only way she would see her sister again. So, for Marie, she would bring an end to those that once ruled over her.

The snow was comforting in a way. She needed that small amount of familiarity to remember who she was. The words of Envy's doll proved to be true, a darkness creeping into her mind.

Her breath came out like a fog as she made her way to the cavern entrance. She wiped a layer of snow from her shoulders before proceeding inside. The screaming of the souls no longer made her skin crawl.

She wasted no time finding Wrath's quarters for she had been here once before. The very room sent a chill down her spine. Her eyes fell onto the form of a doll as she bled, chained to the wall. Wounds had torn apart her back.

She wept softly though she couldn't move. Lavanah hurried over to her, unchaining her before healing the wounds. That had been her once, and though she could not stop this torture permanently she could delay it for the others.

"Go now." She said, standing up. "I will take care of Wrath."

The doll looked at her in confusion, before disappearing from the heart of the mountain.

"I should have never left Gluttony alone with you."

"He would have reached me regardless, Wrath. This was inevitable."

"And what do you call this, Pride? Revenge?"

"No." She said, holding her hands out. "My release from servitude."

"You still serve a master." Wrath said standing, crossing his arms over his chest.

"I am fulfilling my end of the bargain." She said, walking towards him. "Which is unfortunate for you. I need your head."

He grabbed his sword, bringing it over his head, a wicked smile across his face. "I won't give you the chance."

She held her arm in front of her face, the arrays glowing again. Wrath stopped where he stood, frozen in midair but only for a moment, the sword coming down where it sliced through Lavanah's arm.

"Use your spells now, Pride."

Lavanah frowned, her pain immense as she watched the sword come around again. She ducked out of the way, watching as it struck the ground. With an arrogant smile her left arm met the demon's face, his skull exploding. His blood covered her flesh and clothing, though she paid it no mind as she picked up her arm from the ground.

Lesser demons charged inside led by Lust who slowly clapped as he stared at Wrath's corpse. "When I heard that you'd slain Pride, I had to come see you for myself. You weren't difficult to find seeing as you healed one of Wrath's dolls. She was able to point me to you."

"Oh Lust, you bring joy to my heart. I almost don't want to kill you." She said with a sweet smile, holding her arm's hand against her chest. a look of madness in her eyes. "*Almost.*"

"Well, Dollie, that shouldn't be so hard." He said as the demons ran up to her, seizing her, taking her arm from her. "And neither is your capture I see."

She laughed hysterically as the guards dragged her away. "It's the blood loss, I'm afraid! You see Lust, I seem to have misplaced my arm! Do let me know if you find it."

##

Lust stared at Lavanah from the observation room above her cell. Greed stood beside him, Envy spinning on a chair behind them, giggling like a child as she played with Lavanah's arm.

"I want eyes on her at all times. Those doors should never be opened again. Whatever it is Gluttony is trying to do, he's using her to do so."

"Why not kill her?" Lust said, watching as Lavanah sat still in her chains. They were no different than the chains Gluttony had once been bound to.

"Because anyone who goes near her will die. She's mad enough to allow Wrath to chop off her arm. Without it she can wield her blood stronger than any weapon." Greed sighed in defeat. "One of two things will happen, Lust. Either Gluttony is breaking in or she is going to escape on her own. I can't imagine who would be foolish enough to stay. I for one don't want to be around for either."

"Then I will stay to watch her. I do love a good show."

"It's your funeral." Greed said, taking his leave.

Envy fell out of the chair, breaking one of the fingers on the arm. "Lust, I broke it!"

Lust sighed. "What do I look like? A healer? There exists only one demon who can heal, and it's our job to make sure she doesn't escape."

"I need the arm fixed!" She said stomping her feet as she approached Lust. "Let me go inside!"

"No."

Envy turned around, kicking over the chair she had once spun in, its wooden frame breaking on impact. "*Fine.*"

Lust continued to watch Lavanah, eventually calling for one of his dolls. If he was going to remain bound to the room, then he was going to make the best of it. The doll approached him as he stood, removing his trousers for him. Lust held onto his head, watching him even if only for a moment.

Envy was quiet as she snuck out of the room, making gagging sounds as she made her way to Lavanah's cell. She opened the door quietly, tiptoeing in though she knew Lust would find out soon enough.

"You're a healer, right?" She said from the entrance.

"Yes, Child." Lavanah said softly encouraging Envy to come closer.

"Because I broke a finger on my new toy." She said with a sadness Lavanah did not expect as she approached.

"Let me fix it for you, Child."

Envy approached Lavanah, holding the arm out. Lust watched from the observation room as he dismissed his doll. The doll wiped its mouth before leaving through the door.

"Damn it, Envy." Lust said pulling his trousers up.

Blood still dripped from Lavanah's arm as she heard a cawing in the distance, a small black bird entering from what seemed like nowhere. It met eyes with Lavanah, landing in front of her.

"Damned bird." Envy said, stomping on the bird where she crushed its body. "Lust, I killed Gluttony!"

"No, you didn't," Lust sighed, watching them.

Lavanah laughed, her arm reattaching itself to her body, separated from the chains that held her. The arrays glowed, shattering the chains. As she landed the blood covering her body combined with the blood below her, forming a spike that pierced through Envy.

"I never thought revenge was contagious, but if you share the same soul as someone I don't see why it wouldn't be." Envy choked out.

The bird stood from the ground as if it had never been crushed. "That would certainly explain a lot, don't you think?" The bird cawed in response as it flew through the air, landing on her shoulder.

"Well played, Gluttony, I suppose you've solved the puzzle." He said meeting her eyes though she could not see him. "Tell me, Lavanah, what will you do next?"

Envy's blood followed behind Lavanah as she approached the doors, the guards forcing them open, their weapons drawn. Lavanah stepped forward, splattering blood against the floor before them. It rose in the form of spikes pinning the demons to the walls like it had with Envy.

She walked around the spikes, her pace lighthearted as she wandered the halls, the raven remaining on her shoulder though it weighed nothing.

"Lust, I know you've been thinking about me. Where is it you hide?" She said looking at the raven. "Find Lust." She said meeting the bird's eyes.

The bird leapt off her shoulder, flying quickly through the halls, Lavanah following close behind it. She pushed open the doors, the bird flying at Lust who grabbed it by its neck, but the bird became shadows in his fingers.

"You may not be Gluttony but you are equally irritating. The dark arts are a curse Lavanah though you have not realized it yet."

Lavanah curtsied though she did not wear a skirt. "I do not fear the consequences of my actions, Lust. I am willing to do anything to retrieve my soul.

"And what good does having a soul do? I've never felt better."

"Because I have a sister waiting for me." She said fondly. "That's the difference between me and every archdemon before me. I have something out there that protects me from this curse."

Lust laughed. "Whatever gets you through the day, Lavanah."

He struck at her, watching almost in amusement as she grabbed his arm, breaking it before kicking him into the wall. Lust leaned forward, picking up the wooden chair that Envy had lashed out on kicking it at Lavanah attempting to distract her even if only for a moment.

Lavanah caught the chair, flipping over it, bringing the chair with her as she forced it into Lust where it bust, the pieces falling to the floor as she dropped the one piece she held.

Lust used her landing to his advantage, catching her leg where he broke it, throwing her into the floor. She clenched her teeth as Lust's foot came over her face. The floor twisted, stretching towards Lust to push him out of the way. Lavanah took quick and heavy breaths before forcing her bone back into place where her arrays healed it. She screamed in pain, struggling to stand again.

"You are just full of surprises. And here I had thought I was lying to Envy. It turns out you are capable of healing. Who knew?"

"I can name one person." Lavanah said, throwing Lust through the glass of the observation room. She followed behind him, leaping through the broken window, the glass forming a spear that pierced his body as her feet met the floor.

"Gluttony won't let you go." He said, his eyes falling on Envy's body.

"He may not have a choice." She said, watching as the demon breathed his last.

##

Gluttony stood outside his home, preening his feathers with his fingers, the snow soothing as it fell against his skin. Lavanah approached him watching for a moment as the snow melted upon contact. It was one of the few things that made him different from the demons.

"Your bird seemed so real. I had considered bringing him back to you until he became shadows."

"Illusions always seem real."

"I suppose they do." She said looking towards the sky. "You've given me great power, Gluttony. It's saved my life."

"It isn't without its sacrifices, Lavanah." Gluttony said, looking at her, smiling. "Though I am grateful it has protected you."

She looked at him, taken aback. "You are grateful?"

"If you die, then I may never leave here." He said bitterly. "And you'd never see Marie again."

"I am seeing my sister again. With or without you."

"Without me you *can't* see her again. One of those arrays keeps you bound to our contract. Every human receives one, though some never learn of it. The contract is made from magic like the arrays."

Lavanah held her arm. "I'm beginning to think the other demons are right about you."

"Don't be racist." He said with a snarl. "I'm the only one who has tried to help you."

"Sloth was rather kind." She said remembering her time with Sloth. In some ways, she saw Marie in her.

Solas frowned. "Lavanah." He said with a melancholy tone. "Let me make myself clear. Regardless of how you feel about me or what I'm doing you don't have a choice."

Lavanah stared at his face, surprised by the sadness she saw behind his black eyes. She scratched names off a list in her mind. Her heart was heavy in her chest as she realized only two demons remained. Tears streamed down her eyes as she turned on her heels, running away from Gluttony.

He stared into the snow unable to watch as she left. "It's like having a child." His words though cold did not match the voice behind them. For the first time, he heard his own sorrow.

##

Lavanah was quiet as she opened the door, careful as she stepped over the filth that covered the floor of the chambers. Sloth lay in her bed, smiling as her eyes fell upon Lavanah. She closed her book, the raven's feather sticking out of the top. She reached for Lavanah her arms wide open.

"Has the Harbinger of Death sent you?" She laughed, patting the side of her bed. "Come, sit with me." Lavanah sat beside Sloth, closing her eyes as the demon struggled to wipe the tears from her eyes. "Oh sweetie, I didn't mean to make you cry. It's a joke among the other demons."

Her tender heart only brought more tears. "I've done some awful things, Sloth." She said, pressing her hands to her arms.

"Lay your head on my lap, sweetie." Sloth said, her smile remaining strong.

Lavanah laid her head in the demon's lap, hugging one of her pillows close as she cried.

"I know about the things you've done, Lavanah." She said, patting her soft curls. "But know that you are no worse a person than I am."

"They call me Pride now." She said though she no longer enjoyed the title.

"But you're not Pride. You never belonged here, Lavanah, and Solas knew it."

"Solas." She whispered having nearly forgotten Gluttony's real name.

"That's his name." She said with a long exhale. "And like you, he doesn't belong here either."

"He's using me to escape." Lavanah said, taking Sloth's free hand, holding it against her face. "Did you know of any of this?"

"No. He was afraid to tell me, but in truth I enjoy surprises. Even this one." Sloth said, pushing her soft curls behind her ear. "If I may ask of you one thing, will you clean my room before you leave?"

Lavanah sat up wiping the tears from her eyes. "Of course I will." She stood up, beginning with her chambers, adjusting the frames on the walls so they sat straight.

"You can take those down if you wish, I no longer need them with you here."

Lavanah's hands trembled as she removed the frames from the walls, placing them on top of the dresser. "Sloth I'm sorry-"

"No." Sloth said, smacking her fist on her bed. "You have nothing to be sorry for. You may not see it but what you are doing is kind. It is the greatest display of love I have ever been shown."

"How can you say that?" Lavanah said, picking the clothing up from the floor, taking it into the bathroom where she washed each piece, taking her time. She was in no rush to see Gluttony.

"I have been around for a very long time. As a doll, I knew nothing of emotions. I was foolish as any doll of Pride is and took advantage of the weakened state of the Sloth before me. I felt such great power that when I succumbed to the curse, I felt nothing but sorrow and regret as I lay in my bed. Day after day, I would beg my dolls to kill me, but they were wiser than the doll I had been."

"But you seem so happy."

"Because one day Hell became a home for angels too, and it was on that day that I met Solas."

Lavanah hung the clothes to dry, barely able to see through her tears. "You act as if he's a saint, but he's more a demon than any I've met."

Sloth shook her head. "Solas was not an archdemon from the time he came to Hell. Like Envy, he killed the archdemon before him. He knew that if he was to ever have a chance of escaping that he would need our power." She said running her fingers over the feather. "He came to me because I was the only one who had yet to ridicule him for being an angel. At this point, I was desperate, hoping he would be able to kill me. Archdemons don't kill one another for we have nothing to gain from it. Except you of course, you had something to gain."

"Lucky me."

Sloth tried to lift her arm from her bed, to reach for Lavanah but she was too weak. "I hoped because he was an angel that he could save me."

"But he can't." Lavanah said.

"He came to me still distraught over what had happened to his head. Even to this day I've no idea what Solas truly looks like.

He was still in so much pain from his skull being forced to change in such a horrific way, but I offered no words of comfort. Instead I told him that he could never know what true suffering was."

"What did he say?" She grabbed the familiar bucket, filling it with soapy water, getting on her knees where she scrubbed the floors.

"Nothing. He left but when he returned it was with a stack of books. He has brought me many books over the years and somewhere along the way I remembered how to feel happiness. Solas however, didn't. He continued to fall deeper into the hole that I had once dug for myself."

"He deserves it."

Sloth shook her head. "You've only seen one side of a man who's long since learned from his lesson."

Lavanah threw her towel into the bucket, little drops of water splashing onto the floor. "He ate my eye out of my skull!"

Sloth blinked for a moment, looking up from her book. "He's a sucker for beautiful eyes."

"So what in him changed?"

"He found hope." She said looking at her. "In you. Though you were small the little rebel in you enthralled him. I could see it in his eyes each time he came to me and spoke of you. I knew from those moments that he needed you in his life."

"So he's a creep and a murderer."

Sloth laughed watching as Lavanah finished the bathroom. "You're still staring into the past when you need to look to the future. You don't see it now, and I don't expect you to."

"Why do you speak of him as if he is virtuous when he has killed people? *Children.*"

"Did you not kill your sister's husband?" Sloth said though she knew the answer. "Lavanah we all make mistakes. That's why we're here but unlike angels, we have the capacity to change. It's whether we make the sacrifices necessary to do so. Solas has and so have you."

"I don't want to believe him, Sloth." Lavanah said making her way into the main room where she swept the rubbish from the floor, placing it into the trash.

"You've no reason *not* to trust him, Lavanah. He could have let you die. He could have let you become a lesser demon. But I think somewhere along the way he has gained a soft spot for you. The two of you are more similar than you give yourselves credit for. For example, you both have black hair. There's one."

Lavanah tried to resist chuckling. "That may be the only one." She stopped for a moment, looking at the candlesticks as they lay upon the floor. Their flames were still strong, the candles no shorter than the last time she had seen them.

"Is there nothing in this world that isn't fueled by magic?"

"Love." Sloth said. "Like you feel for your sister, and Solas feels for you."

"Just because the man *might* have a soft spot doesn't mean he loves me." Lavanah said, her cheeks reddening.

"I think he may surprise you."

"Why did he call me creation?" She said, changing the subject.

"Because despite the change he has experienced, Solas is still held back by revenge. You are driven by hope. You are young and naïve and therefore blind. A day will come, however where you see that he made the right decision."

She lifted the plates from the floor and into her arms, taking them into the kitchen. "I don't know if I will ever be as wise as you, Sloth." She filled the sink with water, cleaning off each plate before putting them away in the cabinets. Their smell, however, was far more tolerable than then the first time she had washed them.

"Angels. Demons. Humans. We're all just people trying to live our lives to the best of our ability. I know that after you and Solas escape that the two of you will be an excellent pair."

"We are *not* a pair." Lavanah said, stacking the dishes in the cabinet before dusting the room as well as the main room. She lifted the pillows into her hands, straightening them on the sofa.

"Yes you are. And that's why you will return to him after you've finished here." She said. "Don't worry about the sofas, Sweetie."

Lavanah ignored her, fixing the pillows anyway. "Why are you so confident that I will go back to him?"

"Because you need each other. He already sees it and soon you will too."

"Over my dead body." She said grabbing her bucket of soapy water, getting onto her knees again, scrubbing the floors clean.

"Maybe mine will suffice."

Lavanah threw the towel into the bucket again. "What are you trying to say Sloth?"

"I love you Lavanah for cleaning my *entire* room, but you are only preventing the inevitable."

Lavanah dumped the water out where she then placed the bucket in a cabinet below the sink. "I don't know what you're talking about."

"Don't act like a fool, Lavanah. You are better than that."

"I'm not convinced. Look where I'm at." She said entering Sloth's chambers.

"Don't get used to it. You won't be here much longer. Solas will not let you."

Sloth sighed, removing the feather from her book before setting it down. "Could I trouble you for a bath?" She struggled to make her way to the edge of the bed, putting one leg down at a time. Lavanah tried to stop her, but Sloth held her hand up.

Lavanah watched with a heavy heart as Sloth held onto the covers on her bed. She motivated herself in a string of whispers as she inched her way to where Lavanah stood. Her legs trembled with every move, but she didn't let go. She held onto Lavanah with all her strength as she placed the feather in her hair. With a smile Sloth collapsed onto the floor.

"Yes, I did it!" She laughed. "I walked across my room! Do you have any idea how long it has been?"

Lavanah forced a smile, tears forming in her eyes. She had never seen someone so happy to walk a couple of feet.

"Lavanah, I'm going to be frank with you." Sloth said as she was lifted into her arms. "We both know that I will not be alive when you leave here today. I know it pains you, but I have wanted an end for as long as I can remember. This curse has burdened me for far too long. That said I didn't wish to die in filth."

"I would clean forever if you could stay alive." Lavanah shook her head as she carried her into the bathroom. "I don't mind." She said, running a bath. She removed her nightgown, placing it to the side before lowering her into the bath carefully. She started with her hands, kissing her knuckles, knowing the truth behind her words.

"But I don't want to Lavanah. I have enjoyed our conversation but know that there is nothing that is meant to last forever. Even gods fall sometime."

"Sloth, you deserve better than this."

She laughed, enjoying the feeling of the warm water against her pale flesh. "I thought the same thing about you. So, get your soul back and get the hell out of this place." She said trying to resist a smile.

"I just want to see my sister again."

Sloth struggled to sit up, looking into her eyes as she spoke. "Then do it." She looked more serious now than Lavanah had thought her capable of. "But you can't do it without Solas. You are bound to him. So please, free him, Lavanah."

"If you're asking me to—"

"I'm asking you to free a man who has suffered long enough. I'm asking you to make sure my sacrifice is not in vain."

Lavanah struggled to breathe, moving her silver hair around her neck. "What if you're wrong?"

"I'm too old to be wrong." Sloth said with a laugh,

"I think you might be right." Lavanah said, draining the bath.

The girls shared in a laugh as Lavanah helped her into another nightgown. She then carried Sloth back to her bed, fluffing her pillows.

Sloth picked up the book that the feather had rested inside. She ran her hand over the leather fondly until she no longer had the strength.

"This one was my favorite. Gluttony gave it to me a long time ago when I was learning so much myself. It reminds me a lot of the two of you. I want you to give it back to him when you leave."

"I will." Lavanah said, holding onto Sloth's hands.

"I've never seen a man cry before much less a bird man."

"I am going to miss you." She said as she began to drain the life from Sloth doing her best to keep her death painless.

Sloth held onto Lavanah's wrists. "Don't. There is much more to life than the past." She took a deep breath, closing her eyes.

Lavanah could feel the last of her life slip away, placing her hands on her chest. She tried to fight the tears as they fell down her face.

When she was finally able to leave Sloth's chambers she only found darkness waiting for her, the lights of the candlesticks now extinguished.

"Sloth wanted you to have this." Lavanah said, handing the book to Gluttony, keeping it safe from the snow.

He looked at the spine of the book, opening it where he forced a smile. He could see the wear on the book from the many times she had read it. He flipped through the pages, reading the occasional message from Sloth. They began confused, wondering why he had given her the book. He continued to flip through the pages. She had scratched out many of her messages, replacing them with new ones. On the last page, Sloth had drawn little pictures depicting the ending for the characters with the names Solas and Thea beneath them.

"She said it reminded her of you and I."

"I see that though I can't imagine why." He said closing the book. "Is there something you wanted to say?"

"There are many things I want to say." She said approaching him. "But I will say only one of them. I have killed five demons with only Greed remaining. If I help you, then you must stop eating eyes. Please."

Gluttony looked at her for a moment, trying to decide if she was serious before laughing. "All right. No more eating eyes."

"No removing them from skulls period, Solas."

"You have my word."

##

Lavanah entered Greed's chambers, the room empty except for the large table as it sat the first time she had been here, covered in food. She approached the table, flipping it over, the food spilling everywhere, a blue orb rolling down the pile of food. It was all too familiar.

"I have no time for your games, Greed. You have something of mine."

"And you think by making a mess of my chambers that I will suddenly give it back?"

Lavanah turned around, staring into the eyes of Greed. "I would be disappointed if it were so easy."

Lavanah bared her teeth as she struck Greed, the hands on his body reaching out as they caught her before throwing her back into the farthest wall.

She hit the wall with enough force to knock the air from her lungs. The table's legs turned to spears, reaching towards Greed. The many arms on his body deflected them, protecting him.

Greed laughed even as one of her arrays glowed, dismembering him. The many arms and heads fell to the floor below him but only grew back.

Lavanah fell to her feet, having exhausted much of her magic. She smiled at Greed, using the last of her strength to light him on fire, watching as he burned.

"You could say thank you." Lavanah said as Gluttony appeared beside her.

"I have no reason to," He said, throwing her out of the way. "If you're going to kill him, then you should eat those souls."

Greed stepped towards him, the flames beginning to die. "I always knew that one day you would find a way to turn on us."

Gluttony held his hands out, concentrating as he stared at Greed. Though the flames were weak, Greed screamed for they felt stronger than ever.

Lavanah hurried over to the table searching through the food, consuming each soul she came across. Her energy return in quick bursts allowing her to fuel the flames before they died.

Gluttony stepped back, leaning against the wall to regain his strength. He had faith that Lavanah could handle Greed despite her scrappy fighting.

The walls around them began to peel, the floors beneath them rotting away the closer Greed came to his death. Lavanah screamed, her using the last of her energy to turn Greed's body to ash. Among the ashes a colorful pile of souls glowed unable to be destroyed by the flames.

Lavanah fell over as Gluttony approached her. He pushed the souls aside, lifting one up. In it he could see her memories of Marie and herself.

He knelt beside her, holding her up with one arm. Though she could not speak, he was confident he could hear her words.

"Lavanah, once you consume your soul, you can never come back. If you die again you will be in limbo for eternity."

He knew, however, that neither of them had a choice. He parted her lips feeding the soul to her.

She screamed, the pitch shattering glass.

Gluttony held her tightly in his arms as she struggled. Her soft platinum curls fell out, straight black hair growing in their place. Her horns and tattoos remained, their damage impossible to be undone.

Her soul was like fire as it destroyed the fake soul that Gluttony had implanted within her. She gasped seeing Greed's ashes before pushing Gluttony away. She stumbled to her feet, running towards the entrance, despite much of the floor having disappeared.

She cried out in fear when she reached the edge, swinging her arms wildly as she struggled to regain her balance.

"Thea!" Solas shouted, running to her side where he grabbed her hand, pulling her close. "Thea, look at me!"

She stomped on his feet, fighting against him. "Get away from me!" Her arrays glowed bright, setting the walls of the chambers on fire. This only scared her more, her legs weak.

Gluttony did not let go instead, sitting in the floor with her. "Thea." He said, more calmly this time as he patted her head.

"Let go of me!" She screamed, struggling in his arms. "You killed me and made me into a monster!"

He held her more tightly. "You are *not* a monster." He said patting her hair. "I need you to trust me when I tell you that I only want to protect you."

"*I can't trust you.*"

"You trusted me when I was but a raven in your window. Trust me again now."

Her screams quieted as she collapsed in his arms, the fire crackling behind them. She placed her hands on her head, feeling her horns. She made a small noise, pulling at the horns.

"What happened to me?"

Gluttony sat on the floor, holding her in his arms, petting her hair. He closed his eyes; relieved that she no longer was the doll they had created.

"Why do you have a raven for a head?" Her voice was soft, *innocent*. It scared him to see her so broken.

"It's a long story. One that we must finish." He said, thrown off by her broken state. He had become so used to seeing her act with bravery and confidence.

"What's your name?"

He was quiet for a moment having nearly forgotten his own name. "My name is Solas."

"Appropriate. You seem pretty soulless to me."

"I deserve that." He said standing up, helping her to her feet. "But Thea, you and I have been through so much in such a short time. I ask that you look past my mistakes."

She sighed, beginning to remember the events that had led her here. "You saved my life despite the events that it caused. I can look past your mistakes but only if I get my revenge." She said with a familiar smile. "You're not my fiancé, so I suppose I can play nice for a little while."

"No, I'm definitely not." He said, holding onto her hand. "But I am your ally, and I'm going to start by getting you out of here."

"Good. I have a sister waiting for me." She said, squeezing his hand as she approached him.

He couldn't resist a smile as he lifted her arm, placing his hands on one of the arrays.

"Tell me something, Solas, before we leave." She said, staring at the tattoos that covered her arms. "Who will protect me from myself when I am no longer the me I used to be?"

"I do and have by giving you my power." He said, squeezing her hand in return, the glow of her array filling the room.

"Like the prison."

"Only this time I won't leave you." He said with a chuckle.

Thea blushed as she found herself standing on a familiar grassy field. He stared at her as the sun set behind them. The wind blew through her hair as she looked into the distance, lost in her memories. He was able to reteach her how to use some of her power by showing some of his memories. It would be quite some time before she could use them as proficiently as before but he was confident she would learn again.

"There is something I must do, Solas."

He ran his fingers along the pale horns that peeked out from underneath her dark hair. "Then you should go. I'll come see you in the morning."

"Thank you." She said kissing his cheek, the feathers smooth against her lips.

Solas turned to look at her, watching as she disappeared into the distance. "I can't wait to be rid of this bird head."

##

When she arrived home the sun had fallen. The night was beautiful without a cloud in the sky. Marie's garden had died, what remained was no more than wilted hedges. It sickened her stomach to see that they wouldn't keep that much of her alive.

She entered the estate, avoiding the servants and guards as she made her way to the kitchen. She didn't want them to be alerted to her presence too soon. She stole a bowl filling it with water before returning to the garden. She mixed handfuls of dirt into the water to create a thick mud, using it to draw small arrays onto all the exits of the house, even the windows. She was careful to remain unseen, keeping her arrays out of their sight.

She returned to the entrance to the garden, marking it before entering the estate, going to the entrance of the prison. She fought back her memories shivering as she marked it too. She wouldn't allow them to find safety in the very place they had left her to die.

She returned to the kitchen, washing out the bowl before putting it away. She cleared her mind of her past as she prepared hot water, taking the cucumber sandwiches that had been prepared for the next day. She was almost giddy having not had tea for so long much less cucumber sandwiches. She took the plate of sandwiches back to the garden where the little bistro styled chairs and tables waited, white with three legs. She placed the plate on the table she'd all but written her name on before returning inside. She grabbed a book from the library as well as some tea bags, balancing the cream on the book as she carried it outside. On her final trip, she carried the hot water, making sure she had turned the stove off. Her other hand carried a cup on a saucer, a small spoon sticking out of it.

She sat at the table, pleased with the set up. She lifted one of the tea bags, placing it in the saucer. She poured the hot water over the bag, cream joining it after a moment. She stirred it until it looked similar to the way she drank her coffee.

She lifted the cup from its saucer, her arrays glowing, the seals setting on fire in unison. She sipped at her tea, watching as the blaze consumed the estate. She set the tea down after a moment, pleased by the sight. She reached for one of her sandwiches, confident that her seals would hold beneath the flames. She watched as the fires continued to spread, spilling into the estate.

She lifted her book up, flipping the pages until she reached the middle, running her finger down the page before tapping on a line with a smile:

"*The strength of a nation derives from the integrity of the home.*"

She then closed the book, throwing it into the flames. "There was a time where I might have believed those words but that time has since passed." She said, finishing her sandwich as the first scream sounded. "*And the show begins.*"

Fear consumed them first as she watched them run past the windows on occasion. Screams sung from the flames like a choir. She grabbed another sandwich, savoring it more than the last. The smell of burning flesh began to stain the air.

She watched as the fire burned, the screams quieting one by one. She sipped at her tea, watching the fire, listening at it crackled in the darkness, little orange sparks dancing against the black sky. After a few hours, the fire died out. She frowned, her sandwiches nearly gone, her teacup empty. She flicked her wrist, another fire beginning to consume the estate. She threw the old tea bag into the flames, placing a new one into the cup, pouring the water onto it. She emptied the last of the cream into her cup, throwing the pot into the fire, listening as it shattered.

The fire continued to burn as she finished her pastries, dying out after some time.

Thea threw her empty plate from the pastries onto the pile of ash that once was her home before setting fire to it. Not even ash deserved to remain.

She fixed another cup of tea without cream, sighing. "With each new fire my tea tastes worse."

The fire continued to burn, her table eventually clear.

"Thea." Solas said, approaching her, the sun rising in the distance behind the fire.

"No." She said shaking her head. "I've had a lot of time to think, Solas. I'm not Thea. And I'm not Lavanah. Yet I am both. I'm still me, I'm still that same girl willing to watch the world burn."

"Perhaps literally." He said, watching as the fire died out for the last time leaving little behind. "What are you trying to say?"

"I want you to call me Lathea." She said. "A name is just a name, but it's still my name. I won't choose to forget the past but I will not stay there either."

His eyes fell on the one thing she could not erase though the fire had damaged it a bit. In the ground before them were the cells where she had once been tortured, debris lying around its floors.

"I think it's time we left." He said, feeling uncomfortable as his eyes fell on the bloodied remains of her nightgown.

"You don't want my soul first?"

"It will just have to wait until I've visited someone."

"Sariel." She said breathily, Solas nodding in response.

The two of them entered the palace, watching as its guests walked past them, whispering harshly about their "costumes." The servants stayed out of their way, avoiding their eyes. The throne room was disconcertingly empty.

Lathea took a seat in the Queen's throne, Solas taking a seat in the King's throne.

"I always wondered what it was like to sit here."

"And?" Solas said meeting her eyes.

"I feel like a pretentious fool." She said with a smile. "I do not belong in a throne."

They watched as Sariel appeared, leisurely making his way to them. "That's because you are still a child continuing to play pretend. You're only nineteen. You know nothing of the world."

"I'm wiser than my age would suggest. I've seen more of this world than I had ever wished to see. I have been forced to know the ugly side of this world."

Solas stood up, placing his arm in front of her. "Leave her be, Sariel. She has been through enough."

"Then why bring her here? Why not come alone?"

"I have promise to keep to her and so does she. I promise that our meeting will be short."

"Tell me, Solas? How many times must I put you down before you stay down?"

Solas slowly stepped down the stairs as he spoke. "Are you so overconfident in your ability that you believe yourself safe from death?

"And with good reason. You haven't exactly been practicing yourself, Solas."

"I think you may be surprised."

Lathea stood from the throne, starting down the stairs when Solas grabbed her wrist. "Stay out of this. Marie will never forgive me if harm comes to you."

"You're a fool if you think I am going to stand here and watch."

"Then look away." He said, his foot hit the last stair, his wings propelling him forward towards Sariel. The two angels took off towards the ceiling, fighting in the air.

Lathea walked towards the entrance. If she could not fight with him then she would be better off outside the palace.

Sariel kicked Solas, drawing his sword as he watched him crash into the ceiling above them. His impact caused a crater to form in the ceiling, debris falling below him. A large piece of debris hurled towards Sariel who slashed through it effortlessly. Solas took advantage of this, folding his black wings as he dove at the angel. His feet landed on Sariel forcing him to the floor, the impact causing a wave of dust and debris to spread through the room.

Solas took to the air again as Sariel struck with his sword. Angered, Sariel followed close behind, plunging his sword through the abdomen of the angel, pinning him to the wall. Solas screamed, the sound like that of a dying animal.

Lathea covered her ears, gritting her teeth, doing everything she could to stay out of their path.

"Stop toying with me, Solas." Sariel said, twisting the blade.

Solas pierced his eyes with his beak, swallowing his eye. Sariel fell back for a moment, focused on his eye. Solas took advantage of this, removing the sword from his abdomen.

"My curiosity has been sated." He said with a laugh though his body writhed in pain. He flew at Sariel as he produced another sword, avoiding it as he plunged the angel's sword through his abdomen. Sariel took advantage of this, piercing him with the new sword as the blade tore through his abdomen.

The angels fell to the floor with a loud sound. "Lathea set this palace ablaze!"

Lathea bit her lip, setting fire to the palace. "Get out of there, Solas."

Solas could smell the smoke, laughing as he struggled to remove himself from the sword.

"Using her to kill me? That's playing dirty, Solas." Sariel laughed though he struggled to see.

"What can I say, Sariel? *I need her.*" He lifted his body off the blade, disarming the angel. He pulled the sword from Sariel's abdomen, piercing his skull with enough force it pinned him to the floor. He stepped away from the angel, holding his abdomen as it bled through his fingers. His movements were slow as he struggled to escape the burning building. Debris fell, landing on him. It crushed his arm leaving him to be consumed by the flames. Solas took a deep breath, focusing on the debris, watching as it slowly moved off him.

Lathea watched from outside as the flames devoured the palace, the only sound being that of the fire as it consumed all that it encountered. Her nostrils flared, tears coming to her eyes as she waited for Solas to come out.

Solas stumbled out of the burning palace, the walls beginning to collapse behind him. Much of his flesh had charred, many of the bones in his arm crushed. His face no longer had a beak but was also undistinguishable. His wings too had disappeared though she could not tell if it was because of the fire or because of Sariel's death.

She forced a smile as she looked at Solas, the smell of charred flesh and blood stinging her nose.

"You smell like a roasted chicken." She said trying to fight against her tears.

"I'm not amused by your bird jokes." He said resisting a smile, sitting on the stairs. "I never was."

She pressed her hand to the part where he was the least charred beginning to heal him though it took much of her strength.

"What happened to your arm?"

"Debris fell on top of me while I was escaping. I wasn't expecting to be away from you for so long."

She looked away, words difficult, tears escaping from her as she continued to heal his wounds. "I suppose you're out of practice." The holes from the sword were first to close, flesh repairing itself over muscle.

Solas winced as his face healed. "I promise you that I'm in better shape than Sariel."

"Good. I never want to see him again."

He waited until more of his flesh returned before looking up at her. "Lathea, I know that consuming your soul is the only thing that remains of our contract. After that you've no reason to stay, but I need you."

She looked down at him her tears dripping onto the face of a man. "You can't say that." His flesh finished repairing itself, black hair now replacing the feathers, his skin smooth, steel eyes replacing the beady ones of the raven.

"That's not fair. *You're handsome.*" She said her emotions defeating her words.

"How is that *not* fair?"

"Because I always thought you should look like some kind of troll. Only monsters eat eyes."

"You're never letting that go."

"Nope." She said approaching the flames of the palace. "But now there is something I must do because I will not allow my sister to think of me as a demon."

"I—wait—what are you doing?" Solas said, standing, reaching for her.

She grabbed her horns, forcing a smile as she ripped them from her skull, throwing them into the flames. Her skull repaired itself, but the horns did not return.

"You stupid girl!" Solas said, grabbing her hand as she fell, pulling her close, her hair wet from the blood.

She gave an exhausted laugh as she stared into his face. "I'm okay. Really. I just can't let my sister see me as a monster." She said pressing her hands to his face. "I don't want her to look at me in the same way I once looked at you."

"*You're not a monster.*" He said, whispering into her hair.

"Admittedly, *neither are you.*" She said as they sat on the steps of the palace, the fire still strong behind them.

"I can't keep holding you like this, Lathea."

"Then perhaps one day I'll return the favor." She said closing her eyes, the sound of hooves stomping along the ground echoing in her ears.

"Thea!" Screamed a woman with platinum hair as she rode a horse.

Solas stared at the woman in disbelief, the horse coming to a stop beside him. "It's been a long time, Marie."

Chapter 16

"Do I know you?" Humility said, meeting the man's eyes as she dismounted from her horse.

He stood, holding Lathea in his arms. "No, I suppose you don't. I watched your sister — and you — for many years."

"You weren't the only one." She said, turning her attention to her sister. "Thea, can you hear me?" She said, touching her hair.

"She's dead." The woman's voice said. "You went through all of this for nothing."

"She's not dead." Marie said in a whisper,

"Marie, I know it might be hard to face it but—"

"Lathea, Sister." She said as she struggled to put an arm around Solas. "Help me stand."

"I would advise against that." He said.

"I didn't ask for your advice. Help me stand. I want to hug my sister."

Solas held Lathea by her waist as her feet hit the ground. She wrapped her arms around her sister, leaning into her. Marie pressed her hand to the back of her head, pulling it away when she felt the blood.

"It seems we have a lot to talk about, Sister." Marie said, hugging her sister tightly.

"Preferably away from the flames." Solas said, looking back at the palace as one of its pillars collapsed behind them, sparks flying in their direction.

Marie looked at Solas with an apologetic expression. "I only have one horse."

"Go. I'll keep the flames under control. They will be extinguished by the time you return,"

"Thank you, Stranger." She said, helping her sister onto the horse.

"Solas." He said with a smile. "I see you've taken your sister's sense of humor."

"We are twins." She said before turning the horse around. "Just one question before I go, why is her hair wet with blood?"

"It seems you and her have a lot to catch up on."

"So the stories about Hell are true?"

"That depends on what you have heard." Solas said with a smirk. "Though I am very curious as to what you have heard."

Marie laughed. "You sound just like my sister."

"Solas, could you find a wet cloth?" Marie said, sitting with her sister's head in her lap as she lay along the sofa.

He grabbed a cloth from the sink, running warm water over it before bringing it to her. "She's going to be fine."

"Of that I have no doubt." She said wiping the blood from her sister's hair. "But I have many other questions."

Solas sat across from her in a small armchair, leaning into the plush cushions. "Where do we begin?"

"Let's start with why my sister told me to call her Lathea." She said, moving the cloth to her sister's face cleaning the blood and dirt. "And why her arms are suddenly covered in ink."

"You should see her back."

Marie looked up at him, narrowing her eyes. "Oh really? You've seen my sister's back?"

Solas put his hands up. "Relax, kitten, I've not laid with your sister. I am responsible for the ink however. The arrays help her control her magic."

"I see. And the mural?"

"Something to remind her of how far she's come." He said looking at it fondly. "Your sister has done great things."

Marie set the cloth aside, hugging her sister, struggling to hold back tears. "There was a time when I thought I might never see her again."

"I'm happy that I could help bring her home."

"Do not misunderstand, Solas, I am very grateful for your help. Thea—"

"Lathea." He said, correcting her. "She combined her birth name and demon name."

"*Why?*" She said. "She could have chosen any name."

"I agree but she doesn't want to act as if the past didn't happen. She recognizes that it happened and that these experiences are what make her the person she is."

Lathea sat up looking at her sister. "Thank you, Marie."

Marie smiled, sitting closer to her sister. "I'm just glad you're alive."

"I'm sure by someone's definition I am."

"Why must you be so literal, *L*athea?"

"How else would I keep you grounded to reality?"

Solas looked at her. "Lathea."

She looked at him, taking a deep breath before speaking to her sister. "There is something we must do, Marie. I made a deal with him a long time ago, and I must hold up my end of the deal. I promise you though that I'll come see you as soon as we have finished."

"There are a couple of empty houses around town. You're welcome to one of them. Do try to stay close, Sister."

Lathea laughed as she stood, Solas joining her as they made their way to the door. "You aren't getting rid of me that easily."

"I wouldn't have it any other way,"

Solas watched as Lathea wandered in and out of the houses never allowing Marie's home to get out of her sight. She finally settled on one near the tavern that was just far enough that Marie wouldn't hear her if she screamed.

Solas closed the door behind them, watching as she walked into the kitchen, sitting at the table. "Are we going to talk about what happened?"

Lathea propped her feet onto the table. "What's there to talk about, Solas? I killed my parents—"

"You failed to mention that to your sister."

"Now isn't the time for that. I just came home. Give her some time to process the fact that her sister is a demon."

"All right." He said grabbing a chair, sitting in it. "Then let's talk about us for a minute."

Lathea laughed, holding her stomach. "*Us?* You think there's an '*us*'? Just because you told me you need me?"

He leaned back into the chair, crossing his legs. "I'm sorry, was that not you crying on the stairs of the palace?"

"I won't deny that I care about you, but I'm not going to pretend that you're still going to be around after you take my soul."

He frowned, leaning forward. "You think that lowly of me?"

She lowered her feet, leaning forward. "Give me a reason not to."

"Ironic coming from a demon."

She smirked, standing up to lean closer. "Do something about it, Birdie. You want me trust you? Prove to me that I can."

He held her by her chin. "Very well then but you still owe me a soul."

She took his hand, looking at him from under her lashes. "There's no changing your mind?"

"Not a chance." He said grabbing her by the back of her head, meeting her lips.

##

Marie was sitting on the sofa when Azrael returned home. "My sister has returned home." She said, standing, looking at him disappointedly. She couldn't mistake the smell of sweat and perfume.

Azrael tried to kiss her, his heart sinking in his chest when she looked away. "I'm assuming you brought her into town."

"Of course I did. There isn't another for miles."

"Then give her a horse and send her on her way. Marie, I don't expect you to see it but she's dangerous."

"She is no more dangerous than you and I."

He grabbed her by her arms. "*We're nothing like them.*"

She pushed his arms away. "For someone who has watched us our entire lives, you know nothing about us. In fact, you know nothing about humanity. Whatever you have done to these people is only going to hinder them. Humanity doesn't need us to be strong."

"They are like children, Marie." Azrael said, knocking over a nearby chair before wrapping his arms around Marie. "They're weak and need someone strong to hold their hand. Without us they would fall." He said squeezing her,

Marie struggled, pushing him away. "You sound exactly like Sariel the very man who had me killed and my sister framed because he felt threatened by *human children*."

"Sariel was weak." Azrael said, his eyes narrowing from listening to her compare him to the disgraceful angel.

"And so are you."

Azrael slapped her.

Marie held her cheek, staring at him in horror.

"Marie, I'm sorry." He said grabbing her arms tightly. "I would *never* hurt you."

"You just did." She whispered, tears streaming down her face. "But I promise you that it is *not* my cheek that hurts."

"Marie, I love you."

She shook her head, pushing him away. "Maybe you did once and I thought I did too. However, I will not stand here and listen to you judge my sister. I will not let you destroy humanity because of your misguided beliefs. And I certainly will never let you touch me again!"

"Let's stop for a minute and talk about it."

She slapped his cheek. "How does it feel Azrael? Knowing that I'm about to leave you for my sister. The only difference is I'm not having sex with her."

Azrael looked at her, his heart aching for the first time.

Marie stepped around him, opening their door. She didn't hear the final words Azrael said as she gently closed the door behind her. She didn't turn around to see if he was following her, looking for her sister's house.

##

Lathea stared at the wall, studying the details in the wood. She could feel Solas' rough hands as they ran over her flesh, his body pressing against her. They stopped at her stomach as he pressed his lips against her neck.

"You're thinking about something, Lathea."

"I'm fine."

"And now you're lying to me." He said nibbling on her ear. "You and I have been through too much for you to start lying to me. Tell me what's on your mind."

She rolled over, wrapping her leg around his waist. "I thought you lost your magic."

"I did but I don't need magic to know what you're thinking." He said adjusting their position to something more pleasurable. "Is it my face?"

Her cheeks reddened as he pressed into her. "I much prefer this over a bird's head."

"That isn't what I asked you."

She sighed sarcastically. "Yes Solas, your face pleases me."

He smirked, rolling her onto her back. "I'm aware of that."

She punched him in the shoulder wrapping her other leg around his waist. "What do you want me to say, Solas?"

"That you trust me. That you don't want me to leave. To admit that you need me." He said pushing her arms above her head. "But you won't."

She grinned, sitting up, still attached to his body. "Perhaps you know me better than I am willing to give you credit for." She said, stroking his cheek with her hand. "So you want the truth?"

"I already know it." He said, lying down with her on top of him. "But I think you need to hear it more than I do."

She looked into his eyes as she reached to meet his lips. He stopped her, holding her by her neck. She wrapped her hands around his arm though he wasn't hurting her.

"Is it really too much for me to ask you to say three little words?"

"I've never needed anyone before."

"You need your sister."

"I've never loved anyone before."

"You love your sister."

She narrowed her eyes. "That's completely different, Solas. She hasn't spent the last few hours trying—"

Silence fell over them as the sound of Marie's cries flooded their home, the door slamming closed behind her. She sat in the floor of their living room, hugging herself as she cried.

Solas exhaled in frustration as Lathea stood up, throwing on her robe. "We're not done talking about this."

"What more is there to say, Solas?" She said, making her way towards the door. "We're going in circles."

Solas stood on his knees, looking at her with pain in his eyes. "That's because in the thousands of years I've been alive, of the millions of people I've known: angels, demons, humans.... You are the most stubborn woman I've ever met." He was almost desperate to hear her say something, anything at this point. "I just want to hear my wife say—"

"I love you." She said giving him a small smile. "And do put your trousers on."

He sat down, resting his arm on his knee. It was as if she had stolen the air from his lungs.

"Okay."

Lathea tucked a loose piece of hair behind her ear as she made her way down the stairs. Her chest ached both from her conversation with Solas and from seeing her sister in tears. She knelt beside her, wrapping her arms around her as she led her to the sofa.

"What happened, Marie?"

"Azrael came home after sleeping with one of those creatures he created. He's absolutely enamored with them. The worst part is—" Marie said through choked sobs.

Lathea shushed her sister as Solas came down the stairs. He sat on the other side of Marie, rubbing her back.

Lathea stood up, lifting her sister's chin so that she'd look into her eyes. "I'm going for a walk. I want you to stay here tonight with Solas and me when I return. You can teach him to cook. He will need to learn at some point."

"Don't lie to me Lathea." Marie said, wiping at her eyes.

"Now that I'm a demon everyone assumes I'm a liar."

Marie laughed. "You've lied to me before. Not successfully but you've tried."

Lathea knelt before her, staring into her sister's eyes. "I am *not* lying to you. I'm going to walk my happy ass to your house and introduce myself to your husband. I think it's time he knew his sister-in-law."

"Be careful." Marie said taking her hand.

"What's he going to do? Slap me?"

Marie took her hand back at her sister's words.

"*Did he hit you?*"

"I hit back." Marie said quickly, standing up.

Lathea's nostrils flared as she left the house, closing the door firmly behind her.

Solas sighed. "How about those cooking lessons?"

Marie laughed, wiping the tears from her eyes. "I'm afraid that once my sister is done with him I won't have a home to return to."

Solas held his breath for a moment. "If only you knew."

##

Lathea stood at the doorstep of Marie's home, knocking firmly. Her patience was growing thin but she wasn't leaving until she had met Azrael.

He opened the door, staring into her face with disgust. "Did Marie send you?"

Lathea pushed him into his home, closing the door with her foot. "I'm starting to notice a pattern in my own behavior. You see, Azrael, when people disrespect my family, I deal with them. You're a smart man, do you remember what I did to the last man who laid a hand on my sister?"

"You killed him." A woman approached, but Azrael stopped her, pointing at the stairs. "I'll join you in a minute."

The woman looked at Lathea bitterly.

"Go on *pet*. I'm not here for you."

She scoffed but took to the stairs.

"Why do you do that? Insult everyone. Your sister is intelligent and kindhearted. You're a beast though that may be too kind seeing as you're a demon too. Tell me, what was *your* deformity?"

"Horns." She said pointing on her head to where they had been. "But I ripped them out. I couldn't let Marie see me as a demon."

"*Aw, sweet.* This little demon has a heart."

"You must have me confused with my husband. I'm here to kill you. I just wanted to know your face before you breathed your last."

"Your audacious enough to come at me while I'm expecting it?"

"You must really not know me." She said extending her hand.

He took her hand, gripping it firmly. "I suppose not."

"Allow me to introduce myself. I'm Lathea Ares Leighton." She said with a smile before pulling him forward bashing into his forehead with her own. "And no one fucks with my sister."

He laughed, wiping the blood from his head. "She didn't seem to mind it the first time."

Lathea struck out, punching him in the face, the floor extending down, separating them. "What have you done to these people?"

Azrael stepped around, smiling from ear to ear. "I've made them stronger, *better* than the humans you and your sister wish to protect."

"You're creating monsters."

Azrael looked at her, offended by the *demon's* words. "I'm fixing humanity, Thea—"

"*Lathea.*" She said, taking a step back as the floor came down again, closer this time.

"I apologize, Lathea, but you see—" He said holding his hands in the air. "I'm no longer an angel but a God among men."

"No one will worship you."

"My children will and that's all I need. Their faith is the key to restoring my power."

"Then I suppose you find somewhere else to get started." She said, pressing her hand to the wood, setting fire to the house.

##

Marie threw a bucket of water onto the stove, laughing. "It's funny, Solas, of all the books my sister has read none have been cookbooks." She said, opening a window as smoke filled the room. "In fact, none of us require food to survive. So why is it that my sister suddenly has an interest in *food?*"

Solas watched as the smoke escaped through the window. "She's just not quite herself without her soul." He could feel Marie's gaze on him. It was the same look she used to give her sister when she knew she was guilty.

"From what you've told me about your past with my sister I don't see how... *this* happened."

"Must there be an answer for everything, Marie? Can't you allow some things to remain a mystery?"

"I don't want my sister to end up like I have."

He turned to look at her, placing a hand on her shoulder. "You have great things ahead of you. All it takes is for you to look in the right direction."

Lathea slipped in through the door almost unnoticed. She entered the kitchen, paying no mind to the smoke as she threw her hands around her sister.

"What's wrong?"

"He's gone." Lathea said looking at both of them. "But I've no doubt that he will be back."

"How do you know he left?" Marie said, holding her sister's arms.

"You see Marie, I'm starting to notice a pattern in my own behavior."

Marie crossed her arms over her chest. "*Lathea what did you do?*"

"Don't be mad." Lathea said taking small steps away. "But I might have set fire to your house."

"Overlooking the *how* you set the fire I want to address the *why* you set fire to *my house.*" She said doing her best to control the urge to shake her sister. "You couldn't have just punched him?"

"I did that too and it didn't work. His pets can control *things*. I'm not sure what the extent of their power is but she warped the floorboards to strike at me. Wooden things are susceptible to fire. It seemed like a reasonable idea at the time."

Marie took a deep breath. "I can understand you doing so to protect yourself."

"Good because I was hoping you would spend the night regardless."

"I don't see much of a choice now." She said. "What's this about it being a *pattern.*"

"The fire at the palace was my doing too."

Solas stepped in front of Lathea. "In her defense I told her to."

"Terrific. Then Sariel can be anywhere." She said with a sigh. "Sariel is—"

"Dead." Solas said. "How do you know about him?"

"I met him while I was still in Heaven. It's part of the events that led me here."

"Then I am pleased to tell you that I killed him. Otherwise I'd still have a beak."

"And black beady eyes." Lathea chuckled.

Solas looked at her over his shoulder. "Why don't you take Marie to visit your parents' tomorrow?"

Lathea narrowed her eyes. "*You're sleeping on the sofa.*"

Marie looked at her sister. "Tell me you didn't."

Lathea held her sister's hands. "I need you to understand where my head was at the time. I had just escaped Hell after killing so many people. I was angry over what they had done to you, and forced me to do."

"I'm not saying I don't understand or even that I don't approve. I just wish you had given me the opportunity to say goodbye first."

"I promise, next time there's a big decision that you'll be a part of it." She said, giving her sister's hands a squeeze.

"I liked that house, you know. It needed to be redecorated, but overall it was a nice place to call home."

"I'll rebuild it for you one day."

"You can do that?" She said her own abilities limited.

"There are a lot of things I can do now. Not all of them as pleasant." She said, forcing a smile. "So where's my nephew?"

Marie's heart sank in her chest as she sat at the table with her sister. "I suppose there is a lot that we need to catch up on."

The next morning Solas attempted to prepare breakfast for the girls. A few ruined dishes later he had prepared eggs and toast with bacon on the side. He placed both plates down for them, whispering into Lathea's ear as he sat beside her.

"Did you tell her?"

"*We can't be sure. Let it go.*"

He leaned against the back of the chair, watching as Marie took small bites. "Is it that bad?"

"For someone with no experience, it's quite good. I just..."

"Angels don't need food. Does it feel strange to eat?"

"Not really just unnecessary." She said looking at him. "Have you eaten food before?"

"Never touched the stuff."

"That explains a lot about your cooking ability."

Lathea took her sister's plate after clearing her own, quickly consuming what remained. "Well one of us in this house still eats."

Solas coughed words into his hand quietly.

Lathea narrowed her eyes at him. "*Stop. It.*"

Solas stood up, kissing Lathea's cheek. "I'm going to go clear some things from upstairs."

Marie looked up at him. "There are some stores in town that you can trade in. I'd be happy to show you where."

"Thank you, Marie." He said, making his way up the stairs.

Lathea sighed once he had left, looking at her sister as she smiled from ear to ear. "What?"

"He's *perfect* for you. He's just as bad as you are."

Lathea rolled her eyes. "I suppose he will do. I doubt there are many men looking for a six foot, tattooed demon for a wife."

"I'm not six feet tall, Lathea."

"Give or take a few inches." She said with a laugh. "Take him into town. I'll see you tonight."

##

Haven, as many of the locals had come to call the small town began to grow slowly once Azrael had disappeared. He took his creatures, moving to a large town in the southwest. Lathea did not hide her past from their people, aiding in the construction of new buildings for the new residences.

Marie served as the town's healer, taking care of the wounded and the sick. It was unfortunate that not all their residents had fared well in their travels. However, she would not accept their money and instead enjoyed hearing their stories, both the happy and the sad. It helped distract her from Azrael.

Lathea would disappear from time to time, never too long for her sister to notice. She wanted to watch Azrael, to protect her family should he come back. However, in the weeks she spent watching him he never made a move. Instead it appeared that he too was grieving. So Lathea returned home allowing the man to be left alone. She couldn't help but worry in the back of her mind.

Thea had insisted that her sister continue to live with them though she hadn't explained to her why. She had simply told her that it was in her best interests to stay with her family. For Marie it was more than enough of a reason though she always had a suspicion that they were hiding something from her.

"Tell my sister that the food is ready."

"I'm not sure she's hungry."

"It's not for *her* to eat. I want her to give it to the townspeople to show her appreciation. They are keeping her in good health."

The towns people were welcoming of their family and their *conditions*. Those who had rejected them left the town but more always came in their place. Their reputation had begun to spread, their people feeling safe knowing they could hold their own. However, it had also quickly been discovered that Lathea was weak outside of Hell. Without essence from the souls she was losing her power and some days it showed more than others. Though she had removed her horns she could not rip away her title as an archdemon. The town's people shared their life with her in exchange for her assistance as well as protection.

"I'll let her know." Solas said making his way up the stairs.

"Lathea stood bare in front of the mirror staring at her body. Her magic had made her hyper aware of the things around her but also within herself. She could feel her heart beating and count each beat. She could feel every time her lungs filled with air and count the second it took for her to exhale.

"Lathea, are you okay?" Solas said entering their chambers. He placed his hands on her shoulders, kissing her wet skin as he slowly slid them down her body.

"I need you to feel this and tell me if I'm crazy."

He laughed. "You're definitely crazy."

She didn't laugh as she stared at him in the mirror.

He turned her around, looking into her eyes. "I apologize. What's wrong?"

"Just feel this. *Please.*"

She placed his hands on her stomach as she looked in the mirror. She could tell that she had gained weight, her stomach beginning to form a small bump.

"I don't feel anything." He said cupping her face.

She pressed her hands over his, fear in her voice. "*I do.* It's very small but—"

"Are you pregnant?" He whispered.

She nodded. "I can literally feel our child growing inside me." She said, almost trembling. "I don't know how to feel. My sister was always the one that was going to have a husband and a family."

"She has a family and we are part of it. She'll be happy to have little feet running around the house again."

Tears streamed down her face. "What if they have horns? *Or a beak?* Solas what if they look like you!"

He laughed, shushing her. "They will have ten toes and ten fingers and look *exactly* like their mother."

She squeezed his hand. "I needed to hear that. I'm scared that something will go wrong."

He met her lips briefly. "Our children will be *beautiful.*"

"How do you know?"

"Because they will be Nephilim."

"How do you know?"

"Demons are made, Lathea. *Not born.*"

Her heart swelled in her chest as she used her magic to clothe herself in a loose fitting blue dress that stopped just below her knees.

"No puffy sleeves?"

"I hate those dresses. I will never make my children wear them." She said as Solas stopped her.

"You're going to be a great mother, Lathea Leighton."

"Leighton was my parent's names." She said with a groan as she dragged him out the door.

"Here you go again changing your name." Solas said with a sigh, following her down the stairs.

"Is Lee simple enough for you to remember?"

"It's perfect." Marie said, looking at her sister. "I think Lathea's right. It's time for change."

Solas pushed Lathea forward. "*Speaking of change.*"

Marie looked at her sister, dropping her wooden spoon, icing on the end of it. "*Tell me.*"

"It's not a big deal, Marie." Lathea said stepping forward.

"She's pregnant." Solas said watching as Marie's face lit up. "You're going to be an aunt."

"You bitch." Marie laughed, throwing her arms around her sister. "I can't believe you were going to try and hide that from me."

"I just didn't want to upset you."

Marie shook her head. "I'm going to bring Ciel home one day. I promise."

Chapter 17

Azrael lay in his bed, an empty bottle in his hand. A woman lay against his back. Another lay against his front, and several more piled at the end of his bed. He pushed one of the women onto the floor, climbing out of his bed, approaching the window. He held his hand up over his eyes, his head pounding from the multiple bottles of wine.

"Azrael?" The woman said, climbing back into the bed. "Come back to bed."

He glanced at the woman. "Get me another bottle and I might consider it." The woman climbed out of the bed, sluggishly making her way down into the cellar.

It'd been like this for months, maybe years. He had given up on keeping track of time. There was never enough wine in the cellar, enough women in his bed. It wasn't enough to fill the void in his chest from where he had left Marie. He wasn't sure which of them had fallen off the path or where the path was anymore. Everything had become one large blur.

The woman returned, handing him the bottle of wine before pressing against him. He took the bottle, forcing it open with his thumb before pushing her onto the floor.

"Tell me what I can do to please you?"

"Go check on my child." He could remember his son having been born but he couldn't remember how old he was now. Had he spoken his first word or learned to walk? He felt ashamed for having spent such little time with him. Though he was his flesh and blood, he couldn't look at him any differently than he did his experiments.

And so he took another drink of wine.

The woman stood up, pulling a shirt on before leaving to check on his son.

He wasn't even sure if that was his son's mother. He couldn't remember which woman had become pregnant. He had tried impregnating nearly all of them by now. For all he knew he had a bastard child floating around out there.

Azrael lifted the bottle up higher. The wine was beginning to go down more smoothly, the buzzes requiring more wine every night.

"I deserve to be a God." He mumbled, turning around to look at his women.

"You are a God." The women said.

He finished the bottle of wine, approaching one of the women who had spoken where he proceeded to smash the bottle over her head. "Gods don't look like this." He said, pressing his hands to his chest. "I am weak. I am no better than humans." The women wrapped their arms around him but he pushed them away.

"Azrael, let us get another bottle of wine."

"No! I don't want your wine!" He said throwing over the bedside table, empty bottles smashing against the floor. "I don't want your pussy!" He said, staring at the mess that had become his life. It was time for a change.

"You women are disgusting, get a shower, but first clean this mess." He said before dressing himself, leaving the room with his shirt only halfway on.

He made a stop inside his son's room, looking down into the woman's eyes. "Where did his crib go?" He said to the woman as she played with him in the floor.

"Azrael, he's almost five. We made him this bed two years ago."

Azrael pressed a hand to his chest, looking down into his son's face. Five years had passed and he didn't notice them go by. He couldn't even remember them.

Azrael walked over to his son placing his hand on his shoulder. "I'll be home tonight son. Maybe we can... go do something. Just the two of us."

The child smiled widely. "Yes, Father."

Azrael stood, looking down at the woman. "Are you his mother?"

The woman looked offended. "Yes!"

"Calm yourself, Woman. I've had some rough couple days."

She rolled her eyes, speaking under her breath. "*You've had more than a couple.*"

Azrael lifted the woman by her throat, pressing her against the wall. His son watched, studying him.

"Don't let me catch you speaking under your breath again. If you are going to say something, then make sure I can clearly hear you. Otherwise hold your tongue."

"I said nothing." The woman said as she held onto his hand.

"You lie to my face?" He said clutching her throat more tightly.

"I apologize, Fuhrer. It won't happen again."

Azrael dropped the woman, glancing at his son. "One day, you will understand why I do the things I do."

The child nodded as he watched his father leave his room.

Azrael stepped outside, his creatures coming to a stop where they stood. It surprised him to see many of his females with round bellies, the males carrying various objects to and from places. They had begun building without him. A fire was fueled in the pit of his stomach despite the aching in his chest and the pounding in his head.

"Come closer my children." He said, raising his arms.

He felt fortunate that they had not rebelled against him for his absence. He quickly learned that his creatures were logical beings that listened to their animalistic instincts over emotion. Though they had gained much with the rise of their talents they had also been changed even more over the last few years. The corruption in them caused them to develop a taste for blood with the appearance of their talents. He had been able to make an agreement with the local humans in exchange for their blood they offered protection, jobs, homes.... It was a lot to ask of them but so far it had proved beneficial to both races.

Azrael liked the direction the world was going in but quickly realized he needed to fix their blood problem. Humanity again was holding them back.

"Our numbers continue to grow and I am grateful but the land we occupy is too small to keep up with our growing needs. We must take neighboring lands for ourselves, to convince the people of the lands that they are safer among us than against us. Have we not proven ourselves worthy to stand above them?" Azrael spoke, addressing both creature and humans alike. "With our borders expanded we will have space to flourish when summer arrives and the sun is at its hottest. We will have the ability to build cities fitting our needs, to separate our people into districts."

Silence fell among the people at the thought of separation. Azrael walked among his people, placing his hands on the shoulders of men and women of both races.

"Do not fear the idea of separation, my children. I do want people to fear their houses being set aflame or their children drowning. If we separate you by your talents, then you will have a safe place to learn how to control these gifts that I have given you. Those who live among the trees will not have to fear the flames. The flames will not have to fear the water. However, we will remain at one another's side when the need arises."

He returned to his spot at the top of the stairs, looking at the hopeful eyes of his people. "I have spent a lifetime studying the laws of man. Now is the time that I create my own with your interests in mind. We will give birth to a new country that is safe for both humans and Sun Vampires alike!" He said raising his fist, ideas racing through his mind.

Sun Vampires. It was spontaneous, but it worked for him.

The people cheered for a moment before one stepped forward, a woman with a swollen belly. "Fuhrer, what will we call this new country?" She said, her eyes meeting Azrael's.

"Eithne." He said, approaching the woman. "We will name our country Eithne."

He watched as the Sun Vampires separated into five groups. He approached each group choosing one man from each to step forward.

"The five of you will lead your districts for I cannot have my eyes on all of you at once. You will report to me for I am your king and your God."

The men knelt before him. "Thank you, Fuhrer."

"Together we will eliminate the evil forces that are at work in our world. Some of you may suffer and others may die but know that by remaining faithful to me that your sacrifices will not be in vain. It is through you that we may conquer all who oppose me: your king and your God. However, we must prepare before we strike."

The district leader of fire looked up at Azrael. "And where shall we strike first, Fuhrer?"

"Haven. It is there that we will face our greatest threat." The ache in Azrael's chest grew with his answer. Though it pained him greatly, he knew there was no other way. It was time that he set aside his emotions like his children had.

"The twin sisters and the fallen angel? They are no match for our numbers."

Azrael placed his hand on the man's shoulders as they stood. "I agree with you, my son, but we can't underestimate our opponents for they too possess great power. That is why we will wait, expand our walls and our forces before we strike. Tend to the women, we leave tonight for the east."

"East? Don't you think it will be wiser to start North?"

"Perhaps but I hate the cold."

His men dispersed, tending to the women as well as their various duties. The humans approached Azrael, placing their hands on his arms.

"Fuhrer, what will become of us with the separation of the Suns?" Said one of the humans as he held the hand of his wife.

Azrael cupped the face of the man. "Fear not, the separation of my children is for your safety more than theirs. You have the freedom to live in the districts of your choosing. Nothing will change if you uphold your end of our agreement."

"Thank you, Fuhrer, your kindness knows no boundaries."

"Of course. Now if you will excuse me, I must prepare for tonight. Watch over the women while we are away. They are the key to our survival."

The humans nodded before taking their leave.

The mother of Azrael's son approached, now fully dressed in a red silk gown. "So you plan on separating our people. Then what?"

"Then we carry on. We build our country over the years and then train until the moment to strike comes."

"Why not strike now? They will expect you regardless."

"Our army is too small and too inexperienced to successfully win. Preparation is key when fighting angels and demons."

"Of course, Fuhrer." She said, reaching to kiss him.

He turned away, grabbing her wrist. "I will come back to bed but only for a moment."

"I'll bring the wine."

"Leave the wine. I only want my wife."

Azrael watched the sun fall, his women asleep in the bed behind him except the mother of his child. She approached him, straightening his clothes for him.

"So you are going east. What is it you expect to find?"

He took her hands in his, squeezing them firmly but not enough to hurt her. "I expect nothing but regardless of what is waiting for us out there. We will take it."

"And if it is a frozen wasteland or nothing but trees?"

"That is where your talents come in. You have the capability to change this world to whatever fits your needs. I do not worry and neither should you."

"Yes, Fuhrer."

"Watch over my son while I am away."

She grabbed his arm. "You promised him that you would be home tonight."

"He will understand. I do this so that one day he will be able to fill my shoes. I build this country so that he may take over when the time is right. I refuse to rule forever."

"Tomorrow, Azrael. You owe your son at least one day." She said, her eyes narrowing.

He placed a hand on her face. "I will not be here tomorrow nor the day after but upon my return you have my word."

She sighed, accepting his answer.

Azrael could see his men gathering below. "I must leave now. Take care of my son."

"Cassiel." She said.

"What?"

"Your son's name is Cassiel."

Azrael's pace was light as he walked down the city's street, watching the people run from his men. Their houses burned, the smoke painting the evening sky grey.

They had declined his offer to join them.

He did not believe in slavery but he also couldn't leave without this land. It had many good properties and had multiple farms though they too were in flames now. It was disappointing to him for they had to waste the hard work of many good men.

His five generals stood beside him, commanding their men.

"I see you are becoming comfortable with your new positions."

"Yes, Fuhrer." They said in unison.

"I want those people remaining alive herded away from the flames. Create a cage to hold them until we arrive."

One man sank into the ground, another taking into the air as they chased after the humans, the men of the air and earth districts following.

"And what of us, Fuhrer?"

"I want to see this town burn. We will rebuild it later. For now, we send a message."

Two of his other generals broke off, lightning striking the homes from the sky, flames consuming them at an alarming rate.

"Do you smell that?" Azrael said, looking at the remaining general.

"Smoke?"

"No." Azrael said putting his hand on the man's shoulder. "Victory." Azrael said as they reached the outskirts of the town, stone cages built around the humans.

"Push them into one cage. It will be easier to speak with them that way."

The general held his arms out, the multiple cages dragging along the ground before forming one large cage.

"I warned you that I would see your city fall if you declined to join us. I understand your decision but there are things in this world to be afraid of. We seek to protect you."

"You want to use us as a food source." One of the humans said.

"Life requires business. I offer you a service in exchange for another. Perhaps some of you have enough wisdom to see that what I offer is more than reasonable for what I ask. Those of you who have changed your minds, please, step forward."

They watched as some men stepped forward, these men freed from the cage. One man stole away Azrael's attention. He was a burly man covered in ash, an apron draped across his front.

"You, Sir, please come here. I wish to take a closer look at you." The man approached Azrael. "Show me your hands."

The man's hands were covered in burns, cuts, and scars. "What is it you do, Sir?"

"I am a blacksmith. So is my son." He said pointing at the cage where a young boy stayed towards the back of the cage. "Please, save my son and I will forge for your men the strongest armor and weapons."

Azrael placed his hands on the man's arms. "You see, humans! This is how you do business. Offer a service in exchange for another." Azrael looked at his generals, the final two joining them. "What do you think, men? Should we save this good man's son?"

The general of the earth district spoke first. "It depends on the boy. We don't take prisoners."

"Tis true." Azrael said, looking at the blacksmith, letting him go. "Either he joins us on his own or he is buried in the ground with the rest of your town."

The blacksmith approached the cage. "Boy you better get your rear to the front of that cage. You are too young to die."

"But father, these men are monsters!" The boy said.

"I would rather live among monsters than die by their hand. I can't bear the thought of losing my son to these same monsters."

The boy nodded, approaching the front of the cage where others joined him. They were released from the cage, the remaining towns people staying away from the front of the cage. The man kissed his son's head, joining those who had chosen to join the Sun Vampires.

"You betrayed your own kind." The humans yelled from the cage, shouting insults at those who had chosen to leave.

"Do not listen to the men before you. They are ignorant and will only hold you back."

Satisfied with those who joined Azrael turned his back to those who remained, speaking to the general of the earth district. "Crush them and send some of your men to return the humans to Eithne so that they may meet our people. We have still have other cities to visit." Azrael said turning away, four of his generals following.

The earth general raised his hands before bringing them down towards the ground. The cage sank quickly into the earth. The arms of men, women, and children could be seen from the wet dirt, marking their graves.

"That could have been you, Boy." The blacksmith said to his son as they watched the fingers of their arms wiggle in desperation.

Azrael visited many cities, making his way clockwise around their homeland. It surprised him how many humans agreed to his terms, possibly sharing the same view as the blacksmith. Those who refused shared the same fate as the first city. His generals continued to prove their strength, some cities burning, others flushed out. He had never expected his children to display such power, believing it to be limitless until proven otherwise.

Upon his return, Cassiel came running out of their estate. "Father, you've returned!"

Azrael looked down at his boy, patting his hair. The children seemed to show more emotion but with age it gradually faded, instinct taking over.

"Will you be home tonight?"

Azrael looked at his men as he lifted his son into his arms. "Take some time to check on your people. Make sure everyone — human *and* Sun Vampire — is in good health and that spirits are high. I'm sure we will be expecting many births in the coming months. Know that the days ahead will be long but they will ensure a bright future for our people."

"Yes, Fuhrer." His men said before dispersing.

Azrael carried his son into their home, the child's mother watching from the entrance. "What is it we will play first?"

"I want to play Fuhrer, May I."

"And where did you learn that game?" Azrael said with a chuckle as he set the boy down in their living room.

"From the other children at school."

Azrael looked the boy's mother. "You didn't expect me to teach him myself, did you? One of the human women has taken one of your children as her aid and together they educate the children."

"Once they reach fifteen they should be pulled out of the schools. We have to prepare—"

She placed a hand on his shoulder. "I understand, Fuhrer. I will let them know immediately."

He grabbed her wrist. "Thank you. I... appreciate your help."

She smiled, taking her wrist back. "Spend time with your son before you lose the chance. I will come for you tonight. Just the two of us." She said kissing his cheek before taking her leave.

Azrael watched her leave, turning to his son as he ran to the farthest wall. "I'm the Fuhrer."

Azrael chuckled, joining his son. "Yes, one day you will be."

##

Azrael waited until his son's mother had taken him to school before joining his men in the field. Before them the land stretched endlessly with the occasional hill or stone path. He breathed in the fresh air as one of his generals spoke.

"Fuhrer, I was afraid you weren't going to join us."

Azrael put his hand on the man's shoulder. "I wouldn't miss it for the world. How are the people?"

"The humans are adjusting, the blacksmith and his son are preparing their workshop, and our men are building them a forge. They will begin next week."

"Good. If they need anything, bring it to them. Humans have their place and we must show them our appreciation if we expect them to continue to hold up their end of the agreement. This is a partnership between two races."

"As for our people, the women have been delivering children, more than half of them were males. We expect many more births over the coming months."

"Then I suppose we should get to work men. There will be many mouths to feed." Azrael said, his generals behind him, their men in tow.

"What do you see?"

"Land, Fuhrer."

"I see potential." He said, kneeling where he ran his fingers over the blades of grass. "Don't misunderstand me. It is undeniably beautiful but this flat land offers us no protection. Our enemies can just walk right in."

"What do you suggest?"

"Build mountains." Azrael said, laying down a map of the land he had drawn out.

His men lined up raising the earth before them, shaping it as they stretched higher. Azrael was wide eyed as he watched stone and dirt become mountains. His men came to a stop after a moment, catching their breaths.

Azrael approached his general. "I'll leave you and your men to finish. We must move on, build the other defenses. Meet us in the north when you've finished your district.

The man nodded, incapable of words.

"Good then let us continue."

Azrael did not touch wine that night, nor the many nights after it. He wasn't over Marie; he often had multiple women in his bed. However, he was moving on, building their countries defenses and training their men.

After ten years of this his son had been pulled out of school, allowing them to spend more time together in between his training sessions with the generals.

"Father, why did you separate our people?" He asked him one night while pouring over the maps of their lands."

"Our people require structure, Cassiel. Without someone like us in power then disaster will fall over Eithne. Our people are too powerful, like animals freed from their cages but not from their leashes." He looked up from the maps, meeting his son's eyes. "Do you know how many people we have?"

"No, Father."

"Nearly two hundred and three times as many humans."

"There is no mountain here, Father." His son said pointing to a spot on the map.

"That's because it was taken down. We are fortunate to live in a country where we can change the terrain to meet the needs of its people. There can never be an accurate map of Eithne but with that in mind please keep the changes minimal."

"Yes, Father. Wait, what?"

Azrael walked around the table to his son, placing his hands on his shoulders. "I am taking leave for sometime, my son. I don't know when I will be back but you must trust that I will return. Until then I must leave our people to you until I return. Your mother can assist you."

"Father, I am not ready."

"You must have confidence in yourself. You have studied and practiced very hard for this. Learn as much as you can in my absence. One day you will be Fuhrer." Azrael said, making his way towards the door.

"Where are you going, Father?"

"I will see you soon, Son. Do not stay up too late."

Azrael felt bad for leaving his son after telling him his news but he was onto something. Something big. He remembered the rumors in Heaven of the lamb who protected the scrolls. If he could get the scrolls...

He stopped, leaning against the wall in the hallway where he collapsed.

"Azrael!" His son's mother said as she ran to his side, pulling him into her lap.

He couldn't move, couldn't speak. All there was before him was a bright white light. He could see the Elders looking down upon him disapprovingly, Seraphim around him singing praise though not to the Elders like they had so many times in the past. Now they sang praise to him.

"Azrael." The woman cried, her lip trembling.

He stood up, holding his chest as he looked into her eyes. "I am your God."

Chapter 18

"Josephine. Put the sword down." Lathea said as she approached her daughter who swung wildly at a dummy she had created. She had found the sword while out with her father and they had been keeping it a secret from her mother... until now.

"Mother, I can explain." She said backing away.

"Lathea." Solas called to her, another of their daughters, Vasilisa, beside him. She watched her sister curiously, familiar with the situation. It wasn't the first time Josephine had been in trouble for her adventures.

Their last daughter, Alethea, sat with Marie at a table on the patio. She was nose deep in several books, always focusing on her studies. They took a moment to watch, these moments few and far between.

"You know once upon a time I thought raising triplets would be easy because I conquered Hell of all things. Can you imagine my surprise when I learned that I was wrong?" She said, disarming her daughter of the sword. She held it firmly in one hand, her daughter's wrist in the other as she led her back to the house.

"Mother, let me explain." She pleaded, looking at her sisters. "Help me."

"Mother." Vasilisa said, taking her father's hand for support as she spoke. "I think it best that we at least hear her out. Perhaps she had good reason."

"This is not a toy. It's a weapon. Have you ever been cut or stabbed?" Lathea said coming to a stop before her husband, letting go of Josephine.

"No." Josephine said with a pout, kicking the dirt in front of her. "But I want to learn to fight!"

"Your father and I have been in many fights and there is nothing glamorous about it. You should have seen the condition your father was in when we defeated Sariel."

"We?" Solas said with a raised brow. "As far as I recall you set the palace on fire."

"Because my dear husband *asked* me to." She said turning her attention to Josephine. "Sweetie, I'm trying to protect you—"

"Which is why I think it's a good idea to let her train with a sword." Lathea looked at him horrified. "Under our supervision of course." He said giving Vasilisa's hand a squeeze causing her to smile.

"You're serious. My daughter. A swordswoman? I think not." She said with a hand on her hip.

"Lathea, we've talked many times about the situation at hand. Do you expect our children to run when he strikes?"

"Yes, I do." Lathea said, pressing her hand to her chest.

"I don't. We aren't raising them to be cowards."

"We're raising them to survive and sometimes that means running." Lathea's lip trembled as she placed her free hand on Josephine's shoulder. "She's my daughter."

"Lathea *you* never ran from danger. Why would you expect our girls not to do the same?"

Lathea hugged Josephine with her one arm. "If anything were to happen to you I would be devastated."

Josephine smiled, meeting her father's eyes. "But I'm gonna be fine because you'll be watching, right?"

"*Like a hawk.*" Lathea said, handing her daughter the sword.

Josephine took the sword, twirling it as she made her way back to the dummy. Lathea pointed at her as she looked at Solas.

"Do you see what I mean? She's twirling a sword like a baton. You're more experienced with weapons than I am. Will you teach her?"

"Of course I will but she may surprise you."

"She does every day." Lathea said in defeat. "If she's going to fight, I want her to defend herself too. I'm going into town to visit the blacksmith."

Solas placed a hand on her face. "Breathe, Lathea. He's not striking today."

"*You don't know that.*"

Solas forced a smile though he knew she spoke the truth. He joined Josephine, correcting her form, showing her how to strike properly.

Lathea took a deep breath turning to her other daughters, Alethea placing her book down as she spoke. "Mother, are you alright?"

"She worries too much." Marie said, placing her hand over Alethea's, assuring her. "Careful sister, you may develop wrinkles like our mother. Crow's feet." She said putting her hands to her face, using her fingers to mimic wrinkles on her face.

Lathea ignored her sister's comment, turning to meet Vasilisa's eyes. "Will you come with me into town today? I could use an extra set of hands."

"Of course." She said, joining her mother.

Alethea started to speak but Lathea kissed her head. "You have studies with your Aunt. You should stay home."

"I *always* have studies." She said with a pout.

"And you will continue to have studies."

"Vasilisa never has studies. Or Josephine."

"Yes I do." Vasilisa started. "I have to combine them with training just like you."

"*Enough.* You all have studies. *And* training. We teach you girls different things so that you may help one another. You cover each other's weaknesses like your father and I do." Lathea said, looking at her sister. "I'll be back before dark. Do you need anything while I'm gone?"

"Pick up some things for dinner. You know how much Josephine can eat."

##

It never ceased to surprise Lathea the amount of growth their town had gone through over the past fifteen years. The streets were often full of people. These new people had opened shops, a select few gathering in the center of town with their open stands.

They had moved outside of town after the girls were born where they had built a house to fit the six of them comfortably. While they were small Lathea always had to take her sister with her into town to keep the girls under control. Alethea was wary of strangers and would always onto Marie's hand as they walked. Vasilisa would stand between them and Lathea would hold onto Josephine's hand lest she run off.

After the girls were born Marie had suggested returning to town, to give their family space but Lathea insisted she remain. She couldn't stand the thought of her sister living in an empty house alone and with three daughters she needed all the eyes and hands she could get.

"Mother, I've had a question for some time."

"Ask away." She said, knocking on the door of the blacksmith.

"What's a Nephilim? You and father told us when we were small that we were Nephilim but all you said was that it made us 'very special'. I think we've reached an age where we can handle the truth."

"Demons are made from humans. Because your father is an angel and I was once human... well, here you are without horns, feathers, or a tail."

"Not *all* demons have those things according to father."

"You're right because some of us are crazy enough to rip them out."

"Why are we studying and training so much?"

"Because I'm your mother." She said, watching as the door opened, the blacksmith smiling before them.

"And she's a good one at that." He said with a chuckle. "How is your family, Lathea."

"Josephine found a sword."

The blacksmith stroked his beard as he laughed. "I told you, Lathea that she would be a warrior. I have seen those eyes before."

"As have I." Lathea said handing him a piece of parchment with their equipment list on it.

"I would think so. All you need to do is look in a mirror."

Lathea smiled. "Well my husband and I agree that she should be trained with the sword. She will continue to toy with it regardless. May as well make a proper swordswoman out of her."

"I'll make her a sword that she may call her own. On the house."

"You needn't do that."

"Nonsense. You've been coming here for many years. It's the least I can do."

"I can't thank you enough for your assistance. Be sure to tell your son I said hello."

"Me too." Vasilisa said getting on her toes, blushing. "Perhaps he and I could go to the river sometime and catch up. It's been quite a while since I have seen him."

"I think he'd enjoy that, Lisa."

"Thank you, Sir."

"Thank you again." Lathea said putting her hands on her daughter's shoulders, leading them away. "When were you going to tell me that you were fond of a boy?"

"I think you're misreading the situation, Mother. I simply wish to see an old friend."

"You listen to me talk too much, Vasilisa. You're beginning to sound like me." She said as they entered the market, weaving through the various stands. "You know you can tell me anything."

"I also know that you and Father don't keep secrets from one another."

"It's not that we *don't*. It's that was *can't*. He may not have his power any longer but he can read me like a book. As for me, I have my magic. If I think he's lying, then I look in to his head."

"Where's the trust?" Vasilisa laughed.

"I trust your, Father. I just don't like surprises."

"I've noticed what with you reading our minds whenever we plan something for your birthday."

"I'm too old to be celebrating birthdays." She said, beginning to fill her basket with food, paying the woman as she handed the basket to her daughter.

"You're barely in your thirties, Mother! Father is at least one hundred times your age."

"I'm not sure how old your father is." Lathea said curiously. "I never thought to ask though I suppose it has never come up either."

"If the town's people didn't know our family already they would suspect you were my sister." Vasilisa said with a laugh.

"Nonsense, you're all blonde."

"That's another thing I want to talk about. Only your sister is blonde and she's not even supposed to be."

"Your father was blonde before he fell." She said as they approached the butcher. "Chicken or beef?"

"Beef." Vasilisa said pointing at a piece of meat.

"That's lamb. I suppose we could do that for a change but don't tell your sisters." She said, paying for the meat. "When did you become so inquisitive, Vasilisa?"

"I just figured now was as good of a time as any." She said, watching as the butcher wrapped the meat for them. "Josephine would torture Alethea if she knew this was lamb."

They were quiet for a moment, Lathea looking over their baskets. She wanted to make sure she had picked up everything for dinner before making their way home.

Vasilisa looked up at her mother once they were out of town. "Did he really have a raven head when you met him?"

Lathea shivered. She didn't enjoy talking about Hell but only because her only memories of Hell were being imprisoned and Solas eating her eye.

"Yes, beak, feathers and all."

"I'm really glad he doesn't anymore." She said, giving her mother's hand a firm squeeze. "May I ask another question about Father? I've never felt comfortable asking him about this."

"What is it?"

"How did father lose his magic? I'm grateful that someone in our family is proficient with a blade but doesn't he miss it?"

"After defeating Sariel he lost everything but I don't think a single day goes by that he regrets it. After all he has three beautiful girls now. That's the difference between him and Azrael."

"And where is Azrael, Mother?" Vasilisa said coming to a stop, still holding onto her mother's hand. Their house was within their sights.

"I don't know."

"I don't believe that. I know you don't want to worry Aunt Marie but you aren't the kind of person to let a grudge go."

"You are too smart for your own good Don't tell anyone that I've been watching him."

Vasilisa motioned her fingers across her lips like a zipper closing.

"He has taken his creatures into the southwest and created a country he calls Eithne. The most alarming thing is that these creatures can control the world around them, the dirt beneath our feet and even the air that we breathe."

"Is this why you train us? Because you think he will attack."

"Your father and I are very confident he will return and that it will not be with open arms. My sister isn't a fighter and honestly neither is Alethea. Do you remember when she begged Josephine not to kill a spider?"

"Poor spider."

"My point exactly. These people are the reason I'm still sane. They rely on us to protect them and so we shall until our last breaths. Humans are very important. We must keep them safe lest Azrael eliminate them all."

"Have you ever thought of returning to Hell?" Vasilisa said as they began to close the distance between them and their home.

"Not even once." Lathea said confidently, smiling at her daughter.

"Father says they would kill you at first sight if you tried."

Lathea laughed as they opened the door to their home. "I would like to see them try."

Lathea sat at her vanity, combing through her hair as she watched Solas undress behind her. She could hear their girls giggling outside their door as they ran down the hall to one of their chambers. They often acted like she and her sister had as children, sleeping in one of their beds together. They had quickly realized while the girls were young that they needed larger beds to accommodate all three of them.

"Lathea, what's on your mind?" He said, watching her in the mirror as he sat on the edge of their bed.

She placed her brush on the vanity, turning to look at her husband. "Vasilisa is fond of the blacksmith's son."

"So you visited the blacksmith after all. Earlier you seemed very adamant that Josephine not use weapons."

"I can't win every battle." She said, amused. "Vasilisa invited his son to join her sometime by the river. When I questioned her she said she simply wanted to catch up with an 'old friend'."

"She's sounding more like you every day." He said, leaning back on his elbows. "As for their reminiscing of the *old* days they can do it here. *Where I can watch them.*"

Lathea stood, dropping her robe as she straddled her husband's waist, running a finger down his chest. "We're not raising them to be cowards, remember?"

"I meant in battle."

"Not every battle is fought with swords." She said wrapping her arms around his neck. "Our girls are headstrong but intelligent. Vasilisa is a very diplomatic woman. She won't act foolishly."

"*Woman?* She's still a girl."

"Hardly. She's fifteen, Solas. She's not the flat chested little girl we used to see running around naked with her dolls in hand."

Solas pulled her closer. "Don't remind me. I don't want to imagine my daughters as *adults*."

"Oh but I will." She said with a smirk.

"My own wife barely looks—"

"Do not bring me into this conversation. It's not my fault I died at eighteen." She covered his mouth before he could speak again. "My time in Hell has aged me. I don't look like I did before I died. You can't deny that."

He moved her hands from his face. "Give me one reason to allow this boy the time of day."

"He's about her age, Solas. The boy is kind and works very hard. You and I both know that it can't last so allow them some time together."

He breathed through his nose, pulling her closer by her hair. "You're right."

"*Occasionally.*" She whispered into his ear, pushing him onto his back.

##

The following week there was a nervous knock at the door. Solas opened it to find the blacksmith's boy standing on their doorstep. The young boy's legs trembled as he looked up into his face. Vasilisa watched from within their living room, rubbing her hands together nervously.

"Who invited him here?" She asked, staring at her sisters who shook their heads in response.

Lathea stood up, joining her husband at the door. "I'm so glad you could deliver them to us. Take this for the trouble." She said handing the boy a little sack with coins in it. "Come inside. We can get you something to drink while my husband takes the shipment to the back." She said closing the door behind the boy.

Solas looked at her, speechless but leaving through the back door, doing as his wife suggested.

"Hello, Vasilisa." The boy said nervously, looking at Lathea's daughters.

Josephine smirked, looking him over, her mother speaking first. "Alethea, Josephine, why don't you go help your father? I'm pretty sure there are some new weapons."

Josephine jumped up. "New weapons?" She couldn't hold her excitement as she ran through the house, pushing the back door open as she stared at the cart of weapons and armor. "Mother had this ordered?"

Alethea gave Vasilisa's hand a squeeze before following behind her sister, closing the door behind her.

Vasilisa cleared her throat. "Mother?"

Lathea sat on the sofa, pretending to read a book. "Oh no, I am not leaving the two of you alone in here. Your father already disapproves."

Vasilisa smiled, approaching the boy, lifting his hands up. "You've been well, I hope."

"Business is growing what with more people moving into Haven. Not all of them are as kind as your family. Ironic since you're... uhh...."

"Three Nephilim, two angels, and a demon. We've had many laughs about it ourselves." She said, running her thumbs over a burn. "You should be more careful."

"It comes with the job." He said smiling at her worry. "My father gave me the rest of the afternoon off. I thought maybe we could go into town for ice cream."

"That sounds delightful." She said with a blush. "My sister is determined to be a swordswoman."

"I think that's great. Maybe you should learn too."

"You think so?" She said, taking her eyes off his hands though she continued to hold them.

"Someone has to have her back too. Who better than her sister? From the stories I've heard of your mother, it sounds like it's in your blood."

"Perhaps you are right. What do you think, Mother?"

"Oh what the hell, if you want to then we might as well. It's time Josephine learned magic anyway."

She looked at the boy. "Do you fight?"

"A little bit., Ma'am."

"Perhaps you can come spar with us one day."

"I'd like that." He said, looking at Vasilisa. "I mean if you're okay with it."

"Of course." She said, squeezing his hands. "So you said your father gave you the afternoon off? Perhaps you could stay through my studies."

"What studies? According to Alethea you learn nothing." Lathea said with a wink, approaching the door where she opened it. "And it appears I've left the door open. Do close it on your way out."

Vasilisa bit her lip, pulling the boy with her as she left. "Thank you, Mother!"

"It was nice seeing you, Mrs. Lee." The boy stammered, pulling the door closed behind them.

Solas entered the house several minutes later where he looked around. "Where's Vasilisa?"

Lathea rested her head in her hand as she leaned against the arm of the sofa. "It seems I left the door open. *Oops.*" She said patting the sofa beside her. "Come join me."

"If something happens—"

"Nothing will happen. Vasilisa is the first of our girls I would trust with a boy."

"Who is the last?"

"Josephine. It'll take a strong man to tame her heart."

"Sounds like her mother."

"The only reason you had a chance was because I didn't have my soul." She said, throwing her legs over his lap. "Otherwise you'd still be chasing me."

"Nah, I think I'd give up."

"Not a chance."

Solas laughed, leaning forward. He held her legs close with one hand, lifting the sofa cushion with another where he pulled out a book wrapped in black leather. He handed it to her with a smile.

"Does this look familiar?"

"Should it?" Lathea said, taking it from him, running her hands over the cover.

"This was your journal in Hell."

Lathea gasped as she opened it, flipping through the pages. "How did you get this?"

"One of us is still able to go to Hell occasionally."

She flipped through the pages until the handwriting wasn't hers anymore. "I didn't write this." She skimmed the pages, her chest tightening. "Solas, what is this?"

He closed the journal, taking her hands. "I spent a few years filling its remaining pages with many of the things I've seen throughout my lifetime. My favorite part tells of the woman I fell in love with and her journey to become herself again."

"I have no words."

"Then read mine." He said, opening it towards the end. "I also wrote down every spell I've ever known and how to perform them. Drawn every array. All of my knowledge on magic is in this book."

"It's a grimoire."

"Of a sort I suppose." He said closing it again, setting it aside. "You can look at it later."

"Why do this? You can just tell me."

"Because our children will need to know one day too. And their children. There is nothing left of your family's estate to pass down to them. Let this take its place." He wrapped his arms around her. "One of us can still perform magic. Instead of sitting here and explaining everything in detail, you can now look it up yourself. Consider it to be my cheat sheet."

"That's very kind of you to do this, Solas. I love it."

"Hell wasn't all that bad... just mostly. I want you to remember the good things too."

"Name one good thing about Hell."

"Sloth."

"Do you still think about her?"

"All the time. She was a good friend; someone I could trust in the darkness."

Lathea sat up, looking at him. "I wish I could understand how you feel."

"Maybe you will once you read your journal. I have filled every page with every meaningful detail of my life. My favorite ones are about you."

"Of course they are." She said kissing his cheek, lifting the grimoire. "Now move along. I wish to read until Vasilisa returns."

"Josephine is eager to try out her new sword. You should have seen her reaction."

"Write it down."

"You said Nephilim. What is that?" The boy said, watching as Vasilisa ate ice cream for the first time.

"We're half human and half angel. We're not the first but according to my father we have the most potential because our parents are tainted." She paused, ice cream on her lip. "But not in a bad way. You've met them—"

The boy laughed wiping the ice cream from her lip. "How are they tainted? Your parents are really kind though your father scares me a little."

She laughed. "He should. He used to eat eyeballs."

The boy laughed with her, looking into her eyes. "You're serious?"

She nodded taking another bite of ice cream.

"Why?" He said, trying to rub the chills from his arms.

She took his hand. "It has something to do with when he was in Heaven. He doesn't like to talk about it but mother constantly teases him about it."

"Why?" The boy said, stealing a bit from her ice cream.

"I think it's because while in Hell he ate my mother's eye. It grew back but she still gets chills thinking about it."

"When did you learn this?"

"They've been telling us pieces of their history since we were young. Our family doesn't keep secrets what with two parents that can practically read minds."

"I thought your father didn't have magic."

"He doesn't. He just knows my mother well. He's really old."

The boy, held her free hand as they approached the river. "So what do you study?"

She finished the ice cream, taking her hand away to wash them in the river before drying them on her skirt. "Magic!" She said throwing her hands into the air. "Want to see?"

"If that's okay with you." He said sitting on the grass.

"It's really quiet something. Alethea can heal and Josephine can light things on fire."

"And you?"

"A lot more." She said the rocks along the river behind them floating into the air. "Mother wanted to make sure I was adept with magic. Josephine has always been a hands-on kind of person. We used to wrestle all the time as kids. Alethea would cry whenever Josephine got rough with her. She's so tender hearted."

"Yeah I hear you but Lisa... the rocks." He said both amazed and worried.

She smiled, the rocks lowering back into position. "I got telekinesis but we can all cast spells. Mother says we may develop more powers as we grow older but she wants us to practice what we can do now."

"Is that why your mom has all those tattoos?" He said, grabbing her hand, pulling her into the grass with him. "Don't misunderstand, I really like them."

She nodded, covering his mouth with her hands. "You talk a lot."

"I apologize." He said moving her hands off his mouth, holding them firmly in his own. "Let me make up for it."

She blushed as he met her lips briefly.

##

"She's too young to have a... a..." Solas started, sitting at the patio table with Marie.

"A boyfriend?" She said as she held his hands, amused at how torn up he was over his daughter spending the evening with a boy. "My sister is right, Solas. If any of your girls are ready for a boyfriend, it's Vasilisa. Alethea is too tender hearted and shy. Josephine is... well, you know." She said, watching as Josephine struck the dummy, its head falling from its shoulders.

"What if he kisses her?"

"Then she's going to be one happy lady." She said with a laugh. "My first kiss was with a man my father's age on my wedding day. Be grateful your daughter isn't about to be forced into marriage."

"The times have changed, Marie."

"It's only been twenty years."

"And the earth is now occupied by vampires and a demon alongside with humans and angels. Give me some credit, Marie."

She sighed. "The times have most certainly changed."

Solas let go of Marie's hands looking to see Alethea running over to him, the dummy ablaze behind him. Josephine was running around searching for a way to put the dummy out.

"Father, it was an accident—" She started, a slight panic to her voice.

He and Marie shared a laugh. "Go tell you mother. She can put the fire out much faster than I."

"Okay." She said, taking a step back. "Where is she?"

"Probably on the sofa still."

Alethea wasted no time, running into the house. Solas had been right, Lathea had remained on the sofa nose deep in the grimoire. She'd made it a third of the way through, past her own entries and finally getting into Solas' life. It brought tears to her eyes, her cheeks still damp.

"Mother there's a— are you all right?"

She wiped her eyes, closing the book. "Don't worry about me. What's going on?"

"Oh, yes, there's a fire."

"*Josephine.*" Lathea said, standing. "It's time that girl got some real lessons and not from a dummy."

"The dummy is on fire."

"Your Father?"

Alethea gasped, following behind her. "Don't say that, Mother."

Lathea pushed the doors open, Alethea joining her father and Aunt at the patio table.

"You couldn't have handled this?" She said, looking at Solas.

"I had to get you off that sofa somehow." He said with a smile. "You may want to hurry before our lawn gets scorched."

Lathea's brow rose. "Our lawn scorched? Not while I still breathe."

Josephine came to a stop, dropping her sword. "I can explain."

"No. You can't." Lathea said as she approached her daughter, a strong breeze whipping through her hair, nearly knocking Josephine over. The flames flickered for a moment before going out. Lathea poked the dummy watching it crumble before her.

Josephine sighed. "It took me forever to make that thing."

"And only a second to burn it." Lathea said, crossing her arms over her chest. "We've talked about this, Jos."

"I got it, I swear."

"And you had it under control when you burned the drapes last month? Or burned your dinner the month before that? Oh, and the time you—"

"Okay. I get it. You were right." She said putting her hands into the air.

Lathea lived for these moments for they didn't happen often. Their children learned from one another's mistakes for the most part. Mostly Josephine's but that was something she loved about her. She was stubborn, always determined to learn things on her own. She hardly ever asked for help and most of the time she didn't need to. This, however, was not one of those moments.

"Say my favorite words." Lathea said almost giddy.

Josephine hated these moments. "Mother, I need your help. Care to give me a hand?"

Lathea gave her daughter a light squeeze. "Of course I will you stubborn fool. I swear you girls need to take after your father a little more."

"If we do that than one of us might start eating eyeballs." She said, hugging her mother back.

"I should have never told you girls about that." She said, letting go.

"See, you make mistakes too. Now, could I maybe have a new dummy?"

"No." Lathea said, picking up her daughter's sword where she carried it over to the patio for Marie to hold onto. Marie immediately leaned it against the wall behind them, watching her sister curiously.

"No? What do you mean no? What will I train on without one? The ground?" Josephine said kicking at the pile of ash, jumping back when it caught on fire.

"And have you scorch my beautiful lawn? Absolutely not," Lathea said, putting out the fire. "You will train with me."

Josephine looked at her wide-eyed. "I don't think that's a good idea."

"I think it's perfect." Solas said, amused.

"What if I burn you?" Josephine said, concerned.

Lathea joined her daughter in the field. "You couldn't burn me if you tried. Do what feels natural and we'll work from there."

Josephine held her fists up. "Lovely." She said, watching as her mother came at her.

##

"I'll come see you the next time I have a day off." The boy said, stealing one more kiss from Vasilisa as he brought her home.

"That sounds lovely but next time let's talk about your family."

"My family is full of blacksmiths and seamstresses. Yours is far more interesting."

"We're like a retired circus."

"I don't think retired is the right word." He said pointing up above her home, watching as flames shot into the night sky.

She covered her face in embarrassment. "Josephine must have finally allowed mother to train her. I bet she set something on fire again."

The boy laughed, giving her a hug to comfort her. "And this is why we talk about your family."

"Could you imagine if you stayed for dinner one night."

"Maybe he should." Solas said, opening the door. "That is assuming you like my daughter. You do, don't you?"

"Yes, Sir! Very much, Sir!" The boy said, his cheeks turning red as he removed his arm from Vasilisa.

"Good, then I'll speak to your father and have a night for you to come over arranged."

"Thank you very much, Sir!" The boy said, his eyes wide as he stared at Solas.

Vasilisa looked at her father, grateful when her mother pushed him away. "You're late but I'm glad you had a good time."

"Yes, it seems I have missed the 'fireworks'." She turned to the boy. "I'm sorry for my father's behavior. He's protective of all of us."

"I never thought I'd be more scared of an angel than a demon."

"That's because you have yet to see me on my bad side, Son." Lathea said, leaning against the doorframe.

Chapter 19

"Azrael, I can't just walk into Heaven without cause. The terms of my stay on Earth are that I only return if I have something to report. If I were to decide to just waltz in, the cherub would kill me." A Grigori said. "Do you have any idea how easily they can replace me?"

"A lot easier than they can replace me." He said, pulling out a map, circling a large area of land. "The best part of this little arrangement of ours is that you *do* have news."

"What is this Azrael? What are you trying to pull?"

"I offer you a trade, my feathery friend. This..." Azrael said poking at the spot on the map. "Is Eithne. My country. With my people."

The Grigori's eyes widened. "I've heard the rumors."

Azrael leaned back in his chair, putting his feet on the table. "They aren't rumors. I succeeded."

The angel stood up, placing his hands on the table. "What? When?"

"Twenty years ago. Now I have an army that bends to my will." Azrael said, holding his arms out as if the world were in his hands.

"Then why do you want to go to Heaven? Why go back?"

"You let me worry about that." Azrael let the chair's feet fall to the floor, grinning as he met the Grigori's eyes. "I've given you news to deliver."

"I don't like the sound of this Azrael." The angel said pushing the map away. "You're a shady—"

Azrael grabbed the angel by its hair, slamming its face into the table. "I tried to be civil about this, Brother."

The Grigori picked up the map glancing at it though his head remained pressed to the table. "Well you certainly have delivered, Azrael. Let's go."

Azrael let go of the angel's head, wiping his hands on the leg of his trousers. "Don't I always?" He said, walking around the table where he grabbed the angel's shoulder with a firm grip.

"No." The angel said wiggling away from his hand. The world around them became a bright white, a pale stone path appearing beneath their feet. "Been a long time since you've seen this?"

"You could say that." Azrael said, following behind the Grigori.

The cherub stepped forward, blocking the path to the gates. "Halt! Grigori, you aren't welcome here. Turn back now."

"I have news." The Grigori said.

"Not you." The cherub said, its sword pointed at Azrael. "*You.*"

"My news is on this Grigori."

Azrael grinned, meeting the cherub's eyes. "I've been a very bad boy."

The cherub though disgusted by their presence let them pass through the gates. Authority angels approached, dressed in full sets of armor as they escorted them to the large temple that looked over the others. Though it had been twenty years it felt like only yesterday that they had ripped his wings from his back.

The Elders stood as they looked at Azrael. "What is he doing here?"

"I bring news—" The Grigori started.

Azrael approached the angel, snapping his neck. "I thought it was time we had a little chat. Don't you think?"

"What have you done?"

"Oh I have been very busy as of late. I think you've already noticed." He said stepping over the Grigori's corpse as he approached the Elders.

"Seize him." The Elders commanded.

Azrael held his wrists out to the Elders as he got on his knees. "Oh yes! Please, throw the chains on me."

The authorities however did not move. It was as if they had never heard the order.

"What have you done?"

Azrael stood, laughing. "I did what you couldn't. I became a God. Your angels will not arrest me because I am of a higher power than even you or your Seraphim."

"Did you come here to gloat?"

"I wouldn't dream of it. No, I'm here so you can watch me walk out those doors with the scrolls."

"You wouldn't."

Azrael laughed again. "Come on, Gentlemen, I think we know that I will." He said approaching the doors.

"If you are so consumed with power that you have become a God then do not return here ever again, Azrael!" The Elders said, realizing they could not stop him.

"I will do so but in exchange you leave the fate of Humanity in my hands. Your precious Grigori need to mind their own business, no more incidents like we had with Sariel."

"Sariel and his men have been dealt with." Said one of the Elders.

"We cannot allow you to do such a thing." Said another.

"Then I make no promises regarding my return."

The Elders stopped, speaking amongst themselves. "Then let us agree on this. We allow you to control humanity's fate but you must leave at least a third of them alive. We cannot allow humanity to die."

"I will agree to this and in exchange I will visit Heaven no more." He said taking his leave. "Perhaps tonight calls for extra wine and women; to celebrate." He said as he approached what looked like a dead end. He knew the structures of the temples better than that however. They had no dead ends. The angels liked their circles.

Azrael ran his hands over the wall until a symbol appeared in gold, the wall separating. He had a similar path in his old temple that opened to the east wing. Before him sat a small child holding onto a book. On the back of the book were seven seals. The child's head had no hair but instead an old scripture decorated his flesh from his head to toes.

"Hello little lamb." Azrael said, kneeling before the child. It was the one creature that he knew for sure was older than himself and he had been around since the birth of humanity. Even the Elders were younger than him, rebel angels having killed many Elders over the centuries.

The child looked up at Azrael.

"You wouldn't happen to be feeling a bit generous would you? Just hand me the book and save us both the trouble."

The child shook its head, turning away as it continued to hold the book.

Azrael sighed, kneeling behind the child where he covered his mouth and nose with one hand. The child did not struggle, did not scream, just waited. Five minutes seemed like a very long time but eventually the child's eyes closed and Azrael laid him down.

"Perhaps you will finally speak upon waking." Azrael said removing the book from the child.

##

Azrael returned to his home where his son's mother hugged him tightly. "I thought you would never return."

Azrael froze for a moment before patting the woman's back. "This is the most emotion I have seen you display in twenty years."

She let go of him, smiling. "Your son waits for you. He has missed his father."

Azrael held the woman's face, running his thumb along her jaw. "Thank you for all that you have done."

"It does not compare to what you have done for this country and its people."

"My work isn't finished yet."

He didn't have to go far to find his son. He was pouring over a table in the operations room looking over the map of Eithne. He stood when Azrael entered the room, bowing in respect to his father.

"I am grateful for your return. I still have much to learn."

Azrael placed a hand on his son's shoulder. "Rest easy, Soldier. You have more time than you realize to learn the politics." Azrael said placing the book onto the table.

"Has the time come, Father?"

Azrael looked at his son, now a man of twenty years himself. "Yes, the time is almost here."

"Let me help you, Father."

"No. I will do this part alone. I will return when it is time for you to lead our army into war. For now, we send a message."

"A message?"

"We will lose fewer men if we weaken our enemy's forces before attacking them."

His son looked down at the table. "You truly care for these people, don't you?"

Azrael smirked, placing his hand on his son's shoulder. "Between you and me? Yeah. I do. Like you they are my children and I will protect them. So will you one day as well as your children."

"Yes, Father."

Azrael stayed away from Eithne with the book in hand. He worried that he may not be able to control the power once it had been released and would not allow Eithne to know such suffering. If it came to that, he would end the force himself even if it wounded him a great deal.

Azrael set the book aside, drawing the seals into the earth as he spoke. "I have given my people fire to cleanse this world of impurity. I have given them light to pierce the darkness. I have given them earth to protect themselves. I have given them water to bring life. I have given them air to bring them closer to my vision." He stopped staring at the seals in the earth before him. "Together we no longer stand still."

Azrael took a deep breath, opening the first of the seven seals.

It was as if thunder rumbled beneath his feet, a white horse appearing on the first seal he had drawn on the ground. The man that sat on him was also dressed in white, a bow in his hand and a crown on his head.

"You have summoned me but to what purpose?"

"It is time I sent a message. Go west and find the town of Haven."

"What are my orders?"

"Conquer."

Chapter 20

Josephine hit her shield with the hilt of her blade as she stared her sister down across the field. "You learn quick, Sister but I will come out victorious in the end."

Vasilisa smiled as she held her sword. Her other hand remained empty to allow her to use her magic. With her mother's help, she had developed quite the range of magic but preferred to rely on telekinesis for its variety of uses.

"You won't if you continue to stand there, Sister."

Josephine began running at her sister until she heard the thunder, coming to a stop. The sky above them was blue without a cloud in the sky. The two girls put their weapons down looking at one another.

Lathea threw the doors open, looking at her daughters. "Join us in the living room, girls."

"Is it happening, Mother?" Vasilisa said as the two of them approached her.

"I can't be sure." She said, closing the doors behind her girls.

They entered the living room, sitting on opposite sides of Alethea. Marie sat on the sofa opposite them beside Solas reached for Lathea's hand as she entered the room. Lathea tried to give them a comforting smile as she took her husband's hand.

"We have raised you to be aware that this day was coming. I can't even be sure that this is Azrael's doing." Marie flinched at the sound of his name. Solas rubbed her knee with his free hand trying to reassure her.

Lathea continued to address their children. "I want to go on my own to check it out."

"Absolutely not." Solas said, standing.

Lathea put her hand on his shoulder. "It is safest this way. If this is something — anything — I am the most prepared to deal with it. While I am away the five of you need to split up and warn the townspeople. If this turns out to be no more than a storm coming our way then great."

"But you don't think it is." Marie said.

Lathea shook her head. "I will grab a few supplies and head out. I expect the five of you to immediately go warn the townspeople. These people count on us to protect them. Arm yourselves and head out." Lathea left the room, heading upstairs to her chambers where she removed her jewelry, staring into the mirror. "It's been a long time since I've had the opportunity to just let go."

"Try twenty years." Solas said approaching her from behind, his hands on her waist. "I know your plan is wise but in no way, do I approve of it."

Lathea reached behind grabbing his hair, his lips meeting her neck. "I don't seek your approval, Solas. I seek to protect my family and our town's people."

"And I love you for putting others first but you need to worry about yourself once in a while." Solas let go of her, watching as she laughed, changing into her old leather outfit that she had worn while in hell. "You still have that?"

"Obviously." She said lacing her boots up. "And I have been dying to wear it again. I've become rather attached to it."

"Don't tell our kids but I love it when you wear that."

"I know you do." She said kissing him. "I'll be home for dinner. Tell Marie I want beef stew." She said patting his chest before taking her leave.

Vasilisa helped Josephine into her armor before slipping into her own which was considerably lighter. She then approached Alethea helping her into a similar set. Even though her sister wasn't much of a fighter their mother had insisted they each have some form of protection.

They met their father at the bottom of the stairs who wore a heavy set of armor. "I never thought I'd see my daughters dressed for battle."

Marie approached them, opening the door. "We should move with haste. I'll cover the north—"

"No." Josephine spoke up. "You'd be better to cover the center since you aren't wearing armor. If they strike the town then you will be safe. Father can get the south end with the weight of his armor. Not to mention it's closer to home. Alethea will get the west. I've got east, and Vasilisa can get to the north end since she's the fastest of the group."

Marie smiled. "Sounds good. While I'm in the center I'll pick up dinner. Any suggestions?"

"Lathea wants a beef stew tonight." Solas said as he checked to make sure each of his daughter's armor was secured correctly.

"Very well. I will see you all soon." Marie said as the five of them seperated.

Vasilisa hurried to the north side of town using her telekinesis to get through the crowds of people. She was nearly out of breath when she reached the outskirts of the town. She rushed into the blacksmith's shop, clutching her chest.

"Vasilisa?" The blacksmith said, his son bringing her a glass of water.

"You need to leave, now." She said, drinking the water. "Go to the center of town and find shelter."

"I'll grab a few things and then we will leave." His father said, leaving to pack them a bag.

"Lisa, what's going on?" The blacksmith's son said.

She met his lips before stepping away. "I would be much happier to see you if it were under different circumstances."

He blushed for a moment, looking her over. "You're wearing the armor I made."

"I am. In fact, we all are. However, you must leave. Take no longer than five minutes to grab what you need."

"Lisa, where's your family?"

"Doing as I am." She said pushing him playfully. "I have to go. I will see you this weekend as promised."

He approached her, stealing one more kiss before letting her go. "Be safe out there."

"I will do my very best." She said, leaving his shop, running towards her home. The other town's people were right behind her, rushing as they made their way towards the center.

She came to a stop as her eyes fell upon a black horse.

##

Lathea pushed her hair out of her face, an unusually strong wind whipping through the plains. She had two small daggers strapped to her thighs per Solas' request. He had as much faith in her magic as he did any weapon. If it gave him peace of mind, then she was more than happy to have them with her.

She watched as a white horse charged at her, the man sitting atop it meeting her eyes. Once the horse grew near it came to a sudden stop, neighing loudly. It sounded more like thunder than an animal.

"You dare challenge me?" The horseman said his voice hoarse.

"You underestimate me horseman." Lathea said, an array on her arm glowing brightly. "Let us be quick. My sister will be upset if I am late for dinner."

The blue glow of the array died, the horseman drawing his bow quickly. He watched her for a moment before releasing his arrows towards her head. Lathea created a barrier around herself as she drew a dagger, striking the horse. The horse reared, attempting to come down on her. Lathea slipped beneath the horse, drawing her daggers and stabbing it in its stomach.

The horse cried in pain backing away from her, the horseman continuing to shoot her with arrows. She stepped forward, the ground before her rose, curving over her to stop the arrows. However, one arrow plunged into her side as the horseman rode around her, continuing to fire off arrows.

Lathea created a stone dome around her as she pulled the arrow out of her side. The pain was intense but nothing she hadn't experienced before. The array glowed again as she healed her side, fixing the leather of her corset. She threw the arrow down exploding the dome, stone spikes striking in every direction.

While the horseman was distracted trying to protect himself from the spikes Lathea ran at him, drawing her other dagger. She jumped plunging the dagger into the skull of the horse, grabbing the horseman by his robes, yanking him off the horse as it fell. She pressed both her hands to his chest destroying it, separating his body in two. She retrieved both her daggers before returning to the horseman, making sure he was dead.

##

Solas couldn't believe his eyes when he saw the red horse approaching, the man that sat upon it like a soldier dressed in red clothing. Upon his head was a crown of gold, a sword in his hand.

Marie stood beside him, groceries in hand. "Solas—"

"Head inside, Marie. I'm sure Lathea will be ravenous when she returns."

Marie nodded, closing the door behind her.

Solas stood in his path a sword and shield in his hand.

"Step out of my way, little man. I have been sent here by my master to take peace from the earth."

Solas charged at the man striking with his sword. The horse reared back, coming down on Solas who held his shield up, striking with his sword again grazing the man's leg as well as the side of the horse. The man brought his sword down as his horse's feet met the ground. The sword met the shield with a loud sound, Solas stepping back before striking again.

The swordsman laughed, his horse charging at Solas, flames coming from its nostrils. Solas got on one knee, his blood boiling within his veins.

Lathea stopped in the distance, watching for a moment as her husband fought the horse. She wished he had his magic again. The horsemen wouldn't have stood a chance.

She hurried toward him, her arrays glowing as she neared. The horsemen however did not come to a stop.

A gust of air pushed Solas out of the way, a stone spike piercing through the horse, holding them in place. Solas recovered from the hold of the horseman, piercing him with his sword.

"What is going on Solas? I encountered a similar man and horse in the distance."

"The four horsemen have been released. We need to find the girls." Solas said running towards the town, Lathea at his side.

##

Upon the black horse sat a man who looked like a valiant warrior but instead of a sword he held in his hand balances. All the food in the merchant's stores rotted in his presence. The people watched from the safety of their homes including the blacksmith and his son.

"Leave now and you may be spared."

Vasilisa held her sword up. "I'm afraid I cannot. You have already provoked me by depriving our people of food."

"Then I hope whatever waits for you is kinder than this world." He said holding his hand out towards Vasilisa, an intense dehydration falling over her.

"It's a damn shame she'll never have the chance to find out." Josephine shouted, joining her sister though she stood on the opposite end of the horse. She spoke her words quietly, the ground beneath the horse going in flames. The man however absorbed the flames, turning his attention on Josephine.

Vasilisa was relieved when the sensation passed, extending her hand out, trying to hold the man and his horse in place. However, her power wasn't enough.

The horse leapt through the flames, Vasilisa striking at it with her sword as it passed. It charged at Josephine, relying on its strength as it struck at her with its hind legs. Josephine held her shield up though the force of the kick sent her back several feet. She lowered her shield, striking in unison with her sister, their swords piercing through the belly of the horse.

Vasilisa slid beneath the horse while it was distracted, standing up before using her power to pull the swords completely through the animal. She threw a sword to her sister, the two striking down the man.

Lathea ran up to them, wrapping her arms around them while Solas examined the horse and man.

"Well done. Where's Alethea?" Lathea said, a hand on each of her daughter's faces.

"Here!" She said, helping people into one of the buildings before joining her family.

Lathea hugged her daughters with relief for a moment more before stepping away. "Return home immediately and protect your Aunt."

"We want to stay and fight!"

"No." Solas said. "Your mother and I will take care of the final horseman. If he strikes our home—"

Lathea held her hand up as she stared at her children. "I'm not asking. I am giving you orders. Return home immediately."

"Yes, Mother." The girls said before leaving.

Lathea looked at the dead horse. "You said four horsemen. Who is the last?"

"Death." Solas said, holding his shield and sword up. "And I don't imagine we will have to wait much longer." He said trying to defend Lathea as his eyes scanned the land looking for the final horse.

Buildings collapsed, the wood that had supported them forced to rot, people pouring out from them in fear. Some were caught in the rubble. Some were slaughtered while others escaped. Lathea turned, creating a great wind to push the people out of the path of the horseman.

"Solas, distract him. I will return as soon as I am able." She said turning around as a building began to collapse, holding it in place to allow time for the people to escape.

Death did not look like the reaper they had always imagined him to be. Instead he appeared before them as a man with a withered face and cruel eyes. A long silver beard hung from his head, beasts behind him tearing their city apart. He rode a pale green horse, its color no different than a corpse.

With him followed destruction, rust and rot spreading over their town. He carried a sword in his hand, striking at Solas as he passed but did not stop like his brethren.

"Lathea!" Solas said, watching as Death approached her.

She let go of the building, hoping that everyone had escaped. She knew however if she were to sacrifice herself here then more lives would be lost. So, she allowed the building to fall, using the rubble to protect herself from Death's blow.

"You will not leave here." She said, creating a wall of stone before Death.

Solas charged at Death, his sword meeting that of Death's the two locked in a vicious fight as the horse tried to dodge their blows.

Lathea kept her distance trying to hold the horse in place like she had done before with Conquest and War but could not. She watched as Solas took a blow to his armor, watching as the sword pierced him, his sword piercing Death in return. She hurried to his side, her arrays glowing as the horse disintegrated before them. She healed his wounds, trying to remain brave as she looked into his eyes.

The townspeople returned with the sounds of battle becoming silent.

Lathea looked into their eyes expecting hatred and fear but was shocked instead to see gratitude.

"You saved us."

"I'm sorry that I could not act faster." She said looking at the destruction that had fallen over Haven. "Scavenge whatever you can and come to my home. I will prepare shelter." She said helping Solas onto his feet.

They hurried back to their home, the smell of beef stew unable to comfort them as they joined their family in the kitchen. Their daughters had changed out of their armor and were helping Marie prepare dinner.

"Change out of your armor." Marie said. "I'll be done in fifteen minutes."

Lathea smiled making her way upstairs, Solas behind her. She was quick to change, kissing Solas on the cheek before making her way down the stairs. She stepped out into the backyard, Josephine and Vasilisa joining her shortly.

She took a deep breath, approaching the open land, her arrays glowing in the darkness. Simple structures rose from the ground, little cots forming beneath them.

"Create a bonfire in the center." She said, finishing the last of the cots. "The townspeople will be here soon."

"The entire town?" Josephine said, setting fire to the woodpile once her sister finished placing the wood.

"They have no homes, Josephine. Where are they supposed to go? We have enough food and supplies to get them through a few days." She said, joining her girls around the fire. "And now warmth and shelter for them."

"Yes, Mother."

"Let's go eat." She said, guiding her girls inside the house.

The family gathered around the table, Marie placing the stew in the center of the table.

Lathea stared at Solas concerned. "What's on your mind?"

"We need to talk about the situation. I think I have a solution but you won't like what I have to say."

Chapter 21

"You're right." Lathea said having already looked into her husband's mind. "I don't like what you're about to say but do try to explain it to your children."

"So now they're *my* children?" Solas said.

Lathea narrowed her eyes. "*Our* children. Are you happy now?"

"Lathea, stop." Marie said, looking at her sister. "Can't you wait until after dinner?" Marie said as their children began to eat.

"I don't think we can, Sister. This is something we must address now."

Solas took Lathea's hand, giving it a firm squeeze. "I'm doing what is best for my family."

Lathea took her hand back, slamming her fist onto the table. "Azrael is tearing apart our family over his childish and selfish—"

"What is going on?" Marie said, standing up. "Solas, what is this plan of yours?"

He sighed, sympathizing with his wife. "Girls, take your dinner into the living room tonight." The girls glanced at one another before looking into his eyes. "*Please.*"

The girls stood up with their dinner, taking it with them into the living room. Concern fell over them when their mother didn't make a comment. She normally would have told them to make sure they didn't make a mess. Sometimes it was to make sure they kept their voices down. Tonight, she did not care if the girls went wild.

Once Solas was sure the girls would not hear him he spoke, keeping his voice low. "I was once in Heaven — much longer than you were, Marie — and the book containing the seven seals was very well protected. Few knew of its existence but mostly because many who had known had been killed, many by my own hands.

By using the horsemen instead of outright attacking us Azrael is showing us that he isn't willing to risk the safety of his people so easily. Though their numbers are larger, it can't be by much. He is preparing for a fight but he wants to try and wear us down first, no doubt.

We only defeated the four horsemen because Azrael didn't release them all at once. He released one by one issuing them orders. He isn't looking for destruction so much as to clean the slate. He wants to create a new world."

"How would you know?" Marie said. "In all the time I spent with him he never—"

"Because if he wanted this world to be destroyed, we would already be dead. *All of us.*" He took Lathea's hands again, this time she squeezed back. "My wife is the strongest of our group. I believe that wholeheartedly but even she isn't enough to take down his army. We need numbers."

"The humans." Marie said. "But we can't prepare them armor soon enough."

"I understand that." He said. "And that's why Lathea will bestow her power upon them. Give them the strength to fight back. She's read my grimoire. She knows the spells, what to do, and how to do it."

Marie looked at her sister, her face looked distraught. "I take it there are consequences for using these spells."

"Severe but not for Lathea. The humans will suffer and may even die. The spell she will use is to create dolls but it will have a different effect since the humans still have their souls. There's no telling what will happen to them. There's a chance that we create monsters. Azrael may show up here and find that we've done the work for him."

"Then why would you suggest we try such a thing?" Marie said.

Lathea sat closer to her husband, her eyes on her sister. "Because we have no other option, Marie. It could work. It could make them as strong as me. Or we could all die. But if we don't do something then we die anyway."

"Please, tell me, that this is the worst of the news." She said sitting down.

"I'm afraid not." Solas said, watching as steam no longer rose from the stew. "Lathea though powerful cannot perform the ritual in her current state. The soul I placed within her is decaying from her constant use of magic. It can't handle much more."

"Then make her a new one." Marie said, tears welling in her eyes. "I told you to limit your use of magic, sister."

"Marie, it's not that easy. She needs her soul. Her soul has experienced the same corruption that fuels the magic. It's why she can perform this spell. I can't. My soul has never experienced the corruption that hers was forced to undergo."

Marie bit her lip. "So she goes upstairs and takes her soul." She took Solas' hands from her sister. "Please tell me it's that easy."

"None of this is easy, Marie." He said holding her hands tightly. "Your sister must kill me if she wants to take her soul back."

"Why?" Marie said standing up. "It's sitting in a damn box in your chambers!"

"Because I physically can't touch it, Marie. I can't even go near it." Lathea said, standing up. "I made a contract and since it has been fulfilled, my soul belongs to Solas. Why do you think I killed Greed when I was in Hell? Because he owned my soul and I needed it back."

"And the same principle applies here."

"Yes." Solas said, taking both their hands as she sat down.

"Even if I were willing to take my soul back — and I'm not saying that I am — how does that make me any different from Azrael?"

"Azrael knew exactly what he was doing. He has proven his ill will." Solas said, his voice rising, offended she would even ask.

"He experimented on people." Lathea said. "The only difference is I don't know what will happen."

"You're doing it to protect people."

"He believed he was making a better version of the same people we are trying to protect." Marie said. "Maybe you're right Lathea. We are going to his level, but if it saves hundreds of people then isn't it worth it?"

Solas threw his napkin at Marie. "My wife is *not* on his level." He said holding Lathea tightly. "Azrael isn't leaving us much of a choice. We can either lose a hundred, or we can lose everyone. I will not lose my family to this man."

Alethea sat on the sofa watching as her sisters peered into the kitchen from the archway, one on each side. Their eyes were wide as they listened to their conversation.

"We're adults, right?" Josephine whispered, looking at her sister.

"Technically speaking, *yes*, but this is something way above our heads." Vasilisa said.

"They're talking about killing Father, Lisa."

"I understand that, Jos." Vasilisa said before watching her sister storm into the dining room. Alethea took her place on the archway.

"If you don't want to risk the humans then let me step in their place, Mother. We have to do something."

Lathea's eyes widened as she stood up. "*Absolutely not!*" She said, pointing at the living room. "I admire your bravery, Josephine but isn't it bad enough that I may have to lose my husband? I am not risking my daughter's life with him!"

"*Daughters' lives.*" Vasilisa corrected her, joining Josephine. "I agree with her. The angel in our blood may help us." She said, holding her hand out as Alethea joined them. She gave her sister's hand a firm squeeze as they looked at their mother.

"Solas, help me." Lathea pleaded, sitting down when her husband remained silent. "I don't want to do any of this I can't lose my family. *Not again.*"

"But we must do something, Lathea." Solas said, cupping her face. "If we do nothing then not only will you lose me but our daughters and the lives of the town's people."

Lathea cried as she stared in the face of her husband. There was only one other time she had seen fear in his eyes: the day their daughters were born. Only instead of joy accompanying it she could see a never-ending sadness.

"And if our daughters want to do this as a family—"

"Do you hear yourself?" She said. "We're not going camping or taking a trip to the lake for the weekend. You're asking me — *all of you* — to kill my husband and perform a ritual on my daughters that may or may not kill them."

"*Yes.*" Josephine said.

Solas held his hand up. "Girls. Living room. Now."

"But—" Josephine said, looking at her father's face as Vasilisa led them away.

"Are you really asking me to do this?" Lathea said, taking her husband's hands as she looked deeper into his eyes. "I will never see you again if I do. I'm not sure I can live with that."

Solas kissed her hands. "Never again? Don't be ridiculous, Lathea, one day someone will kill you too."

Lathea wanted to laugh at his response but wrapped her arms around his neck instead. "I hope you're right. I don't want to live forever if my family isn't complete."

"You won't live forever so enjoy life while you can. I don't want to see you too soon." He said. "If anyone can do this, it's you."

"That doesn't make it any easier for me."

"I don't expect this to be easy for you but I expect you to follow through with this. You have my grimoire. And soon you will have my soul."

Marie looked outside their window. "The townspeople have arrived."

Lathea held onto Solas' hands as she stood, fighting tears. "I'm going to help them get comfortable for the night. Will you tell our children the decision?"

"I will. Put on a strong face, Lathea. You are the hope these people are searching for." Solas said, letting go of her.

"I wouldn't be so sure of that." She said, a tear slipping from her eye.

Solas wiped it with his thumb, smiling. "Then why are they here? Not every building was destroyed."

Lathea forced a smile before she opened the patio doors, her sister on her heels. "I want to start by apologizing for the losses you all have suffered both in blood and in shelter. My family and I will act with haste to restore your lives to the best of our ability. In the meantime, we are happy to share our home and food with you. We must face these troubling times but together we can overcome them." She paused shocked to see people smiling, few with tears in their eyes.

"You destroyed the threat. That is more than we could have asked for." Said one man.

"If they hadn't come here I'd still have my, Shaun!" Said his wife, her husband holding her back.

The townspeople argued amongst one another until Lathea cleared her throat, projecting her voice. "I understand that some of you will blame us for your loss. Let me be the first to tell you that we aren't responsible for this. However, if you are about to stand before me and accuse us and dare I say it — demean us — then get off my property. I will not allow any of you to treat my family with ill will. If I hear someone speaking out against me then you will be forced to leave. I could have left you to fend for yourselves, to die, but I didn't. You should be grateful for that alone."

She watched as the woman yanked her arm from her husband, leaving the property. "Are you coming with me or not?" She said to him.

"Without Lathea and her family we would be dead. Just like Shaun. I'm not done fighting."

"Then I don't need you either you worthless—"

Lathea put up a wall between the woman and her husband. "Anyone else?" She waited a moment, watching as a few others left. "Good. Then let's get some sleep. Tomorrow will be a long day."

Lathea met with the townspeople individually, her sister covering half of them. They did their best to comfort people and accommodate their needs but there was only so much they could do on short notice.

Once the humans had settled in they returned to their home, her daughters wrapping their arms around their mother.

"You told them?"

Solas nodded. "I think it's time we went to bed, Lathea."

Her daughters let go of her, watching as she disappeared up the stairs with their Father.

"Twenty years isn't enough time with someone. Not when you have forever." Alethea said.

"I think your father has always known that he would have to leave." Marie said, walking the girls to their rooms.

"How is that possible?"

"I don't know and perhaps I never will." Marie said, closing their doors. "Perhaps I don't need to know everything. At some point, you have to accept that some things just are."

"Like how you're responsible for the death of your sister's husband?" The woman's voice said. "Ironic how your sister once killed your husband."

Marie ignored the woman's voice kissing each of her nieces on the forehead.

"I don't think your sister deserves to be happy. She's killed how many people now? Her husband makes ten? Fifteen? *Twenty?*"

"Shut the hell up." Marie said as she made her way to her room. "My sister doesn't deserve the pain she's been forced to endure. She certainly doesn't deserve to lose her family."

"She's a cold-blooded killer. Maybe this will make her accept who she is. And when she does she'll come for you too."

"Lathea would *never* hurt me."

"That depends on if her children live or not." She said. "Maybe she will instead take her own life and leave you *alone*."

Marie came to a stop. She wanted to believe her sister wouldn't take her own life, but she had tried once. What was to stop her from doing it twice? If both her husband and children were to die, what would stop her?

##

Lathea lay in bed with Solas watching the sunrise. She hadn't let go of him since their bodies had fallen onto the sheets. She wanted every kiss, every touch to last longer than the one before. Seeing the sunrise was a painful reminder of the day ahead.

"You're a pessimist, Lathea."

She looked up at him. "That's an awful thing to say on a day like today."

"There are no days like today. This one is special." He said, smiling as he held his wife, memorizing her face.

"It's our last day together, Solas. Even the most special days reach an end."

"You aren't talking about the day, are you?" He said though he already knew the answer. "I love you more than I can express in words, Lathea, but you must understand that neither you nor your sister reach an end."

Her eyes widened as she looked at him. "But last night you said—"

"I know I did and I'm sorry that I lied to you. That was wrong of me. But the truth is I... have reached my end and my journey has been blissful. I have a beautiful wife with three beautiful daughters. A sister-in-law who I know will watch over my family in my absence—"

"Does that make losing your family worth it?"

"Only a pessimist would ask me that." He said kissing her head. "Today is the day you save the world, Lathea."

She buried her head in his chest. "I don't want to save the world. I want to save my family."

"Is there a difference?"

"No. I suppose there isn't."

"You should put your clothes on." Solas said, sitting up, pulling on his underclothes.

Lathea did the same. "You heard them too?"

"They can't sneak in on people who never sleep." He said lying in bed with Lathea again now that they were covered.

Three blonde heads poked around the corner. Lathea was grateful their daughters took something physically from their father.

"Can we come in?" Alethea said, her head on the bottom.

"Of course."

Josephine stopped her sisters. "Are you guys wearing clothes?"

"Yes." Lathea and Solas said in unison.

The girls climbed into the bed with their parents still dressed in their nightclothes. They remained quiet, watching the sunrise with their parents, occasionally looking into the youthful face of their mother. They did not see fear or sadness for she hid it from them well this morning. Instead, she looked at peace though she knew today would be the last she would spend with her husband.

Josephine was first to speak. "Mother?" She said quietly, her head resting against her father, Alethea between their parents, and Vasilisa lying against Lathea. "What were your final days like?"

Lathea pat Vasilisa's hair as she met Josephine's eyes. "I was very afraid until your father appeared in my window in the form of a raven. He gave me hope and though it was taken from me soon after, he never let me fall off my path. Though his methods weren't the kindest he continued to push me forward."

"And I will continue to do so." He said. "I wasn't the same man back then. I was corrupted. After I lost my power and our contract was complete I thought your mother would leave."

"I thought you were going to leave." Lathea said with a laugh.

"Never. I couldn't go a day without looking into those blue eyes." He looked into the equally blue eyes of his daughters. "They're spellbinding."

"Why do you ask, Josephine?" Lathea said. "What's on your mind?"

Josephine balled her fist, Solas placing his hand over her fist. "Because I would be lying if I said I wasn't afraid." She held her father's hand tightly.

Lathea's breath caught in her chest. She had nearly forgotten about the ritual that she was about to put her daughters through. Her mind had been trying to wrap around the fact that Solas was leaving them. She hadn't even thought about how her daughters felt about the situation.

She squeezed Vasilisa. "Everything will work. You're going to be fine." She said though she was sure she was trying to convince herself more than them.

"See, optimism." Solas said. "They're going to be more than fine. They're going to be great. Who knows, maybe you'll be like your mother and stop aging. Though you can expect your Aunt to still joke about you aging."

"Talking about me again?" Marie said as she stood at the door.

"Think we can squeeze one more?" Alethea said.

"Of course we can." Lathea said as they made room for Marie.

Marie laughed, squeezing in behind Vasilisa. They laid in silence for a moment the sun having risen beside them. After some time Vasilisa sat up, climbing out of the bed. Her sisters followed behind her, disappearing out of the room. The sound of feet running down the stairs seemed to echo through the house.

"I wonder what they have planned." Solas said pulling Lathea closer.

Marie sat up when she smelled smoke. "Oh no. They're trying to cook."

Lathea looked at her sister though she continued to hold onto Solas. "Could you—" She started, watching her sister disappear out the room. "Never mind."

Solas laughed, squeezing her tightly. "We need to get out of the bed."

"I don't want to."

"I won't spend my last day in bed even if it is with you, Lathea." He said getting out of the bed, approaching the tub, running a hot bath. "However, if you want to join me..." He said watching as she removed her clothes.

"Way ahead of you." She said pushing him into it, water splashing onto the floor as she met his lips.

Marie wiped the sweat from her brow. "Josephine, stoves are for cooking. Not practicing magic."

"The stove is too slow." She said, crossing her arms over her chest.

"Cooking takes time. Patience."

"Patience? Josephine? I don't think so." Vasilisa said, chopping vegetables. "Why don't you go help Alethea check on the townspeople?"

"I want to help cook."

"And you did. You grabbed the pans." She said with a laugh. "It's the thought that counts."

Josephine groaned, embarrassed as she made her way onto the patio. She watched as people cooked what food they had salvaged from the city sharing it among one another. It tugged at her heart to see them struggling. She wanted to help them but she was so focused on her father, on her sisters, on *today*. She wanted to believe that she would be able to worry about them tomorrow but she couldn't be sure.

The blacksmith's son approached her, his eyes filled with worry. "Josephine have you seen your sister?"

"Which one?" She said with a chuckle, stopping him before he could speak. "She's inside. You should go talk to her."

The boy knocked on the patio door, stepping inside when Vasilisa met his eyes. Her heart sank inside her chest as she met his eyes. She had completely forgotten about him with her world being turned upside down. Now she had to do the same to him.

"I'm so sorry." She said, Marie nudging on her to go. "Can we go for a walk? I need to tell you some things."

"Of course." He said taking her hand as they walked around the property.

Vasilisa did her best to hide her tears as she struggled to tell him about the events that had taken place. Her tears fell as he wrapped his arms around her. Their chests ached as they held one another.

"So you could die from this ritual."

Josephine nodded. "It's the same ritual that made my mother into a demon. She was unconscious when it happened she said. My father told me that demons performed it differently because not all magic is the same. My mother's soul was literally ripped from her chest."

He looked at her. "She would never do that to you."

"She may not have a choice. It depends on what my father wrote in the grimoire." She said as they stopped by the river where they had their first date. "I worry for my father more than myself. I will miss him and I hate that we must lose him. I hate that any of this happened."

"So let's assume this ritual works and we win the battle. What happens then?"

"I don't know. I don't think my mother has thought that far. I don't think she wants to. I certainly don't."

He hugged her tightly. "It's going to work, Lisa. I just hope you don't forget about me with all that power you'll gain."

She cried harder, squeezing his hands. "I'm not losing you. I certainly won't allow myself to change. My sisters and I will still have our souls. I think that's what scares my mother the most. The ritual is meant for the soulless. It's to create dolls."

"Dolls?"

"They're basically demon slaves but really all demons are." He sighed. "Your family is... complicated."

"Can you handle it?" She said.

"I have for the last five years. I think I'll be okay for at least five more."

She laughed, kissing his cheek before they made their way back to her home. "I'll come find you in the morning, okay?"

He kissed her head. "Vasilisa, I doubt it will be that easy."

She looked at him, surprised to hear him say her whole name. "You might be right but I'll try anyway." She said making her way into her home. Her family was gathered at the table like it was a normal day.

"You're late." Solas said with a smile.

"I'm sorry." She said, sitting beside Alethea. "We wanted to make you breakfast."

He held his hand up. "Regardless of what happens today, everything is perfect."

Lathea tried to hide the tears from her eyes behind her food. Solas however, knew her too well and placed his hand over hers. She had to be strong for him and those around her.

##

Lathea couldn't hide her tears as she sat at the river with Solas watching as the sun set before them. He held her tightly wishing she would stop crying. He had spent the day trying to convince her it wasn't the end that this was something good but she couldn't look past the truth before her.

"How are you able to accept death so easily?" She said through her tears, holding onto him.

"Because I've lived for thousands of years, Lathea. If I could think of another way, then I would. I don't want to leave my family, *to leave you* but I refuse to watch you die either. I know it's cruel to put you through this but if it were I in your shoes, I couldn't do it. You're stronger than I am."

"You're a bastard." She laughed through her tears.

"This bastard loves you for this. For everything you do and will continue to do."

"Solas, let's say it works. Let's say everything works in our favor and this battle ends. Haven is still in ruins. There is no food left in our city, no shelter, nothing. There are mouths to feed and I can't fix everything in a day."

"You rebuild. You might have to do things you don't want to do. You might have to take another city by force but I know you. You won't let these people go hungry. They know you will protect them."

"What if I can't?"

Solas pushed her playfully. "Don't be ridiculous. *You can.*"

She stood up, staring at him. "You act like I can deal with everything that is thrown at me. We have to accept that at some point I'm going to be thrown something I can't handle."

He stood up, the night sky beginning to cover them. "Because such a thing doesn't exist. You have four shoulders inside that house to lean on even if one of them isn't mine. You are a leader not a loner. These people are following you because if someone can handle this it's you. That's why you are here, Lathea." He said, his voice rising. "I love you and your sister but she can't do half the things you have done. She will support you but in the end, it is you leading these people. I won't leave this spot until you accept that."

"Then I won't. I'd rather you stand there forever."

"But I can't." He said grabbing her by her arms, resisting the urge to shake her. "I love when you show me weakness but this isn't the time. There is real danger out there and it's on our doorstep." He said, looking up to see many of the townspeople gathered around them.

Lathea wiped her eyes, embarrassed that they were seeing her at her lowest moment. "I'm sorry if we disturbed you." She said, taking Solas' hand. She took a deep breath as he squeezed it hard.

"No one will be sleeping tonight." One man said. "Solas has been a part of this community for a long time. Everyone will be feeling your loss."

Solas' heart ached in his chest. He was leaving more than his family behind. He put his free hand on Lathea's shoulder holding her close.

"It's time, Lathea. You have a very long night ahead of you."

The people created a path allowing them to make their way towards their house. "I stand corrected." Solas said as they made their way to the house. "You have four hundred shoulders to lean on."

"None of them are you."

"They don't have to be." He said as they entered their house. "Girls, go outside."

Their daughter's eyes went wide. "We want to be here!"

"Absolutely not. This is between your mother and I. You can comfort her after this is over but I do not want you to see me like... that."

"You mean dead." Josephine seethed.

"Yes. The last memory of me that you have needs to be of today. We had a great day together."

Josephine hugged him, crying. "I'm sorry, Father."

"Don't be, just listen to your mother more. It will make her life a little easier."

Lathea nudged him. "I can handle it, remember?"

He kissed her head, a tear slipping from his eye as he heard her finally accept his own words. "Your damn right you can."

Marie followed behind their daughters. "I'm right here, call me when it's done and I'll take care of Solas."

"Thank you, Marie." He said. "Please, don't let my girls see."

She nodded. "You have my word."

He hugged her as well as his daughters one last time, kissing their heads. "I will see you again but hopefully not for a very long time."

Lathea took deep breaths with every step as they made their way back to their chambers. She watched as he climbed into the bed, holding her hands as he pulled her in beside him. She wrapped her arms around him, holding him close.

Solas pushed away from her, laying his head in her lap. "If I let you hold me, you will never let me go."

"I can't promise I ever will."

"I don't want you to. I just want you to remember what good will come of this. If you continue to focus on the negative, then you will never be happy again. I can't die knowing that you may never smile again."

She forced a smile, running her fingers through his hair. "I will do my best to continue to smile."

"That's all I ask of you. Our daughters need you to."

She kissed his forehead, Solas squeezing her hands. "Lathea, you have to do this now. If you want I can talk to you the whole time."

"I'd love it if you would do that for me." She said, her hands trembling as she slowly began to drain his essence.

He shared her smile. "Lathea, I never wanted to live forever. It was a catch twenty-two for me. I didn't want to leave you but I also was tired of living. I'm sure it sounds crazy."

"No. I'm sure one day I'll feel the same."

"And I would love to say that on that day my arms will be wide open. I want to say that one day I will be able to have eternity with my wife and children but the truth is that you are meant for greater things. *Marie too.* You will *never* be alone."

"You really believe this isn't the end for us."

"I know it isn't. Despite what I've said in the past, *not everyone reaches an end.*"

She kissed his head again. "I believe you."

"I'm glad you will hold onto my soul forever. I will literally be a part of you."

She laughed through her tears. "It's kind of ironic, really. Your name sounds like soulless. I used to write mean comments in my journal while in hell about it."

"*Very mean comments.* I read them." He said, taking her hands in his as he sat up, meeting her lips. "But you never left so I must have done something right."

"You got me pregnant."

"Like I said, I did something right."

She laughed again, placing one of her hands on his face. "I'm glad Josephine has your sense of humor. I won't have to miss it."

"All of our girls have something from me. They got your eyes and looks."

"They all have your hair." She said, running her fingers through his hair. "Vasilisa and Josephine look like you."

"They can't. They're triplets, Lathea. You just don't want to admit that I figured out how to clone you. Don't expose my secret though."

"Because two of me wasn't enough."

"You and your sister only look alike. Your personalities are like day and night ." He said, his grip on her hand beginning to loosen up. "I need to lay down."

Lathea's lip trembled as she watched him lay against their pillows. He pulled her down to lie against him.

"Don't leave me yet." Lathea said. "I'm not ready for you to go."

Solas kissed her knowing his next words would be his last. "I will love you evermore." He said closing his eyes, his lips still against her skin.

Lathea screamed at the top of her lungs, the pain unbearable as she held her husband's body in her arms. She had never felt so distraught. Her entire body shook with her screams, her tears landing on his chest. She wanted him to move, to hold her, to tell her to stop crying but instead the comfort came from her sister.

"Lathea you have to let go." She said pulling on her sister.

"My husband is dead because of me!" She screamed. "I can't do this, Marie! I thought I could but I can't!"

Marie was able to pry her sister's arms off Solas where she immediately wrapped them around her, squeezing her tightly. Marie forced her sister out of the bed and away from Solas, holding her just as tightly as her sister cried against her chest.

"Your husband is dead because of me. This isn't your fault. If you need someone to blame, then blame me. I can't let you take responsibility for this." She said, the words painful to say but described exactly how she felt.

Lathea struggled to breathe as she stared into her sister's eyes, her voice a whisper. "I would never blame you for this."

"I'm the reason why Azrael's creatures exist."

"No, *you aren't* and even if you had never been involved with him, he would have found another way." Lathea reassured her, hugging her sister. "This still would have happened regardless. So, I will *never* blame you."

Marie cried, holding her sister. "I'm so sorry you had to do this. You don't deserve this." She said crying as hard as her sister.

Lathea's heart was able to feel more at ease seeing her sister share her pain. It had always been easier for her to comfort Marie. She was good at comforting her.

She tried to look at Solas once more but Marie stopped her. "Don't let your last memory of him be on that bed. Let it be with him in your arms."

Lathea took a deep breath. "Okay. Take good care of him."

"You're not the only one with magic, sister." She said wiping her sister's tears. "Don't worry about us. Go see your daughters."

"I'm sorry that your last memory of him has to be this."

"It's a burden I am willing to bear to preserve your memories of him." She said kissing her sister's head. "Go be with your daughters, Sister."

Lathea stood up, using her hand to avoid looking at the bed as she left the room.

Marie stood up approaching Solas, crying silently as she smoothed his hair. "Thank you for your sacrifice." She said as his body was bathed in a white light.

##

Lathea forced a smile as she met the eyes of her daughters, tears falling from their eyes. They wrapped their arms around her holding her as tightly as she had with Marie. She hushed them as they cried. She sat on the floor, wrapping her arms around her daughters. Through them she was able to find the strength to stop her own tears.

"We heard you scream, Mother." Josephine said through choked tears. "We were scared that something had happened."

Lathea took a deep breath, her voice struggling to return to normal. "That's because our lives will no longer be the same. Your father has passed but his soul will be with me forever."

"And yours, right?" Vasilisa said. "You reclaimed yours."

"Not yet. I was worried about our girls."

They smiled through their pain. "Go get your soul, Mother."

Marie came down the stairs with a small wooden chest in her hands. In its wood were iron pieces decorated in ornate designs. On the bottom Solas had etched a message but had never told Lathea about it.

"I have something for each of you." She said setting the box aside, five necklaces in her hand. Each had a different symbol hanging from the chain, a small vial with white ash next to the symbols. "I made these a long time ago when the girls were still small. You girls used to collect the strangest things. At one point Alethea, you brought home handfuls of dirt because I told you to never forget where you came from. I filled these vials with ashes from your father. Again I ask of you to never forget where you came from."

"What did you do with what was remaining?" Alethea said smiling at the memory.

"I have them waiting for you upstairs."

Lathea nodded. "I'll retrieve them when I go for the grimoire." She said taking the box from her sister. She could feel the souls calling to her from inside it.

Marie handed each of them a necklace, placing one around her sister's neck, the last one around her own neck. Lathea hugged her sister, trying to resist her tears again. It became harder once her daughters joined.

"Thank you Marie."

"It's the least I could do." She said turning the chest, forcing a smile. "I need to show you something."

Lathea looked at her daughters. "Go outside, tell the townspeople the news. I will join you soon. The hardest part has yet to come."

The girls did as their mother asked, opening the patio doors to see the townspeople gathered in front of the house.

"We heard the screams." One said.

The daughters joined hands as Vasilisa spoke. "Our father is in a better place now but he will never truly be gone."

"You knew about this chest, right?"

Lathea rubbed her hand over the wood fondly. "Yes. Solas let me choose it. Back then my soul was snuggled comfily in his sock drawer."

"Did you know about this?" She said as she watched her sister read the inscription.

"No." She said with a smile

Lathea, by the time you have found this message I believe you will have learned that I always knew I would be first to leave.

I can't wait to meet our children and I know that when I'm gone you will continue to be the excellent mother I know you will be. So, until the day that I do leave I'm going to leave little secret messages like this for you to find. My words can't express my love for you so I hope my soul can tell you just how much I loved you.

And if it can't know that I tried.

##

Lathea laughed unable to resist the few tears that escaped. "He wrote this when I was still pregnant." She said handing the box to her sister to read. "I'm proud of the man he became."

"Once upon a time I told you he was perfect for you." Marie said.

"Because you said he was just as bad as I am."

"And I was right." Marie said with a laugh, handing the box back to her sister. "But he was also just as *good* as you are."

"Yes, he was." She said looking at the box. "I will wait until you've returned to reclaim my soul. If this is anything like last time, then I will need you."

"I'm going to retrieve the grimoire and ashes from your room. Then I will be here for you."

"Thank you, Marie." She said opening the chest, staring at the blue light of her soul and the green light of Solas' soul.

Lathea took her sister's hand as she returned from upstairs, the grimoire under her arm, the ashes in her hand as she watched her sister stare into the light. "What is it Lathea?"

"His soul is *green*." She said surprised. "I always imagined it to be orange."

"You must remember sister that he was still an angel at heart. After all, look at your children."

Lathea continued to hold her sister's hand as they sat on the sofa. The chest rested before them on the coffee table, Solas' ashes and the grimoire on opposite sides of the chest. Marie's hand trembled though her sister tried to comfort her, lightly squeezing it. She didn't know what to expect, her sister's words tormenting her.

Lathea consumed Solas' soul first, taking deep breaths as it devoured the fake soul that he had given her. Her hand trembled as she reached for her soul, its call growing louder the longer she waited. She swallowed it, the fire returning in her chest as it warred with Solas' soul for control. She screamed, squeezing Marie's hand as she wrapped her arms around her sister. Lathea cried for a moment, the strength of the angel's soul almost too much for her demonic body.

The souls eventually settled, existing in harmony within her. She shivered as she stood, looking around her home as she walked around the living room, her eyes wide.

"Lathea? Can you tell me your daughter's names?" Marie said having heard the stories from Solas long ago.

"Alethea, Josephine, and Vasilisa who are the most beautiful women in the world." Lathea said, looking at her sister with a smile. "I remember *everything* and so much more. Not only do I feel more like myself than I have in years but I feel... wise."

"Wise? I don't understand." Marie said, joining her sister.

"I don't know how to explain it to you. I have all my memories and his. I can see the fierce battle that took place in Heaven. I can see Azrael's corruption long before we were born. I can see *everything*. Most importantly my power is different. I have my husband's power but it's *vast*. I don't know where it ends. I don't understand why he never showed me this gift of his?"

"Perhaps because he understood what it could do." She said with a smile. "He once told me it could destroy-"

"But it can also *rebuild*." Lathea said. "And that is what we will do with it." Lathea took her sister's hand as they made their way towards the patio doors. "Marie, I feel something else but it's not from me or Solas. I can't explain it."

Marie shook her head, her hand on the patio doors. "We have all the time in the world to find out." She said pushing the doors open.

Lathea's daughters stood to the side. The townspeople still gathered around their house. Many shared looks of concern while others were in tears. Some had even left unable to bear the fact that she had killed her own husband. Marie joined her nieces, holding them close to comfort them.

Lathea took a deep breath, breathing easier with her soul returned. She looked over the faces of their people knowing that the hardest thing had yet to come: the ritual.

She spoke confidently, hiding her fear well. "Tonight has felt longer than any other night I could compare it to. My time in Hell felt like one long day and even then, it does not compare to tonight.

I have lost my partner, my husband, the father of my children, and the man I had once hoped to spend eternity with. Many of you lost a friend. Tonight, we all grieve but we may not have long to do so."

A man stepped forward holding his wife's hand, tears falling from her eyes. "I'm sorry for your loss, Lathea, but we must know what happens next. Does the threat remain?"

Lathea nodded slowly. "I'm afraid it does and it may be closer than we know. That is why tonight is not yet over. My husband gave his life so that I may reclaim my soul. By doing so I have the strength necessary to perform a ritual known only to the worthiest of sinners. Knowledge passed onto me by my husband. My daughters have volunteered themselves for this ritual."

She wasn't surprised to see eyes widen, many speaking amongst themselves about the decision.

"Are you okay with that as their mother?" Said one woman. "I can't imagine it's easy for you."

"My husband told us last night that he believed that this was best. I will continue to put my faith in him though he no longer walks beside me."

"Is there anything we can do?"

"There is nothing I can ask of you other than your continued support. Like my daughters, I too am afraid."

The woman approached Lathea and though she was timeworn and frail she held onto Lathea's hands. "You saved my family and so I will pray for yours. Godspeed, Lathea."

Lathea cupped the woman's face, kissing her forehead. "I would have done more if I had been able."

The woman pressed her hands to Lathea's face. "You are but one woman trying to protect a thousand more. You carry a burden that most cannot. You must remember to breathe and accept that you have done all that you can. I promise you that regardless of the outcome it will be enough. The people of Haven are with you." The woman smiled before returning to her family.

Lathea stood, looking at the faces of the townspeople realizing that the woman was not far off. She had never realized just how large their small town had become despite those who had left. She smiled at them before joining her daughters.

"Are you ready for this?"

"No but we have a duty to protect these people." Josephine said as she led her sisters beside her mother.

"Yes, we do." Lathea said, placing her hand on her daughter's shoulder. "We're going to do this by the river so that we are a safe distance away from the people. I want them to try and rest. Do we have enough beds?"

"Barely but the people have managed. There have been a few groups of people who joined us over the last day." Alethea said. "Azrael has been attacking many cities over the past few years. Many abandoned their homes before Azrael could attack. When they saw the destruction of Haven they believed he had come for us and eagerly joined our numbers to fight back."

"I'm pleased to hear that there are survivors."

"According to them many in his army are not experienced. Some are as young as fifteen."

"He's sending children to their deaths." Lathea said stopping before the river. "I suppose I should get started."

"We." Vasilisa said. "We should get started."

"Thank you." Lathea said looking at her daughters. "I want to get this over with as soon as possible. I know you girls will do great."

Marie handed her the grimoire, holding onto the large bowl that held Solas' ashes. "You may need this."

Lathea opened the book flipping through it to the last couple pages. She skimmed the pages until she found the ritual that spanned over multiple pages. She flipped over pages until she came across a recipe, her eyes on Marie.

"Can you prepare this while I draw the array?" She said flipping the page to the recipe handing the book back to her sister. In the ground beside her daughters a copy of the array formed, words within it though not of a language known by man.

Marie skimmed it, nodding. "How much do you want?"

"As large of a batch as you can manage. My daughters have our height."

Marie laughed. "I'll see you soon then."

"What can we do to help?" Alethea said.

"Draw the words as I go." Lathea said standing in the center of where the array would be the circle forming in the earth around her. It was large enough to fit a legion of men. She didn't understand why Solas' instructions asked her to make a large array but she trusted his judgment.

"Words?"

Lathea stopped approaching the miniature version she had made. "These are words though I only understand some of them. It's in your father's memories. I can't make sense of them. It's a dead language but it still holds prominence."

"What do the words mean?"

"I can only make out a few like flesh and blood and darkness. Then there others like this one that mean birth and light." She said tapping on the words as she spoke. "They're coming to me in bursts. I think I'll be able to understand the language more fluently soon."

Lathea returned to her place drawing the array by hand. She wanted to save her magic to perform the ritual. Her daughters stood near her writing in the symbols along the way.

It was beautiful though intimidating. None of the arrays on her arm were as complex as the one she was creating. It was a large circle with seven inner rings each with their own symbols and words. In the center of the array three circles overlaid with one another, symbols connected to their lines with one large symbol in the center of them. Each circle had a different kind of meaning and pattern though she could barely tell what they meant. On the outer ring of the array were three large circles connected to the smaller circles. Each of the large circles had a circle within them filled in with dirt. Symbols decorated around the outside of these circles. Finally, a variety of smaller thin circles appeared around the middle ring.

Marie returned with a basin placing it beside the array. "That's quite the circle you have there."

Lathea smiled. "Let me see the grimoire." She said as Marie handed it to her. She flipped back to the first page to find a list of notes left by Solas. Many of them were warnings but at the end he clearly stated that he hoped she would never have to use the array. She sighed realizing that he truly believed there was no other option.

"There's one more thing to do." She said flipping to the next page where over the two pages before her he had drawn a human body profile from the front, the back, and both sides. On these drawings of a human he had drawn symbols that covered from head to toe. Below the drawings were notes.

"I need you to remove your clothes."

The girls leaned forward looking at the images in the grimoire. They then looked at one another before meeting their mother's eyes.

"Oh please. I gave birth to you. I am well aware of what you girls look like."

Vasilisa was first to remove her clothing though she tried to hide behind her hands, her sisters doing the same. Lathea dipped two fingers into the basin beginning to paint the symbols onto her daughters. The mixture was pale in color made from the ashes of their father.

"What are these symbols for?"

"Your father modified the ritual to include this as a last resort to protect those inside the array. He never wanted things to come to this but wanted to prepare us if they did."

"Father holds so many mysteries."

Lathea turned her daughter continuing to paint the symbols down her legs. "Yes, he does and I look forward to learning more about him for the rest of my life."

By the time Lathea had finished painting the symbols the townspeople had migrated down to the river and circled the array. In the beginning, only a handful were on their knees, praying as they watched Lathea prepare her daughters. By the time Lathea looked up she could see nearly everyone in prayer. Their presence comforted her but it did not ease her fear. If even one word or symbol was out of place it could mean the end for them all.

She lifted the grimoire into her hands flipping through the pages. "There must be something missing. I... I don't know what to say or what to do—"

Marie took the grimoire from her looking over the pages before closing it. "Lathea, it says that you will know. We've done everything right."

Lathea looked at the grimoire for a moment before her eyes fell on her daughters and then the townspeople around them. The timeworn woman approached Lathea taking her hands.

"How old are you Lathea?" The woman said.

"I'm thirty-eight." She said though she didn't look a day above eighteen.

"Nine. You're thirty-nine." Marie reminded her. "Our birthday was a few weeks ago."

Lathea was amused that her sister had to correct her. "Thirty-nine."

"You are young but you have a heart older than my own. You worry though you have no reason to do so. Every soul before you has faith in you, prays to you. So, have faith in yourself, child." She said kissing her hands.

"Thank you." Lathea said, watching as the woman returned to her family. "Marie—"

"Stop it, Lathea." Marie said hugging her sister. "You can do this because you have to. You've always succeeded in these situations." She said before joining the timeworn woman who held her hand as she prayed.

Lathea turned to her daughters taking a deep breath, sharing their smile. "I am so proud of you for doing this. No matter what happens I want you to know that."

Her daughters nodded, linking their hands together.

Lathea approached the array though she did not stand inside it. The arrays that decorated her arm began to glow activating the larger array. The symbols on her daughter's bodies went from white to blue glowing with the array.

She wasn't sure where the words she spoke came from or how she knew to speak them. Perhaps it was another part of Solas' soul that she had yet to understand. Still she continued to speak them, a breeze picking up around them sending chills over her daughter's skin.

The townspeople remained on their knees, continuing their prayer as they watched Lathea. The breeze picked up becoming a strong wind that surrounded the array. Lathea watched as her girls looked at the faces of the townspeople and their aunt seeking their strength unable to resist their fear.

Pain struck them bringing them to their knees. They let go of one another's hands pressing them to the ground instead watching as their blood left their bodies painting the lines of the array red. It scared them until that fear became weakness. They no longer had the strength to hold their bodies upright, laying down in the grass as their blood flowed through the array around them.

Lathea's chanting came to a stop., tears streaming down her face as she watched her daughters lay still before her. "No!" She said, screaming as she fell to her knees. She reached for her daughters unable to cross the array to them.

The townspeople turned their attention to Lathea, a white light consuming her. She could no longer see the people she was trying to protect nor her sister. Worst of all she couldn't see her daughters or hear their cries.

She could only see Solas.

She ran to him, wrapping her arms around him. "*I failed you, I'm so sorry.*"

He laughed, meeting her lips. "You're wrong, Lathea. I couldn't be more proud of you." He said pushing her away. "My magic runs through your veins and the faith of the people of Haven have caused you to transcend. I told you that you were meant for something greater. *This* is it."

She cried, holding desperately onto his hands. "I don't want to leave you."

"You don't have a choice. Your people need you."

She wrapped her arms around him again. "I can't stop crying, Solas." She said, burying her head into his chest. "Angels and demons don't get an afterlife."

Solas laughed, looking into her eyes. "And neither do Gods."

"What are you talking about?"

"I know you could feel their faith. It is that faith that creates Gods. Not the other way around." He met her lips before stepping away. "I may never get to see my wife again but I know that she will be watching over the world."

"I don't want this! *I want you!*" She pleaded as he let go of her. "*Solas!*" She cried, reaching for him.

"Lathea." He said calmly, stepping away. "You exist to protect people, to give them strength. If for no other reason you are preparing our daughters to deal with the future. I love you but there is no place for you in the afterlife. There never will be. Not for you and not for your sister."

Lathea reached for him but suddenly before her eyes she watched as the array slowly turned from red to black before the blood of her daughters returned to their bodies.

Marie knelt beside her sister, holding her tightly believing that she too had died. Lathea pressed her hands to her sister's arms as she cried. She screamed at her daughters, begging them to move, to stand up.

Marie held onto Lathea tighter, relieved to hear her sister's voice. Her relief was quickly replaced by fear as they stared at the bodies of her daughters.

Still they did not move.

The wind settled, the air around them still. Lathea pushed her sister away, crawling to her daughters though her body was weak from dread. She held her daughters close as she cried. Marie sat beside her, holding onto the hands of her nieces.

"Lathea, you have to stop."

Marie looked at the bodies of her nieces gathering her strength to pull Lathea away. She struggled, holding onto the bodies of her daughters with what little strength she could muster. Marie pulled her away from the array again, her sister's body almost limp in her arms as they cried.

"I can't lose them too." She said crying as she pushed her sister away. "Have I not suffered enough?" She screamed at the sky, her eyes clouded from her tears.

Marie pulled her sister into her arms, trying to avoid her eyes falling onto the bodies of her children. She could barely see them herself as she struggled to comfort her sister.

The townspeople lowered their hands onto the ground, many leaning forward to bow, their heads on their hands as they prayed that Lathea's daughters would stand again. Some like the frail woman joined Lathea, placing their hands on her as she cried, trying to soothe her pain.

That was when something unimaginable happened; Marie wiped the tears from her eyes to make sure they did not deceive her.

Josephine was the first to sit up.

"*Lathea.*" Marie said, wiping the tears from her sister's eyes.

Lathea looked at her daughter, stumbling to her feet as she ran to her side, wrapping her arms around her as they collapsed onto the ground. She kissed Josephine's hair and face, her eyes aching from her tears. She turned around when she felt a hand grab her shoulder.

Vasilisa sat up next, wrapping her arms around her mother's neck for support. Her body felt tired, changed, but strong.

Lathea pulled them both her daughters close to her chest as she cried into their hair. "Please let Alethea be okay. *I can't lose my daughters.*" She begged into their hair.

It was several long minutes before Alethea sat up. Lathea wished she had a third arm as she struggled to squeeze all her daughters close.

"Mother, you're hurting me." Alethea said finding herself being squished by her sisters.

"*I don't care.*" She laughed, letting them go as she placed her hands and head on their faces. "As long as you're alive."

Lathea took several deep breaths, wiping the tears from her eyes. Her daughters smiled, assuring her that they were fine.

Though the symbols she had painted on them were no longer there she couldn't accept that her daughters were unchanged. She looked them over, taking their hands in hers, looking at the underside where she could see their veins. Lathea ran her fingers over their necks and wrists, her daughters' veins now silver in color.

"How do you feel?" Lathea said, concerned as she looked at them.

"I feel tired but I'm glad it's over." Vasilisa said, Alethea nodding beside her. "It was frightening."

"Never. Again." Josephine said, breathing through her nose.

"Never again, I promise." Lathea said, before kissing each of their heads before sending them over to Marie.

"I'm going to take them inside and let them rest. I'll monitor them and let you know if anything happens." Marie said putting her arms around them.

"Thank you." Lathea said kissing her sister's head.

"I think the townspeople have something to say. We will talk later. I want to ask you about that white light."

"Later then." Lathea said watching as her sister led her children away before turning to look at the townspeople as they continued to bow to her. She watched as one by one many of the townspeople stood up, their fists over their hearts as they looked at her. "Allow us to undergo the ritual."

She looked at the many faces both men and women as they offered their lives to attempt the ritual.

"Absolutely not. You saw what it did to my daughters. You could die."

"We cannot allow you to fight alone." One man said stepping into the array before he took a knee. Others soon joined him, the array nearly impossible to see beneath them.

"I can't promise any of you will survive." She said approaching them, the bowl in one hand as she marked their foreheads and arms. It was the only amount of protection she could offer them.

"Then we give our lives to the Goddess."

Lathea froze in place, looking into the eyes of the last man as she marked his forehead. "I'm... you shouldn't call me... what I'm trying to say is—" Lathea looked down at her dress noticing it had become white. "Thank you, *all of you.*"

She returned to the other townspeople, taking their hands as the arrays on her arm glowed once more. She spoke the words again watching as the larger array glowed as well as the symbols on the townspeople. The blue glow seemed to overpower the darkness around them, the townspeople outside of the array kneeling to pray again.

Lathea returned to her sister once the townspeople returned to their beds to try and rest. She was relieved to see her daughters sleeping soundly in their beds. Marie smirked, her eyes on her sister as she sat beside her.

"You're a Goddess now."

"I don't feel any different."

"Well you're practically glowing. Kind of like when you were pregnant but a bit brighter and no belly."

Lathea laughed as her sister wrapped her arms around her, the two watching the sunrise until they heard her daughters screaming.

Lathea ran upstairs where her daughters stood in the hallway with burns covering their faces and arms.

"What happened?" She said looking at her daughters.

"I don't know. I woke up and the sunlight was burning me." They said stammering over one another.

"Is it because of the ritual?" Marie said closing the curtains to help block the light. "It would make sense that there are side effects to it."

Lathea smiled, patting their hair. "Then I will keep you out of the sunlight until it subsides. Why don't the three of you stay in Vasilisa's old room? There are no windows and plenty of books. I'll work on covering your windows while you sleep." She said healing their burns. Her daughters nodded making their way to Vasilisa's chambers.

Lathea made her way down the stairs, the townspeople entering her home wrapped in blankets to protect them from the sunlight. Many were covered in burns, some with exposed muscle. Those in the center removed their blankets allowing Marie and Lathea to use them to cover the windows. They pinned up several blankets over each window to make sure sunlight didn't get in.

Thea lit candles around the home while Marie tended to the wounded. Thea was grateful she had built such a large home for the family but even despite its size the rooms still felt cramped.

"I apologize for the side effects." Lathea said. "I will do my very best to accommodate you until it subsides. My daughters too are feeling these same effects."

That night the house emptied, the townspeople as well as Lathea's daughters developing the same hunger for blood that Azrael's creatures had developed. Most of the townspeople who'd remained out of the ritual were happy to assist with their new diet. Lathea couldn't help the guilt that seized her as she watched her daughters biting into innocent people.

"Lathea." Marie said, taking her hand. "You have done the very best that you can."

"You sound like the wise woman." She said, lacing their fingers together. "I can't help but feel that I did something wrong."

"Demons are corrupted people, right?"

"Yes."

"Then this ritual has corrupted their souls. You did nothing wrong. It's just the way the magic is."

"I wish we never had to resort to such dark magic." She said, letting go of her sister. "I should go. I need to make sure my... people are all right."

"Still feels strange to think of yourself as a Goddess?"

"Yes." She said, crossing her arms over her chest watching the people interact with one another under the protection of the night. "I hear Azrael has named his creatures the Sun Vampires."

"I suppose what with the side effects it would be only natural to call your men and women the Moon Vampires." Marie said smiling from ear to ear.

Lathea wanted to return her smile but could not get past her guilt. "Once they are finished I want you to take those unaffected by the ritual far away from Haven. I will send Alethea to accompany you."

"Don't you need her when Azrael attacks?"

Lathea shook her head. "She's not a fighter. I don't want her to be a part of a battle that she can't fight."

"Then I will take good care of her as we travel."

"I know you will. You're going to have many people accompanying you. It will be good to have the extra set of hands." She said. "That and I will be able to find you a lot easier."

"What do you mean?"

"I can't explain it but I know where everyone is right now. Josephine is in the back, Vasilisa is over to the right and Alethea is over to the left. I can also tell you the name of every person that was in that circle and where they are right now. It's like I can see through all their eyes but at the same time I do not feel burdened by it. It explains why the archdemons were always able to call their dolls on a whim, how Solas could always find me."

Marie took her sister's hand. "I'm proud of you. I know these events have been hard on you."

Lathea finally smiled. "It was but there is still one more challenge to face."

It was several hours before the Moon Vampires finished eating, many of them returning to the house. Lathea's daughters stayed beside her counting heads as they returned.

"There's just over one hundred of us. Do you think we have a chance?" Vasilisa said as the last person entered the house.

"I have to believe that we do." Lathea said watching as the sun rose before them into a grey sky, thunder rumbling close by. "And if we're lucky it will rain."

Chapter 22

Lathea watched as Marie led away the remaining humans, Alethea at her side. The Moon Vampires stood behind her, watching as their loved ones disappeared into the distance with little more than the clothes on their backs. Josephine and Vasilisa were dressed in their armor, thick clouds protecting them from the evening light. The thunder was growing nearer and more frequent.

Lathea turned to her people. "There is nothing I can say now that I haven't already said. Know that I am at your side on the battlefield and that your safety matters more to me than the outcome of this fight."

"We can't lose against Azrael." One of her men said.

"I will do whatever I deem necessary. There is no strategy here. We are entering this battle with one eye closed." She said, her voice strong despite her burden. "I know the Sun Vampires possess power and I know they've had many years to train with this power. However, you are stronger and faster. Use that to your advantage whether you are causing our enemies to fall or falling back. Do not throw your lives away senselessly."

"You are considering the possibility of a retreat?"

"I am considering all possible outcomes of this battle. I understand that it's unlikely that we will all walk away from this. If we do not win here today, then at the least Azrael knows we are fighting back. We can prepare and strike again and when we do we will be victorious."

Josephine and Vasilisa pressed their fists to their chests, their men doing the same as they met Lathea's eyes.

The thunder continued to call to them.

"It's time." Lathea said, making her way towards the source of the thunder.

They crossed the field beyond Haven, lightning in the distance striking repeatedly in the same place. Lathea's chest tightened as she saw the Sun Vampires. She was surprised to see that their numbers were twice of their own, many of his men — no women stood in his army — younger than her own children. One of them specifically caught her attention, a man about the same age as her own daughters. He stood next to Azrael and looked the spitting image of him.

"He has a son." She said though they were still far away.

"Will you trade words with him, Mother?" Vasilisa said.

"You don't always have to speak to convey your words. Despite my words to our people, we are only here to buy your sister and Aunt the time they need to escape."

"Mother, they pose no threat." Josephine said confidently.

"I might have shared your feelings if there were twenty of them but they have had time to prepare. You need to fight expecting to lose but trying your hardest to win. Victory is sweeter when you don't expect it."

Josephine turned to their men. "We strike first. Do not underestimate the enemy."

Their people pressed their fists to their chests again, the sound like that of a drum. They closed the distance between them and Azrael, his Sun Vampires manipulating the earth around them causing it to rise and fall.

"Lathea, I was beginning to wonder if you heard my call." Azrael said approaching her, his men creating stairs with each step he took. "Where is your husband? I thought he was trained to use a shield and a sword or is he a coward?"

Lathea held her tongue waiting until he was in arms reach to strike at him, her arrays almost blinding, the white light a sign to her people to strike.

Azrael's son stepped forward, summoning fire as he struck Lathea back. Her men ran past her like a blur, striking the Sun Vampires. A small group of Sun Vampires took to the air using strong winds to try and hold them back. Moon Vampires immediately took down a handful of them by hurling their weapons at them, piercing their chests and abdomens. The men retrieved their weapons from the fallen Sun Vampires immediately seeking new opponents.

It worried Lathea to see his men so confident in their ability that they refused to wear armor nor wield a weapon.

"Ooh, you're just like me." Azrael said giddily watching as Lathea stood. "You experimented on humanity!"

Lathea continued to hold her tongue, drawing her daggers as she lunged towards Azrael, cutting the cheek of his son instead as he landed before her.

Lathea put away her daggers as the sky grew darker, rain beginning to fall, lightning now striking directly at her men.

Azrael laughed, holding his hands out in the rain. "I hope being a mother was worth the deaths of your men. Until we meet again, Lathea. Give my regards to your sister." One of his men in the sky used the air to lift him away to safety leaving his son with Lathea.

She ducked out of the way of his fist, flames landing against the wet ground behind her. She lunged against him, striking his stomach with her hand, an array glowing in the darkness. The man grabbed her arm as the array glowed burning her flesh before kicking her back.

Lathea suppressed the pain using the momentum of her fall to roll onto her feet. She continued running, striking the man with her fist, another array glowing, the force enough to throw the man back several feet providing Lathea with the chance to escape and join her men.

She watched as Vasilisa threw aside her sword to use her magic to rip the arms from one of the men preventing him from striking their people with lightning. She then kicked him to the ground, holding her hand out where her sword returned to her as she plunged it through the young man's chest.

Lathea was confident that Vasilisa would be able to hold her own as she continued to put down those who struck their people with lightning. She pressed forward towards Josephine's location, stepping over the bodies of men and women from both sides of the field.

Josephine held her shield up as large stones were hurled at her. Her new strength allowed her to maintain her footing from the impact. She lowered her shield charging at the man where she plunged her sword into his chest, turning around to grab the head of another where she lit him on fire watching, as he burned alive. She lifted her sword from the corpse before cutting the burning man's head from his shoulders.

The rain gathered together into a large pillar, striking her like a battering ram. The force threw her off her feet, her body sliding in the mud and the blood of the battlefield. She was quick to climb to her feet, running towards the source, his water turning to steam this time as it collided with Josephine.

Lathea deflected the water as someone attempted to strike her. He was a boy who had he been her son, wouldn't have been allowed to date unsupervised much less fight. He stepped back creating a spear of ice as she grew near a look of terror on his face as he reached for the weapon. She kicked the boy down before he could grab the spear, taking it from him as she crushed his skull with her foot, turning around to strike another Sun Vampire through his jaw and out the top of his head with the spear.

In the distance, she could hear Josephine cry in pain, fear taking over as she ran to join her. *Vasilisa if you can hear me, meet me beside your sister.* Lathea called out to her daughter in her mind. She hoped that her people could feel her presence in the same way she felt theirs.

I'm coming, Mother. Vasilisa answered in return, running as fast as she could towards her sister until a man crossed her path. He held his hands out, lightning surging through the air in her direction. She dropped her sword, holding her hands out to create a barrier protecting her from the lightning.

One of the Moon Vampires appeared, grabbing her sword as he ran at the man creating the lightning. He turned his power onto the Moon Vampire electrocuting him before he could plunge the sword into his chest. Vasilisa ran at him, taking her sword from his body before slicing through the man's neck. Upon her landing, she continued running towards her sister.

Lathea narrowed her eyes as she saw the stone spike that had pierced through Josephine, suspending her in the air. Memories flooded her mind of the time she had spent in Hell, the many demons she had killed. She slid along the wet grass into the stone spike, her array glowing as she touched it, shattering the spike. The momentum didn't let up, Lathea sliding through the stones as they fell around her.

She climbed to her feet as she slowed, joining Vasilisa as she caught Josephine in her arms. Lathea pressed her hands to her daughter's wound; healing it enough that it no longer threatened her life. She then turned to meet the mad eyes of the man who had wounded her.

He was a very large man with thick muscles covering his arms and a twisted look on his face. He had been training almost daily for the last twenty years. He took a step towards Lathea stone spikes rising from the earth attempting to skewer Lathea like he had with her daughter.

Lathea held her hand up, her arrays glowing creating a transparent barrier around them. The spikes rose quickly, hitting the barrier with enough force to shake the ground beneath them.

"Take your sister with you and leave the battlefield." Lathea said, the barrier disappearing, another array glowing as she placed her hand against a spike destroying them.

"Heal me and let me fight with you!" Josephine demanded, her arm around her sister as they stood.

"I will not waste my magic to heal you when your sister can do it. I will send you her location but you need to leave now." Lathea said using the blood on the battlefield to strike at the man. "I will send the rest of our people behind you. We must fall back."

Vasilisa began to drag her sister away though she fought against her. "We can't leave her, Lisa!" Josephine argued though she was in severe pain.

"I'm not losing my sister." She said as they were confronted by one of the Sun Vampires in the air. He used the air to pin them down where they stood.

Josephine held her shield up to protect them from the winds as Vasilisa used her telekinesis to plunge a sword from the battlefield through the man. "We have to keep moving, Jos!"

"You are a coward sending your men away in the midst of battle." The man said as he clashed with Lathea.

She let go of the blood she had gathered as her weapon focusing on the man instead, watching as his blood boiled within his veins. The man screamed in agony before exploding, his hot blood splattering against Lathea. As the rain fell around her it created steam that closed in on her, burning her face and arms.

She clenched her teeth, running through the steam, ignoring her wounds, continuing to suppress the pain as she carried the blood of the fallen with her, striking another man through his skull with it, adding his blood to the mix.

She turned, watching as another of her men fell, their numbers halved as the storms began to clear, sunlight piercing through the clouds above them. Her army paid it no mind, however, continuing to fight.

Lathea used the air around her to jump into the center of the fight, the impact of her land sending those around her off their feet. She used the air to push her men back, creating a stone wall to keep them in the shadows.

"Fall back!" She screamed at them, holding off a group of Sun Vampires as she brought forth cloud to protect her men as they made their escape. Her men watched her for a moment before disappearing into the distance.

"You dare fight us on your own?" Azrael said, watching her from afar. "I've heard the stories about your power but I feel like you're holding back. Don't I deserve your best?" He pretended to be offended though he remained behind the protection of his son.

Lathea ignored Azrael however, grabbing a Sun Vampire by their head burning the flesh of his skull as his blood boiled within him before she pushed him into the center of the battle where he exploded, his blood searing the flesh of those around him.

She could feel as her men created more and more distance between them and the Sun Vampires. She held a spear of blood, her daggers remaining on her thighs as her last resort. To fight monsters she had to become a monster and so she let go. Her arrays were like a light show, different ones glowing with her every strike. The blood of the fallen swirled around her, far more than she had ever controlled at once. She created a similar pillar like the child once had, shaped like a fist, striking Azrael's men.

She fell to the ground below her, the men in the air using the wind to hold her down. She redirected the blood turning the fist into a hand to strike them down freeing her from their grasp. Stone spikes pierced through her abdomen, shoulder, and legs. She destroyed them before using the last of her strength to create a wall to shield her from their blows as she escaped.

"Do we pursue her?" Azrael's son said looking at the many corpses on the battlefield, most of them Moon Vampires.

"No. I want her to see her sister again. I didn't realize how capable she was on her own. Before I had only heard stories of her power, now I've seen it for myself. If I had known sooner what I know now we wouldn't have allowed them to escape. I underestimated her power."

His son took a deep breath, their men falling back.

"Uaine's leader has perished."

Azrael sighed, disappointed. "Find someone else good with rocks to lead them."

His son nodded. "What will you do now, Father?"

"I will study our enemy. This is an act of war." Azrael said approaching one of the bodies of the Moon Vampires. His son nodded, satisfied with his father's answer as he led their men back to Eithne. The sun shined bright above them, not a cloud remaining in the sky.

##

Lathea no longer had the strength to suppress her pain, barely able to walk as she tried to make her way back to her people. She took a knee, standing among the ruins of Haven. Her wounds had only grown worse the harder she pushed herself.

I need assistance. I can go no further. Lathea called out to her people though she was unsure of what they could do to help her.

The light of day was bright as she searched for something to bandage her wounds. Instead what she saw brought a smile to her lips.

She understood Marie's words now as she watched her sister approach. There was a light that surrounded her, an air of joy and healing as she knelt beside her, putting her arm around her shoulders.

"You've transcended, Sister."

Marie wiped the blood and dirt from her sister's face as she helped her through the city. "The faith the humans have is strong though divided."

"Divided you say?"

"Some are afraid and don't wish to be a part of a war that they had no say in." She said. "Some remain loyal to you however and want to bring an end to the Sun Vampires, to Azrael. It's understandable really. Those whose loved ones did not return don't want to remain where they are constantly reminded of this day."

"Then let's take them somewhere where they won't be reminded of the massacre that happened today." Lathea said. "Marie, I want you to take them somewhere safe, far away from here. If they see you as their Goddess, then you should be the one to lead them home and help them rebuild."

"Speaking of which, Sister, they have taken to calling me Alayna. I can't imagine why." She said almost nervously.

"Because it means beautiful." Lathea said. "I have to agree with them, Alayna. It's very fitting for you."

"I wonder if they know a name that means stubborn like a bull. Your men told me how you commanded them to leave you alone on the battlefield."

"I think between the two of us we've had enough names." Lathea said. "I did what I felt was best for my people regardless of what happened to me."

"Your daughters are worried sick."

"Then I suppose they will be grateful to see that I still live and breathe." She said looking into her sister's eyes. "So will you lead the human's home?"

"I will. Where can I find you once I have finished?"

"Is your twin telepathy not working?" Lathea laughed as they approached the tents. "Meet me where our parent's estate once stood."

"Why there?" Alayna said, helping her sister onto one of the cots. She waved over to Alethea who began to clean her mother's wounds.

Lathea closed her eyes. "Don't keep me waiting, Alayna. You are all too familiar with my patience."

"You have but a handful of it." She said with a laugh, leaning down where she kissed her sister's forehead. "I wouldn't dream of it."

She approached the humans who had already separated after a large dispute refusing to speak to one another. "Let's go home." The humans looked up at Alayna with a twinkle in their eyes as they followed her, more than half of the humans disappearing into the distance with her.

Alethea placed a wet rag on her mother's forehead as her sisters joined her. "Mother, where is Alayna taking them?"

Lathea sat up despite Alethea trying to keep her down. "I told your Aunt that if they did not want to remain here with us that she should lead them home and help them rebuild."

"And what of our people? We can't live in these tents forever." Vasilisa said.

"Someone bring me a map if you will."

"Mother please, let me clean your wounds."

Lathea took the rag from her daughter. "I can handle this, Alethea. I need you to listen to me, all of you. What I say next is very important."

Lathea cleaned out her wounds before healing the flesh and fixing the leather of her corset and trousers though it took what energy she had left.

Josephine handed her mother a map as she cleaned her hands, setting the rag on the cot. She took the map from Josephine, approaching a long table where she rolled the map out. She used an inkwell to hold down one corner while her daughters held the other three. She grabbed a quill from the inkwell dipping it into the ink. She circled a large area in the southwest of the map.

"This is where Eithne is. I've been watching it grow for a long time now."

"Explains all those father and daughter weekends we used to have."

"Your father though he didn't approve of me going alone allowed me to do so. He knew I would regardless." She drew little lines through the circle, separating it into five pieces. "Each of these sections is a district in Eithne. Azrael has his people separated by what element they can perform. As we saw today they can only perform one of fire, light, earth, water, or air. Azrael leads them from here." She said making a dot in a district in the Mideast of the country.

"Each district is named, this one being Orlaith and home of those skilled with fire. The others are Kiva, which is light, Uaine is earth, Finnegan is water, and finally Saoirse that is made of air. He's molded the terrain to fit the needs of these districts such as these mountains here." She said circling the western side of Eithne. "The

Shea Mountains were created by Azrael's men as a way to defend their people."

"How much time did you spend over there?" Josephine said.

Lathea laughed. "Too much it seems. I started once you girls had been weaned from my bosom."

"Why? What good does it do us?" Vasilisa said. "We've lost too many men. We can't attack Eithne."

"We don't have to." Josephine said, her eyes wide. "Where's Alayna taking the humans?"

"Here." Lathea said circling an area in the southeast on the other side of the river that was on the side of Haven. "It's where her son lives."

"Alayna has a son? I thought she couldn't have children."

"Before we died she had a baby named Ciel. If I know her as well as I think I do — and I do — she's going to ask Ciel to lead the humans."

"That should go over well." Josephine said. "Hello there, I'm your mother but I'm also a Goddess. Sorry I haven't been around for the last twenty years. Do you mind being a king for the rest of your life?"

Lathea smiled though she tried to resist chuckling. "I didn't say it would be easy. I know Alayna has been dying to see him again. She's been watching over him for a very long time. He's only a year older than you girls."

"We should meet him." Vasilisa said. "Especially if Alayna succeeds despite Josephine's sense of humor."

"In time. It will be a lot for him to process that his mother — who he hasn't seen in almost twenty years — has become a Goddess."

"That is assuming he doesn't reject her. He could be angry and dismissive." Vasilisa said.

"Would you reject Alayna regardless of the past?"

"No. I don't think I would. There is a kindness about your sister that makes her magnetic." She said looking at her mother.

"The same kindness you have, Vasilisa. That is why you girls never got in trouble around her. My sister has a very tender heart though it is now wise of the world." She said tapping on the area her sister was travelling to. "It will take them some time to get there which is good because we will be moving our men here." She said circling the entire north side of the map.

Josephine and Vasilisa looked at the large circle with confusion. It was three times the size of Eithne with a natural mountain range creating a border along the south. Much of the area was covered in trees and to the west it was covered in tundra.

"Mother, it's going to be freezing in a matter of months." Josephine said.

"I understand that but I don't think our people will have too much trouble adjusting. We need to go here. The land is natural. No one has gone this far north before."

"Probably because they couldn't. They would have to cross this body of water." Josephine said taking the quill and striking an X through the large lake in front of the mountains. "Even if they were able to cross the water they would then have to somehow make it over those mountains."

Lathea nodded. "And we're going to. We *must* set up here. We will be able to watch over our allies and enemies."

"Allies. What allies?" Vasilisa said. "In case you haven't noticed, Mother, we don't have any allies. They called the humans who remained otklonil - *the rejected*."

Lathea smiled. "If Alayna succeeds in getting her son into power then we can send you to make peace between his people and our own. He is family and can use this to your advantage."

Vasilisa's eyes widened. "I hate to say this but you're right especially if we arrange a few marriages between the people and create trade routes with them. With all this natural land, we can trade things like timber and metals with them. There's no telling what we might find."

"So let's say we gain the humans as an ally. What then?" Josephine said.

"That's up to you girls." Lathea said. "I won't be staying with you any longer."

Alethea looked up at her. "But mother our people need you. We need you."

"No." She said. "They need you to lead them, to guide them. Remember how I always told you girls that you would do great things."

"No." Josephine said. "It was always tie your shoes. Stop running through the house. Josephine, did you set the curtains on fire? And so on."

"You did set the curtains on fire *a lot.*" Vasilisa said.

"*By accident.*"

Lathea laughed. "I was always so grateful I had triplets. Think of yourselves like a triangle. There are so many meanings of the triangle. Love, truth, and wisdom for example, Alethea means truth. Then there is creation, preservation, and destruction. I think we know which of you is destruction. And it can even be as simple as past, present, and future. Vasilisa your name means queen and I believe that you will live up to its meaning. The three of you are the future of these people."

"Wait just a minute." Vasilisa said taking a few steps back. "Mother, you can't mean—"

"You have to, Lisa. I'm a healer, Josephine is a warrior, and you kind of talk too much but only sometimes." Alethea said blushing, smiling brightly.

"I do no such thing." She said stepping forward, her finger in her sister's face. "I am persuasive at most."

"I'm giving a new meaning to the triangle." Lathea said drawing one inside the circle she had drawn for her people. "Divine, Shield, and Voice. Alethea will keep the faith in these people strong."

"They already worship you, Mother. I suppose we will need a priestess." Josephine said, her arms crossed over her chest. "Can you handle it, Alethea?"

Lathea was at a loss for words but she couldn't deny that her daughter spoke truth. She had become a Goddess because of the faith of their people.

Alethea nodded. "Of course. These people haven't had a place they could feel safe in for a long time. If we build temples throughout the country, then no matter where they are they have somewhere that is undeniably safe." She said taking the quill from her sister to draw seven dots around the circle that represented their country.

"Alethea will be a priestess of... me." It felt strange for Lathea to think of herself as a Goddess instead of just being their mother. "Josephine you will be the shield for this country. I expect you to use what your father taught you to train these people. We can't allow this to happen again."

"You have my word, Mother. Never again will our people suffer as they did today." Josephine said, taking her mother's hand.

"Which means I am the voice." Vasilisa said, shaken up by the entire concept of being a queen. "Please tell me you don't expect me to—"

"I am grateful that you are a capable warrior on the battlefield, Vasilisa, but now it is time you use your words like you wield your sword. You will be queen and lead these people. You won't be alone though. Your sisters will always be at your side."

Josephine let go of her mother's hand to hold her sister's hand, Alethea joining her.

"Divine. Shield. And Voice." Lathea's daughters said together.

Lathea nodded. "I have a name for your country if you girls are open to suggestions."

"Of course." Vasilisa said, looking up at her mother as her sisters stood beside her.

"Lytharia."

"Then so it shall be." Vasilisa said. "I suppose we should go tell the people."

"No, you have to go tell the people." Josephine said, standing beside Alethea. "We get to stand there and look pretty."

Alethea laughed, looking at Vasilisa. "It seems we have a lot of work to do."

Lathea remained at the table as she watched her daughters approach the people both humans and vampire.

Vasilisa stood between her sisters who held her hands to comfort her but only for a moment. "Lathea has aided myself and my sisters in deciding on a plan of action. We will not remain under these tents forever. We must show the Sun Vampires that we aren't done fighting."

The people cheered for a moment before some stood up.

"I understand you have questions and I will do my best to answer them."

"Where will we go? The Sun Vampires have taken the southwest and the traitors—"

"They are not traitors." Vasilisa said. "We must understand that they have suffered a great loss. If they choose to go their own way, then we will wish them safe travels and prosperity. We will not reject someone just because they feel differently. They are still our family and our friends. They are just a lit bit farther away."

"I apologize, Milady." They said. "They are moving east. In the north it's nothingness."

"That's why we're going north. The land is rich in materials and the days are still long so we have time before the cold months come. We can set up shelter and plant enough crops to get us through the winter. This will be no easy task and we will face many problems along the way but there is nowhere safer for us to go than north."

"How will we get over the mountains?"

Lathea watched her daughters proudly from the table. "You let me handle that."

"So let's say we get there, shelter is made and we can rebuild, what then?"

Vasilisa climbed onto one of the tables, stabbing its wood with her sword. "If you will allow me, I would like to be your leader, your queen, as we struggle together through these trying times."

The people looked at her for a moment, before conversing amongst one another.

"Why do you believe you are in a better position to lead us than any of these people?"

"I understand your doubt. I felt the same when Lathea approached me about leading but I believe my mother is right. Over the course of my life I have proven to her and to the people of Haven that I am willing to step up in any situation. When the four horsemen attacked, I stood with my sisters against them. When we realized we were outnumbered against the Sun Vampires I stood with my sisters again as we offered our lives to a ritual that could have killed us. I am fit to lead you because I am not only a capable warrior but because I am compassionate. You don't have to take my word for it but I would like the chance to prove to you that I am who I stand here and claim to be."

"Why should we choose you over your sisters?"

"My mother said it best in only three words: Divine, Shield, and Voice. Alethea is a healer and Josephine is warrior. That leaves me as the Voice and I want earn my place as your leader."

"Our queen." They said. "Don't let us down, Your Majesty."

Vasilisa resisted the urge to rub her arms, the final two words they spoke sending chills over her skin. Instead she removed her sword from the wood of the table, holding it in the air above her as she spoke.

"I will not let you down."

The people cheered as she climbed down from the table. She returned to her mother who held a tiara in her hand that she had created from a sword she had found lying nearby. Hopefully no one would need it anytime soon.

"When in doubt, seek your sisters. And if together you can't find an answer then I will always be here, Vasilisa. I will stay in the shadows while you lead them from the light."

"Alayna is going to be doing the same thing, isn't she? That's why she's looking for Ciel."

Lathea nodded.

"Thank you, Mother, for everything."

"Don't thank me yet, Vasilisa. You have a lot of work to do." She said watching as the blacksmith's son approach. "Beginning with finding your king."

Vasilisa turned, taking his hand as he approached. "I think he found me a long time ago, Mother."

"I think you're right." Lathea said kissing her cheek. "I will give you a moment alone."

"I'm sorry that our weekend was ruined." Vasilisa said smiling at him as he met her lips. When he pulled away she looked over him, her eyes widening, tears flowing down her cheeks. She had become so wrapped up in helping her mother and sisters that she hadn't even noticed that he had been one of the volunteers for the ritual. That he had become like her.

She kissed him back, wrapping her arms around him. "I'm so sorry—"

He laughed, pushing her back, sitting beside her on a nearby cot. "There will be many more weekends, Lisa, or should I say Your Majesty?"

"Don't you dare." She said. He was the last person she wanted to hear those words from though she knew it was out of respect.

"I overheard your mother mention you finding your King."

"Then you should have heard what I told her." She said taking his hands. "You and I have been together for five years now and I've known you for far longer than that. I never expected that my life would go in this direction but I would be honored if you would continue to follow me down this path."

He smiled, placing his hand in his pocket. "While I too am disappointed that we couldn't share this weekend together it's because I had planned to give you this." He said producing a small ornate wooden box from his pocket.

Vasilisa took it from him, opening it to find a silver ring with a floral pattern engraved around it lying on a thick layer of blue velvet. She looked at him unable to speak. She watched as he pulled the ring out of the box, holding her left hand with his free hand, their eyes locked on one another.

"I'm sorry that I can't afford something better for you so I made this ring—"

"*No.*" She said, her chest tight as she looked into his eyes. "*It's perfect.*"

"I had planned to ask you by the river at our favorite spot."

She took a deep breath, placing her hand on her chest. "Are you sure you want to be a part of my strange family?"

"Are you sure you want to marry the son of a blacksmith?"

"Only if he's willing to become used to the title of King instead."

He placed the ring on her finger. "I can get used to it."

Lathea stood with her daughters, the three of them watching Vasilisa as she wrapped her arms around the blacksmith's son. His father joined them as he watched, the other townspeople cheering.

"I always did think of your girl as my daughter."

"Now you don't have much of a choice." Lathea laughed, putting a hand on the man's shoulder. "Did you ever think your son would become a king?"

"Of course not though once upon a time I didn't believe in angels and demons either."

"Neither did I and then I became one."

"Lathea you became so much more than a demon."

She watched as her daughters left to join their sister and her fiancé. I will be sad to be away from my daughters, from my people but I must go."

He turned to look at her. "What happened out there after you sent our men home? I was relieved to see my son return though everyone questioned what became of you."

"Walk with me. I don't want them to hear what I am about to say." She said as the blacksmith joined her beyond the tent. She waited to speak until they were out of earshot, walking to the river. She spent a minute watching the sun set, the night sky like a blanket above them, protecting them. The sound of the water travelling downstream was the only thing keeping the silence at bay.

"I had to kill children. *Children.*" Her heart raced in her chest as she spoke, tears brimming her eyes. "In the heat of battle I knew what I was doing was right. I knew I had to protect our people from these *monsters* but these monsters were still living and breathing people. Most of them should have been studying not slaying."

He took Lathea's hand in his, rubbing her back with his free hand. "You saved my boy, Lathea. You saved the children and husbands and wives of many other people."

"And I also killed the children and husbands and wives of many other people! I forced my children to kill children! What kind of mother am I to experiment with dark magic on my children and then force them to go through this? I should have sent all my daughters away. Not just Alethea who was probably crushed seeing all these wounded people especially her sisters. I can't imagine the damage I have brought upon my own children."

"Alethea was strong the entire time always helping those in need whether they were physically or emotionally wounded." He said, holding her face in his hands. "You did not force anyone's hands. Your children would have gone into battle regardless because they understand that this is about protecting those who can't protect themselves. No one blames you and neither should you, Lathea."

"My husband would still be alive if I'd had the strength to face this alone."

"*And you would be dead.*" He said icily, squeezing her hand. "Can you honestly say that you would rather your family suffer through that instead?"

"I don't know what I should have done but surely there was a better way. Our men were slaughtered. I led the people I swore to protect to their deaths." She said standing up. "I feel numb when I should feel guilty. I became the monster I sought to destroy."

"You did no such thing."

Lathea shook her head tears streaming down her face. "He said I experimented on humanity but I did something far worse. I killed my husband corrupted their souls. That's why they can't go out into the sunlight. Maybe never again. For all I know there could be more side effects. I ruined the lives of these people including your boy." She fell to her knees, her head in her hands. "I'm sorry. I'm so sorry."

The man laughed, holding Lathea close, rubbing her arms as he spoke. "You didn't ruin my boy's life. You ensured he would live a long and happy life. Now he's getting married to the woman he loves and is about to become king!"

She pulled away looking down at her hands. "I miss my husband. I would give anything to have him back for one more minute." She said. "I should have never killed him."

"You act as if his sacrifice is in vain but what you fail to see is that he has ensured that not only the lives of his wife and daughters but of our entire town get to live to their fullest. He gave you the strength to save these people."

He took her hands, leading her back to the tents. "There is something you need to see, Lathea. I promise you will feel better."

When they returned, the townspeople stood around the table that held the map. On top of the map sat Solas' grimoire.

She ran her hands over the leather, tears in her eyes, the blacksmith standing beside her. "We weren't going to leave your book behind. We know how much it means to you."

She hugged the man, crying against his chest. "Thank you."

Vasilisa held her fiancé's hand as they watched the clouds roll across the night sky, a new moon above them. "Okay people, let's move."

"You should take the time to clean up." The blacksmith said when Lathea let go of him. "You're still covered it blood and dirt. We have long night ahead of us."

She laughed. "I suppose I am. Tell my daughters I'll kill them if they leave without me."

The blacksmith shared in her laughter. "I will make sure they know."

Lathea returned to the river removing her clothes where she washed the blood and dirt from them before laying them in the grass to dry. She dipped her feet into the cool water, her heart still racing in her chest. Across the water she could see stones, one rolling into the water only it seemed to be coming at her across the water, growing bigger as it came closer.

"No." Lathea said through her teeth as she focused on the rocks before her.

She took a deep breath allowing herself to sink beneath the surface. When she surfaced, the water seemed bluer than it had before and she could swear the grass had become a brighter shade of green. The moon was almost blinding, as was its reflection off the water.

"*Breathe, Lathea.*" A voice spoke, startling her, the sound chillingly close to her husband.

"Solas?"

"No." The man's voice spoke. "Though if that is what you wish to call me then so be it."

She submerged herself under the water again, swimming as she thought of a response. "So are you here to tell me that I'm losing my mind?"

"You and your sister have many things in common. You have both lost the ones you've loved, seen war, and now hear our voices." He said calmly. "However another thing you share is the ability to overcome though you heavily rely on one another. What would you do if your sister died?"

Lathea surfaced, laughing. "She won't die. She's a Goddess now." She said, making her way towards the shore.

"It's no more than a title. So, I will ask again. What would you do?"

"If you are referring to Azrael then let him come. My men will be ready."

She returned to the shore where the water evaporated from her body. "You're avoiding my question, Lathea."

"What would you do if your sister died?"

She held her leather clothes in her hands as she stared at them. She recalled the many faces of Greed as her husband helped her slay him. The fire that consumed her estate as she avenged her sister's death.

"I would do what I do best: *revenge*." She said pulling on her clothes.

"That is an answer I can accept." The man said. "But never forget who you are, Lathea."

"A demon?" She said returning to her people, watching as her daughters helped take down the tents. They smiled through the pain, helping their people as they began to leave the camp. Vasilisa stood in the front, Josephine at her side as they guided them.

"*A mother.*" He said. "And a mother can also *forgive*."

She watched as Alethea stood towards the back, watching over the elderly as they headed north.

"And that includes forgiving yourself."

Lathea crossed her arms over her chest. "You sound a lot like my husband for someone who isn't."

"I *know* you." He said with a laugh. "I also know how strong your spirit is."

Lathea closed her eyes as s smile decorated her lips. "You don't know the half of it."

##

"Where will you go, Mother?" Alethea asked as Lathea joined her to aid her daughter.

"I will stay with you girls long enough to make sure that Lytharia becomes home for you, for your sisters, and for these people. As soon as you girls have a plan of action I will return home."

"Will it be hard without Father being there?" She said, handing her mother the grimoire.

She shook her head, holding Solas' grimoire close. "I considered setting our home aflame but in the end decided against it. Your father used to make jokes about how quick I am to set fires. So I will leave Haven as it stands. People need to remember what happened on this day. If nothing else it is a sign of the future," She said watching as the timeworn woman who had once shown love and support for her now followed behind her daughters.

"You said a sign of the future. What kind of sign?"

Lathea met her eyes, the smile that had once decorated her face becoming a solemn expression. "I don't know. Make sure your sisters are prepared."

"Prepared for what?" Alethea said, her eyes widening.

"For war." She said, placing her hand on her daughter's shoulder. "I'm returning to the place where Alayna and I grew up. I burned it down in an act or revenge but I know now that it was a mistake. I want to surprise my sister when she returns home."

"How will I find you?"

"You will always be able to find me, Alethea. I will return to the shadows. You sister needs to be in the spotlight leading our people. You know I exist. They will know I exist. I want you to recruit more priests and priestesses. Build temples and help our people expand over the entire country. I want our people to not only survive but to *thrive*."

"I will do this." She said with more confidence then Lathea had seen in her before.

"I have faith in you, my daughter." She said, taking her daughter's hand.

"You have a good heart mother."

"Is that so? Well let me know when you find it."

Chapter 23

Ciel stared at the large painting that hung before him. The woman within it sat before a large garden of greens and pinks with little spots of blue and purple along the bottom. She tended to her flowers. Platinum hair draped around her shoulder and a smile on her face. She wore a simple white dress, her belly swollen.

He pressed his hand to the image, clutching his fist.

He wanted to leave this place, to find her. He wanted to do something great that would bring her home. He didn't care that it'd been twenty years. Any chance to know her would be better than accepting her death.

"Ciel." The woman who had once been Marie's wet nurse called.

"Yes, Ma'am?" He called. He had decided many years ago that he would never call her mother but he wouldn't show her disrespect either. Her mother had been kind. After she passed they had built a relationship built on resentment.

"You have a visitor. She's quite beautiful. When were you going to tell me about her?"

He looked up at the painting, his chest tightening as he walked into the living room. "It never came up." He said approaching the door.

His hands sweat with anticipation as he pulled it open, his eyes widening as they fell onto Alayna.

Her heart raced in her chest as she stared into the eyes of the dark-haired man. "Would you care to join me for a walk?" He said.

"I'd love to." She said as he took her hand leading her to the courtyard where a garden towered above them extending forever in every direction. Her heart seemed lighter than air as he led her through it.

She couldn't help stopping to look at the different flowers as well as the variety of topiaries. Her eyes seemed to glisten at the familiar surroundings and the care that had been taken for the flowers. She had missed her garden and hadn't thought to plant another after the birth of her sister's children.

"Who tends for this garden?" She asked as she held a delicate flower, its petals soft against her fingertips. She felt at peace, so much so that the days before felt like a bad dream.

"I do." He said watching her with an almost childlike fascination. "I was told once that my mother loved gardens. So, I keep one in her memory."

Alayna looked at him with tears in her eyes. "What happened to your mother?" She was afraid of his answer.

She had sworn to come back but never had. She wasn't sure where she had fallen of her path. When she put Ciel second but there wasn't a day that passed that it didn't haunt her.

She worried what the woman had filled his head with after the passing of her mother. The lies she had fed to him about not only herself but of her own mother. It made her heart ache to think about what her son went through when he could have grown up with his cousins instead. He could have been happier.

But she had left him behind.

"She was taken from the world too soon while I was still an infant. She used to bring me into her garden all the time I've been told." He said meeting her eyes. "The woman who had looked after her, my grandmother, told me many great things about her but unfortunately she too was taken from this world when I was seven."

"I'm sorry for your loss." She said, reaching for his hand but quickly taking it back. "Was your mother ill?"

"No." He said, taking her hand holding it firmly as they walked. "Some say her sister took her life but growing up my grandmother always insisted that I never believe her sister would do such a thing."

She held her tongue, desperate to tell him the truth but instead she turned back to the flowers. She tried to hide as she wiped away the few tears that had managed to slip. He placed an arm around her, closer to her shoulders than her waist.

"They tell me my mother was a good woman, beautiful and strong. That she had a big heart and a lot of love."

"I can only imagine." She said, struggling with the words as they reached the center of the garden.

"I know you from somewhere, but I can only name one place." He said having a seat on a bench as he continued to look at her. "I don't want to believe it. You look no older than myself when she should be in her late thirties."

She swallowed nervously. "And where might that be?"

"There is a painting of my mother in her garden while she was with child. *With me.*" He swallowed, his chest tight as he spoke. "I look at it every day and I dare say it but you look exactly like her. It's almost as if a day hasn't passed."

She was at a loss for words as he spoke.

"Are you Marie Elizabeth Leighton?" He said standing up.

"I used to be... before I died." She said. "Your grandmother is right; my sister isn't to blame. I had returned home for her wedding but your father had insisted that you stay."

"What happened to my father?"

"My sister is, however, responsible for his death. After she learned of the way he treated me she ended his life. You could say my sister is my guardian even to this day. I was upset at the time because I was afraid to raise you alone so I went to see my father but he poisoned me."

"And you died." He said approaching her, cupping her face. "It's so hard to believe that you're here. You should be in your late thirties."

"Thirty-nine to be exact. My sister and I celebrated our birthdays last month." She placed her hands over his. "I'm so sorry I didn't come back for you. There's not a day it doesn't haunt me."

"When I was twelve I ran away from home to look for you because I refused to believe that you were dead. It's the same reason why every day I look at the painting of you. Because I wanted to believe you were out there." He said pulling her into his arms. "But there was never a day that I hated you. *Or blamed you.* My grandmother raised me to have faith in you."

"And I love her for that but I don't deserve-"

"You don't deserve the kind of treatment you keep subjugating yourself to. Why do you continue to bully yourself when all I ever wanted was the chance to know my mother? I don't hate you for what you've done. I want to thank you because you gave me something to live for."

"Ciel-" She said, tears streaming down her face as he pulled her into his arms. He held her tightly but only for a moment before pulling her over to the bench where they sat together, their fingers laced together.

"You must forgive me; I have many questions."

"So do I."

His eyes widened. "You have questions?"

"Just the one really. I've always wondered if you hated me for leaving you. It's haunted me for a long time. I could have given you a different life, a *happier* life. You could have grown up with your cousins—"

He wrapped his arms around her, pressing her head to his chest. "*Never.* I don't think I would have been as accepting as a child. Now is as good of a time as any."

She held onto him, tears streaming down her face as her son held her in his arms. "Your turn."

He took a deep breath as he ran his fingers through her hair. "How do you still live? You *died*."

She sat up to look him in the eyes as she spoke. "When I died I became an angel through an unlikely series of events."

"Unlikely series of events? What do you mean? They tried to tell me all the time as a child that after we die we become angels."

She shook her head. "I was born with the holy spirit. It's why my hair is different from my sister's." She pulled away, wiping the tears from her face before taking his hands. "As an angel I was obsessed with finding my sister and you. The Elders didn't approve and I became a Grigori. A lot of time passed and... well most recently I... became a Goddess." She said with a sigh. "I understand if you don't believe me."

"I believe you." He said, pulling out a handkerchief, offering it to her. "Though I want to know what it is you stand for."

"What do you mean?"

"What do you expect your followers to practice? What do you want them to see you as?"

"I want my followers to stand for justice. To seek it out like I did while I was in Heaven." She said, taking the handkerchief, wiping at her face. "I'm a mess, I'm sorry."

He smiled, pleased by her answer. "You're a beautiful mess, Mother." He felt relieved to finally say mother. Perhaps it was because his grandmother had always spoken about her or because he had always dreamt of this day. Only in his dreams she appeared older even time worn.

She laughed, looking into his eyes again. They were bluer than the day sky above them. "My followers have taken to calling me Alayna. I would have said no if my sister hadn't said it was fitting."

"Your sister is right." He said with a blush. "I apologize. I never imagined my mother would look as young as myself."

She placed her hand on his cheek. "And don't you forget where you get your looks from. Though your hair is more like my sister's which I suppose is fair. Her daughters have platinum hair like me."

"Will you tell me about her daughters?"

"You have three cousins, triplets — Alethea, Josephine, and Vasilisa — who until recently had been Nephilim. Their father was a great man. I wish you could have met him. He always put his family first and was the entire reason why I'm able to see my sister again. There was a time where I thought I'd never see her again."

"What happened to him?"

"He was brave and sacrificed his life to save his family as well as our townspeople."

Ciel looked down, holding her hand. "I'm sorry that you lost him." He said. "What is your sister's name? My... aunt."

"She was born Thea Ares Leighton. After she left hell she began to call herself Lathea. The La comes from her demon name, Lavanah."

"Your sister spent time in hell?"

"She can tell you all about it but yes. From what I've heard it's quite the story. That's where she met her husband."

"That's a strange place to fall in love." He said. "I want to meet them, Mother. I want to know my real family."

"Then you will." She said holding both his hands, watching as he stood up.

When she did not stand up he began to frown. "Is it safe for me to assume you aren't here just to see me?"

"Ciel, I've wanted to come see you for a long time but recently I realized that I *had* to come see you. Not just for me but for my people."

"You once said that I would do great things. What did you mean by that?"

Alayna stood up, squeezing his hands as a breeze played with her hair. "At the time I assumed that you would one day become a duke. A great and powerful duke. I know in my heart that you are such a man."

He let go of her hands, turning around. "There's no chance of me becoming a duke now, Mother. I'm sorry."

"I'm not asking you to be a Duke." She said placing her hand on his shoulder. "I'm asking you to be a King."

He placed his hand over hers, looking at her from over his shoulder. He was in disbelief but when she did not waiver he understood that she meant her every word. She was choosing him to become king.

"Are you asking me because I am your son?"

"I'm asking you because there is no one else I'd trust with an entire population of people. People who need a leader after the horror they've been through. I know you're capable of leading people."

He turned around looking at her. "Let's assume I say yes. What happens then?"

"We rebuild. I did not come alone. My people are camped not far from here, at least five hundred people. I am their Goddess not their queen."

He nodded. "You realize the leaders of the territories—"

"I'd like to see them try to argue with a Goddess. Wouldn't you?" She said with a smirk, her brows raised. "The territories will either try to join you or move on. It's for you to decide if you allow them to become a part of Adamaris."

"Adamaris?" He said.

"Unless you'd rather name it something different." She said, embarrassed. "It's up to you since you'll be leading—"

"Mother, I love it." He said kissing her forehead. "*Breathe.*"

"I find it very hard to today. I don't know what's wrong with me. Might be something in the air."

He laughed watching as she continued to walk around the garden. "I suppose I should pack a bag."

She looked at him, peeking from behind a topiary. "If you come with me, there's no coming back, Ciel."

"I have no intention of coming back." He said taking her hand, leading her back into the house. "I will be but a moment. Thank you for coming home." He said kissing her cheek.

"On the contrary. I'm taking you home." She said watching as he disappeared.

The wet nurse entered the room, looking at Alayna. "It's so nice that Ciel has found a girlfriend—"

Alayna approached the woman, striking her with the back of her hand. "Do not act as if you don't remember me. I haven't aged a day." The woman held her cheek as she looked up at Alayna. "How dare you treat my son as malevolently as you have for all these years?"

"You should be dead." The woman said attacking her with a knife.

Ciel grabbed her by her wrist; squeezing it with enough pressure the she dropped the knife. "My things are packed, Mother. I think it's time we left."

Alayna took Ciel's hand as he held a small bag of clothes. "Did you not grab anything else?" She said. "I thought you had paintings—"

"We can always paint new ones."

She laced her fingers with his. "Yes, we can."

##

That evening Alayna watched from a distance as her people told Ciel stories of the last twenty years, of his family, and of the battle that had taken place recently. They had welcomed him with open arms and believed that he too was the best choice for king though he was still struggling to believe it himself.

He waited until many of their people had retired to their tents before approaching Alayna. "These people are good people. I hope I don't disappoint them."

"You are the son of a Goddess. You just might surprise yourself."

"I've learned that many are farmers. I thought maybe we should make our way further east to begin rebuilding. The ocean will provide us with a lot of water to grow crops. We could build farms there and continue to expand from there towards the north."

She turned to look at him. "See, you're ready for this. A good king thinks of his people first. I know my sister well; she's going to take her people north and conquer the snow."

"North? Those mountains are impossible to climb."

"She won't be climbing them. My sister will create a path for her people to literally walk through the mountain."

"Your sister can manipulate the land?"

"Lathea possesses a great power but I worry for her mind. I can't imagine she came out of the battle unscathed."

"Is that why you will be leaving after we've rebuilt?"

She nodded. "Part of the reason. These people know I watch over them. I don't have to be here for them. That's what you're here for. You will become their shoulder to lean on but I expect you to come visit me. *Often.*"

"Of course I will." He said looking at her. "So your sister is taking the north. Who will lead?"

"Her daughter, Vasilisa. I have no doubts about that. I think that it would be wise if you married one of their people. If you want to marry."

"You keep saying their people. If I am to be king, Mother, I need to know what I may face. I understand about the Sun Vampires but the Moon Vampires are still a mystery to me."

"Your cousins are the first. The originals. I don't know much about them as a race either but you will meet them soon enough. Form your own opinions. I will support you regardless of your decision."

"Vasilisa, you said. Is she kind?"

"Very kind. But she is also wise and fair. She is a capable warrior both in and out of battle."

"We have to take down the Sun Vampires." He said placing his hand over hers. "I'm sorry you have to go through this. I know you and Azrael—"

"That was a different time, Ciel. Do what you must to protect these people, to protect yourself. Your family will support you."

He took a deep breath, wrapping his arms around her. "I suppose we have a lot to do, don't we?"

Alayna looked into the night sky, the moon shining bright above them. "Ciel, there is a future ahead for you that you never imagined. I have faith in you and so do these people."

"Does that mean I get to be a God?" He laughed.

"I don't think so. You'll have to settle for being king." She said hugging him, his lips on her hair.

Chapter 24

Lathea took her time as she walked down the halls of the estate. She had spent the last six months changing the décor from what it had once been. As children, her mother had loved the colors of gold, burgundy, and yellow. It was enough to make her stomach sick that she had copied the house with such accuracy. Now many of the walls were purple with the occasional peach such as the kitchen.

Most of the house remained the same. She wanted it to feel familiar to her sister when she came home. It had been two years since she had seen her and wanted the surprise to be perfect. She was happy that she could finally reconnect with her son. She couldn't imagine her life without her daughters.

She approached a set of yellow curtains in the kitchen, pressing her hand to them where they turned to white with little rose fastens. She peered out the window into the garden where she watched her daughters enjoy tea together. It reminded her of her childhood though none of them tended to the flowers or read a book.

Alethea had done well so far as a priestess and wore elaborate robes of white and blue that draped around her. The material was light and would flow behind her when strong winds came in from the mountains. She was grateful to be surrounded by the warmth of the plains again. Lathea had built her a large temple in the center of a lake with a bridge leading to shore. Alethea had been busy recruiting priests and priestesses around the country and had chosen a special six of them to represent the other temples. They called her the High Priestess. She was often receiving letters and with the help of Vasilisa aided in their troubles.

The blacksmith had created an entirely new set of armor for Josephine who wore it proudly. It covered her entire body in ornate metal with the occasional blue design while keeping her feminine form. Josephine had requested a special breastplate as a joke after her mother had suggested she look for a husband. However, when the blacksmith presented it to her it became what she wore everyday outside of battle. It was designed to appear like a corset made of metal, blue fabric hanging from where it stopped, an ornate design like the wings of a bird covering her breasts. Lathea had realized that if she were going to have a grandchild from Josephine she had to settle for the slightly provocative armor. At least her daughter wasn't flaunting her assets.

Lathea had to compromise with Vasilisa too. She refused to wear dresses outside of the formal parties. She was too in love with the idea of armor and Lathea blamed Solas for that. However, her armor was made of leather now instead of metal, her husband kind enough to create something that still gave a regal presence. It was black like night with a short coat; it's collar standing up. Because the armor itself stopped at her thighs she wore tall boots to minimize the amount of skin that showed. Draping from the armor was many layers of elaborate fabrics of white and blue that flowed behind her as she walked. Around her waist remained her sword.

"Ooh! Your daughter is about to have a daughter of her own!" Spoke the woman's voice. They did not speak often but when they did it was enough to drive Lathea mad. "See, you *are* old."

Lathea sat with her girls wearing a simple black dress. "I wish you girls would wear something... bulkier. Because of the cold."

Josephine leaned forward, the wings struggling to hide her bosom. "Oh but you said you wanted grandchildren."

"Do not use my words against me." Lathea said. "I am grateful that very, very minimal skin shows—"

Alethea laughed. "She wants you to hide your figure, Josephine."

"Absolutely not." Josephine said leaning back. "This figure distracts my men long enough to allow me to show them their general is more than a piece of ass."

"You don't need your *figure* to prove that." Lathea said. "You're just amused by catching them."

"Like cat playing with a mouse." Josephine said jokingly.

Vasilisa rested her hands on her stomach, grateful that she was finally starting to show. Her only regret about having a child was that she would be forced to wear the dresses her mother was dying for her to wear.

"You should see her fight now, Mother." Alethea said. "These men think that because they're vampires they will be able to hold their own."

"I am proud of all of you. Have the side effects been manageable?" Her daughters still had to stay out of the sunlight. The only reason why they sat in the garden was because Lathea was keeping the skies thick with clouds.

Her daughters hadn't told her much about the side effects but she could sense when they were bothering them. They didn't seem to struggle with it as much as those who had once been entirely human such as Vasilisa's husband. In exchange those affected by the ritual had gained extraordinary powers to go with their speed and strength. No two vampires had the same power though occasionally they seemed similar. Her daughters hadn't lost the powers they had been born with. They gained another one such as Josephine's ability to create lightning.

"We're doing great, Mother. You shouldn't worry so much." Vasilisa said, placing her hand over hers.

"I will always worry about my girls."

Vasilisa looked at Josephine giving her a kind of signal. Josephine nodded, looking at Alethea who nodded in response, following her out to the front of the estate.

"Vasilisa, what do you have planned?" Lathea said.

"We have a gift for you, Mother." She said standing up, taking her mother's hand, her free hand remaining on her stomach. "Josephine makes an excellent general as you had predicted she would. However, her heart is beginning to soften just a little what with Lytharia growing, our people treating her just as they treat Alethea and myself."

Alethea and Josephine carried together an enormous marble statue of Solas, placing it in the center of Alayna's garden. Lathea had spent a lot of time bringing life to the flowers again. To see Solas among the flowers brought tears to her eyes.

She ran her hands over the smooth marble, looking into his face. The statue was twice the size of her but displayed him just as she remembered him.

"Mother?" Josephine said, nervously. "Are you... okay?"

Lathea approached her daughter, wrapping her arms around her, kissing her cheek. "Thank you for doing this for me."

"I thought it might be nice to have someone to talk to other than yourself." She said with a laugh. They were aware of their mother's condition since after the battle.

Alethea and Josephine each put a hand on Lathea's shoulders when she let go of Vasilisa. "It will be nice for us all to come talk to father once in a while."

"I hope you're including me in that statement, Vasilisa." Came Alayna's voice as she walked around the estate and to her garden.

"Welcome home, Sister." Lathea said, wiping the tears from her eyes. "I hope this serves as a nice surprise."

"The statue or our home? Because right now I can't decide which surprises me more. You must have put so much work into it. Everything feels... familiar and yet new."

"Do you like it?" She said as Alayna hugged her nieces.

"I love it but I didn't come home empty handed either." She said turning around. "I want you to meet your nephew. I know you've been waiting over twenty years to see him."

Ciel approached them dressed in a blue and silver shirt with black trousers. "It's nice to meet you." He said looking at his cousins. He was astounded more by their height than their beauty. They were just as tall as he was.

"My name is Alethea." She said extending her hand, pulling back the fabric to her wrist so that he could shake her hand.

Instead he brushed his lips against her knuckles, bowing respectfully. "I've heard many great things about you. You keep the faith of your people strong."

"Someone must keep their spirits high. Even after two years some men struggle to keep faith when they can't walk into the sun. We learned the hard way what happens."

"I'm sorry for your loss." He said letting go of her hand. "Perhaps you could teach some of my people how to heal like you do."

"Perhaps. We will see if they can learn magic. Many of the humans of Lytharia have picked up on it. If our Queen allows I will take a group of them with me to Adamaris to see if we can pass on the knowledge."

Vasilisa laughed hearing her sister refer to her as Queen. "Of course, you may. We will make arrangements once we've arrived home. It may take some time seeing as Alethea can only travel during the night."

"I can send some men to make the journey easier."

"I'll have my general send a handful of her men to accompany them. Your men need to remain at home. I'm sure it's been quite the journey to rebuild."

Josephine nodded in agreement. "It would be safer for my sister if she were accompanied by some of our warriors. We've been preparing in case of another attack by the Sun Vampires."

"I've heard stories about the battle. I'm sorry for the men you ladies lost that tragic day." He said. "Magic would definitely make things easier for our people. It would help us defend against them. I've heard that Azrael has a history of taking cities. I appreciate you for sharing your knowledge with us."

"Of course, you're family. *They* are family." She said.

Lathea and Alayna sat at the patio table watching them almost amused. "Can't you discuss politics later?" Lathea said. "Why don't you get to know one another first?"

Vasilisa blushed. "I suppose she does make a point. Would you accompany me for a walk?"

"I would love to." He said walking beside Vasilisa. Josephine stood to his right, Alethea on Vasilisa's left.

"Your sisters accompany you everywhere?"

"When they are around, yes. We're kind of like a triangle you could say."

##

Lathea screamed. Before her she could see the men and women from the battlefield, her people who she had led to their deaths. They stood up their clothes becoming white robes as they cried with a loud voice.

"Will you not avenge our blood, Lathea?"

Lathea tried running away from them but the world around them shook like an earthquake. Out of the darkness she could hear Alayna's voice.

"Lathea!" She said, shaking her sister. Come back to me. It's not real."

Lathea sat on the floor in her sister's arms as she held her. "I killed them Alayna even if it wasn't by my own hands."

"You have to stop blaming yourself. Tell your voices to shut up. You are still in control, I promise."

Lathea closed her eyes and when she opened them the walls around her seemed to be melting. "I don't want to keep looking at the world if this is all I will see from now on." She said closing her eyes again.

Marie shushed her as she held her more tightly. "If you live with your eyes closed you will miss the moments that make it worth it. Remember Vasilisa's wedding?"

"I do." Lathea said. "She looked so beautiful, just like you at your wedding."

"Only your daughter was able to marry a man she loves." She laughed, helping her sister to her feet. "Go sit in the garden, I'll make some tea and join you."

Lathea did as her sister asked walking slowly, the walls around her eventually returning to normal. She sat at the patio table looking into the evening sky, the smell of tea soon accompanying her.

"I completely understand what you're going through."

"It's madness." Lathea said as she poured cream into her tea.

"Yes, but madness is like a painting that's never finished and traps the artist within. It is both beautiful and frightening, ever changing."

Lathea took a sip of her tea, contemplating the words for a moment. "What will you do now, Sister?"

Alayna stirred cubes of sugar into her tea. "I think I might go visit Ciel. It's great to finally get to know my son. I've never seen him so happy as he is now being king. He's a good king." She said sipping her tea. "And what about you sister? What will you do?"

"I'm going to write a grimoire."

Lathea and Alayna's journeys have reached their end.
However, the story has only begun.

Turn the page for a teaser for Book 2:

Kismet

An Era of Dawn Novel

An Introduction to Insanity II

1. Madness is defined as "the state of being mad". Frenzy. Rage. Insane.

2. Habit is defined as "an acquired behavior pattern regularly followed until it has become almost involuntary".

3. Insanity is doing the same thing over and over again and expecting different results.

##

I'm not a scholar. I'm not a scientist. I'm not a psychologist. Hell, I never went to college. I have spent more time than I can recall researching on the Internet about *many* things especially madness. And in all this time I have been educating myself I've come to realize many things.

Madness is not something that can be defined so easily. There are many words to compare it to, many ways it has been defined but none understand it better than those who experience it. I often wonder if they see it as *madness*. I do not see it as an emotion but as a different way of thinking. People with madness see the world in a way that others can't. *And it's beautiful.*

Habit is a routine of behavior that occurs subconsciously. Routines are developed through repetition. Doing the same thing over and over. Therefore I believe that the quote you have read simply defines habit. Madness is something that can't be defined. It is something that we all experience differently and I think that's why I find it beautiful. It's something that is always changing even if not for the better.

Everything remained the same. The sun would rise every day at exactly five forty-five and set at eight. They would bring her breakfast: two eggs, bacon, and toast. At six thirty she was on the treadmill. At noon they brought lunch: pizza. But never did she eat it. Then she would spend her afternoon nose deep in the same book. Dinner came at six: steak, greens, and potatoes. At nine she was in bed.

This was her everyday and had been for twenty years. She could no longer remember what led her here but she was content to remain. Though she had spent weeks learning this routine, practicing it over and over, she genuinely believed one day something would change.

But change never came.

"I can't imagine living my life in such a routine." Whispered a man as he watched her. "It's absolute madness."

The man beside him reached to press his hand against the glass, the woman before him flipping the page of her book. His partner reached for his hand, grabbing it by his wrist before it could meet the window.

"Don't touch the glass." He said. "She will see you and you'll have ruined the experiment."

"Your experiment doesn't create *madness* but instead delusions. I almost wish she were mad. She would then have the strength and the will to set herself free." The man said, placing his hands against the glass regardless of the man's words. "Animals belong in cages. She deserves freedom."

And that's when she noticed the screen from which the sun set, the heat from the man's hands distorting the image before her. It took but a moment for the anger to consume her as she grabbed the chair from which she sat, throwing it into the glass. Like the glass, the illusion she had lived was now shattered and in pieces before her.

"Your routines have allowed you to live an illusion, my dear." The man said. "For the first time, you are free."

The woman stared at him, afraid of the world before her.

Made in the USA
Charleston, SC
17 January 2017